Live th

...and get carried away with the passion, drama and desire!

We're offering you a very special chance to experience three fabulous books that will give you a taste of our three bestselling series!

Modern Romance™

Medical Romance™

Historical Romance™

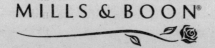

Live the emotion

TWO-WEEK WIFE
by
Miranda Lee

THE REAL FANTASY
by
Caroline Anderson

MISTRESS OF HER FATE
by
Julia Byrne

MILLS & BOON®

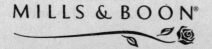

Harlequin Mills & Boon Limited,
Eton House, 18-24 Paradise Road, Richmond, Surrey, TW9 1SR

LIVE THE EMOTION © Harlequin Enterprises II B.V., 2003

Two Week Wife © Miranda Lee 1997
The Real Fantasy © Caroline Anderson 1996
Mistress of Her Fate © Julia Byrne 1995

ISBN 0 263 83677 0

024-0703

Printed and bound in Spain
by Litografia Rosés S.A., Barcelona

CONTENTS

Modern Romance™ presents...

TWO-WEEK WIFE
by
Miranda Lee

Miranda Lee is Australian, living near Sydney. Born and raised in the bush, she was boarding-school educated and briefly pursued a career in classical music, before moving to Sydney and embracing the world of computers. Happily married, with three daughters, she began writing when family commitments kept her at home. She likes to create stories that are believable, modern, fast-paced and sexy. Her interests include meaty sagas, doing word puzzles, gambling and going to the movies.

CHAPTER ONE

'ADAM,' Bianca said in that softly persuasive voice he knew oh, so well. 'I...er...I...um... Well, I have this little problem, you see, and I'm afraid I need your help...'

Adam's stomach contracted. He turned slowly from where he'd been pouring himself a drink, the whisky decanter and glass still in his hands. He'd just walked in the door after one hell of a Saturday afternoon at Randwick races and wasn't in the mood for one of Bianca's 'little problems.'

All sorts of possibilities flittered through his mind. She'd clobbered some poor bloke who'd patted or pinched her on the bottom—Bianca had one of those bottoms men could not resist.

Or she'd given all the housekeeping money away to a good cause. *Again.*

Or... His eyes darted swiftly around the unit. God, don't tell me she's brought home some starving stray dog or cat she's found on the streets!

This she did with regular monotony, even though she knew the lease didn't allow pets in their apartment block. It always fell to him in the end to take the damned bag of bones to the RSPCA, after which

5

Bianca would glare balefully at him for days, as though he himself had personally murdered the wretched worm-ridden animal.

Relief flooded through him when the spacious and relatively uncluttered living room showed no sign of such a stray. Besides, Bianca wouldn't be nervous about something like that, he finally realised. She would be defiant and rebellious.

And she *was* nervous. More than he could ever remember seeing her before.

His stomach tightened another notch.

Hell, he hoped she wasn't pregnant by her latest beefcake boyfriend, and wanted *him*—her schnook-head flatmate and first best friend—to pay for an abortion.

Oh God, not that. Anything but that!

'For pity's sake, Bianca,' he said, almost despairingly. 'What have you done *this* time?' Adam's normally cool grey eyes projected total frustration as he glared at the woman he'd loved and hated for the past twenty-eight years.

No, not twenty-eight, he amended bitterly in his mind. Only twenty-three. He hadn't met her till their first day at kindergarten together, when he'd been five.

He'd been blubbering in a corner of the classroom, all by himself, when this amazingly grown-up and self-assured four-year-old, with big blue eyes and a glossy black ponytail tied with a red ribbon, had put an arm around his shaking shoulders and told him not to worry. *She'd* look after him. *She* wasn't at all scared because her mummy was a scripture teacher at this school and she'd been coming here for simply ages.

This little she-devil—who had been cleverly disguised as a guardian angel back then—had even known where the toilets were, which had been of real concern to him at that moment in time.

He'd been her devoted slave from that point.

He still was.

And she knew it!

He watched wryly as she made those big blue eyes look oh, so innocent. If there was one thing Bianca should not have been able to look these days, it was innocent. But she could, and it always made him melt.

'It's nothing bad, Adam,' she said, as though butter wouldn't melt in her mouth. 'Really.'

'What about dangerous?' he muttered drily. Bianca thrived on danger of the physical kind.

As a kid she'd been a tomboy and a thrill-seeker, always having to climb the highest tree in the yard, always having to play whatever sport the boys were playing and then become the best at it. She'd been able to run faster, throw further and jump higher than any of the boys in her class.

But that had all changed when she went to high school and puberty pulled her back on the field. Talent and determination alone hadn't been able to

compete with the boys once the sheer disadvantage
of height, weight and size had become evident.

To Bianca's chagrin, she had stopped growing at
five feet three and a half, and she was burdened for
ever with a very slender fine-boned figure. Even so,
she'd fought to be allowed to play with the boys'
soccer team, going on to become their highest goal-
scorer each season.

'You're not going to try out for the Australian male
soccer team now, are you?' he asked, somewhat caus-
tically.

Bianca was still into sport in a big way. *And* sports-
men. If there was one thing guaranteed to turn her
on, it was broad shoulders and a bulging set of biceps.
Brains didn't come into it. Only brawn. She liked her
men tall too, which was rather ironic considering her
own lack of height.

Though six feet tall himself, with a far better body
than Bianca gave him credit for, Adam knew he
would never fulfil the criteria necessary to capture
Bianca's sexual interest. Nothing sparked when she
looked at him. There was no chemistry—on her side.

Adam knew this because Bianca had told him so
herself, with brutal but well-meant frankness, on the
night she'd turned twenty-one and he'd wasted two
dozen long-stemmed red roses in trying to woo her
one last time. When he'd confessed he was crazy
about her, she'd declared she loved him to death, but
that it was the love a girl felt for a big brother or a

best friend. She was sorry, but if he couldn't accept that, then perhaps it would be better if he stayed out of her life.

She'd been right, of course. It would have been better if he'd stayed out of her life.

But he hadn't. He just couldn't. He remained her best friend, lending a fairly broad shoulder for her to cry on occasionally, and money when she was desperate enough to ask; Bianca had been brought up by her Scottish mother to 'neither a borrower, nor a lender be'.

'Don't be silly.' She pouted at him. She had pouting lips to go with that equally pouting bottom. 'I don't do things like that any more. I know I'm far too small to play with the really big boys.'

Only on the soccer field, he thought testily. It didn't stop her playing with the really big boys in the bedroom. And the bigger the better, from what he could gather.

'I wouldn't put anything past you, Bianca,' he ground out as he slopped some much needed whisky into his glass.

'You make me sound so…so…'

'Crazy?' he suggested bitingly. 'Irresponsible? Impulsive?' She was all of those things. Not to mention warm, wacky, wild and wonderful, he added to himself on a silent groan.

Lifting the glass to his lips, he downed a good gulp

of straight Johnny Walker. It burnt a fiery path down
his throat and into his knotted stomach.

Bianca's beautiful lips pursed further, her blue eyes
narrowing, giving her an exotic, oriental look. This
was enhanced by her high cheekbones, and the way
her long black hair was pulled back tightly from her
face. Adam had often fantasised about her being his
own private geisha girl, especially when she wore the
colourful red and white flowered kimono dressing-
gown he'd given her last Christmas.

Bloody stupid fantasy, he thought ruefully. Bianca
was as far removed from a geisha girl as any female
could get!

'Just because you don't know how to have fun,
Adam,' she tossed at him with haughty disdain.

He snorted and strode across the sable-coloured
carpet, flopping down into his favourite brown leather
armchair. 'Is that what you think you're doing when
you keep changing direction in your life at the drop
of a hat?' he threw up at her. 'Was it fun you were
having when you came to me last year, stony broke
and without a roof over your head? Was it fun earlier
this year, after that loser of a boyfriend dumped you?
Do you really find it fun having others pick up your
pieces?'

'I do not expect you or anyone else to pick up my
pieces,' she huffed and puffed. 'And I'll have you
know that *I'm* the one who usually dumps my "losers
of boyfriends," not the other way around.'

'At least we agree on one thing,' he said drily. 'They've all been bums so far.'

'Maybe,' she countered blithely. 'But they all had very nice bums, those bums.'

'You'd know, I suppose.' He quaffed back half the whisky, congratulating himself on the offhandedness of his reply—especially when the image of his Bianca being intimate with any part of another man's anatomy nearly killed him. 'But we have digressed. Back to your present little problem. Out with it, Bianca. I'm not in the mood for any of your female manoeuvrings tonight.'

'All right, then, you meanie. I was just trying to tell you nicely, to make you understand that I had no idea this would eventuate. When the situation first arose, I didn't *have* to involve you personally at all, but something unexpected has happened and now I have no alternative.'

Adam didn't have a clue as to what she was talking about. But he feared he would. Soon. Only too well.

Bianca sat down on the sofa-end nearest his chair and leant towards him with the most heart-warmingly pleading look on her lovely face. 'Please don't be mad at me, Adam,' she said, in a voice which would have melted concrete.

For a split second Adam felt himself begin to go to mush, before cold, hard reality had him getting a firm handle on his ongoing weakness for this incorrigible creature. She was going to use him again, as she had used him for years.

No more, he vowed staunchly. No more!

'Out with it, Bianca,' he snapped. 'No more bull. Just give me the facts, and *I'll* decide if I'm going to be involved or not.'

Her startled eyes betrayed surprise at his hard stance. She straightened her spine, then rocked her shoulders slightly from side to side in the characteristic gesture which usually preceded defiance or outright rebellion. Her chin shot up. Her eyes flashed and her mouth tightened. 'There's no need to take that tone.'

'I'll best be the judge of that, thank you. Now just spit it out, woman!'

'Very well. It's to do with my mother.'

'What about your mother?' Adam frowned. Bianca's mum was a widow and had gone back to Scotland to live several years before. She'd been very lonely after her husband had been killed in a drag-racing accident.

Bianca was her only child and not much company once she'd finished university and had started flitting round the world on never-ending backpacking holidays. She only returned long enough to pick up a few months' work, thereby saving up enough to be off again.

Mrs Peterson had several brothers and sisters back in Scotland, so it had made sense for her to return to her homeland. Then, six months ago in May, she'd been diagnosed with breast cancer.

'Is she worse?' he asked worriedly. 'Do you need some more money to go and see her again?'

'No to both those questions. Which is just as well. I haven't finished paying you back for the last ticket to Edinburgh you bought me.'

True, he thought ruefully. Which was the only reason she'd stayed in one job and one place for so long. No doubt as soon as her debt was paid she'd be off again on some new adventure, trekking through the Himalayas or skiing down the mountain slopes of St Moritz.

'No, Mum's much better,' Bianca was saying. 'And there's every chance that the cancer won't come back.'

'Then what's the problem? I don't understand.'

'She's coming out here for a fortnight's visit, that's what. Her plane touches down next Saturday afternoon—a week from today. Her brothers and sisters all pitched in and bought her a return flight to Sydney.'

'Well, what's the problem in that? You should be thrilled. Oh, I see…you want her to stay here. That's no trouble, Bianca. I don't mind. I'm hardly here these days anyway, and there are two beds in your room, aren't there?'

'That's the problem,' she muttered.

Adam blinked his confusion. 'The beds in your room are a problem?'

'Yes.'

'Why?'

'Because Mum won't be expecting me to occupy one, that's why.'

'You've lost me, Bianca.'

Her sigh was expressive. 'It's like this, Adam. Mum thinks we're married. Naturally she'll be expecting me to be sleeping in *your* bed. And she'll also expect you to be around a bit more than you have been lately. God knows what you've been up to. If I didn't know better I'd think you were avoiding me.'

'She…thinks…we're…married,' he repeated slowly, his eyes narrowing with each word.

'Don't look at me like that, Adam. I didn't mean any harm. Honestly. But when I was over there in May she looked so darned ill. Try to understand…I thought she was going to die!

'I knew she'd always wanted to see me settled— preferably with you—so I told her what would make her happy. I said we were engaged and going to be married. Then after I came back and she kept hanging in there I had no alternative but to follow through. So I sent her some selective photos from Michelle's wedding and said it was ours.'

Adam was shaking his head in utter disbelief. 'How, in God's name, did you pull *that* off? You weren't even wearing *white* that day!'

'My bridesmaid dress was pale pink and could easily pass for a wedding dress. Besides, Mum wouldn't have expected me to have a traditional wedding with a big white dress. And you looked suitably bridegroomy in your best man outfit.

'Luckily with it being your sister's wedding, all your family were there. And on top of that, we had a lot of shots taken together, being partners for the day. Mum thought you looked very handsome, by the way. Oh, and remember those queen-sized sheets she sent, and which I gave you for your bed? They…er….they were our wedding present.'

Adam's hand clenched tightly around the glass he was holding. Fury that she would perpetrate this fiasco without even consulting him had his blood bubbling with heated anger along his veins. Naturally she hadn't expected to get caught. She'd probably thought her poor mum would safely pass away before her outrageous lies came to light.

That was always the way with Bianca. She never thought things through to all their possible eventualities and consequences. She always just plunged into some mad caper or other, without worrying or working out how it might affect others.

Never had this been more evident than on the occasion she'd come to him at the age of seventeen and asked him to relieve her of her virginity. Not for reasons of romance, mind. Simply out of curiosity. And she was tired, she'd said, of being the only girl in her group who hadn't done it. Tired of having to defend her lack of male admirers.

Back then, boys hadn't gone for Bianca all that much. Of course, *she'd* always thought it was because of her lack of boobs, but that hadn't been so at all. It had simply been because they were used to treating her like a mate, not an object of male desire.

He'd been the only boy in school who'd fancied her like mad. And she'd known it. What she *hadn't* known, when she'd asked this favour of him, was that he'd been a virgin too, back then. A bit of an embarrassment, really, being a male virgin at eighteen. His mates had used to rag him about it all the time.

He cringed now to think of the total mess he'd made of 'relieving' Bianca of her virginity—and himself of his own. He'd been so bloody nervous. Terrified, in fact. He'd been scared of hurting her, scared of coming too soon, scared of not being able to get the damned condom on properly.

The act itself had turned into an absolute disaster, with most of his fears coming to pass. In the end, he *had* hurt her, *and* it had all been over too soon. As for the damned condom…he had no idea how that had eventually assumed its rightful position. No doubt more by accident than design.

What should have been the most marvellous moment of his life had deteriorated into being the most embarrassing and definitely the most humiliating.

He could still recall the various expressions on her

face during the ten-second event. Pain had been followed by a few moments of frowning frustration, culminating in something even worse...relief when the act had come to a very rapid conclusion, obviously without her experiencing one single moment of pleasure, let alone satisfaction.

Afterwards she'd been uncharacteristically silent, and he'd skulked off home feeling utterly crushed and totally deflated.

The only good to come out of that night had been that the experience had seemed to turn Bianca off sex for the next few years. She'd probably concluded it wasn't worth bothering about, till a super-macho martial arts instructor, whose class she'd enrolled in during her last year at uni, had taken her uninterest in him as the ultimate challenge and then proceeded to show her that sex was nothing like what she'd experienced that night. He'd apparently been a fantastic lover, with a body any girl would drool over and a technique to match.

From that moment she'd been hooked—not only on the pleasures of the flesh, but on that sort of male. After Mr Black Belt, she was programmed to believe that arousal and satisfaction were synonymous with an ultra-fit, muscle-bound body and a super-stud mentality.

Adam had always wanted the opportunity to show Bianca he was no longer the sexual klutz he'd been at eighteen, but she would never give him that opportunity. Her mind was fixed against him, her pre-conceptions set in concrete. He'd thought he'd come to terms with this, but now he realised he hadn't. Not for a moment.

He wanted her now more than ever, and could not bear the thought of spending a single second in the same bed as her without being able to touch her.

Which was what she would surely ask of him if he agreed to go along with this masquerade of a marriage. She would expect him to allow her to climb into his bed every night for the duration of her mother's stay. And she would also expect him not to lay a single hand on her.

Such a prospect was beyond the pale. He would not do it. He was a man, not a mouse, and it was high time Bianca recognised that fact.

Uncurling his white-knuckled fingers, he placed the empty glass down on a side-table and stood up.

'No, Bianca,' he said, his face stony, his voice quite cold. 'No.'

And he stalked off down the hallway towards his room.

CHAPTER TWO

'WHAT do you mean...*no*?' she shouted after him as he disappeared down the hallway.

'I mean *no*!' he called back over his shoulder. 'I won't go along with it. You married us, Bianca. Now you'll just have to divorce us.'

Bianca gaped after him for a moment before snapping her mouth shut. Exasperation mixed with irritation as she rolled her eyes. She'd had a feeling he was going to be difficult about this. And she'd damned well been right!

Underneath, however, she still felt confident she could bring him round. Michelle always said she could twist Adam around her little finger. Bianca wasn't fond of that phrase, but she could not deny there was some truth in it. Just as there was some truth in Michelle's belief that her brother was still in love with his old schoolfriend.

Bianca sometimes felt guilty about taking advantage of Adam's lingering and largely unrequited passion for her. She'd shamelessly used his affection for her in the past. She supposed she was still doing it to a degree.

Though, to be fair to herself, she'd warned him

never to hope things would change. She loved him to death but she did not desire him. It was as simple as that.

Actually, now that she thought about it, she wasn't so sure Adam *was* in love with her any more. There'd been a steady stream of girlfriends paraded through this place since she'd come to live here a year ago— all blonde bimbo types, with legs that went up to their armpits and busts which made Bianca go green with envy. If he was pining after *her*, then he was making a darned good fist of hiding it.

This realisation piqued her somewhat. She'd become used to the notion that Adam was still in love with her. It had become a secret balm to soothe her battered ego on occasions, to reassure her that she was worthy of being loved, that there was more to her than being just the flighty piece of goods several men had called her.

Bianca frowned dissatisfaction at this train of thought. It seemed she just wasn't ready yet to give up Adam's status as her secret admirer. Knowing he was always there for her was the one steadying factor in her life—he was a rock she could rely on when all else failed.

A type of panic began to set in. She could not bear the thought that he might one day cut her out of his life. For ever. She'd be lost without him. Yet if he wasn't in love with her any more, then it was bound to happen one day…

Maybe he isn't still madly in love with me, she amended in desperation. But he *does* care about me.

Just as she cared about him. Deeply. He'd touched something in her from that first day at kindergarten, when she'd spied him in a corner crying his heart out. All during their school days she'd felt compelled to look after him, for he'd been such a sweetie. And such a hopeless nerd of a boy!

Around sixteen, he'd shot up suddenly—all gangly legs, long, greasy hair and pimples. Talk about unattractive! By their last year at school he'd improved somewhat in looks, but by then he'd become shy and awkward around girls. One day she'd overheard several of his so-called mates taunting him over his lack of success with the opposite 'sex. They'd called him cruel names and made him look small.

Bianca had felt sorry for him, *so* sorry that she'd decided to sacrifice her own virginity for the sake of his. It was the least she could do, she'd felt, for her very best friend.

Oddly enough, she still could not think of that night without being besieged by the most confused feelings. He'd been absolutely hopeless at it. And it had hurt like hell. Yet, for all that, she'd been unbearably moved by the experience—had had to battle hard not to cry afterwards. There had been something so incredibly sweet about his appalling nerves, not to mention the look on his face.

Bianca tried to blot out the disturbing memory as

she launched herself up from the sofa and raced after Adam down the hallway.

Of course there'd been something incredibly sweet about it, she dismissed with irritable impatience. Adam was an incredibly sweet person. Thank God. And as such, he could not keep saying no to her once she pointed out how much the truth would distress her mother. He liked her mother, almost as much as her mother liked him.

Bianca made it into his bedroom just in time to see him slam the *en suite* bathroom's door shut. She heard the lock snap into place, followed by the sound of the shower being turned on full.

Pummelling on the door didn't seem like a good idea, so she decided to wait patiently for his return. Meanwhile she picked up the clothes he'd strewn around the room in his anger.

Bianca shook her head in disbelief as she hung up his shirt and trousers. Messiness was as unlike him as his outburst of anger. The adult Adam was a quiet, coolly controlled individual—a highly intelligent but rather reserved man who liked order and tidiness. He was a maths lecturer at Sydney University, and his chief hobby was working out mathematically based systems for winning money at the races.

With some success apparently, since he was now driving a new BMW. His salary alone would not have provided that, and his family had no more money than hers.

She was tucking a sock into each shoe when the bathroom door was wrenched open. A cloud of steam emerged first, through which strode Adam, swathed from neck to ankle in his favourite red towelling robe which was as huge as it was thick.

Amazingly cold grey eyes settled on her as he sashed it tightly around his waist. 'That won't work either,' he said brusquely.

'What?'

'Picking up after me. Sweet-talking's a waste of time too. You've overstepped the mark, Bianca, and I'm not going to save your butt this time. Your mother will probably live for donkey's years and I'm not going to be permanently saddled with the ridiculous role of pretending to be your long-suffering husband.'

'R-ridiculous!' she spluttered. 'Long-*suffering*?'

A coating of dry amusement brought a gleam to his steely gaze. 'You don't honestly think any sane man would want to be your *real* husband, do you? Only a fool or a masochist would volunteer for *that* job.'

Bianca blinked her shock. This was her sweet Adam talking to her like this? And looking at her like that?

'You look surprised, darling,' he went on with chilling indifference as he casually raked his hands through his wet dark hair. 'Don't tell me you've believed all that rubbish my sister's been feeding you all these years about my still being in love with you?'

Bianca's mouth fell inelegantly open. Adam's laugh scraped down her spine like chalk on a blackboard.

'Michelle's such a romantic,' he said, his voice as cynically amused as his eyes. 'I admit I had the most awful crush on you all through school. I even clung to my warped passion through our university days. But I finally outgrew it—for which I have you to thank, Bianca.

'You really made me see the truth that night you turned twenty-one. I was wasting my time wanting you. So I turned my futile fantasies from fiction to fact with another female later that evening, and frankly I haven't looked back since.'

Bianca was stung to the quick by his words. *And* by the images they evoked. 'You mean I wasted my guilt on you that night?' she burst out angrily. 'There I was, thinking I'd broken your heart, when in truth you were off…you were off…' She huffed and puffed to stop herself saying the crudity which had sprung onto the tip of her tongue.

'I was off making some other more grateful girl happy?' he suggested sarcastically.

'Who was it?' she demanded to know, her mind racing along with her heart. 'Not that awful Tracy. My God, she'd sleep with anyone, that trollop!'

'Thank you for the compliment, darling. But, no, it wasn't Tracy. It was Laura.'

Laura!

Bianca was speechless. Laura had not been one of their group. She'd been a friend of a friend of a friend, who'd somehow been at her party by accident. Thirty if she was a day, but an absolutely stunning blonde with an absolutely stunning figure.

'I don't believe you!' she choked out, hurt beyond belief by this almost ancient betrayal of his so-called love for her.

'Don't you? Poor Bianca.' His smile was not at all sweet. 'Has someone stolen your lollipop, darling? Won't naughty Adam play the game any more?'

Her mouth returned to its earlier goldfish imitation.

Adam reached out and flicked her chin upwards, so her teeth snapped together. His eyes were narrowed and cruel-looking. He was nothing at all like the Adam she knew and loved.

'I suggest you toddle off now, sweetheart, and make up a new story to tell your mother. I'm sure you can come up with one, being such an inventive and imaginative little minx. If you're really stuck, you could always try the truth!'

Bianca's startled tongue-tiedness didn't last for long, and was quickly replaced by indignant and sceptical outrage. 'I don't believe any of this! Have you been drinking? Did you lose all your money at the races? This isn't like you at all, Adam.'

He gripped her shoulders and pushed her down into a sitting position on the end of the bed. 'Yes, I've been drinking,' he agreed in a steely tone. 'And, yes,

I did lose a good deal at the races today, which didn't please me at all. But you're quite wrong when you think this isn't like me. It is. It's the new me.'

'The new you?' she repeated blankly.

'I've been too soft with you for too long, Bianca. It's done your character no good. No good at all. You think you can do as you please where I'm concerned. You think you can run rings around me. Well, you can't anymore, sweetness. I'm awake to you now. Actually, I have been for ages, but it didn't suit me to make a stand. It does now.'

'Why now?' she threw back up at him, feeling suddenly angry. How dared he let her think he loved her all this time when he didn't?

'Because I've met someone,' he said. 'Someone I intend asking to marry me. Hard to do that when I'm pretending to be married to someone else, don't you think?'

Bianca felt her world go slightly out of kilter for a moment. Adam had fallen in love? He was going to get married?

Her heart squeezed tight. Her stomach flipped over. 'I don't believe you!'

He straightened, laughing. 'You do seem to be having trouble with believing me today. Tell me what you don't believe.'

She levered herself to her feet, shaken to find that her legs felt like jelly. 'I don't believe you've met someone. You haven't brought a girl home here once this last month. You're just making her up.'

But at the back of her mind Bianca was remembering all those nights Adam hadn't come home lately. She'd presumed he was sleeping over in his room at the university, which he sometimes did. Now she saw there could be a very different explanation for his many absences.

He laughed again. 'You're really grasping at straws, you know that? The reason I didn't bring Sophie here was because I wanted our relationship to last. What chance did I have with any of my other girlfriends after they'd met *you* as my flatmate?

'They always took one look at you and were instantly jealous and suspicious. Nothing I could ever say would convince them our friendship was purely platonic. They were all convinced we were secret lovers. An impression you deliberately seemed to foster, I might add.'

'I did not!' she denied hotly. But underneath she knew she had. She'd never felt any of those bimbos were good enough for Adam. She'd only been protecting him by getting rid of them.

'You never wanted me, Bianca,' he swept on, a cold rage settling into his eyes. 'But you didn't want anyone else to have me either. You've been a very greedy little girl. And very selfish. It's time you stopped thinking of no one but yourself.'

'But that's not true,' she wailed, hating this new

Adam and the way he was making her feel. 'I was thinking of my mother when I told her...what I told her.' Tears filled her eyes, tears of temper more than distress. 'You have no right to say these rotten things to me. You're being so hateful!'

'The truth often hurts.'

The truth, she thought savagely. The truth was that *her* Adam was going to marry someone else! Just the thought of it was like a dagger in her heart. God knows why. She didn't want to marry him herself. She didn't want to marry *any* man.

Marriage, in Bianca's opinion, would be a living death for someone like her. She was just like her father in that respect, craving change and excitement all the time. She didn't like the idea of settling down and having children any more than he had.

Her dad had married in the throes of a whirlwind passion, then spent the next twenty years finding satisfaction outside of the marital bed. Bianca suspected she might be just as fickle. There hadn't been a male yet to hold her sexual interest beyond six months. She suspected none ever would.

'So who is this Sophie you're going to marry?' she demanded to know.

'Oh, no, you don't,' Adam retorted with a dry chuckle. 'I'm going to keep her well away from you, Madam Mischief-Maker.'

'Where do you sleep with her?'

'None of your business. Do I ask you where you copulate with your latest boyfriend?'

'You can, if you like. But Derek and I have parted company. He was beginning to bore me.'

'Gee whiz, what happened? Didn't you fall asleep straight afterwards one night? Were you actually forced to make conversation with Mr Macho-Man?'

Bianca could feel a smile begin to tug at her lips. It was a good description for Derek, who was a professional weight-lifter with more muscles than mental capacity. 'Something like that,' she said.

Their eyes met, and that old camaraderie which had sustained their friendship all these years struggled to the surface. She'd always been able to tell Adam pretty much anything. And she'd never been able to shock him. He'd always listened and always given her sound advice, but never condemned. He was still her best friend, she realised, her heart squeezing tight as a wry smile began to play around his mouth.

Instinctively she reached out to place an intimate hand on his arm. 'Sophie doesn't have to know, Adam,' she said pleadingly. 'Mum will soon be gone, back to Scotland. Please...I don't want to spoil her trip by telling her the truth just yet. I promise I'll write to her after she's gone back and make up something to get you permanently off the hook.'

She held her breath as he simply stared at her.

Please say yes, she was silently willing him. Please...

His sigh was weary as he removed her hand from his arm. 'You never know when to give up, do you? Now let me make this quite clear. I am not going to play happy husband for you and your mother. I am not going to let you sleep in my bed while she's here, unless I'm not in it. I am not going to be at your beck and call, or dance to any tune you might choose to play.'

Bianca's dismay was only exceeded by her panic. 'But whatever am I going to tell her?'

'Tell her whatever story you fancy, Bianca, only make it convincing. You have a choice: either telling the truth, or inventing a temporary separation or impending divorce. Believe me when I tell you I have somewhere I can lay my head for the duration of that fortnight, so you don't have to worry your pretty little head about where I'll sleep.'

Bianca glared at him while he shepherded her out of his bedroom. 'Now, if you don't mind, I'd like to get dressed. I'm going out.' And he firmly closed and locked his door.

CHAPTER THREE

ADAM closed his eyes as he leant against the door.

God damn Bianca for making him lie like that!

He had no intention of asking Sophie to marry him.
Hell, he'd only just met the girl the previous week.

He also hadn't been going to go out tonight. He
was tired after his unsuccessful foray at the races. He
would have liked nothing better than to settle down
in front of the TV with his feet up and have Bianca
dish him up one of her interesting meals.

She was a fantastic cook, and spoiled him whenever he was at home in that regard. It was one of the
plusses among the many negatives in having her
around.

But he'd be blowed if he'd stay at home tonight
now! He'd have to sleep over at the penthouse, he
supposed, even though it would still smell of paint.
He didn't have a date with Sophie, as Bianca would
undoubtedly conclude. But he wished he had.

A night in bed with Sophie would blot Bianca out
of his mind for a few hours at least. Sophie was everything Bianca wasn't. Tall and curvy, with long
blonde hair, wide hips and breasts like melons. He'd
learnt from Laura many years ago never to date a girl

who reminded him in any way of the heartless creature who'd told him she felt nothing when she looked
at him. Generally he confined himself to bedding
busty blondes, with the occasional redhead thrown in
for variety. Brunettes never stood a chance.

Sophie was a minor actress, sleeping her way up
in the world with gay abandon. He'd met her last
Saturday night at the new Darling Harbour Casino,
where she was working as a croupier between bit
roles in movies. No doubt she'd thought he was a real
high-roller, laying thousand-dollar bets. Which he
was, he supposed.

Gambling had always paid off for Adam, because
he approached it with a cool head and mathematical
skill. Bianca would be stunned at how much money
it had brought him over the years…if he ever chose
to tell her. She thought he confined his gambling to
the races. She also thought he lost more than he won.

Racing was all very well, in small doses, but the
really big money was to be made in the casinos.
Unfortunately, he had to keep changing venues, because management soon spotted professional gam-
blers, and had a dim view of clients capable of counting cards or who used other systems which could
regularly beat the house.

Bianca had no idea of his weekend trips interstate,
to the casinos in Melbourne, Hobart, Adelaide and
even Perth, nor of the elegant, sophisticated and very
accommodating women who threw themselves at him

on those occasions. It stroked his ego to note that they had no trouble with 'spark' when they looked at him, as Bianca did. Hell, they fairly went up in flames when he touched them.

Fortunately, the opening of a new casino in Sydney had brought him a much closer venue—for gambling and otherwise. The night he'd met Sophie, he'd been trying one of his newer systems on the blackjack table, though his concentration had been shot to pieces. He'd been thinking about Bianca spending the weekend up the coast at some sleazy motel with darling Derek. She hadn't been bored with him seven days ago. Far from it!

Sophie had given him the eye as she'd dealt him the cards, so his bruised ego had taken her home to her place after she finished up. He hadn't given Bianca a single thought till he'd woken the next morning to brown eyes instead of blue, and blonde hair instead of black.

Swearing at the memory, Adam levered himself away from the door, throwing off his robe as he strode over to his built-in wardrobe.

He began to agonise, as he dragged on some clothes, about whether he'd ever marry.

Probably not, came the savagely rueful acceptance. He'd only ever wanted one girl as his wife and the mother of his children. How could he settle for second-best?

No, he'd be having one-night stands with blonde

bimbos when he was eighty—paid for, by then—and dreaming of what might have been, if only he hadn't been such a useless schmuck at eighteen!

He glanced down at the old jeans he'd automatically pulled on and thought of all the swanky clothes he'd recently installed in the penthouse instead of the boot of his car—the ones he wore in his secret life as gambler and lover extraordinaire. The Italian suits. The tuxedos. The black silk pyjamas and dressing gowns.

He shook his head at himself, for he knew that that life wasn't real. It would one day come to an end. It was a game. Thankfully a prosperous game, while his wits and courage were up to it, but still essentially a game—to be played as a boost to his ego and bank balance as well as a much needed diversion from the distress real life kept bringing him.

Real life was outside this door, waiting for him, waiting to try to change his mind about being her pretend husband.

He would have to be strong. Already he was feeling guilty. Already he was weakening. Tempting thoughts began infiltrating his brain. Maybe he would enjoy the pretence? Maybe he could lie there at night beside her and fantasise? Maybe she'd be so grateful to him that she'd let him…?

His teeth clenched down hard in his jaw. He didn't want her bloody gratitude. He wanted what she willingly gave those other guys. He wanted her passion and her desire. He wanted her sexy little body, naked and panting beneath him, begging him to go on, desperate for him...

Adam swore as he became hotly aware that his fantasy had swiftly transferred to a hard, aching reality. He dragged a sloppy Joe down over his thudding heart and vowed not to weaken one iota.

Even if she got down on her hands and knees before him, he would not budge an inch.

A darkly ironic smile creased his mouth as he shoved his feet into battered trainers.

Let's not go too far, Adam, came the wicked thought. Bianca on her hands and knees was a perverse and powerfully persuasive prospect. Too bad it would never come about. He would give anything to have her at his mercy. Anything!

Bianca spun round from the kitchen sink when she heard Adam's bedroom door bang. Oh, dear. He still sounded very angry. What to do? How best to approach him?

Appeal to his sense of compassion, she decided, and raced out to head him off before he could leave. The sight of him dressed in old clothes distracted her for a second.

'Oh!' she exclaimed. 'So you're not taking the soon-to-be fiancée out tonight?' she asked tartly, and immediately bit her bottom lip. Wrong tack, you fool.

'We're staying in,' he drawled. 'Watching videos and searching for the meaning of life.'

Bianca was taken aback by his sarcasm. He really was in a filthy mood. Perhaps she should leave appealing to his compassion till tomorrow.

But what if he didn't come home tomorrow? He was staying away from the flat more and more these days—obviously at this Sophie's place.

'Adam, when can we talk about this further?' she asked, in her most apologetic and reasonable tone. 'I know you're angry with me, and I'm sorry. I should have told you before this.'

'You shouldn't have done it at all!'

'Yes, you're right. I'm sorry.'

'Bianca, saying sorry is not always enough.'

Bianca could feel mutiny brewing inside her heart. Why was he being so damned difficult about this? Was she asking so much? Two miserable weeks of pretending to be her husband and then he was off the hook to marry this...this Sophie creature.

'You always said I could count on you,' she pointed out rather sulkily.

'You can. In things that count.'

She pouted her displeasure. 'I would do it for you.'

'Do what?'

'Pretend to be your wife.'

'Really? That's an interesting thought. But I don't need a pretend wife. I'm going to have a real one.'

Bianca still hadn't come to terms with that. Still,

there was a many a slip twixt the engagement and the altar. If this Sophie was anything like his previous girlfriends he'd soon be bored to death with her. None of those bimbos had had enough brains to boil water.

'So what do you expect me to tell Mum?' she asked defiantly.

He shrugged. 'That's your problem.'

'I'm not going to tell her I lied, Adam.'

'Heaven forbid. Tell you what, though. I'll stay away the whole fortnight. You tell your mum we're having a trial separation. Then, later, you can write and say that it didn't work out and we're divorced.'

'She'll be very upset.'

'Only if you are. Tell her that it was an amicable parting and that we're still good friends. That's the best I can do.'

Bianca pressed her lips tightly together to stop herself from saying what she thought of him and his so-called friendship. When the chips were down, it had proved about as strong as his so-called love! 'Is that your final word on the matter?'

'It is.'

'Then to hell with you, Adam Marsden. You're not the man I thought you were. As soon as Mum goes home to Scotland, I'll be finding somewhere else to live.'

His sudden stillness raised one last grain of hope in her breast. She could have sworn regret flashed momentarily in his eyes. But then they cooled perceptively and her heart sank.

'I think that would be best for all concerned, Bianca,' he said, with casual indifference.

All of a sudden she wanted to cry. Or to scream. Or both. Instead, she gave him an icy glare. 'I will never ask you for another thing. Not as long as I live. I will have trouble even speaking to you!'

His face hardened. 'Good.'

'I had no idea you were such a bastard! To think I once believed you loved me!'

The cruellest little smile pulled at his mouth. 'The things we have to live with,' came his sarcastic remark.

Bianca could only stare at him. 'I don't know you at all, do I? You've become a stranger!'

'A stranger?' he repeated idly. 'Yes, you could be right.'

And, with that devil's smile still playing on his lips, he picked up his car keys from where he always left them in the ashtray on the coffee-table and walked out on her.

CHAPTER FOUR

BIANCA was as good as her word. She didn't ask Adam for another thing all week. Neither did she speak to him.

Hard to, when he wasn't there.

He'd come back briefly on the Sunday evening, collected some clothes, told her curtly he'd be staying elsewhere for the following three weeks and departed again.

It turned out to be the loneliest, most wretched week Bianca had ever spent in her life. She missed Adam terribly. OK, so they hadn't been living in each other's pockets lately, but he was usually there a few nights a week, and always on a Sunday afternoon. She liked having him around to talk to and cook for. He gave her life purpose, especially now she'd given Derek the flick.

Truly, she didn't know what she'd ever seen in that big lug. He had a great body to look at and touch, but this time—amazingly—she'd wanted more. She'd wanted a boyfriend with brains as well as brawn.

Adam had been so right about dear Derek's lack of grey matter. This had come home to her during their drive up to Foster last Saturday. Four hours had

never seemed so long. She'd been bored to tears before they'd even arrived at the beachside town.

Derek had not been pleased when she'd told him
she wanted separate rooms. She hadn't actually been
to bed with him as yet, and he'd no doubt been expecting a real orgy that weekend. Still, it hadn't been
long before he'd started talking about some other girl
he'd met down at the gym that week. Clearly, his
girlfriends were just interchangeable sex objects.

A bit like *your* boyfriends, darling, came that horrid
voice which had seemed to keep popping into her
head ever since her fight with Adam. It told her all
sorts of things she didn't want to hear about herself.
Like how shallow she was. And how selfish.

Which she obviously was! Otherwise she would
have been happy that Adam had fallen in love and
was going to get married. Instead, she resented the
thought. She certainly resented this Sophie. More than
resented her. She hated her. And she didn't even
know the girl.

Depression began to set in as each day dragged by.
November was a fairly slow month in the section of
the accountancy firm where she was currently employed. Her job description as 'taxation consultant'
sounded far grander than the actual work she did—
giving tax advice to clients and preparing their tax
returns.

She'd have to find herself a new job soon. This one
paid well, but it was as boring as anything. She'd only

stuck at it because she owed Adam money. There were far too many moments during each day when her mind was not occupied, and then she would begin thinking of what she was going to tell her mother about her supposed marriage to Adam.

Night-times were worse. It took her ages to fall asleep, her thoughts going round and round. She started taking extra aerobics classes at the gym every evening, working herself so hard she should have slept like a log every night.

Instead, she tossed and turned, guilt warring with irritation.

Irritation was definitely winning by Wednesday night.

If only Adam had been co-operative, she started thinking furiously. If only he hadn't fallen in love with that stupid Sophie. If only he was still in love with *me*!

By Thursday night her conscience took over again. She was being shallow and selfish, thinking of no one but herself. She should never have lied to her mother in the first place. Lying was never a good idea. Honesty was indeed the best policy.

By the time she fell asleep on the Thursday night, Bianca had decided to ring Adam at the university the next morning, beg his forgiveness and promise to tell her mother the truth if only he'd come home to live.

Friday dawned to the sound of the telephone ringing in the flat, and she jumped out of bed, certain it was Adam. After all, a friendship such as theirs could not be destroyed so easily. He was probably feeling as guilty as she was, she thought as she raced to answer, her heart pounding as she snatched up the receiver.

'Hello? Is that you, Adam?' Even as she said the words she knew she was wrong. For the beeps on the line told her this was a long-distance call.

''Fraid not, lass,' a male voice said, with a Scottish accent. 'If that's Bianca, this is your Uncle Stewart.'

'Uncle Stewart?' Her heart squeezed tight. Something had gone wrong with her mother. She wasn't coming. She was dying!

All the blood drained from her face and she slumped against the telephone table. 'Oh, God,' she groaned. 'What's happened?'

'Now don't jump to conclusions, lass. Your mother's fine. She's just taken an earlier flight. It arrives around five this afternoon, not on Saturday. Is that OK? Can you meet it?'

'Yes, of course!' Bianca exclaimed, relief making her feel better than she had all week. 'But why did she do that?'

'A friend was able to upgrade her to business class on that flight for no extra money, so it seemed silly not to take it.'

'I'll say.'

'I won't keep you, lass. This is costing me a fortune. Look after your mother.'

'I will, Uncle Stewart. And thanks so much for helping with her fare.'

'No trouble. She deserves it. Bye for now.'

'Bye.'

Bianca hung up, feeling excited yet slightly sick. Her mother's imminent arrival brought home to her the fact that there was one thing less advisable than lying to her mum, and that was owning up to lying to her.

Bianca knew then that she just couldn't do it. She was going to stick to her marriage story, which meant it was better if Adam stayed right away. So there would be no phone call to the university, no begging for forgiveness. She would just have to make up some plausible story to explain Adam's absence.

Perhaps she could say the university had sent him on an unexpected mission to deepest, darkest Africa, to teach calculus to underprivileged pygmies!

Five-fifteen that afternoon found Bianca parking her car in the international terminal car park, feeling more than a little flustered. She'd had no trouble getting time off from work, but her old rusted-out heap of a car had decided not to start after sitting in the hot November sun all day, and she'd had to ring the Road Service Company to come and get it going.

Luckily, the problem had only been dirty points, and she was soon on her way. But time had been lost, peak hour had arrived and it had taken her much longer to get from the office in Crows Nest through

the harbour tunnel and out to busy Mascot. Her watch
said twenty past five by the time she made it inside
the blessedly air-conditioned terminal building.

A check of the overhead screens showed the flight
had landed pretty well on time, ten minutes earlier.
Bianca hurried along to Gate B, still feeling hot and
bothered, and very grateful that it would be a while
before her mother got through Customs.

A quick trip to the Ladies' revived her melting
make-up and limp hair, which she secured high on
her head in a shiny blue scrunchie. Her mother always
complained she never made the most of her looks, so
she'd made a special effort to look pretty today, wearing one of the few feminine outfits she owned—a
flowing skirt and matching blouse in a flowery print
of blues and mauves.

Bianca gnawed at her bottom lip as she washed her
hands, hoping the old friendship ring Adam had given
her once long ago would pass as a wedding ring. She
was not the owner of much jewellery, and it was the
best she could rustle up at the last minute. At least it
was fairly plain and made of gold.

Taking a deep, gathering breath, Bianca smiled at
herself in the mirror and told herself to be natural, or
her mother would know something was up. May
Peterson had a nose for lies, and liars.

Bianca was shocked on her return to Gate B to see
her mother already there, frowning as she looked
around the milling crowd for a familiar face. It

seemed business class passengers were shunted through Customs a darned sight faster than the economy section in which Bianca usually travelled.

Mrs Peterson spotted her daughter and tears swiftly replaced the worry in her eyes. Bianca felt her own eyes flood as she hurried forward and threw her arms around the only person in the world who truly loved and understood her.

Till this week, she'd thought Adam did as well. But she'd been wrong about that. The thought hurt her more than she liked to admit, even to herself.

The hug was long and touchingly silent. The two women embraced tightly, no words necessary. Or perhaps neither was capable of speaking for a few moments. Finally, Bianca drew back to look her mother over.

'God, you look good!' she exclaimed.

And she did. Nothing at all like the frail, wan woman who'd been lying in that hospital bed last May. There was flesh on her bones, colour in her face and that old sparkle in her pretty blue eyes. For a woman of fifty who'd been battling cancer all year, she looked bloody marvellous!

Bianca stood there, a silly grin on her face as she thanked God for the miracle He'd obviously performed in answer to her many prayers. Yet, down deep in her heart, she still feared that the battle was not yet over, the fight not yet completely won. As such, she was not going to say or do anything to cause her mother extra stress.

Her mum believed Adam was her adoring, loving husband, and Bianca was going to make sure she continued to think that till she was well out of the woods.

'Where's Adam?' May asked straight away. 'Parking the car?'

Bianca swallowed, smiled, then started on her newest invention. 'Actually, no, he couldn't be here with me, Mum. Your surprise visit has unfortunately co-incided with a series of conferences in America Adam simply *had* to attend. He was wretchedly disappointed, but this trip was very important to his career at the university.'

'Oh, what a shame,' her Mum sighed. 'And I was so looking forward to seeing him again. I do so love that boy. I always knew he was the right one for you, Bianca. I'm just so glad that you finally realised it too. Still, maybe you and he can come over to Scotland some time in the near future. I'd love the rest of the family to meet him.'

'Er...yes, of course, Mum.' Bianca could not trust herself to say any more. Resentment that Adam had put her in this awkward position had begun to sizzle inside her again. She also bitterly resented the thought that she would have to lie like this for a whole fortnight while he was off having fun with his new lady love and not giving *her* a second thought!

'Let's get out of here,' she said, rather abruptly,

and her mother gave her a sharp and far too intuitive look.

'There isn't anything wrong, is there, darling?'

Bianca found a dazzling smile from somewhere. 'Wrong? What could possibly be wrong?'

'I don't know…'

Bianca linked arms with her mother and dazzled some more. 'You silly billy! I haven't been this happy in years. We're going to have such fun this next fortnight, you and I. I've taken two weeks' holiday off work and we're going to paint Sydney red!'

Bianca started telling her mother all she had planned, and by the time they were on their way— the car had still coughed and spluttered before starting—that slight worry in her mother's eyes had totally disappeared. Thank God.

'What a lovely flat you live in,' her mother said as she walked out onto the balcony of Adam's unit an hour later.

'Yes, I suppose it is,' Bianca agreed with a degree of surprise. Really, she didn't care much about her surroundings, provided there was a shower and a toilet, a comfortable bed to sleep in and some kind of kitchen to cook in.

But, with her mother's comment, she took a fresh glance around at the spacious and modern unit, with its crisp white walls, brown leather furniture, plush sable-coloured carpet and marvellous aspect. They were only a couple of streets away from Collaroy

Beach, and high enough to have an unimpeded view of the beach and the Pacific beyond.

Though not in the luxurious category, the two-bedroomed unit was very comfortable by anyone's standards.

'Do you own it or rent it?' Mrs Peterson called back over her shoulder.

Bianca bit her bottom lip at this question. Did Adam own it or rent it? She didn't know. She'd never asked and he'd never volunteered the information. She rather suspected he owned it, which was why he let her live here free. But she wasn't sure.

'It's…er…still being paid off,' she said carefully.

'It's lovely. But not really suitable for children.' Her mother walked back inside and into the kitchen, where Bianca was making them both a cup of tea. 'Are you planning on having a family soon?' she asked hopefully.

Bianca's heart squeezed tight. She knew what her mother was getting at. She wanted to be a grandmother before she died.

'Not just yet, Mum,' she returned, a little tautly.

'You do realise it might take you some time to get pregnant, with your periods the way they are?'

'Yes, I know.' Bianca was one of those girls who only had a few periods a year. When she'd been playing heavy sport she'd hardly had any. She'd always joked with her mother that if she ever fell pregnant she'd have to have the baby—no matter what the circumstances—because it might be the only baby she'd ever be blessed with!

Earlier this year she'd gone on the pill, in an effort to regulate things and boost her oestrogen level, but it had made her feel so yukky she'd stopped taking it three weeks back. She had no doubt that the artificial period which had naturally followed the next week would be the last period she would see for months.

She sighed her exasperation at her body, which had always been a source of frustration to her. She would have given anything to be an Amazon with big boobs, legs ten feet long and a period every month that you could set your clock by.

'You might have to take one of those fertility pills,' her mother said. 'Though that usually produces multiple births. You wouldn't want that.'

'God, no.' Bianca had trouble picturing herself coping with one baby at a time, let alone several.

'Does Adam want a big family?'

'Let's not talk about babies, Mum. Adam and I have only been married a few months after all. Do you want a biscuit with your tea? Dinner won't be for a couple of hours yet.'

Her mum took the hint and dropped the subject of babies, though not without first giving her a long, thoughtful look. Bianca suspected her silence on the subject was only temporary. She began to dread the coming fortnight.

The evening finally drew to a close. Her meal of

Thai curried chicken and rice had been a surprising success, given her mother's tendency to cook plain food herself.

Bianca had also expected her mother to crash out early with jet lag, but she'd said she wanted to get her body onto Sydney time, so they'd watched the Friday night Ruth Rendell movie, which went on quite late, after which her mother had finally got ready for bed and taken her sleeping tablet.

Bianca made them both a cup of cocoa as a night-cap, and they were sitting on the sofa in front of the television, idly watching the late news and sipping their hot drinks, when an item came on covering the première earlier that evening of a new Australian movie.

Bianca started watching the segment rather cynically, thinking how like Hollywood the Australian movie industry was becoming. A whole lot of hype and not always that much quality!

There was the obligatory red carpet, the white stretch limousines, the screaming fans and, of course, the stars…glamorous women dressed in glitzy gowns and handsome men looking impossibly suave and sophisticated in superbly cut tuxedos. Such a false world, Bianca was thinking, when suddenly a very familiar face filled the screen.

A familiar face, yet *not* a familiar one. Bianca could hardly believe that was *her* Adam, in one of those superbly cut tuxedos, with one of those glamorous women on his arm dressed in a gold lamé gown cut right down to her navel.

'Isn't that Adam?' her mother said in a puzzled voice.

'Shh!' Bianca hissed, desperate to hear what the commentator was saying. She didn't stop to realise how damning his words might be to her story of her supposed husband being over in the US of A at a harmless conference.

'And here's Sophie La Salle arriving. Sophie has only a small part in this new and daring film, but one hopes that some smart producer will realise the public will want to see more of the glorious Sophie in future. Not that we aren't seeing quite a bit of her already here tonight. That's some dress, Sophie!

'It certainly seems to be appreciated by her very handsome escort. Can't say I recognise him. Perhaps he's one of the show's producers. Maybe we'll get a hint as to his identity later this evening at the post-première party. We'll keep you posted, folks.'

Furious disbelief exploded in Bianca's brain as she watched Adam slide an intimate arm around that disgustingly gorgeous creature's incredibly small waist. Or maybe it just looked small, she thought viciously, because of the size of the breasts above it, which not even the thick golden tresses spilling over them could begin to hide!

'Bianca, that *is* Adam, isn't it?' her mother was saying somewhere in Bianca's hazy background. Her whole focus was still fixed on the television screen and the way Adam was smiling into that woman's smugly beautiful face as he shepherded her into the theatre. She'd never realised before what a sexy smile he had. Or how handsome he was.

When had he grown that handsome, dammit?

'Bianca?' her mother prodded impatiently.

'Yes, it's Adam,' she bit out.

'But… But…'

'The bastard!' Bianca added savagely, no longer caring about anything but the rage flooding through her. And the jealousy. A black, black jealousy.

This last realisation had her jumping to her feet and pacing agitatedly around the room. She couldn't possibly be jealous. Being jealous was a symptom of loving someone. And she didn't love Adam. Not like that. It had to be a case of that selfish possessiveness Adam had accused her of, whereby she didn't want him herself but she didn't want anyone else to have him.

'Bianca,' her mother said firmly as she stood up and switched off the television set. 'Will you please stand still and tell me what's going on here?'

Bianca struggled to gather herself. And once she did she accepted that she would have to tell her mother the truth. She wasn't going to pretend that Adam had thrown her over for that blonde bombshell, though it felt as if he had. And she didn't like the feeling one bit!

'I'm sorry, Mum,' she said brusquely, 'but I haven't been strictly honest with you.'

'Well, that's pretty obvious! Adam is clearly not over in America at any conference, since he was here in Sydney tonight, accompanying that...that... actress...to the movies!'

'So it seems,' Bianca agreed through gritted teeth.

'My God, he's left you, hasn't he?' came her mother's shocked conclusion. 'He's having an affair with that...that...trollop!'

'That's the way it looks, I guess.'

'I can't believe it! I thought Adam was different. It just shows that most men can't be trusted—especially where a beautiful woman is concerned. A pretty girl only had to bat her eyes at your father and he was a goner.'

Bianca's sigh was deep and weary. She'd heard about her father's unfaithfulness at some length all her life and didn't want another lecture on the male sex's lack of moral fibre. She also wished to heaven she'd never started this.

Time, she decided resignedly, for the truth.

Bianca was about to launch into a full confession when the sound of a key rattling in the front door lock distracted her.

Both women's eyes turned in time to see Adam walk in, still in his tuxedo—although the bow tie was now undone, suggesting it might have been removed

at some stage during the evening. He looked startled
to see Bianca's mother standing in the room.

He also still looked disturbingly handsome, Bianca
conceded, confusion in her heart. She couldn't stop
staring at him and wondering if she'd really looked
at him lately.

Her eyes swept over him now, taking in the adult
Adam for perhaps the first time in years.

His face, though not classically formed, was un-
deniably *very* handsome: strong male features combined with intelligent grey eyes to project an impres-
sive look of maturity and confidence. His dark brown
hair, which he'd once worn far too long and wayward,
was now superbly cut to fit his nicely shaped head.
His mouth, she noticed, was just as nicely shaped, the
bottom lip sensuously full.

Bianca liked nice mouths on men.

She frowned as she started having decidedly erotic
thoughts, not so much about men's mouths in general,
but Adam's in particular. Annoyed with herself, she
dropped her eyes to follow the full length of Adam's
frame, trying to find something she could happily cri-
ticise.

She found the dinner suit he was wearing—that
very expensive-looking, silk blend, satanic black and
devilishly attractive dinner suit.

Most men would look good in that outfit, she decided waspishly. It was like a magic wand. Pop it on
any male and *poof*, its inhabitant would become in-

stantly glamorous and gorgeous—a bit like Cinderella did once her fairy godmother had garbed her in that beautiful ball dress and glass slippers.

That suit was better than any fairy godmother's wand!

Bianca's now scornful gaze rested on the undoubtedly padded shoulders, which would account for Adam's suddenly superb shape. Not a wrinkle creased either sleeve, nor the long, elegant trousers, seemingly housing equally long, elegant legs.

Bianca scowled as she tried to recall the last time she'd seen Adam's legs in the buff. No image came to mind. Yet she must have, she supposed, either in shorts, or some time around the unit—though he wasn't into shorts, and that red dressing gown he always wore covered a hell of a lot of him.

Her irritation grew as she realised that, although they lived near a beach, she'd never gone swimming with him, so she didn't know what he looked like in a cossie. How *was* it, she puzzled furiously, that they'd never gone swimming together?

His startled grey eyes met her glaring ones, and he gave the wall clock a darting glance. It was just on midnight.

Cinderella, it seemed, Bianca decided with savage sarcasm, had left the ball and finally come home.

CHAPTER FIVE

IT ONLY took Adam a few seconds to get the picture. Bianca's mother must have flown in earlier than intended, and his coming home had completely obliterated whatever outrageous story Bianca had told her to explain his absence from the marital home.

He almost laughed. It was a fitting end to a bloody awful night and a bloody awful week. The only good thing to come out of it was that he'd spent each night at the casino, winning incredible sums of money. Incredible because he'd bet recklessly, with no real system. His mind had been too full of Bianca to concentrate on a system, or even a proper staking plan.

Ironic that he'd come back, trying to do the right thing by her, his conscience having finally got the better of him, only to drop her right in it, obviously. He gave her an apologetic shrug which was met with a glare so fierce he was taken aback.

Good God, what *had* she told her mother about their marriage? He shuddered to think.

'Hello, Mrs Peterson,' he said with a sheepish smile. 'You're looking well.' Which she did.

She'd also always looked upon him with favour.

Till this moment...

'Hello, indeed,' she returned stiffly. 'And you're looking guilty. I hope you've finally seen the error of your ways and come to beg Bianca's forgiveness.'

'Pardon?' He shot Bianca a please-help-me glance, only to have those dagger eyes of hers cutting him to shreds again.

'There's no use playing Mr Innocent, Adam,' Bianca snapped. 'We saw you on the late-night news, escorting darling Sophie to the première of that movie tonight.'

Oh, he thought, and had to smother a laugh again. That would certainly have blotted his copybook, if he was supposed to be Bianca's loving husband. Which, no doubt, he still was. Bianca would not have backed down and told her mother she'd lied. That was not her usual *modus operandi* at all. She would have plunged further into the mire of more deceit and deception rather than confess all.

Admittedly, one look at her mother's stern and disapproving face was even making *him* feel guilty and uncomfortable. And he hadn't done *anything*!

'I tried to cover for your absence by telling Mum you were at an overseas conference,' Bianca raged on, blue eyes flashing and cheeks flushed a bright red. 'But you rather blew my excuse out of the water with your very public behaviour with that disgusting woman tonight. The least you could have done was conduct your affair behind closed doors, not flaunt it for all the world to see. You've made me look a fool, Adam, and I will not have it!'

Adam could hardly believe what he was hearing, and astonishment over Bianca's attack mixed with astonishment over her demeanour.

He'd never seen her so angry. Or so damned beautiful! This level of temper tantrum did become her. And he didn't think he'd ever seen her wearing such a feminine skirt before—certainly not one which rustled around her legs with each movement she made. He was momentarily distracted by the thought of how easily he could slide his hands up her legs with a skirt like that.

'I want you to leave!' she stormed on. 'Get your clothes or whatever you've come for and just go!'

Adam dragged his attention back up to Bianca's scorn-filled eyes, his fantasy fleeing in the face of reality. Any amusement vanished, his heart hardening against her. Who in hell did she think she was, making him look this bad in her mother's eyes?

He decided two could play at this game. After all, he'd vowed never to let her use him ever again. He'd warned her too. She should have listened to him.

'I have no intention of going anywhere, Bianca. This is my home, and you're my wife. I'm back and I won't be leaving again.'

To give her credit, she didn't turn a hair at his counter-attack. He had to admire her spirit. Bianca never knew when she was beaten.

'Really?' she snorted. 'Might I ask what happened to cause this change of heart? Last weekend you told me you were leaving me for good. You even said you were going to marry that Sophie person. Though God knows why. Men don't marry women like Sophie, you know. They just screw them.'

Adam heard Bianca's mother gasp of shock but he didn't think Bianca had. Her blood was too far up. He couldn't make up his mind whether she was mad at being found out in more lies, or just mad at being thwarted. He decided to thwart her some more. He liked seeing her like this. It was almost as if she cared about him.

'Why should you care what I do, Bianca? You never loved me. You only married me to make your mother happy. Why don't you admit it?'

'Is that true, Bianca?' her mother intervened, her expression and her voice holding intense shock and disapproval.

'No!' Bianca denied hotly.

Adam wasn't going to let her get away with that. 'Then you're telling me you *do* love me?'

'I've always loved you, Adam,' she insisted, a guilty red heightening the colour in her cheeks.

He knew she was playing with words, using the love she felt for him as a friend to mean another kind of love—the *only* kind he wanted from her. Her lie infuriated him. 'No kidding?' he said coldly. 'Did you love me when you went away to a motel last weekend with another man?'

'Bianca!' her mother gasped, looking totally appalled now. 'You didn't!'

'Oh, yes, she did,' Adam swept on while Bianca's mouth flapped open. 'His name is Derek. He's a professional weight-lifter. Wall-to-wall muscles. You must know your daughter's predilection for beefy men, May. She's never hidden it.'

'I...I thought she was over that. I thought she'd finally seen some sense.'

'Who are you to talk?' Bianca burst in. 'You with your busty blondes. Sophie wasn't the only one, Mum. There's been a whole line of overblown blonde bimbos before her!'

'You mean you noticed?' Adam tossed back with blithe indifference.

'Hard not to when you paraded them through here for me to see.'

His laugh was harshly dry. 'Careful, Bianca, or I'll begin to think you're jealous.'

'Over *you*?' she sneered.

Adam hadn't thought she could hurt him any more than she already had. But he'd been wrong. He looked at her now and hated her—hated her with a passion which was as annoyingly sexual as his love had been.

'She's exaggerating, May. They were just students I was giving some extra tutoring to.'

'What in?' Bianca scoffed. 'The *Kama Sutra*?'

'No. I leave those particular lessons up to you,' he countered icily, glad to see shamed colour sweep up her neck. 'I swear to you, May, that I haven't been unfaithful since my marriage to your daughter.'

Which was technically true, since Bianca had only announced their married state last weekend. He hadn't taken Sophie out all week. She'd wanted to get her beauty sleep for tonight's première. Neither had they made love tonight. He'd left her at the post-première party, making eyes at an American director.

'Not that I haven't been tempted,' he added snakily. 'My loving wife hasn't been giving me any attention lately. It's been so long since she slept with me, I can't remember what it was like.'

Bianca's eyes narrowed to savage slits. 'Hard to sleep with you when you're hardly ever home!'

'I'm home now,' he said coolly, and watched with bitter amusement as Bianca struggled to control her temper.

'Are you saying that you still love me?' she asked archly. 'That all those other women meant nothing to you? Sophie included?'

'Absolutely nothing. It's always been you, Bianca,' he said, hating himself as his voice shook slightly. 'You're the only woman I've ever loved, or ever will love.'

He cursed himself when her eyes widened, as did her mouth. Slowly. Smilingly. Damn, but she was actually looking smug now. Adam's teeth clenched down hard in his jaw. He was going to wipe that triumphant smirk off her face if it was the last thing he did.

'Darling,' she said with simpering sweetness, and came forward to give him a mock hug and a mock kiss on the cheek.

'Darling,' he returned grittily, and, taking her chin in a forceful grip, turned her face so that he could kiss her full on the mouth.

He wasn't a fool, however. He kept his tongue to himself, so that she couldn't bite it, revelling instead in the feel of her shocked lips and flinching body. God, but it felt good to be able to kiss her like this, knowing she was hating it yet unable to do a damned thing about it. Her lies held her captive beneath his lips.

His satisfaction was savage, and he began to understand the attraction of putting a woman over one's knee and paddling her backside. It would certainly satisfy that deeply primitive need a man had to dominate and control his woman by physical force—especially when that woman was as spirited and defiant as Bianca.

When he lifted his mouth he was surprised to find she was looking up at him with a type of bewildered respect in her eyes. It was a look he could easily get used to, he decided, so he took her firmly by the shoulders and kissed her again. This time he even had the temerity to slide his tongue between her startled lips, hoping like hell that this uncharacteristic respect would last a few more seconds.

Nevertheless, he kept this second kiss brief, for the feel of his own tongue in her mouth pushed him quickly to an edge of desire that was as terrifying as it was intoxicating.

He knew then that it would not be the last time he kissed her this night. Not by a long shot.

'Oh, how romantic,' Bianca's mother was sniffling from the sidelines as he surfaced.

'Say a single word,' he rasped, when Bianca sucked in a sharp breath, 'and I'll tell her the real truth. I swear it!'

Her mouth snapped shut, but her eyes spoke volumes.

'Why don't you go to bed, May?' he suggested, with far more calm than he was feeling. 'You must be very tired. Bianca and I will be just fine now. I think I have your visit to thank for her finally seeing some sense where our marriage is concerned. We were heading for disaster before you arrived.'

'So I can see!'

'I didn't do a thing with Derek last weekend, Mum,' Bianca insisted, sounding like a naughty little girl trying to defend herself, despite her hand being caught in the cookie jar. Adam just stopped himself from shaking his head. Would her lies never stop?

'I...I was just trying to make Adam jealous, to

make him see how it felt to have someone you loved looking at someone else.'

As if she knew what that was like, Adam thought viciously. She'd never really loved anyone in her life!

'It seems you've been two very silly people,' May said. 'You're far too old to play silly games like that.'

'I couldn't agree more, May,' Adam said. 'And there'll be no more games. I promise.'

'I'm glad to hear that.' A yawn took her by surprise and she apologised.

'Go to bed, May.'

'Yes, I *am* very tired. And I took a sleeping tablet just before you came in. But no more arguing, mind. I couldn't bear it.'

He wrapped an arm tightly around Bianca's shoulders, pulling her close and throwing her a sickeningly adoring look. 'I'll be too busy kissing her for that.'

May smiled her approval. 'You do that, Adam. It certainly seems to work. I don't recall ever seeing Bianca this subdued. 'Night, darling,' she directed at the stiffly held and no doubt smouldering female by Adam's side. 'I'm so happy you two have made up.'

'Smile,' he hissed under his breath as he kept up his own mock adoration.

Bianca smiled and said goodnight to her mother.

The guest bedroom door was hardly closed when she rounded on him, wrenching out of his arms and spitting fury. 'How *dare* you?'

'Keep it down, Bianca,' he drawled softly. 'You don't want your mother to hear, do you?'

She took two handfuls of his lapels and dragged him into the kitchen. 'You had no right to tell her about Derek and make it sound like I was an adulteress! I know you don't think much of my morals but I do have some. And I would never, ever commit adultery!'

'Gee whiz, I'm glad to hear that, Bianca, especially now that we're married.'

'Don't be ridiculous. You know we're not really married.'

'We are for the next fortnight. And I aim to enjoy the plusses as well as suffer the negatives.'

'En—enjoy the plusses?' she echoed, all the colour in her face fading. 'What do you mean by that?'

Adam wasn't sure himself, but he was getting some pretty exciting ideas. 'What do you think I mean? I might not still be in love with you, Bianca, but I still fancy you. Since I can't have Sophie or any of my other ''blonde bimbos'' while your mother's here, I'll make do with you.'

He rather enjoyed her look of stunned amazement. At least it wasn't revulsion. 'You wouldn't dare,' she croaked.

Wouldn't he?

Too damn right he would.

His laugh was low and dark. 'Try me.'

'I won't let you.'

'Won't you?' He arched an eyebrow and boldly stroked a slow hand down over her left breast.

She jumped back, but not before he felt her bare nipple peak hard against her blouse. Bianca rarely wore a bra. Her involuntary response sent an electric charge all through him, despite the fact that he knew it wasn't for him especially. He'd always known she was a highly sexed creature.

She was staring at him again as though she didn't recognise him. 'I...I don't want you like that,' she said, as though trying to convince herself.

Adam merely smiled. She no longer had the power to hurt him with that silly statement. He'd crossed back over the line from love to hate once more, and he was finding that a much more daring and quite ruthless emotion. He could make her want him. He felt sure of it.

But he knew if he said as much to her she would fight her feelings. And him. Bianca was as stubborn as she was proud.

His shrug was nonchalant. 'No matter. Just lie back and think of your mother's health and happiness. Or think of *mine*. After all, I'm your best friend, aren't I? And you love me to death. Or so you've told me often enough. You wouldn't want me to suffer because of your lies, would you?'

'Suffer?' she echoed blankly.

'Contrary to your popular opinion of me, I am a highly sexed man who views a whole fortnight's celibacy with something akin to horror. If you wish to stop me straying, you'll have to keep me happy in bed.'

'I should have told Mum the truth,' she wailed.

'Perhaps,' he agreed. 'But it's too late now.'

'It's never too late,' she pouted.

His eyes dropped to her lips and he began thinking of all the ways he wanted them.

'Oh, I think it is, Bianca,' he said. And, drawing her forcefully into his arms, he started on the first one.

CHAPTER SIX

BIANCA could not believe what was happening. Adam was kissing her and she was enjoying it. No, not enjoying. That was the wrong word. She felt too confused for real enjoyment.

But there was no denying that her body was responding to the hungry passion of Adam's lips and the steely embrace she was wrapped in. It was automatically melting into him, avidly welcoming the invasion of that demanding tongue and even wanting more.

He whirled her in his arms, lifting her feet slightly off the floor as he strode back into the lounge room and pulled her down with him onto the large sofa, kissing her all the while.

Bianca felt dazed and dazzled by this new and very exciting Adam. She had never dreamt he could be like this. And, while her mind was still struggling to come to terms with this unexpected side to his character, her body kept responding with instinctive delight. She'd always loved forceful men, loved it when they took charge of lovemaking, sweeping her along with the strength and power of their male passions.

He angled her body beside him, her back pressed

into the squashy leather of the sofa. His mouth on
hers continued its hungry demands, making her blood
sing and her head whirl. Desire for more contact had
her lifting her right leg up to lie along his. When one
of his hands started sliding up that leg all she could
think about was how far it was before he reached its
zenith.

Every ounce of her concentration was soon focused
on that travelling hand as it moved slowly up her
thigh. She moaned softly when his fingers finally fluttered against the lace edge of her panties. His mouth
burst from hers and they both drew in deep, ragged
breaths. Breathing heavily, he buried his face in her
neck and his hand moved on.

It was under the elastic now, finding moist folds
and electric places. Bianca began quivering with pleasure and expectation. Yes, touch me there, she willed
him. And there. Oh, yes, that's it. Keep doing that.
She moaned her excitement, plus her frustration.

Please don't let him stop, she prayed wildly.
Please...

He stopped, his hand withdrawing as he rolled from
her and stood up, coolly arranging her clothes before
raking his own ruffled hair from his face. 'Not here,'
he said, his eyes oddly cold as they moved over her
flushed and flustered face. 'And not like this.'

He was gone before she could assemble her
thoughts into words, stalking off down to the master
bedroom. Bianca scrambled off the sofa, her heart still

thudding heavily, her body screaming with thwarted desire.

She chased after him, only to find him taking off his expensive jacket and hanging it carefully in the wardrobe. He looked totally unconcerned about what had just transpired between them, as though it were nothing out of the ordinary.

Yet it was. It was very much out of the ordinary— both *his* actions and her *re*actions.

'Adam, I...' She hesitated, distracted by the sight of him flicking open the buttons of his white dress shirt then stripping it back off his shoulders. Nicely tanned and very broad shoulders, she noted, attached to an equally broad chest which looked toned beneath the smattering of dark curls.

He walked over and threw the shirt in the cane clothes basket in the corner, the movement highlighting the rippling muscles in his back and arms.

'Have you been doing weights?' she asked abruptly, her voice sounding almost resentful, as though he had no right to be doing things like that behind her back.

A wry smile hovered around his nicely shaped mouth as he turned to look at her. 'Glad to see you still have your priorities right, Bianca. But, yes, I've been doing weights. *And* working out. I have been on a regular basis for over ten years now.'

'Oh,' was all she could say, her gaze genuinely admiring as he walked towards the *en suite* bathroom.

'Care to join me?' he drawled, sending a cool glance over his shoulder at her.

Bianca blinked. *Did* she? Her head was pounding, as was her heart. Suddenly she didn't know where she stood with Adam any more, either with her own feelings or his. He was like a stranger to her…a very sexy stranger who was throwing her for a loop.

She wanted him. Oh, yes, she wanted him like mad.

But where would it all end? An affair with the Adam she'd used to know—or thought she had— would probably have headed towards marriage and babies, to a secure relationship with love and commitment. Because that old Adam had really, truly loved her.

But this new, totally alien Adam was a different prospect indeed. There was a coldness about him, a hardness which she couldn't explain or understand. Had Sophie thrown him over for someone else tonight? Turned him into an instant woman-hater? Bianca could hardly believe how ruthlessly he'd turned this sham of a marriage against her, using it to force kisses on her and then force himself on her.

Oh, come now, Bianca. The voice of brutal honesty intruded. Force? He wasn't forcing you out there on that sofa. You'd have let him do damned well anything and begged him for more.

What a mind-blowing realisation! How had Adam suddenly captured her sexual interest? Where had the spark come from? The chemistry?

It was this new and insidiously compelling chemistry which drew her into the bathroom. She stood there, watching him strip off to total nudity, a lump forming in her throat as she saw why perhaps he'd hurt her so much all those years ago. Yet he wasn't even aroused!

That stunned her. How could he not be aroused after what he'd done to her out there?

'Like what you see, Bianca?' he drawled from across the room.

'Yes…' It wasn't in Bianca's nature to be sexually coy, but the admission was made on a husky note, forced out of dry lips from a very dry throat.

A coldly rueful smile gave his mouth a strange look as he slowly crossed the distance between them. 'Then what are you waiting for, darling?' he asked, in a mockingly sardonic voice which scraped across every nerve-ending she owned. 'I'll bet you weren't this slow to get out of your clothes your first time with dear old Derek. Or is it that you want me to undress you? Do you have a fetish for your lovers stripping you? Is that it?'

Bianca had never felt more torn. She wanted to tell him to go to hell, show him she wasn't going to let him get away with treating her like this. Instead, she slid her arms up around his neck, reached up on tiptoe and kissed him, pressing herself against his splendid nakedness.

'Yes,' she breathed against his suddenly frozen lips. 'Yes, I have a fetish for my lovers stripping me.'

Adam swore under his breath as his flesh leapt. Damn, but she was trying to turn the tables on him, trying to take control. He wasn't having any of that.

Dampening down his desire with another supreme effort of will, he extricated her arms from around his neck and stepped back slightly so that he could begin on the buttons of her blouse.

She was taken aback by his seeming control, he could see, her eyes wide on him as he undressed her with casual aplomb. The sight of her perfect little breasts with their large, hard nipples endangered more than his physical control, but he kept going, sliding the zip of her skirt down and easing the garment over her slender hips to pool on the white-tiled floor.

Now all that separated her from total nudity before him was a scrap of pink satin and lace. He thought of where his fingers had already been as he peeled the panties down her athletic legs, of her hot, wet, pulsing core. It was almost too much for him. It was certainly too much for his repressed but aching flesh, which sprang to life, rearing up with primal urgency.

Whirling abruptly from her, he strode over to turn on the shower taps, standing with his back to her while he adjusted the temperature and battled to get himself at least marginally under control.

At last he felt sufficiently in charge of his emotions—and his body—to face her once more.

Bianca was shivering by the time he returned to draw her with him under the hot spray. Not from cold. From a dizzying excitement. And an exquisite expectation.

Yet beside her almost blind arousal lay a bitter resentment that Adam was not similarly turned on. She wanted to see him as mindlessly impassioned as she was. His cool composure seemed to be emphasising her own lack of control, her own wanton willingness to surrender herself totally to his casual and rather cold sexual demands.

Where was the Adam who'd once followed her around like an adoring puppy? Who'd have lain his life at her feet if she'd wanted him to?

Gone. She had to accept it. Replaced by this cool, enigmatic stranger who was at this moment doing the most wicked things to her body with a bar of soap, turning her this way and that beneath the heated spray of water, sending her mad with desire as he teased aching nipples, massaged trembling buttocks and throbbing thighs.

She was shaking by the time he snapped the water off and began towelling her dry. He carried her back into the bedroom, for which she was grateful—she knew she wouldn't have been able to walk. Her eyes clung to him as he laid her down on the bed, and for the first time she saw a spark of conscience, a moment of doubt over what he was doing.

For Bianca, it was too late for that. She no longer wanted his conscience, or his doubts. She only wanted him, inside her, expelling this almost hateful need from her body. She'd never felt this strung up, or this desperate. Her hands snaked round his neck, her fingers interlinking as she drew his mouth and body down on top of hers.

Her legs opened to wrap tightly around him, her buttocks lifting from the mattress till his flesh fell with driving hardness into the softness of her woman's body. With a powerful thrust which took her breath away he was suddenly there, filling her completely. He cupped her face with his hands and stared down into her wild, wide eyes, watching her while he began moving with a voluptuous and powerful rhythm.

Bianca squeezed her eyes shut against the shame of Adam seeing her so lost to everything but her body's demands. Her mouth fell open as she felt her climax begin to build. She gasped her pleasure, then groaned her torment, grimacing when the knife-edge of tension tightened its grip on her nerve-endings.

The knowledge that he wanted to coldly watch her come brought one last burst of defiance, and her eyes flew open. But she was too late, those tortured nerve-endings giving up the ghost, bringing a twisted cry to her lips as her flesh shattered into a thousand electric spasms. Her contractions were fierce and strong around his flesh, the pleasure unbelievable.

The look of dark triumph on his face frightened Bianca at first, but then his mouth gasped wide with agonised ecstasy, his release as cataclysmic as her own.

'Oh, God, Bianca!' he cried out, collapsing on top of her, burying his face in her hair. 'Bianca...'

She had never heard her name called out with such emotion, or such despair. It moved her unbearably and she gathered him close, instinctively trying to soothe him. The certainty that he still loved her, despite his earlier denial, evoked the most incredibly warm feelings inside her. It made what they had just shared something much more wonderful than anything she'd ever experienced before.

But no sooner had she hugged him tight than he was wrenching himself out of her arms and abruptly withdrawing from her body. The obscenity he used as he rolled over onto his back made her flinch.

'What is it?' she asked, levering herself up on one elbow to look down at him. 'What's wrong?'

'Nothing,' he bit out, slanting her an angry glance. 'I hope,' he added viciously.

'What are you saying?'

'I'm saying I didn't use anything just then, dammit. And you made no move to stop me. Not once!'

'Oh,' she said softly, her stomach flipping over as

she lay back down again. There was no use making excuses. She simply hadn't thought of it.

'Yes, *oh*!' he growled, rolling over onto his side to glare down at her. 'Hell, Bianca, I hope you're not in the habit of getting carried away like that. I know you're on the pill, but that's not the point these days, is it?'

Bianca opened her mouth to tell him that actually she *wasn't* on the pill. But she quickly closed it again, sensing that there was nothing to be gained by the admission. The odds of her falling pregnant on this one-off occasion were so remote as to be almost negligible.

But she had a feeling Adam wouldn't be too pleased with the news of even the slightest possibility. He didn't look too pleased all round.

'You always said the reason you never told your boyfriends you were on the pill was because you wanted them to always use a condom,' he ranted. 'You've always claimed to be fanatical about safe sex. What just happened rather proves you're not infallible when it comes to being Miss Protection Perfect, wouldn't you say?'

Bianca could feel her own blood pressure rising, but she battled to remain calm. 'I have never, ever *not* practised safe sex before tonight, Adam,' she stated firmly. 'And, contrary to your opinion of me, I have not had that many lovers over the years. Barely a handful. Can you say the same?'

'Maybe not, but I can assure you practising safe sex is an automatic way of life with me.'

'You've always used a condom?'

'Too darned right I have.'

'Then why didn't you tonight?' she counter-challenged.

He pressed his lips tightly together, his eyes seething with resentment at her attempt to make him admit he'd got as carried away as she had. 'I guess at the back of my mind I knew you were on the pill,' he muttered at last. 'And maybe, at the back of my mind, I just didn't damned well want to!'

'And maybe *I* had the same damned good reasons!' she threw back at him. 'But be assured I want you to use something in future, because I don't trust you any more than you trust me, Mr Protection *Im*perfect!'

Bianca was shocked when Adam started smiling down at her. It was a wickedly knowing smile, which sent a prickle of apprehension down her spine.

'What are you smiling at?' she snapped. And where had his anger gone to, dammit? She liked him angry. It made her feel safer than when he was...like this.

'At you, Bianca,' he drawled, and reached out to play idly with her nearest nipple.

Bianca was shocked when it sprang to attention with appalling swiftness. Stunned, she knocked his hand away and sat up. 'What do you think you're doing?' she asked shakily.

'What you just gave me permission to do,' he said, sitting up as well.

'I did no such thing.'

'Yes, you did. You asked me to use protection *in future*, which suggests you're expecting a repeat performance. I think the future, my darling wife of the next fortnight...' he murmured thickly as he reached out to play with both her breasts at the same time. 'The future...has already arrived.'

Bianca gasped when he took her shoulders and pushed her back against the pillows, straddling her and effectively pinning her to the mattress. Her cry of outrage was muffled by his kiss, her eyes rounding when Adam used his hands to find her body's most electric and seductive places.

'Hush,' he said when she moaned a pained protest. 'You don't want to wake your mother, do you?'

He kissed her again for an interminable time, only removing his mouth when she no longer had the will to scream—and when he had other uses for her lips.

CHAPTER SEVEN

ADAM carried the breakfast tray into the bedroom, his mouth tightening as his eyes lit upon Bianca's still naked form sprawled face-down across the bed. Her lovely long black hair, no longer confined in that purple thing, was spread out in tangled abandon against the cool, creamy sheets. She looked the picture of erotic decadence—utterly spent from an orgy of sensual delights.

If only her mother could see her now...

But Mrs Peterson was still safely asleep, that sleeping tablet doing a good job. Not that it was all that late. Only eight.

Adam placed the tray carefully on top of the bedside table, sat down on the side of the bed and stared down at the delicious curve of Bianca's spine. He could not resist the temptation, and bent to kiss the small of her back before running his tongue-tip slowly upwards.

'Don't,' she groaned, arching away from him and then rolling over, her arms flopping wide, her eyes still shut.

His gut contracted as his gaze raked over her beautifully formed, perfectly toned little body.

Bianca had always bemoaned her small breasts and her lack of height, but to him she was just right. He adored the shape of her slender curves, loved the way each breast fitted neatly into the palm of his hand, revelled in the fact that she was so much smaller than he was. And correspondingly less strong.

His heart lurched as he thought of how he'd forced the issue with her last night, through his superior strength alone. He wasn't proud of that fact, but, damn it all, she hadn't objected for long. She'd been more than willing to give him what he wanted in the end.

And he'd wanted so much—all those things he'd thought of doing with her over the years and never been able to. Well, he'd done most of them now, and it hadn't dampened his passion for her one bit. Or his love, for that matter. He loved her more than ever. Wanted her more than ever. Hell, he wanted her to be his for forever. Wanted her to be his *real* wife.

But he knew Bianca would never be his, or any other man's, for forever. He was damned lucky to have got this far with her. Her abandoned behaviour with him last night was nothing out of the ordinary, not even those bittersweet moments of total surrender, when any man who didn't know her might have thought she must love him to allow such torrid intimacies.

But Adam knew the truth. A set of unusual circumstances had allowed him to tap into Bianca's Achilles' heel—sex—and she was simply running true to form.

Once sexually attracted to a man, she always quickly became infatuated, even obsessed. She lived and breathed that man. Nothing was too good for him, in bed and out.

But only for a time. Eventually she would begin to find flaws in what she'd once thought was a perfect male specimen. Sometimes it was the man who opted out first, probably because she'd begun to pick him to pieces. At other times she did the breaking up herself.

Oddly enough, the longest lasting of her lovers had been one who hadn't treated her very well at all. The bastard had actually boasted to Adam one day that his success with women was because he lived by the adage 'Treat 'em mean, keep 'em keen'.

Adam personally found that theory distasteful. But, damn it all, it seemed to work. Where had being the good guy ever got him with Bianca? Bloody nowhere. Yet as soon as he'd started standing up to her, and treating her as if he was a selfish, macho stud with nothing to lose, she'd fallen into his hands like a ripe peach. It was perverse in the extreme, but who was he to question the road to sexual success?

And he *was* being sexually successful with her. His loins leapt as he thought of the number of times he'd had her the previous night. Hell, he'd lost count.

Having her body might not be everything. He'd

always wanted the complete woman—body and soul. But sex with Bianca went a long way to making him feel infinitely better about all the years he'd wasted futilely trying to win her heart.

He saw now that she was not capable of loving a man that way. *Any* man. Her relationships were based on lust. Once the intensity of her desire began to fade—which was inevitable—the relationship was dead in the water. Adam knew that this new desire of hers for him would not last. It never did.

But, meantime, he aimed to take full advantage of that desire.

He would have to be careful never to hope for more, however. Bianca had hurt him more than enough for one lifetime. To set himself up for added pain would be insane.

No, he wasn't going back to being stupid old Adam, boring best friend and doormat. He was going to stay being the man who'd shocked her into responding to him last night, the selfish stud who took without asking, who came and went without getting permission, who kept secrets from her and never, ever allowed himself to be taken for granted.

'Wake up, Bianca,' he said brusquely.

Her eyes fluttered but remained sleepily shut while she yawned, then stretched with voluptuous sensuality. Bianca's naked body had been bad enough. Her naked body moving like that was too much for Adam. He scooped her up and set her down on the carpet, smacking her hard on the bottom as he propelled her towards the bathroom.

'Hey, that hurt!' she protested, rubbing those gloriously pouty buttocks of hers as she glared over her shoulder at him.

'Good,' he pronounced. 'Now get that butt of yours into the shower. It's after eight and I've brought you some breakfast.'

She half turned, an incredulous smile on her face. 'You brought me breakfast?'

Adam made a mental note never to do such a stupid thing again. 'If you can call muesli and orange juice breakfast. But don't get used to it. I thought you might need an energy boost after last night,' he finished drily.

'Oh...'

The memory of the night flickered across her face, bringing with it a faint trace of worry, he thought. Or was it shame?

No, not shame, Adam conceded ruefully. Bianca would never be ashamed of what she did in bed. She thought of sex as a beautiful and natural expression of the attraction between a man and a woman. There were no taboos in her mind. She was always scathing of people who tried to make sex into something wicked and dirty. Sick, she called them.

That momentary cloud quickly cleared from her wide blue eyes, replaced by a soft look which twisted Adam's heart. Damn, but she was so good at that, looking at him with the innocence of a child. There again, she *was* a child in some ways, always wanting fun and excitement, never wanting the things a grown woman wanted—except in one department.

'Adam,' she said softly.

'What?'

'Thank you.'

'For what? Breakfast?'

'No. For coming back last night. You…you did it for me, didn't you? You wouldn't have had any idea Mum was already here. You left that Sophie female and came back to help me out.'

Well, of course he had! But he couldn't tell her that, could he? If he did, soon she'd start thinking of him again as good old Adam—loyal life-saver and breakfast-bringer.

He let his eyes drift over her with lazy amusement. 'Actually, Bianca, I hate to disillusion you, but I came back last night to pick up my books to take to the races today. I can't operate my system without them.'

She blinked her surprise before hurt darkened her eyes. 'Oh,' she said. 'Oh, I see.' She stiffened, and suddenly seemed to realise she was standing stark naked before him, her hands moving to cover herself. 'Sorry,' she muttered unhappily. 'My mistake.' And she hurried into the bathroom, shutting the door behind her.

Adam steeled himself against the automatic self-hate which flooded his heart. So he'd hurt her.

Deliberately hurt her. So what? This was self-survival, here. He could not afford to wear his heart on his sleeve with her any more. He had to distance himself from this futile loving which had obsessed him most of his emotional life.

Lust was what he was going to concentrate on from now on, for in the long run that was all Bianca responded to. Real love she scorned as weakness. He could not afford to be weak with her if he wanted to keep her sexual interest. Which he did. Hell, a man would have to be mad not to want a repeat performance of last night. There were other Bianca fantasies he hadn't lived yet as well, and he aimed to live every one of them in the coming fortnight.

Oh, yes…his days of being a push-over were well and truly gone!

Bianca found herself crying under the shower. She had never felt this confused before. Or this vulnerable. Or this hurt.

The reason, of course, was Adam. Not the Adam she'd known and loved all her life, but the stranger sitting on that bed.

Last night, when he'd made love to her that first time and called out her name, she'd been so sure he still loved her. Even afterwards, when his lovemaking had become incredibly daring and increasingly demanding, she'd still felt confident that it *was* lovemaking and not just having sex. She could have sworn she'd felt a very special passion in every kiss, every caress.

Now she wasn't so sure. My God, the way he'd looked at her just then, the way he'd spoken to her.

He'd made her feel so…*unloved*.

More tears streamed down her face, which wasn't like her at all. The thought that she might have fallen in love with Adam at the same time he'd fallen *out* of love with *her* was distressing in the extreme.

And so frustrating.

It just wasn't fair!

But when had life—or love—been fair? she wondered with a degree of cynicism. Her own mother had married a man she'd loved to death, only to have him be chronically unfaithful to her. Bianca had always believed she was tarred with the same brush as her father, because she'd imagined herself deeply in love several times, only to fall out of love within a few months. She'd obviously always confused sexual attraction with love.

Bianca frowned. Since that had always been the case, then why should what she was feeling for Adam be any different? Maybe it, too, was just a sexual attraction and would wear off after a while?

She could not deny that seeing Adam on the television in that dashing tuxedo and on the arm of the stunning Sophie had lifted the wool from her eyes where his physical attractions were concerned. She'd begun looking at him with new eyes last night, and

discovered an Adam she'd had no idea existed—an
Adam who was more like the type of man she usually
went for. Tall, well-built, strong and very macho.

Bianca sighed and switched off the shower. Even
to her own ears that sounded awfully shallow. Yet
hadn't she already decided this week that she *was*
shallow? It was no wonder Adam no longer loved her.
Living with her this past year had probably opened
his eyes to the real Bianca, with all her shallowness
and sexual superficiality.

Still, he didn't seem to mind *sampling* that sexual
superficiality, did he? she thought savagely as she
rubbed herself dry. He had taken outrageous advantage of her last night. He'd taken outrageous liberties
as well! No doubt he expected more of the same tonight, and for the rest of her mother's stay.

Bianca's heart began to pound at the prospect. As
much as she would have liked to feel outrage, all she
felt was an excited anticipation. Tonight could not
come quickly enough.

Bianca was not a girl to keep lashing herself over
her own faults. Very well…so she was sexually shallow—weak as water where the pleasures of the flesh
were concerned. It wasn't entirely her fault this time.
Who would have believed that the gawky boy who'd
taken her virginity with such appalling ineptitude
would develop into such a fantastic lover?

Jealousy re-erupted when she thought of him doing
all those things he'd done to her with Sophie. She

could just about tolerate his not loving her, but she was not going to tolerate another woman in his life. Not while *she* was in his bed. No way!

Bianca sashed a huge cream towel around her and stormed back out into the bedroom, her hands coming to rest on her hips as she ground to a halt.

'I want to know about Sophie!' she demanded hotly.

Adam glanced up from where he was still sitting on the edge of the bed, sipping *her* glass of orange juice. 'What about her?' His bland tone infuriated her.

'I hope you don't think you're going to be juggling the two of us. When I take a lover, I demand his exclusive attention.'

His eyebrows lifted, but his expression remained irritatingly casual. 'How nice for you. But I'm not your lover. I'm your pretend husband.'

'Same thing.'

'Oh, no, Bianca. Not at all. But, if it makes you feel better, be assured I won't be sleeping with Sophie during these two weeks. I don't think your mother would approve of my being absent from our marital bed at night, do you? And Sophie is not a day-time person. Besides, why would I want Sophie when you're being so accommodating?'

Bianca squirmed a little as she recalled just how accommodating she'd been. But any embarrassment was quickly replaced by a burst of defiance. Why should she feel ashamed of what they'd done to-gether? Adam clearly didn't.

Bianca had never been one to abide by those dou-ble standards where sex was concerned, and she wasn't about to start now. Being a hypocrite was not her style.

She'd wanted Adam to make love to her last night and wasn't going to pretend differently this morn-ing—even if he was turning out to be a very different Adam from the one she'd always thought she'd known so well. This new Adam was not at all sweet, or touchingly in love with her. She doubted he was in love with any woman, the selfish, sexy rat!

This realisation brought with it a sudden thought, and she eyed him suspiciously. 'You never did intend asking Sophie to marry you, did you?'

'No.'

Just as she'd thought! 'Then why did you say you were?'

He stood up, shrugging. 'It suited me to say so at the time.'

'You mean you lied to me!'

'Mmm, yes, it seems I did.'

Bianca was shaken by his cool confession, and the small smile playing on his lips. Had she ever really known Adam? Where would the shocks end? Still…she had to admit that he'd suddenly become a very intriguing man to be around. And very exciting.

'Will you be going back to her after this fortnight

is over?' she asked, shaken by how dreadful such a prospect made her feel.

'Who knows? Maybe. It all depends.'

'On what?'

'On you, Bianca. On you.'

She stiffened when his hand snaked around her neck. He drew her slowly against him, his mouth covering hers with a confident possession which brought a moment's indignant rebellion.

But only a moment. She'd always been a sucker for aggressive lovemaking from men she wanted. Her lips parted beneath his as her pulse-rate kicked into overdrive.

Yet, strangely, his kiss gradually grew gentler, and the soft sipping at her lips brought a sweet yearning to her soul which had her clinging to him and wanting him to just go on holding her and kissing her like that. There was no urgency for more. It was just him and her, together, in each other's arms, loving each other with great tenderness. Bianca had never felt anything like it. It was just so beautiful.

'Adam,' she whispered shakily when his mouth finally lifted.

'Mmm?'

'I... I...'

She stopped herself just in time from saying the silliest things. Lord, she really had to stop mistaking these warm, squishy feelings she was feeling for love.

It was just another side to sex, she supposed, a softer side which she hadn't explored as yet.

Adam—especially this new Adam—would laugh if she started telling him she loved him, or promising she would always be there for him. She almost laughed at herself. Silly Bianca. As if she could ever promise a man that anyway.

'Bianca? What were you going to say?'

She ignored the sudden stab of dismay in her heart and smiled brightly into his suddenly watchful grey eyes.

'I was just going to ask if Mum and I could come to the races with you today?'

CHAPTER EIGHT

'OH, NO I couldn't possibly do something as energetic as go to the races today,' May said when she finally surfaced around ten. 'I'm wrecked. But you two go. No, I insist,' she went on when Bianca started to object to that idea. 'I'll be fine here on my own. I'll loll around watching TV, and then I'll have a nap after lunch. What time do you think you'll be home?'

'The last race is at four-thirty,' Adam said, 'but I always leave before that. I'd say six should safely see us back. Would you like to go out for dinner tonight, May?'

'Not tonight, thank you, Adam. But I'll tell you what I would like…'

'Your wish is my command.'

'Some Chinese takeaway. No particular dish. I like just about everything Chinese.'

'Done! We'll bring a selection home with us.'

May smiled at him. 'That would be lovely.'

Adam felt quite pleased at this outcome, though actually he'd had no intention of going to the races that day at all before Bianca had asked about his coming home last night. The previous Saturday's results had taught him to give his system a rest for a while.

It only worked well with top-class horses, it seemed, and they were all out on spells after the recent conclusion of the spring racing carnival, both in Melbourne and Sydney.

But he rather fancied taking Bianca to the races, he thought as he got dressed. He often saw well-heeled businessmen there on a Saturday afternoon, with their latest dolly-birds on their arms. Most of them mistresses, no doubt. They just didn't have that wifely look about their model figures and perfectly painted faces.

He'd imagined Bianca as his mistress more than once in his darker moments. He'd fantasised about becoming filthy rich and buying her for himself with the sheer power of his millions. Her lack of desire for him hadn't mattered in that scenario. She would do whatever he wanted because he was paying her exorbitant amounts of money, dressing her in designer clothes and giving her lavishly expensive gifts of jewellery.

Unfortunately, in reality Bianca was not too impressed with money, or designer clothes, or jewellery. The girl went around most of the time in shorts or jeans, her only jewellery a clunky black sports watch with which she could time her jogging. She had two androgynous-looking suits she wore to work—navy and black—mixed and matched with various cheap blouses and T-shirts. It was no wonder he had been startled to see her in something soft and feminine last night.

Still, the present pretend situation allowed him some leeway when it came to buying her things, and he didn't have to buy her desire now. He already had that. Amazingly.

This thought brought with it an elation and a boldness which, quite frankly, he was having difficulty in controlling. There wasn't anything he wouldn't dare to do. There wasn't anything he could *not* do, he decided as he pulled on a shirt.

Except win her love, came that sly voice, and he stopped buttoning his shirt for a moment, a scowl sweeping his face.

For a moment, this morning, he could have sworn Bianca had been going to tell him she loved him. He'd thought she'd felt the magic between them. But the magic had only been on his side, obviously.

All she wants from you is sex, that rotten voice went on. You'll go the same way as all the others eventually. Tossed in the garbage like a used tissue.

Adam straightened, scowling some more.

'I will not listen to you today,' he muttered to himself. 'You're destructive. And depressing. I'm happy this morning, dammit. Just shut up.'

'Talking to yourself, Adam?'

Adam whirled, his expression wryly amused when he saw that Bianca had dressed in her usual weekend garb of jeans and sleeveless T-shirt. Since he himself always wore jeans to the races—hell, he was usually there to work at winning money, not a fashion-on-the-field award—he could understand her mistake. But that was not how they were going to arrive at Randwick today.

'Just making a deal with the devil, darling,' he told her, and her eyebrows lifted.

'So that's how you win at the races, is it? By the way, Mum thinks it's rather odd that all my clothes are in the spare room, but I told her you had so much musty old junk in your wardrobe there wasn't room for mine. Now, why in heaven's name are you smiling at me like that? Is there something wrong with the way I look? *You're* only wearing jeans!'

'Too true. But I keep my racing clothes elsewhere. I'm going to change on the way, and you, my dear wife, will be changing with me.'

He was delighted to see she was totally flummoxed at this announcement. He was also delighted that the presence of her mother in the flat precluded Bianca launching into an Aussie version of the Spanish inquisition.

But peace only lasted till he bundled her into the BMW around eleven. No sooner had he pointed the car south, in the direction of the city, than she started.

'Adam, I don't like it when you keep secrets from me. I want to know—'

'Why aren't you playing netball this afternoon?' he

broke in, determined not to satisfy her very female curiosity.

Her sigh was heavy. 'If you'd been around lately, you'd know I played the finals of the netball season two months ago! And my team happened to win. Haven't you seen the trophy on top of the television?' she asked in a miffed tone.

The place was full of sports trophies Bianca had won. He was proud of her achievements, but jealous at the same time. He would rather she played with *him* than a silly old netball.

'Congratulations,' he said drily. 'But that doesn't answer my question. Isn't there a summer season?'

'Yes, but it's played at night because of the heat. I don't like playing sport at night. Night-time is for other things.'

'I'm sorry I asked,' he muttered, though not sorry she wasn't playing netball. He had other plans for Bianca this afternoon.

'Adam, you still haven't explained what you meant when you said we were going to change clothes on the way to the races. That is what you said, isn't it?'

'Yes. Tell me, Bianca, do you ever regret not doing a degree in Physical Education, as you always planned to do?'

She frowned her frustration at his changing the subject again. 'No,' she grumped, and folded her arms, obviously giving up on getting answers to her questions.

Adam smiled. Bianca not getting her own way with him had an undeniable appeal. He didn't think he would ever get tired of it.

'You don't miss being a sports mistress?' he asked, before realising what he'd said. 'Sports mistress' rather described her to a tee.

'I was very happy doing a business degree, thank you very much,' she retorted. 'If you remember rightly, there was no scholarship I could win for PE like I managed with business. Dad was dead by then and Mum was just making ends meet. A scholarship *plus* my part-time job at Franklins meant she didn't have to spend every cent on my education and she had a bit left over for luxuries for herself for a change.'

Adam sighed to himself. Just when he started thinking Bianca was a selfish chit he came face to face with her good qualities. She did so love her mother. And she wasn't at all mean and selfish when it came to material things. To be honest, she was a good friend too. When she'd said she would have pretended to be his *wife*, if he'd asked her, she'd been quite sincere. She would have. Without giving it a second thought.

'I was disappointed at first,' Bianca admitted, warming to the conversation. 'But I soon realised it didn't really matter what degree I did. I could still indulge my passion for sport in my spare time. And uni life was fantastic! I've never had such a good time as I had during those three years. It was such fun, Adam, wasn't it?'

Fun! Adam scoffed silently. That was the bottom line where Bianca was concerned. Fun! Well, *he* was going to have fun this afternoon, and he just couldn't wait!

'Indeed it was,' he agreed suavely, hiding his wicked intentions behind a wolf-like smile. 'And we're going to have more fun this afternoon. Trust me.'

Bianca fell into a blinking, wide-eyed silence while Adam simply kept smiling, neither speaking till they arrived at North Sydney and he swung off the road, driving down a ramp into the underground car park of the high-rise building which housed the penthouse unit he owned.

'I hope you're finally going to tell me what on earth we're doing here?' she demanded to know, her silence quickly giving way to angry exasperation. 'Unless Randwick Race Course has been dramatically picked up and moved indoors, I don't think we're at the races yet. Or is this the mysterious place where you keep your racing clothes?' she asked tartly. 'In a basement car park?'

'Did anyone ever tell you, Bianca,' he said smilingly as they both climbed out, 'that you're beautiful when you're mad?'

She rolled her eyes at him over the roof of the car and he laughed.

'Come on,' he said, and walked round to take her hand. 'We haven't got a lot of time.'

'For *what?*'

'For getting My Fair Lady ready for the races!' he pronounced, and, totally ignoring the bewilderment on her face, he started dragging her towards the basement lift.

The next hour was one of the best in Adam's life.

The building above them was not just an apartment block; it housed offices on the first few floors, with the ground floor being devoted to shops of all kinds. Most of these shops catered to the wealthy yuppy career woman, who possibly lived in the building or worked there.

Adam headed for the most expensive and largest boutique, which had a make-up and hairdressing section attached, told one of the superbly groomed salesladies what he wanted done with Bianca—amazing how helpful the woman became when he slipped her a hundred-dollar bonus for herself—then left a still stunned Bianca in her undoubtedly capable hands while he dashed upstairs to change into his grey silk-blend Italian suit.

He returned just in time to see a strikingly made-up Bianca emerge from one of the dressing rooms, hair sleekly up.

She did a double-take when she saw him standing there in his suit, but after a couple of frozen seconds she shrugged acceptance of the craziness of it all and started to parade herself for his inspection and approval.

The cream trouser suit she was wearing was elegant, but not at all what he'd had in mind.

'Well, Adam, darling?' she said in a breathy voice as she catwalked her way around the heavily mirrored display area. Wickedly laughing blue eyes showed him she'd decided to join in the spirit of the dressing-up game. 'What do you think?'

He cocked his head on one side, looked her up and down, then coolly shook his head. 'No. Cream doesn't suit you.'

She pouted prettily and gave the sales-lady a mock desolate look. 'My husband doesn't think cream suits me. Oh, dearie me, whatever will we do? Off with the cream and on with the new,' she tossed back airily as she sashayed off to the dressing room.

Adam smiled to himself. What a wicked little minx she was! But what a woman! It was no wonder he loved her. No other female he'd ever met compared with Bianca.

She came back five minutes later in a slender red silk dress with a Chinese collar and slits up the sides. She looked exotic and pretty, yet oddly innocent, almost childlike as she paraded around in her bare feet, beaming at him. Clearly she liked herself in this dress, but it was not the look he wanted.

He shook his head again. 'Very nice, but I'd like to see her in black,' he ordered. 'Something short and tight. And some high heels, please. Black, with an ankle strap.' He'd noted they had a pair like that in the small range of expensive and very sexy shoes on display in one corner of the shop.

Bianca's blue eyes opened wide for a second, as did her scarlet-glossed lips. Her mouth snapped shut at the same moment her eyes narrowed. Now she didn't look quite so happy to play this game. Her lips pouted further, as they did when she was displeased. She looked petulant, and so damned sexy he almost changed his mind about the races. The penthouse awaited upstairs, as did the king-sized bed...

But, no... He had another fantasy in mind for the penthouse. Today was mistress day.

Besides, tonight would eventually come. And it would be all the better for the waiting.

It was ten minutes before she returned from the dressing room, by which time he was dangling on a delicious razor's edge of sexual tension, the like of which he'd never known before. The sight of her quite took his breath away.

The outfit was black, as ordered. A scandalously short, tightly fitting, figure-hugging dress, with a low, wide square neckline that barely covered her nipples.

Adam eventually dragged his eyes away from Bianca's tiny but well-defined breasts to travel slowly downwards, past the expanse of bare tanned thighs, past slender knees and beautifully shaped calves to her erotically clad feet. The outrageously high heels lent her legs the illusion of great length, the sight of the ankle straps giving his desire for her a piquant push.

He had never seen her looking sexier. Or *less* innocent.

For a moment he imagined all the men at the races looking at her and wanting her, and was torn between wanting to hide her away for his eyes only and flaunting her for all the world to see. Something dark inside him tempted to show her off, to show everyone that at last she was *his*...even if it was only in the most elemental way.

Yes, that was what he wanted, he decided with a devilish satisfaction. There would be no hiding her body away from ogling eyes, no conventional good-guy path.

His conscience pricked a warning, but he would have none of it. This was what she wanted him to be, wasn't it? This was what turned her on. Primitive man. The predator. The possessor.

But then she looked at him and he saw a flicker of dismay in her eyes.

His instant remorse annoyed him. But it was too late. His love for Bianca resurfaced with a vengeance—as did his conscience—and he knew he would not enjoy himself if Bianca was feeling that uncomfortable.

'No, I don't think so,' he said almost regretfully. 'Not for the races. The red silk was better. But I will

take the black as well,' he told the sales-lady in a
husky aside. He just might have Bianca wear it for
him one evening next week in the penthouse. They
could have a private candlelit dinner together. Then
afterwards...

'Would your...er...*wife*...like some jewellery to
go with her dresses?' the sales-lady asked.

Adam was taken aback for a second by the knowing way the woman had said the word 'wife'. Clearly
she didn't believe Bianca was any such thing. He
gave the woman an icy glare but she wasn't fazed.

'We have some exquisite costume jewellery here,'
she went on, indicating a showcase filled with dazzling pieces. 'What about these lovely black crystal
drop earrings and matching bracelet? They could only
enhance madam's striking beauty, don't you think?'

He did think. But when Bianca returned, wearing
not only the red silk dress but the strappy black high
heels, he had a moment's doubt. Once the glamorous
earrings and bracelet were in place, his doubts grew.
Suddenly she looked a lot less innocent than she had
earlier.

Not that Bianca seemed concerned any more, he
noted wryly. Her blue eyes were bright and shining
with a return to her earlier mischievous manner. Why
should he worry if she wasn't?

'I had no idea you had such beautiful taste in
clothes, darling,' she cooed as she slipped her arm

through his. 'I must have you take me shopping more often.'

Adam gave her a droll look while he silently called himself every kind of fool. He should have made her wear the black. It would have matched her devil's soul. There he'd been, thinking she was upset at being dressed up like a sex object. Instead, she was enjoying every perverse moment!

'Any time, darling,' he drawled. 'I don't mind what I spend on you as long as I get value for money.' He looked her up and down with lazy eyes, lingering on the outline of her braless nipples under the thin red silk. 'And there's no doubt you look the part perfectly.'

By the time his gaze returned to her face, Bianca's blue eyes were flashing, the high colour in her cheeks showing that her blood was rising again.

Good, he thought. Bianca in a temper was an incredibly passionate creature. She'd been spitting mad with him last night and look where it had got him. In bed with her. If he could not have her love then he'd settle for her body.

His smile was darkly triumphant as he turned her round and patted her on the backside. 'Now off you go and collect your old clothes, darling,' he said thickly, 'while I pay for your nice new ones.'

All together, counting the dresses, shoes and jewellery, the bill came to a little over three thousand dollars—not counting the tip he'd given the woman.

Still, in Adam's view it had been worth every cent. This was going to be a fun afternoon after all!

He paid with his bankcard, knowing that what he'd won at the casino this week covered it more than twice over. He could have paid cash, but he wanted to keep that for the races. He was going to bet big this afternoon, in keeping with the occasion. He'd never been on such a dangerous high before. Never felt this bold, or this deliciously bad.

Adam was sure that if he could keep his stupid conscience out of play, he was really going to enjoy himself.

Bianca could not stop staring at Adam as he led her back towards the bank of lifts which would carry them down to the basement car park. Partly because he looked incredibly handsome—wherever had that gorgeous grey suit come from?—but mostly because of the expression on his face. There was something dark and dangerous lurking in his cold, yet strangely *hot* grey eyes. Something…wicked.

Adam being wicked held a kind of shocked fascination—especially since Bianca had spent her entire life thinking of him as a bit of a goody-two-shoes. Clearly he was far from that.

Still, his being wicked could be fun. She'd actually enjoyed herself back in the boutique, had revelled in the whole dressing-up game. Yet the finished result was a far cry from the classily dressed My Fair Lady, off to Royal Ascot. She looked more like Suzie Wong, ready for a night on the town. If her mother could have seen her, she'd have had a pink fit! She'd certainly be asking her daughter some pertinent questions.

Bianca herself was determined not to let Adam keep sidestepping her own questions.

'Mind telling me what's going on, darling?' she asked saucily as they waited for the lift doors to open. 'Do you make a habit of tarting up your female friends for an afternoon at the races? Or is this charade just for me, for some reason?'

His smile was irritatingly sardonic. 'Now don't be tedious and start asking more useless questions. I have no intention of answering them.'

Which was another thing that was bothering her. This increasingly enigmatic and uncooperative side of Adam's character. She'd been so right when she'd thought him a stranger before. He was.

'The least you can do is tell me where you got your suit from?'

'Why?'

'Because I want to know! Did you rent it? Yes, I'll bet you did. Like you rented that tux you were wearing last night. There's a clothes rental shop in this building, isn't there?'

The lift doors opened and he walked in, turning to smile at her from the far corner. 'Just get in, Bianca.'

Pursing her lips together, she tried to stalk in with

her usual long stride, only to wobble on the appall-ingly high heels she was wearing. 'Watch it,' he said, reaching out to steady her.

She wrenched her arm away and glared her temper at him. 'If I wasn't wearing these tart's shoes, I'd be fine.'

'I didn't ask you to wear them. Not with the red silk, anyway,' he added drily.

'I could hardly wear my old trainers. Or nothing at all!'

'No, nothing at all would not have been suitable.'

'Neither was that disgusting black dress I was poured into—the one you still bought.' She rattled the large plastic shopping bag at him, which contained her old clothes plus the black bit of nothing. 'If you think I'd ever wear that whore's dress in public, then you have another think coming!'

'I have no intention of letting you wear that partic-ular number in public, Bianca. It's for my eyes only.'

She blinked widely at him as an image of her pa-rading around in private for him in the black mini popped into her mind. She'd exaggerated when she'd called it a whore's dress. It wasn't *that* bad. A lot of girls dressed like that these days when going out at night. Short, tight and sexy was in. But she'd never felt comfortable displaying her lack of any real cleav-age.

Still, she had to admit that when Adam had looked at her in that dress, she'd been…well, she'd been very turned on. She had been quite discomfited by the fact, especially when she'd felt her breasts swell and her nipples tighten.

In truth, she *still* felt turned on. She only had G-string panties on, which had been fine under jeans but made her feel half-naked and very sensuous underneath a thin silk dress. She didn't even have any tights for security, and was very aware of her bare thighs and buttocks. On top of that, her nipples had stayed erect, poking like little pebbles against the cool red silk.

'I still feel decidedly undressed,' she complained.

'Is it my fault you don't wear a bra?'

'You don't want me wearing a bra and you know it,' she countered sharply. 'I'm not dumb, Adam. I finally get the picture. This is the price I have to pay for you pretending to be my husband, isn't it? I not only have to take over Sophie's duties in bed but everywhere else as well! I saw the way she was dressed the other night. You have this *thing* for tarted up women, don't you?'

Once again he said nothing, just leant his back against the far wall of the lift and surveyed her slowly, his eyes darkening as they moved inexorably to her nipples.

'You look incredible,' he said in a desire-thickened voice.

'I look cheap,' she snapped.

He laughed. 'Hardly cheap. That outfit set me back a pretty penny.'

'And that's another thing,' she said, frowning. 'I know what it means when dresses don't have price-tags on them. It's the same as restaurants which don't have prices on the menus. It means everything's hor-ribly expensive. You're not that rich, Adam, that you can afford to throw your money around like confetti. You shouldn't be wasting your hard-earned money like this.'

The lift doors opened and Adam levered himself away from the wall. 'Don't you worry your pretty little head about what I spend my money on, Bianca. You're not my *real* wife.

'Now…' He took her arm and began leading her forcefully across the car park 'Let's get moving. By the time we get to Randwick we'll have missed the first race. But no matter—the first couple of races are never the best ones to bet on.'

Bianca thought of standing her ground and *de-manding* some answers, but, in truth, she suspected Adam would be as good as his word. He wasn't going to tell her where his own expensive clothes had come from, or deny or confirm why he'd had her dolled up like some sex-pot.

Besides, she had to admit that beneath her exas-peration lay an excitement which would not be de-nied. It *was* fun to be dolled up like this, and to have her blood zinging through her veins. She felt not a little wicked herself, so when she climbed into the passenger seat and the slits in her dress parted, exposing most of her stockingless thighs, she made no attempt to cover herself. She might not have big boobs, but she had great legs!

Adam likes to see female flesh, she thought breathlessly. Then female flesh he will see!

When Adam glared down at her expanse of exposed thigh with disapproval on his face, Bianca was thrown completely. Wasn't this the sort of thing that turned him on? Apparently not...if his scowl was anything to go by.

'I think, darling wife,' he muttered as he fired the engine, 'that we'll be standing up all afternoon.'

Bianca could only shake her head in utter bewilderment when Adam reversed rather angrily out of the parking space. Now she had no idea what game he was playing. Or what he felt for her. Or what role he expected her to fulfil this afternoon.

He'd become a mystery man, all right. But a rather fascinating man as well, she realised as she slid a sideways glance over at his closed but very handsome face. Her gaze drifted down to his lips, which at that moment were pressed testily together. His full bottom lip was jutting forward a little. It looked incredibly sexy. *He* looked incredibly sexy.

Desire knotted her stomach and she thought, all of a sudden, of the many hours which separated her from going to bed with Adam tonight.

Too many, she decided ruefully as she felt the blood begin to gallop around her veins. Far too many…

By the time Bianca uncurled herself from the passenger seat of the BMW half an hour later, she had her wayward body only partially under control. Standing up, she skimmed the red silk dress back down her thighs in an unconsciously nervous movement, at the same time trying not to wobble in her five-inch heels.

Adam watched her with another of those unnervingly sardonic smiles he'd suddenly discovered. He was no longer looking disapproving of how she looked. Just drily amused.

Rebellion surfaced along with her ongoing frustration.

He wanted a sexual exhibit on his arm? Well, he'd get one. And to hell with the consequences!

CHAPTER NINE

ADAM wasn't enjoying himself as much as he'd thought he would. The next bloke who leered at Bianca was going to get a fist in his face!

Of course, *she* was having the time of her life, the lying little devil. There she'd been, pretending she didn't like the way she looked, but since she'd started being on the receiving end of ogling male eyes, she'd been lapping it all up like a cat with cream.

She'd sashayed her way around the course, fluttering her eyelashes at every man they passed and wiggling that sexy bottom of hers, which was looking *so* sexy in that red dress it was downright sinful.

On top of that, she'd already downed more glasses of champagne than he'd ever seen a female down and stay standing. No doubt she was as high as a kite, because she'd started to giggle—something Bianca never did—and to drape herself all over him—something else Bianca never, *ever* did, not with any man.

By the fourth race Adam had just about had enough. He wanted to leave, but, darn it all, he was winning again, weirdly enough. A punter never left the track when he was winning, though the next race left a lot to be desired.

'Oh, look, the darling horseys are coming out!' Bianca explained, with the best bimbo vocabulary Adam had ever heard. 'Which one are you going to put your money on, honey?' she gushed, holding onto his arm so tightly Adam suspected it was to keep her upright, not because she was inordinately fond of him.

'I wish I knew,' he said drily. 'The next race is a two-thousand-metre event which doesn't have a single runner tried at the distance. I'll just have to try pot luck with a combination on top trainer and top jockey.'

'Why don't you use that wonderful old system you foisted on us unsuspecting students during our first year at university?' Bianca suggested with a saucy smile. 'You know, the one where you were going to turn our miserable hundred dollars each into a fortune? It didn't do too badly, I suppose,' she went on, her blue eyes glittering with wicked amusement. 'Only twenty-nine consecutive losers!'

Adam cringed at the memory. What a fiasco! 'Trust you to remind me. Still, I've learnt a thing or two about racehorse systems since then. *And* staking plans. You need a damn sight more than a few hundred dollars to start with if you wish to survive!'

'I'll bet I could pick you the winner,' she said, with the blithe confidence of the merrily intoxicated. 'If it's a long race and none of them have run with distance before then the fittest will undoubtedly win. I'm an expert on fitness. Come on...'

She dragged him over to the railing on the saddling enclosure, where the horses were still being led around in circles by their grooms.

'Look at that one!' she pointed out eagerly. 'Talk about rippling muscles. Have you ever seen a fantastic rump like that one?'

'Er...' Adam gave Bianca's own well-defined rump a rueful glance. 'Not too often.'

'That's definitely the winner!' Bianca announced, after another minute's superficial survey. 'There's not another horse to touch it. I demand you put a bet on that one for me.'

'All right. If you insist.' She'd die when she saw the ticket, but it would be sweet vengeance for her amusing herself at his expense.

Smiling, he propped a sozzled Bianca up against the railing, then went to place the bet at the tote window before hurrying back. He had a feeling he didn't dare leave Bianca alone for long. She looked far too delicious. And she was far too tipsy.

He'd been right. By the time he returned, less than five minutes later, some good-looking slimeball with a moustache and money written all over him was chatting her up. Bianca was looking up at him with a rapt expression, as though he were God's personal messenger, and it took all of Adam's control not to walk up and thump the creep right in his perfectly capped teeth.

As it was, his voice was glacial as he joined them

and said, 'Thanks so much for looking after my wife. But I'll take her back now.' And, clamping an iron grip around Bianca's upper arm, he practically dragged her off, not stopping till he found a relatively secluded corner.

'Ooh, how masterful!' Bianca said, then giggled.

'You're plastered,' he snapped, whirling her round to face him.

'You noticed!'

'And you're acting like a cheap whore.'

'Well, of course! Isn't that what you wanted?'

Her words hit him like a low blow in the stomach.

No, of course that was not what he wanted. He wanted her as his wife, not his whore.

Still, he couldn't deny she'd so aroused him that afternoon that he could not stand another moment's torture.

'Let's get out of here,' he said brusquely.

Her lovely but slightly glazed eyes blinked up at him. 'But you just put a bet on that horsey for me.'

'It's collectable any time if it wins,' he growled, and, taking her elbow, began to steer her back through the crowd.

'Where…where are you taking me?'

'Somewhere we can be alone.'

She ground to a halt, swaying on her high heels as she did so. 'I never thought you were the type of man to take advantage of a girl,' she said, her voice slurring.

He laughed. 'Your mistake, then.' And to prove his point he bent to take her startled mouth in a brief, hungry kiss. When his head lifted her eyes were glazed in a way which suggested he could take advantage of her all he liked and she would not object. The thought sent his conscience to hell, and he aimed to keep it there.

This was the life! For the time being, anyway. He was under no illusions that it would last. He figured he would at least have the next fortnight with her, maybe even a month to two...if he could keep up the bad-boy act long enough and well enough.

But sooner or later his masquerade would be discovered, and Bianca would see that underneath he was the same old Adam he'd always been. Once that happened this spark he'd managed to fire in her would no doubt be snuffed out, and she would cut him adrift again.

A black despair invaded his heart at this inevitability, and it was with some difficulty that he blocked it from his mind. He managed quite well once he turned his thoughts to taking advantage of her in the very near future.

'No more chit-chat,' he snapped, and resumed propelling his torment back to the car.

Irritatingly, she did what he asked, not saying a single word during the drive back from Randwick to North Sydney. Her silence grated on his nerves, and he began to worry about what she would say when she saw the penthouse. Not that he intended telling her all. Bad boys never explained, or confided. They simply shrugged off questions then took what they wanted.

'What are we doing back here?' Bianca was finally driven to ask when he directed the BMW into the same basement car park he'd taken her to that morning. 'Do you have to bring your suit back? Is that it?'

Adam frowned his puzzlement. 'What in God's name are you talking about, Bianca? I own this suit.'

'Oh. I…I thought you must have rented it.'

'Your mistake again. Stay there,' he said as he switched off the engine. 'I'll come round and help you out.'

Which he did—not so much to act the gentleman, but to leer nicely at her naked legs, the sight of which had tormented him all afternoon. Looking at her firm brown thighs did little, however, for his resolve not to rush things once he got her upstairs.

'Where are you taking me?' she asked shakily as he led her once again to the bank of lifts.

'Somewhere private.'

'Must you be so mysterious?' she threw at him once they were in the lift.

'It saves answering a whole lot of unnecessary questions.' And unnecessary arguments. He'd brought her here for sex, dammit, not for true confessions.

He should have known that wouldn't be the end of it. When he inserted the key into the lift lock for the top floor, she started up again. 'You're taking me up to an apartment, aren't you? This building is one of those where they've converted the upper floors for city living. Who owns it? A friend of yours? The university?'

'Let's just say I have access to it,' he bit out. 'Now why don't you put a lid on it, Bianca? You're driving me crazy with all your questions. I haven't brought you here to cross-examine me.'

The lift jolted a little as it began its upward ride, and tipsy Bianca rocked against Adam's chest. His arms shot around her, one large palm landing on her bottom. His eyes locked with hers while slowly he pleated the red silk upwards till his fingertips encountered a delicious expanse of pouting and shockingly bare buttock.

Bianca's eyes turned a smoky blue at this point. Her lips fell apart and her tongue-tip moved seductively between her teeth in a tormentingly erotic way.

'I'm beginning to realise that,' she whispered, in the sort of voice which would have aroused a zombie. 'Perhaps you'd better show me exactly what you had in mind…'

'That was the best Chinese food I've had in years!' May pronounced, leaning back in her chair with a big smile on her face. 'But I've eaten way too much. You shouldn't have bought so many dishes, Adam. I've made a right little piggie of myself.'

'Nonsense! Chinese food's like that. In half an hour you'll be wanting to eat something else. Another glass of wine?'

'Just half a glass.'

'What about you, Bianca?'

'No, no more wine.' She placed her hand over her glass, but could not bring herself to look at him.

She'd sobered up considerably since their torrid lovemaking session that afternoon. My God, she had never known anything like it. It had been really wild.

Somehow they had made it inside the penthouse apartment before Adam had shown her well and truly why he'd brought her there. Not that she'd minded his savage haste. She'd been wanting him all afternoon, had been dying for his touch and his body. Neither of them had been able to wait, ravaging each other up against the door without turning on the light. They hadn't even undressed properly.

But that hadn't been the end of it. Adam had then carried her temporarily satisfied body to the biggest bed she'd ever seen, where he'd proceeded to drive her crazy for ages on what had seemed like acres of blue satin sheets. She had never realised any man could know so much about a woman's body, or how to torment it for so long without release. He had dangled her on a bittersweet edge till she'd been moaning

and groaning. And begging. Dear heaven, how she'd
begged!

But it hadn't been the begging that had bothered
her. In a way that had been exciting. For she had
known, in her heart, that Adam had not been trying
to punish her. He'd been making her pleasure last.
When she'd finally gone over the edge, it had been
incredible.

It had been her thoughts afterwards which had upset her. And the inevitable conclusions she'd come to
once she'd really taken in her surroundings.

She'd been lying there on those satin sheets, exhausted, glancing around the spacious bedroom with
its mirrored wardrobes and plate glass windows and
stunning view of the harbour, when she realised that
this could not be the first time Adam had used this
orgy palace for assignations with the opposite sex.
The certainty that he had brought that ghastly Sophie
there, had had sex with her in that very bed, had
turned her stomach.

She just hadn't been able to lie there after that, and
had scrambled out of the bed and dashed for the
shower, calling out to Adam that it was late and
would he please get her own clothes from the car.
She'd bundled up the other clothes, which had been
scattered around the place, stuffed them in the shopping bag, along with the jewellery, and left them
there.

If he had noticed her change of mood he hadn't

said anything—highlighting, to her, the fact that he didn't give a damn about her feelings. All he'd wanted from her was sex. The truth was that he'd dolled her up like a whore that morning and then treated her like a whore. Even worse, she'd *acted* like a whore.

She'd been relieved to leave that hateful place behind, plus those hateful clothes. She hoped Adam thought they were worth the money he'd paid for them. Maybe he could dress up his next bed partner in them! The surety that there would be other silly girls who would do what he wanted in the future was depressing in the extreme.

'You're very quiet, Bianca,' her mother said. 'And you haven't eaten much either. Aren't you feeling well?'

With an effort, she found a small smile. 'I have a bad headache,' she said. Which she did. Champagne did it to her every time, once the initial effect wore off.

'You look tired too, darling,' her mother went on. 'Why don't you go to bed early tonight?'

'I think I will.' She stood up and started clearing the plates away. At least when she was asleep she couldn't think, or feel upset.

'Adam and I'll do that,' May said. 'You go pop in the shower and get into bed. Would you like me to make you a cup of cocoa?'

'No, thanks, Mum. I'll be fine.'

But she wasn't fine. She crawled into bed feeling utterly wretched. Everything was so mixed up in her head. She tried telling herself that she couldn't possibly be in love with this new Adam, that beneath his sexy exterior he was quite hateful, really, nothing at all like the nice, kind, sweet person she'd grown up with—the one she'd always believed really cared about her.

This Adam didn't care about her. And he wasn't at all nice—no matter how well he was fooling her mother out there. He was hard and ruthless and selfish.

What had changed him? Had he been changing all along and she just hadn't noticed?

She lay there for what felt like hours, her head pounding, her heart just as bad. She must really love him to feel this badly. Just a sexual attraction couldn't possibly cause this much misery.

But he didn't love her back. He really didn't. He was amusing himself with her. And using her.

Dismay soon turned to outrage. She wasn't going to let him use her again. Or touch her again. Just let him try!

When he finally came into the room to go to bed, she lay perfectly still under the bedclothes, glad she'd found a big T-shirt of his to wear to bed. It came right down past her knees—knees which were bent right up to her chest. She was curled up in a foetal position, her eyes tightly shut, her back turned towards his side of the bed.

She listened to the sound of the shower, then to the sounds of his coming back into the room. She froze further when she felt the quilt lift, then flinched at the feel of his body settling behind hers.

For an excruciatingly long moment she thought she was safe. But then he took her shoulder and rolled her over against his naked side. 'No,' she said on a strangled sob of despair. For even that small contact made her want to melt against him. 'I…I still have a headache.'

'I doubt that. Care to tell me what's really bugging you, Bianca? I'm not a fool. You've been in a mood since before we left North Sydney.'

'I…I don't want you to touch me any more.'

'Really?' There was ice in his voice. 'What's brought about this change of attitude? You sure as hell didn't mind my touching you this afternoon. In fact, you couldn't get enough.'

'I was drunk.'

'Maybe, but you weren't drunk last night, sweetheart, and you were just as accommodating then. Don't give me this garbage. Tell me the truth.'

'Very well. I don't like being used!'

'Used?'

'Yes, used,' she snapped, scornful of his attempt to sound shocked. 'I'm sure you're familiar with the concept.'

He actually laughed.

Bianca was mortified. 'How dare you laugh at me?' she snarled. 'You're nothing but an unconscionable, hard-hearted, cold-blooded, ruthless rake, and I hate you!'

'Oh, no, you don't,' he returned, still chuckling drily. 'You probably think you're in love with me. God, but it's ironic. But don't worry. You'll soon be yourself again, darling. Being in love is only a temporary passion with you. So I'm going to keep on touching you, *and* making love to you. Let me burn out your unwanted fires that way, Bianca. It's much more fun.'

'Fun! Is that all you can think of these days? Fun?'

'Yep. I was taught by an expert. Now stop this nonsense and let me get on with restoking your flames. Methinks they've temporarily gone out.' He dropped light, teasing kisses on her outraged mouth till she simply didn't have the will to argue.

'You're incorrigible,' she muttered.

'And you're beautiful.'

She stiffened as his hand started stroking softly up and down her thigh. 'You have no conscience at all, do you?' she groaned. 'And you're still using me.' She trembled when that tantalising hand travelled higher. 'Men are all the same when it comes to sex.'

'Do you want me to stop?'

She sucked in a sharp breath as that hand found its mark. 'If you do,' she whispered breathlessly, 'I'll kill you.'

CHAPTER TEN

THE sun was shining brightly when Bianca slowly surfaced the following morning. Adam was sitting up in bed beside her, reading the Sunday papers and looking for all the world as if he'd been doing the same thing every Sunday for years.

His hair was tousled and there was stubble on his chin. But he looked utterly gorgeous, she thought, a wave of weakness flooding through her.

Oh, well. She acknowledged with wry acceptance her own ongoing susceptibility for this man. She'd never been renowned for her ability to resist gorgeous men!

He beamed over at her as she yawned and stretched. 'Guess what?' he said brightly. 'It won. That nag you made me bet on before we left the races yesterday. Better still, it was twenty to one! What say we go buy you a new car today?'

'Don't be silly,' she said, yawning again. 'One little bet isn't going to buy me a new car. Not unless you put a couple of thousand dollars on it.'

'Sorry. I only put one.'

'One dollar. Gee whiz. What are you planning on buying me with that? A toy car?'

'Nope. I thought a brand new Nissan Sports would suit you. With a red stripe down the side. Come on, let's go.'

'*What?*' She sat bolt-upright before she remembered she was naked. 'You've gone mad, haven't you?' she pronounced agitatedly as she snatched the sheet up over her breasts. 'Or you're on drugs. Is that it? You've been taking something?'

'The only thing I'm hooked on is you, darling,' he returned, and leant over to plant a kiss on her gaping mouth. 'Can't have my best girl driving her mum around in a dangerous, rusted old rattle-trap, can I?'

Bianca was shaking her head. 'Now I know you *are* mad. I don't feel I can take advantage of someone who's gone temporarily insane.'

'Why not? I am.' With this cryptic comment, he climbed out of bed and carried his beautiful body towards the bathroom. 'Come on, Bianca. The salesmen await. It wasn't one dollar I had on that noble nag. It was one thousand.'

'One *thousand*!' Bianca squawked, leaping out of bed and chasing after him. 'What on earth are you doing, betting big sums of money like that?'

'Winning,' he replied with a cheeky grin.

'But...but you won't always win, Adam,' she pointed out in a panicky concern for him. 'Sooner or later you'll start losing. No one wins for ever.'

The smile faded on his face as he yanked her under the shower with him. 'You think I don't know that?'

he growled. 'Look, I'm winning now. And it's making me bloody happy. I'll worry about losing when I start losing—fair enough?'

She stared up into his suddenly harsh eyes and wondered if she'd missed something. But then his mouth pulled back into a wicked smile and the moment was gone.

'Here,' he said, lifting up her hand and smacking a cake of soap into the palm. 'Make yourself useful, woman. I washed you last time. Now it's your turn.'

He bought her a new white Pulsar Sports with a red stripe down the side, even getting air-conditioning thrown in with the deal. Bianca was still in a bit of a daze as she followed Adam home in her lovely new car, her impressed mother by her side.

'What a lucky girl you are, Bianca, to have a man like Adam as your husband. He's so kind and generous. And he just adores the ground you walk on. There again…he always did. Never seen a boy so besotted by a girl as he was by you during your schooldays. I always felt rather sorry for him, loving you so much, because I was afraid you'd never see his worth, or feel about him the same way he felt about you.'

Her mother's ravings rather snapped Bianca out of her appreciative daze. For what her mother didn't know was that Adam was no longer that same besotted boy. He was a man. And very different from the slave-like adolescent her mother was describing. His kindness and generosity came with a price-tag these days, she realised as she thought of those clothes he'd bought her. And now this car…

Would he expect to be repaid in kind?

Her mouth went dry at the thought.

'By the way,' her mouth was rattling on, 'I didn't like to say in front of Adam, but that Derek fellow rang yesterday while you were out. It gave me great satisfaction to tell him you were at the races with your husband. You could have cut the silence on the other end of the line with a knife,' she finished smugly.

Bianca frowned. She didn't really care whether Derek believed she was married to Adam—at least it would keep him away—but she would have to remember to click on the answering machine in future, if they ever went out again leaving her mother behind. Otherwise some silly caller might let the cat out of the bag over Adam and herself.

This thought led to another. What if someone just 'dropped in' during the next fortnight? Michelle was given to doing that occasionally. Thank God she was away up the coast, visiting her parents. It was also as well that those same parents had retired recently and moved up to said coast, far away from Sydney. Still, Adam's parents rang him most weeks. She would have to tell Adam to ring them himself, during the day, thereby heading off any awkward possibilities.

Bianca was mulling over what else she might have

forgotten which would expose Adam and herself as frauds, when a small tan dog dashed across the road in front of her. Her heart leapt into her mouth as she braked and swerved, almost sideswiping another car. All to no avail. The awful clunking sound under the front wheels was sickeningly loud and unmistakable.

She'd hit the poor thing.

Her hands were shaking as she pulled over to the side of the road and turned off the engine, dreading what she would see when she climbed out. 'Stay in the car, Mum,' she ordered, sounding much more in control than she felt.

It was worse than she'd expected. Much worse.

The pathetic bundle of matted fur was lying in the gutter, his head lolling limply to one side, one of its back legs twisted at an impossible angle and a bloodied area around the hip. Bianca bent to look closer. The pup didn't have a collar round its throat and it wasn't moving.

It's dead, that's why, Bianca thought numbly as she bent to touch it lightly. I killed it. I'm a murderer.

She straightened and looked away, feeling sick. Adam, who must have seen what had happened in his rear-vision mirror and pulled over as well, came running back up the pavement.

'What happened? You almost hit that car. Dear God, Bianca, you scared me to death. For a moment there, I... Dear heaven, you're as white as a sheet. Oh, darling, don't cry,' he said, and gathered her to him. 'There, there,' he soothed, stroking her hair and cuddling her close. 'There's no need to cry. A miss is as good as a mile.'

'But I didn't miss,' she sobbed. 'I wasn't concentrating. I was thinking of my new car and…and other things, and then…and then it was just there, and I…I… Oh, Adam, I killed it!' she wailed, and buried her tearstained face in the warm expanse of his chest.

'Killed what?'

'That poor little dog,' she said, turning from his arms to point down the gutter.

It was then that the animal lifted his head and whimpered.

Bianca burst out of Adam's arms. 'It's *alive!*' She raced over and knelt down in the gutter, and patted the frightened puppy on the head. 'Oh, Adam, look, it's alive! Look, I didn't kill it.'

He *was* looking, with a wry smile on his face. 'So I see. I suppose you'll want me to take it to the vet now, and pay for all its bills, and then find it a home.'

'Well, it doesn't have a collar, Adam. And it's so skinny and scrawny. If anyone owns it, they're certainly not looking after it. But I can pay for the vet bills myself, if you'll help me get it there. I'm not that poor, and I've almost finished paying you back for my plane trip to Scotland.'

Her mother joining them at that stage rather put paid to that line of conversation. 'What's going on?'

she asked. It was then that she saw the dog. 'Oh, the poor little thing.'

'Adam's going to take it to the vet, aren't you?' Bianca said, looking up at him with pleading eyes.

He squatted down beside her, his hand on her arm as gentle as his expression. 'Of course,' he said softly. 'Did you think I wouldn't?'

Tears pricked at her eyes, for underneath she'd been worried that the new Adam might have a hard heart all the way through. Now she saw that down deep there was still a soft core. He was still someone she could count on, and the sense of relief was enormous. Her gaze blurred and she leant forward to kiss him on the cheek. 'Thank you,' she whispered.

He said nothing, merely patted her on the arm.

After a few seconds he stood up. 'I've got a blanket in my boot. You stay put with the dog while I go and get it.'

'It looks like a terrier of some kind,' her mother ventured while they awaited Adam's return. 'A nice-looking little dog.'

'I'm going to keep him if he gets better,' Bianca suddenly decided, blinking hard to stop herself from crying.

'You can't keep a dog in a flat, Bianca,' her mother said, with typical Scottish practicality. 'Do be sensible.'

'Then I'll move into a house,' she said stubbornly.

'I think Adam might have something to say about that, don't you?'

'What will I have something to say about?' Adam said on rejoining them. He knelt down and began spreading a blue blanket alongside the injured animal.

May pretended not to see Bianca's warning glance. 'Your wife wants to move to a house,' she said blithely, 'so that she can keep this dog. Actually, I agree with her—not so much because of the dog, but because a flat is not the best place to raise a family, no matter how nice it is.'

Bianca's silent groan was echoed in her face, but no one was looking at her. Adam's attention was all on the dog as he rolled it gently onto the blanket and Bianca's mother was watching him for some reaction, burbling on with meddling intent.

'You know, Bianca has always held the opinion she wouldn't make a good mother, but that's not so. My daughter has a wealth of maternal instinct in her. That's why she's always lavishing love on animals. I think she'd make a marvellous mother, don't you, Adam?'

Bianca saw the flash of scepticism in Adam's eyes before he wiped them of all expression and looked up at his pretend mother-in-law. 'I'm sure you know your daughter better than anyone, May,' he said as he wrapped the dog securely in the blanket and scooped him up. 'But I suggest you don't hold your breath on becoming a grandmother. Bianca has a mind of her own, and she just doesn't see herself as a mother just yet.'

Bianca could not have agreed with Adam more. Though the conversation brought back to mind that niggling qualm about the other night, when Adam had slept with her without protection. Still, her conceiving a baby on that one-off occasion would be like a thousand to one shot winning a race. When she looked at it like that, she decided it wasn't worth worrying about. One day a period would come along. And if it didn't…well, she'd cross that bridge when she came to it.

'Mum, you're being a meddling mother-in-law,' Bianca pronounced sternly, though she did feel a little sorry for her mother.

May had wanted a big family herself, but hadn't been blessed with one. And now her only daughter wasn't going to fulfil her very natural wish to compensate by having a tribe of grandchildren. She'd be lucky if she got *one* grandchild at some time in the nebulous future.

Bianca felt rotten about it but could hardly rectify the situation. It wasn't *her* fault she was lacking in the right hormones to become a prolific breeder. Like mother, like daughter, it seemed.

'Adam, do you want us to come with you to the vet?' she asked. 'You might need someone to hold the dog while you're driving.'

'No, I don't think so. This little fellow's not going anywhere, and I can keep a good eye on him in the passenger seat. I suggest you go on home—if you feel capable of driving, that is.'

'I'll be OK. It's only a few miles from here. I'll take it slowly.'

'You do that.'

'Adam…'

'Yes?'

'Oh…nothing.' She'd been going to thank him again, but that would look a bit funny in front of her mother. 'We'll see you later.'

'I could be quite a while,' he warned.

'I'll put dinner on. Is there anything special you want?'

'You know I like anything you cook, Bianca. Now do let me get this dog to the hospital or he'll die on me, and then there'll be hell to pay!'

'You and Adam have a wonderful relationship,' May said, once mother and daughter were on their way. 'Being best friends before you became lovers was probably all for the best.'

Bianca felt a sudden urge to shock her mother out of thinking everything was perfect, Adam included. What would be her reaction, she wondered, if she learnt it was Adam who'd taken her daughter's virginity, when she was only seventeen? May had always thought Adam was such a nice, quiet, good boy. So had I, Bianca thought. Till recently.

But to reveal that old piece of history would be so unfair. That hadn't been Adam's idea.

'We still have our problems, Mum,' she said instead. 'And don't you go believing what he said about that Sophie woman. He slept with her, all right.'

'Oh, no. No, I won't accept that. Your Adam loves *you*, my girl. He was only trying to make you jealous with that flashy piece of goods, like he said.'

Bianca shook her head. Little did her mother know that Adam *liked* flashy pieces of goods in general. He'd turned *her* into a flashy piece yesterday. Her mother would have *died* if she'd seen her.

'Much the same as you were doing with that Derek person,' her mother added. 'I know you too well to believe you were unfaithful to Adam, darling. You're the most faithful girl I know, once you've decided you love someone. In the past, that love has been somewhat misguided, but I can see with Adam that you love him now as much as he loves you.'

Bianca swallowed as tears threatened again. She wished. 'I hope so, Mum. But no more talk about babies, please. I can't even *think* of babies while my marriage is on shaky ground. Having a baby would be the worst thing I could do at this moment.' Which it most certainly would!

'Your marriage, my girl, is as solid as a rock,' her mother pronounced with irritating certainty.

Bianca almost laughed. 'How can you *say* that?

Two days ago my husband was dripping all over another very sexy woman.'

'I just can.'

'Second sense?'

'Common sense. And my own two eyes!'

'Whatever you say, Mum,' Bianca agreed, with a weary sigh. Thank God she was only going to be with them for a fortnight. Bianca loved her mother very much, but she loved her even more from afar!

CHAPTER ELEVEN

'IT WAS so good of you to buy me a business class ticket back home, Adam,' May said warmly. 'You're still a good boy. Now, look after my girl for me, won't you?' And she gave him a peck on the cheek.

Adam nodded, then stood back a little while mother and daughter said their goodbyes, doing his best to watch them without depression setting in. The call had come to board the British Airways flight to Edinburgh. It was time for Bianca's mother to leave, and time for his pretend marriage to Bianca to end.

Perhaps it was all for the best, he reasoned, firmly pushing aside his emotions to concentrate on logic. How long could he have kept playing a combination of perfect husband and perfect playboy?

In May's company he'd been as nice and wholesome as apple pie, but behind closed doors he'd kept up the bad-boy act, never taking no for an answer to his demands, but never answering Bianca's own perfectly natural questions about his gambling habits, and that puzzling penthouse and what he'd been up to in it.

Yet it was the bad boy she'd fallen in love with, not good old loyal Adam.

Which left him *where*, if he wanted to keep Bianca in love with him? Being a bastard for ever? She would eventually grow bored with that as well, he knew, so what was the point?

The point, he decided, with a surge of ruthless resolve, was to keep her in his life and in his bed as long as possible. Maybe he might even marry her for real while she was vulnerable to this new side of himself. Who knew what he might do?

Adam frowned. Hell, was being a bastard becoming second nature to him?

Bianca returned to his side, red-eyed and sniffling. 'She's gone,' she croaked.

He gave her his hankie and put a comforting arm around her shoulder. 'Do you want to stay and watch the plane take off?'

'No, I hate that.' She blew her nose noisily. 'I'd rather go visit Lucky.'

Adam sighed. 'That mangy dog again. You visited him the other day, didn't you?'

'I've been visiting him *every* day. You've been happily at work, so you wouldn't know.'

Happily at work? That was a joke.

It was as well his students had been doing end-of-year exams these past two weeks, as his concentration had been shot to bits. Lecturing in maths required a clear brain and some focus, but all he'd been able to think about all day every day was getting home to

Bianca. He was glad it was Saturday and he had the rest of the weekend with her.

It was only ten in the morning and the sun was shining. The rest of the day stretched ahead, warm and sensuous and theirs alone. He didn't want to waste too much of it visiting a dog, no matter how cute it was. Truly, he was beginning to feel jealous of that animal.

'You don't honestly mean to keep him, do you?' he asked.

'I certainly do. The vet said he'd be ready to go home tomorrow.'

'Might I remind you that all that talk of moving into a house was just talk for your mother.'

'I suspected as much,' she said glumly. 'But I do have friends, you know. Maybe one of them can look after Lucky for a while, till I can find a house to share with someone.'

'Such as whom?' Adam snapped. God, she meant to leave him for that damned dog! It felt as if he'd been kicked in the stomach. So much for his belief that even the bastard in him had captured her love.

She shrugged and stuffed the hankie into her jeans' back pocket. 'I don't know. I'll find someone.'

'I dare say you will,' he said sourly. Bianca had a knack for getting people to do things for her—himself included.

'Oh, all right,' he growled by the time they reached the car. 'I'll look around for a house.'

Her face was almost worth the effort he knew it would take, selling his unit and finding a house which wouldn't break his bank. Of course, if he sold the penthouse he would have plenty of money. But, damn it all, he didn't *want* to sell the penthouse. It gave him a real buzz, using the place—especially with Bianca in tow. He was planning on taking her there tonight.

'I'll go see some real estate agents today,' he added resignedly.

'Oh, Adam!' she exclaimed, and threw herself into his arms, covering his face with kisses. 'I do so love you!'

He grabbed her shoulders and held her away from him. 'Do you, Bianca?' he ground out, his heart thudding with a mixture of desire and anger. 'Do you really? This isn't just gratitude talking?'

Confusion clouded her lovely eyes for a moment. 'No,' she said at last, but in a tentative voice. 'No, it's not gratitude.'

'You love *me*?' He scowled with all the cynicism the years of rejection had put there. 'Adam Marsden? The same Adam Marsden you met in kindergarten?'

'Yes,' she said with heart-wrenching certainty, and went to kiss him again, this time on the mouth.

He stopped her. 'Great sex is not love, Bianca,' he pointed out coldly. 'When are you going to learn that?'

She looked uncertain now. 'I… It's not just that,' she said. 'Surely not…'

Adam's frustration was acute. To place his heart in her hands was unthinkable, no matter how much he was tempted. She had no idea of true love. No damned idea! Dear God, if he let her, she'd tear his heart out completely. She'd already broken it a dozen times over.

'Don't try to make the last fortnight into more than it was, Bianca,' he continued harshly. 'Your mother's gone away happy and we had a great time together. Let's leave it at that.'

'You mean you…you don't want us to…to continue?'

'I didn't say that,' he said roughly. 'But let's not romanticise our relationship. We're friends and flatmates who've discovered we're sexually compatible.'

'Sexually compatible,' she repeated, rather blankly.

Exasperation at her lack of insight had him pulling her against him and kissing her with more impatience than passion. 'There,' he growled, once he'd reduced her to trembling. 'That's sex, Bianca, not love. What we've been doing every night in bed is sex, not love. What we did in the penthouse was sex, not love. Get the picture?'

'Oh, yes,' she said, and the hurt in her eyes nearly killed him. 'I get the picture. Your pretending to be my husband was just for sex. Your being nice to my mother was just for sex. Your buying me that car was just for sex. Yet all the while, down deep, stupid me thought it was because you loved me. You're sick, Adam Marsden. And cruel. Don't bother selling the unit and buying a house on my account. Because I won't be living in it with you. I won't be having sex with you any more either!'

Her tirade pained him terribly. He grimaced and went to say something, but she was too quick for him.

'Oh, don't bother trying to defend yourself,' she bit out. 'I recognise a right bastard when I see one. Occasionally it takes me a while, but once the penny drops, it stays dropped. Funny—all these years I admired and respected you so much. I might not have loved you as I love you now, but I always thought highly of you. Now I wouldn't spit on you if you were on fire!'

He couldn't bear her looking at him like that. He just couldn't bear it.

She wrenched out of his hands and started stalking off.

'Bianca, don't go!' he called after her.

But she kept on walking.

'I love you!' he confessed aloud with a tortured groan. 'I've always loved you. You must know that…'

She stopped, then slowly turned, scepticism warring with hope on her ravaged face. 'Don't say that if you don't mean it.'

His shoulders squared and he looked her straight in

the eye. 'I mean it,' he said, looking strong on the outside while inside he was unravelling. Dear God, he'd done it now. He'd really done it.

Well, if he was going to burn his bridge behind him he was sure as hell going to get across that bridge first. He began walking towards her with a purposeful stride.

'I love you,' he repeated, his eyes locking hard with hers. 'And I don't want you to go.'

She fell into his arms, as he'd known she would. Bianca, he realised resignedly, *was* a romantic. What a pity her commitment never matched her ardour. It was a case of the flesh being willing, but the future being weak.

But, oh…that ardour…and that flesh.

He gathered her to him and began wallowing in both.

CHAPTER TWELVE

BIANCA had never felt so happy. Adam loved her. He'd *always* loved her, he'd said. All those qualms she'd been having over his treatment of her lately had already disappeared in the face of that love.

She lay back in the bubble bath and soaked in her happiness. Even her qualms about *this* place had been put to rest. He'd finally admitted that he owned the penthouse. He'd bought it a few years back while he was still living at home and market prices were down.

He hadn't paid cash for it, of course, just a deposit, then mortgaged the rest and rented it out for a tidy sum to a yuppy American insurance executive who'd been over here for a three-year stint in Sydney. When that lease had expired, two months ago, Adam had come in to do some repainting and redecorating and found himself staying over on the odd night, because he liked the place. But he planned on renting it out again soon.

It wasn't an orgy palace, he'd told her. Even if it looked a bit like one in some ways. Everything was so large and lush and plush—from the thick carpet to the huge bed to the satin sheets.

Bianca glanced around the equally large and opulent-looking bathroom, with its sunken spa bath and huge shower which could house an orgy itself if it wanted. She smiled idly as her toes played with the gold taps, which were shaped like dolphins.

What did it matter if Adam *had* brought Sophie here, she mused, or any of those bimbos he'd once dated? He hadn't loved them. He loved her. He'd *always* loved her, she reminded herself, revelling in the way that made her feel. So very, very special.

Any negative feelings—if there were any—in this wonderful new relationship with Adam were over her own past treatment of *him*. The knowledge that he had indeed always loved her filled her with some guilt, plus a very real need to make it up to him. She didn't deserve such loyalty and such an enduring love, but, since Adam saw fit to lavish such a love on her, she wasn't about to reject it. But she wanted to spoil him shamelessly in return for having put up with her all these years.

So thinking, she rose from the bath, towelling herself dry then massaging some perfumed moisturiser into her skin before pulling on the red and white kimono Adam had insisted she bring with her tonight.

He liked it on her, he said. And he liked her hair up the way she did it sometimes, piled haphazardly on top of her head, with bits and pieces falling around her face and neck.

She fixed it that way, and made herself up similarly to the way the girl had made her up that Saturday

Adam had taken her to the races—with plenty of eye make-up, blusher and bold red lips.

She surveyed the finished product in the vanity mirror, conceding that she looked…colourful.

A downward glance at her reflection noted the peaked nipples pressing against the silk. Two weeks ago she might have thought it was this provocative place turning her on, or the champagne she'd already downed—Adam had bought a bottle on his way here and opened it on arrival.

But it wasn't her surroundings or the alcohol which was causing her blood to fizz and her skin to tingle. It was love. She loved Adam as she had never loved a man before. With her heart as well as her body. He was everything a girl could want. The complete man. Basically good and kind and decent, but also beautiful to look at, with a wickedly sexy side which was as fascinating as it was fun.

She blushed as she thought of how assertive he could be when aroused. How…masterful. But Adam being masterful was not what she planned for this evening. It was *her* turn to be masterful, she decided. And his to be pampered. And loved. And made love to.

'Adam, where are you?' she called out as she came out of the bathroom, feeling a little nervy. She'd never played this role before, but was determined to do it boldly, and with flair.

'In here,' Adam called back from the direction of the living room.

It was in darkness, the only light the lights of the city shining through the window. Bianca sucked in a steadying breath and padded her way across the white shag-pile carpet.

The lounge setting was white too, a deep, low four-cushioned sofa flanked by two two-seaters, all with a view of the bridge, the harbour and the city beyond. The bridge was the focus at that moment, with its coathanger shape outlined against the clear night sky and a steady stream of cars moving like strangely reg-imented glow-worms from one side of the city to the other.

'You like watching the lights?' she asked as she approached his seated form.

His legs were stretched out in front of her, his arms along the back of the sofa. He was wearing jeans and a white T-shirt which hugged and displayed his mus-cles without help or artifice. Bianca still could not understand how she hadn't noticed his lovely body till recently. It was certainly a case of none so blind as they who will not see.

He glanced over at her, then stared, his steel-grey eyes glittering in the dim light. She hoped it was with desire. But she could not afford to question whether it was or not. She had to assume.

Swallowing, she walked around in front of him and sidled between his thighs, kneeling down and leaning forward to spread her hands over his T-shirted chest, revelling in the feel of the hard, broad planes underneath the thin material.

'What are you doing?' he asked. A tad agitatedly, she thought, for her palms had just grazed his male nipples.

'Shh,' she murmured, her tongue suddenly thick in her throat. 'I'm having fun.'

'Oh, I see.' She wasn't sure if she liked the way his mouth lifted at one corner. His expression was vaguely cynical. 'And am I going to have fun too?'

She reached up to smooth her fingertips over his lips, wiping the smirk away. 'You will if you're a good boy and just do as you're told.' She ran a sharply nailed fingertip down his throat and down his chest towards the waistband of his jeans.

He sucked in breath sharply. 'What if I don't want to be a good boy?'

She smiled a wicked smile. 'Then I'll have to punish you. You know what happens to bad boys, don't you?'

He was staring at her as though mesmerised. 'No,' he said thickly. 'What?'

She took his hand and, rising slowly to her feet, pulled him up with her. 'They're made to have a bath.'

'A *what*?'

'A bath. I'm going to give you a bath.'

His chuckle held a secret darkness which teased her

curiosity and inflamed her jealousy. 'Is there something wrong with my giving you a bath?' she asked
archly. 'Has some other woman done that for you
here?'

'No, no. You're the first, believe me. *Anywhere*. At
least the first since I turned ten. I wouldn't even let
my mother in the bathroom with me after that, and
certainly not my sisters.'

'Oh? What happened when you turned ten?'

'I started growing in certain areas,' he said drily.

'And you grew very nicely in those certain areas
too,' she complimented him as she led him towards
the still steamy spa bath.

He actually blushed but she pretended not to see.

'You're not going to undress me, are you?' he
asked, sounding a little panicky.

'But of course! What would be the fun in your
undressing yourself?'

'What, indeed?' he said in a droll tone.

She threw him a questioning look as she stripped
the T-shirt over his head. What was wrong with him?
Wasn't he liking what she was doing? He *seemed* to
be, by the look of the bulge in his jeans. Maybe he
just felt a little unnerved at not being the one in control. She could imagine that most men were like that.

She slid her hands over his bare chest and looked
up at him. 'Don't you want me to do this, Adam?'
she asked gently. 'I mean…I thought you'd like it. I
was going to wash you, and dry you, then give you

a massage, and then…' She gulped down the sudden lump in her throat. She hoped she'd have the courage to go through with all she had in mind—if he let her. 'I…I only wanted to please you…'

When his eyes closed tightly for a second, panic gripped in her heart, but then they opened and they were amused and smiling. He took her hand and placed it on the snap fastening of his jeans. 'Be gentle with me,' he murmured.

Relief had her laughing a low, throaty, sexy laugh. 'Don't worry. I wouldn't want to damage the equipment.'

Adam lay back in the bath, his last fantasy about Bianca coming true. She had stayed out of the bath for quite a while, kneeling beside him and washing his back and body in true geisha style. But gradually her kimono had become water-spattered, and he'd spied those magnificent nipples of hers poking through the wet silk.

The temptation to lean over and take one into his mouth through the material had proved too much for him. It hadn't taken long after that for him to peel the whole damned kimono off her trembling body and insist she climb into the bath with him.

Now she was sitting behind him, her legs wrapped with seductive sensuousness around his hips. It was erotic in the extreme to feel her open like that and pressed up against his buttocks. His fierce awareness of that area, plus her trailing a wet soapy sponge over his front, from his own hardened nipples to his even harder privates was both agony and ecstasy.

'A massage, you said?' he suggested at last, though God knew how he was going to stand that. Talk about self-torture!

He stood it quite well. For it was bearable bliss—provided he lay on his stomach. He kept his eyes shut, though. The image of her doing what she was doing in the nude was bad enough, but the knowledge that if he turned his head to the left side, with his eyes open, he would be able to see her in the mirrored wall, was perturbing in the extreme.

'Higher,' he ordered thickly, then groaned when what felt like her nipples brushed over his buttocks. It was too much for him, and his eyes half opened. He peered through the glazed half-slits at the sight of her, straddled across his thighs, her hard-tipped breasts swinging gently back and forth as she kneaded his shoulders.

'That's enough,' he grated out. She stopped, and he rolled over beneath her spread thighs. Love and desire crashed through him at the sight of her flushed face and wildly glittering eyes. She was beautiful, his Bianca. But never so beautiful as at this moment, caught in the throes of a passion which she sincerely believed was for him. He would be a fool not to see that she really thought she loved him.

It evoked some hope in him that maybe this

time…just maybe…her love might last. But then he recalled what she'd said to him out in the living room. 'Fun', she'd called it. Fun.

His heart hardened a little and he reached out to hand her the small foil packet he'd kept clenched in his fists.

'You do the honours,' he said, and gritted his teeth while she did. Expertly. Smoothly.

His own hypocrisy did not escape him, but still her skill annoyed him. Grasping her quite savagely by the hips, he lifted her up and angled her roughly down onto him.

Her gasp might have been a protest, or pleasure. He didn't know and told himself he didn't care. Blinding himself to anything but a determination to prove a point, he urged her to ride him, groaning with triumph when her initial hesitation was soon lost to her own soaring desire. He'd never asked this of her before, preferring to be the man on top up till now. But this time, he wanted to see for himself how wild a creature she was. And how wanton.

He watched her through narrowed eyes, trying to steel his heart against her, telling himself that this utter abandon had been witnessed and enjoyed by others before him, men she'd *thought* she loved. Where were they now, those men?

On the scrap heap of her life, that was where.

She stopped suddenly and smiled down at him,

making him moan when she bent down to give him a long, lingering kiss.

'In case you've forgotten,' she murmured against his lips. 'I love you.'

And then she went back to what she'd been doing, her hips lifting and falling with athletic and sensuous rhythm, her eyes never leaving his. He saw them grow heavy, saw them glaze over as her climax grew near. Her lips parted to cry out his name as she came, and with that raw, naked cry his body and his heart gave an answering burst of love for her once more.

He pulled her down on top of him afterwards, and buried his face in her hair lest she see his despair. For he would never love anyone as he loved her. He didn't know what he would do if she ever left him. The thought was unthinkable.

'Adam,' she whispered, making no attempt to remove him from her body.

'What?'

'I want you to know that I've never done that before. Been on top, I mean.'

He grasped her face and lifted it so that he could see her eyes. 'That's the honest to goodness truth?' he said, amazed yet moved. For he could see she wasn't lying. He'd always known when Bianca was lying. She could never really look him in the eye when she was telling fibs.

'I know you think I'm some kind of sex-crazed fool who used to fall at the feet of every muscle-bound bum who came my way, but that's not true, Adam. I haven't had that many boyfriends either. There've been times when many, many months have gone by and I've been all by myself.

'I never picked up any men during my back-packing treks overseas. I'm not that stupid! And even when I *was* involved with someone back home here, I never felt comfortable enough to do what I did today. I was always a bit self-conscious about taking the assertive role in sex. Frankly, I was too shy to be on top.'

Disbelief at what she was saying warred with his very deep need to believe her. '*You*, Bianca? *Shy*?'

'In some things I am. I…I've never been happy with my boobs. Or my lack of them. Fact is, I've never thought my body was much cop at all.'

'But you have a gorgeous little body!' he exclaimed. 'I think it's quite perfect.'

'I know you do,' she said, her heart turning over. 'That's why I dared to expose myself to you today in the most intimate way a woman can expose herself to a man. I wanted you to see me making love to you, to see how much I loved you.'

'Oh, Bianca…'

'You do believe me, Adam, don't you?' she asked, a little worried by the clouds of doubt which kept flitting across his face.

He said nothing for a moment, and when he smiled

there was something incredibly sad about it. 'Of
course I believe you. And I'm incredibly touched.'

'Tell me you love me, Adam,' she insisted, something about this conversation prompting panic in her
heart. 'Tell me you'll always love me.'

Why did he sigh? Why did he sound almost…resigned? And that smile again…that sad, sad
smile.

'I love you, Bianca,' he said, and no one could
have doubted the wealth of emotion in his raw voice.
'I'll *always* love you.'

Bianca sighed a deep, shuddering sigh of relief.

'Then let's go home, my darling,' she murmured.
'This is all very nice here, but it's not real life, is it?'

CHAPTER THIRTEEN

REAL life with Bianca, Adam soon decided, was great—despite an initial qualm that she might become bored with him once their relationship settled into a more regular routine.

Both of them returned to work on the Monday, after spending Sunday looking at houses and moving that lucky little dog, Lucky, out of the veterinary hospital and into some boarding kennels along Mona Vale Road, only fifteen minutes' drive away from his besotted new owner.

Monday evening was very pleasantly spent at home watching a movie on television after dinner before they finally went to bed, where Adam made love to Bianca with a leisurely passion compatible with his surprisingly relaxed and happy state.

Bianca seemed to like it, for she curled up against him and went to sleep straight away afterwards. For his part Adam found it a bit of a relief not to have to play the role of bad-boy lover extraordinaire. It was rather nice to have simple straightforward sex, full of tenderness and love. Who knew? Maybe Bianca was ready for this kind of relationship. Maybe she'd finally grown up where love was concerned.

Tuesday evening passed pretty well the same way, although there wasn't much on television, so they listened to music and chattered about the books they'd been reading. They'd always been very comfortable in each other's company and that had never changed.

They liked the same kind of movies on the whole, and the same kind of books, although Bianca was more into Stephen King than he was. They both liked fantasy fiction, with some adventure and romance thrown in. Only in music did they differ largely—Adam preferring jazz and country and western to Bianca's passion for pop and rock.

He came home early from work on the Wednesday—it was the last week of the term and things were really winding down—only to find Bianca already home from her office. She was sprawled out in the lounge, looking rather down in the mouth.

'What's up?' he asked, and dropped a kiss on that mouth as he sat down on the edge of the wide-cushioned sofa.

'I feel yukky,' she said.

'Yukky in what way?'

'Yukky in the stomach. I kept thinking I was going to heave up all day, but I didn't. Still, in the end the boss sent me home, since I was spending so much time in the toilet waiting for it to happen.'

'Hmm. I feel all right, so it can't be last night's dinner. Maybe you've got a virus. Poor Bianca,' he murmured, stroking her hair back from her forehead. 'You do look peaky. Perhaps you should go to a doctor, have yourself checked out.'

She gave him the oddest look. 'Maybe…'

'Don't worry about cooking anything tonight,' he said. 'I'll pick up some takeaway. I dare say you don't feel like eating much.'

'God, no. Nothing at all.'

She fell silent, frowning, and Adam had the feeling she was away in another world. It wasn't like Bianca to be sick. Or to be silent. Something was bothering her, but it seemed he wasn't to be privy to what it was.

He stayed sitting and stroking her hair and she closed her eyes, turning her face a little away from him. He was not a body language expert, but that small gesture bothered him. It felt like a physical as well as an emotional rejection.

The thought that Bianca wouldn't want him to make love to her that night was more perturbing than it should have been. He was being paranoid, he knew, but the niggling suspicion that there was more here than met the eye would not go away.

'Before I forget,' he said at last, taking his hand away. 'There's an end-of-year party of the faculty at the university on Friday night, so I'll be home late.'

Bianca opened her eyes and turned her head back with a sigh. 'That's all right,' she said, still not really looking at him. 'I'll have a drink with the people from work. They all go down to the pub after work on a Friday. Or I'll go to the gym if I'm feeling better by then. No doubt this is only a twenty-four-hour tummy bug.'

And it was. She felt much better the next day, she said, though she was still a little preoccupied, walking out of the door without kissing him goodbye as she had on the previous three mornings.

Adam vowed to ask her what was bothering her that evening, but no sooner was dinner over than an old girlfriend rang out of the blue—God knew where she'd got the number!—and Bianca talked and talked to her for simply hours.

Her name was Roberta, and she was one of the girls Bianca had gone backpacking around the world with—the sort of outrageously flip female one would never imagine settling down. But apparently she'd fallen in love with her dentist—poor bloke—and was getting married. From Bianca's side of the conversation, Adam gathered the stupid girl was pregnant as well, which was good for another hour's chit-chat about babies and such.

Adam went to bed on his own in the end, feeling quite resentful that Bianca preferred talking to a girlfriend than being with him. He was also beginning to feel vaguely unsettled by the atmosphere in general.

Was the rot already setting in?

He was coming to think so, lying there still wide awake when Bianca finally came to bed, though he pretended to be asleep. So he was pleasantly surprised when she snuggled in behind him, her hands wrapping lovingly around his body, her fingers caressing his chest and stomach.

When he groaned and rolled over and reached for her, he was taken aback when she said no, she didn't want to make love, she just wanted to touch him and hold him. Was that all right by him?

He said of course it was, but, while he enjoyed the feel of her hands touching and holding him, there was something strangely platonic in the whole scenario. It was as though she was telling him something with her hands—something he didn't want to hear. I love you, they seemed to be saying. But not the same way as I was loving you a week ago. That old spark has gone out. The sexual chemistry has died.

Adam lay there long after Bianca drifted off to sleep, lay there with his body aching and his heart breaking.

He could not bring himself to talk to her in the morning as they went about their breakfasts. She didn't seem to notice, her mind off in the clouds again. Or was it something far more down-to-earth which was occupying her mind? he began to think with savage jealousy. Had she met someone else? Was she trying to find some way to tell stupid old Adam to get lost?

'You're very quiet,' he said at last through gritted teeth.

Bianca looked up from her plate of muesli, something like guilt in her eyes. 'Am I? Sorry. I was thinking…'

'About what?'

'Oh…this and that.'

'Care to enlighten me on what "this and that" means?' he quizzed, trying not to sound suspicious and accusing.

She opened her mouth, then shut it again. 'It's nothing to worry *you* about,' she muttered. 'Yet.'

'That sounds very mysterious. When can I hope to know this dark little secret of yours?'

She actually blushed, and Adam's stomach tightened. Bianca blushing was as alien a concept as her staying in love.

'What makes you think I have a dark little secret?' she said.

'I know you very well, Bianca,' he returned ruefully. 'I can read you like a book sometimes.'

'No one knows anybody else all that well, Adam,' she mused cryptically. 'If we did we wouldn't flounder around, not knowing what to do and what to say sometimes.'

Now what did she mean by *that*? Was she afraid of his reaction if she broke up with him? Was she worried he wouldn't go as easily as dear old Derek?

Well, she was right there. He bloody well wouldn't! If the worst came to the worst he would revert to Adam Marsden, bastard of the month. No way was he letting Bianca slip out of his hands now. Hell, he'd get her pregnant if he had to. Though God knows how he'd manage that, with her taking the pill.

Thinking of the pill reminded him that Bianca hadn't had a period for a while, and a thought suddenly clicked. She could be suffering from PMT. She'd complained and complained about the effect the pill had on her, especially in the week leading up to her period. Her breasts would be sore, she'd have a bloated stomach and a yukky feeling.

Yes, of course—that was it! Why hadn't he thought of it before? Bianca had always been touchy about her body and her periods.

His relief was huge as he reached over to place a soothing hand on top of hers. 'If you're worried about the intimate side of our relationship once you get your period, then don't be. I know I was demanding at the beginning of this new relationship of ours, but I do realise things can't always be like that.'

She blinked at him. 'What? Oh, yes. Good. Thank you. That…that's a relief off my mind.' She stood up and moved swiftly over to the kitchen counter. 'Can I get you another cup of coffee?'

'No, I'd better get going. Don't forget I'll be late tonight,' he reminded her. 'It's sure to be at least ten before I can get away, which means it will be closer to eleven by the time I get home.'

'No sweat.' She didn't look up, her concentration on pouring boiling water into her mug.

He came over and gave her a peck on the cheek. 'Wait up for me, will you?'

She slanted him a quick smile, but he could feel the tension in her. 'Yes, of course.'

Adam could have bitten his tongue for seemingly putting sexual pressure on her when it was obvious she was not feeling the best. Yet, despite his guilt, an oddly desperate feeling suddenly swept over him, and as soon as she put the kettle down he pulled her into his arms, kissing her hungrily for a few seconds.

'How's that for a goodbye kiss?' he said stupidly and, whirling, strode out of the unit before he made even more of a fool of himself.

Bianca stayed on his mind all morning—and all afternoon. By the time the faculty party started that evening, he was a dead loss where being social and charming were concerned. He was worried about the woman he loved. There was something wrong. He just felt it.

'Sorry,' he told his chums over his first drink. 'But I simply can't stay. Family emergency.'

He dropped into the pub at Crows Nest on the way home, but Bianca hadn't joined her colleagues there that night, he was told. She wasn't at home either, so it seemed likely she was down at the gym.

The gym was Bianca's therapist. Whenever she was troubled or upset, she would work out. She'd once told him exercise was good for PMT, so it was likely she was down there, pumping iron or doing her third step class. That girl sometimes didn't know when to stop.

He decided to go down and stop her.

The gym was within walking distance of their block of units—Bianca always jogged down and back—but Adam was in a hurry so he drove down. He slid his BMW into the kerb opposite, switched off the engine and was about to climb out when Bianca came through the swinging front doors, dressed in purple lycra bike shorts and a matching midriff top.

Adam might have called out to her if she'd been alone.

But she wasn't.

Dear old Derek was with her, dressed in shiny blue boxer shorts and a black singlet top designed to show off his huge chest. He also had one of his huge arms solidly around her shoulder, and she was leaning into him as though for all the world she wanted them to become one right there on the pavement.

Adam wanted to kill them both, so he counted to ten—after which he still wanted to kill them both.

Don't jump to conclusions, he kept telling himself as he watched Derek fold Bianca into the low passenger seat of a sports car which matched its owner's shorts for colour and shininess, watched with a pounding heart and seething soul as they drove off together.

Adam might have scorched after them in the BMW if he'd been pointing the right way. As it was, the shiny blue Mazda accelerated away before he could say 'kill' and was gone. He sat there for simply ages, trying to get his black fury under control. Or was it black despair?

No, not despair. Despair didn't feel like this. Despair wanted to run and hide and cry, whereas Adam wanted to seize and strangle and scream!

She would have to come home eventually, he decided at last, with a cold calm that was as frightening as it was chillingly satisfying.

And when she did…

He drove home with seeming composure, only to have it shattered by the sight of Derek's car parked outside their block of units. She'd brought him *here*? A glance upwards at the unit showed that the lights were on in the front living room and master bedroom. As he watched the light in the bedroom clicked out.

Adam's pain knew no bounds. He could not believe she could be this wicked. Or this cruel! It was bad enough she'd taken up with Derek again, but to do so in *his* flat, and in *their* bed!

The only reason he didn't go upstairs then and there was because he knew he would not be responsible for what he did. She wasn't worth going to jail for life over.

What to do? How to handle it?

He stayed in his car and waited till Derek left at around ten-thirty. Then he waited till well after midnight, making sure Bianca would be asleep when he went in.

Icy tentacles wound round his heart as he stared down at her, curled up with seeming innocence in the middle of the bed. How could she just go off to sleep after what she'd done? Still, sex did exhaust one, he thought bitterly.

He hated having to climb into that bed with her, knowing what he knew, but it had to be done. Vengeance had to wait till morning. Besides, he wasn't ever going to let her suspect he'd witnessed her treachery. His male ego could not take that kind of punishment.

Lying there beside her, unable to sleep, he wondered how long she'd been planning to juggle both of them.

It wasn't like Bianca to be this treacherous, Adam agonised. To give her credit, she usually only had one lover at a time. And she was usually tremendously loyal while she was with her one and only. This type of deceit and double-dealing was something entirely new to her character.

Her mood over the past couple of days suddenly explained itself. She was feeling guilty. Very, very guilty.

But guilt hadn't stopped her from having her fun tonight, had it? Obviously she hadn't been as happy with the tender loving sex he'd been giving her this week as he'd thought she'd been.

'Adam?' she said dreamily from her half-sleep. 'Is that you?'

'Who else?' he bit out.

She yawned and rolled over. 'Did you have a nice party?'

Not as nice as yours, he thought savagely.

Shock crashed through him when she began to stroke his thigh. He stiffened in more ways than one.

'Too tired?' she asked when his hand abruptly closed over hers, only inches from the evidence of his unwanted and involuntary arousal.

'Let's just say I'm not in the mood.'

'Oh…'

Adam's resentment over her reaction to his rejection was acute. How dared she sound hurt? And how dare *he* still be tempted?

'Too much whisky,' he muttered, and rolled his back to her.

'You shouldn't drink and drive, you know, Adam,' she said, now actually sounding worried about him. Was there no limit to her perfidy?

'Yeah, well, there are a lot of things people shouldn't do, Bianca,' he growled, giving some vent to his simmering outrage. 'But that doesn't stop them. It's not a nice world. Now let me go to sleep, for pity's sake. I don't know about you but I'm wrecked.'

More than wrecked. Totally destroyed. But she would never know that. Come morning, she would be out on her ear, never knowing what she'd done wrong!

CHAPTER FOURTEEN

BIANCA woke the next morning with butterflies in her stomach and trepidation in her heart. Who would have believed her being pregnant by Adam would cause her so much concern? It wasn't that she wasn't happy about it. She was. She was ecstatic. It was Adam's possible reaction which worried her.

A few days ago she would have been positive Adam would be just as thrilled. Now…she wasn't so sure.

What was it Roberta had said the other night? How once you really fell in love you couldn't wait to get married, settle down and have a baby with the person you loved? While such sentiments coincided exactly with what *she'd* been feeling lately, Bianca wasn't at all sure Adam felt the same way. He hadn't once mentioned marriage, despite his agreeing to buy a house so she could bring Lucky to live with them.

Then last night…

Bianca threw a worried glance over at Adam's still sleeping form and bit her bottom lip. Adam had been *very* late home. He'd said he'd been drinking whisky but he hadn't smelt of alcohol at all. He'd been lying to her. And then he hadn't wanted to make love.

Had he been with someone else? Had Sophie loomed on the horizon again, with her big boobs and highly accommodating nature?

Bianca heaved in a deep breath then let it out again with a shuddering sigh. Immediately Adam rolled over, settling oddly cold grey eyes upon her.

'Oh,' Bianca said. 'I…I thought you were still asleep. I was just about to get up and make coffee, but I have to go to the toilet first.' She scrambled out of bed, dragging on her kimono before dashing for the bathroom.

When she returned, Adam was still looking at her in that peculiarly cold fashion. 'Is there something wrong?' she asked as she sashed the kimono tightly around her waist.

'That depends.' He stretched, then linked his arms up under his head.

'On what?'

'On how you're going to handle what I have to say.'

A nameless fear gripped Bianca's insides. She tried to keep her cool but it was hard. 'Then perhaps you'd better just say it. Whatever it is you have to say…'

'Very well. This isn't going to work out, Bianca.'

Bianca swallowed. 'What isn't going to work out?'

'You. Me. Us.'

Spots began to swim around Bianca's eyes. 'Why not?' she choked out.

He sat up abruptly, throwing back the quilt and

swinging his feet over the side of the bed. His face, she noted, was uncompromisingly hard. He shrugged on his red dressing gown then stood up, looming over her.

'Too much water's gone under the bridge with us, I'm afraid,' he said. 'I loved you for a long time, Bianca. I thought I still did. But I see now I don't. It was a hangover from the past.

'I wanted you for such a long time and…well, now I've had you—and while it was very satisfying in one way it wasn't quite as good as I'd anticipated. To be brutally honest, Bianca, my fires for you have burnt out at long last. There's no spark left in me. No…chemistry. I'm sorry. There's no use my pretending. I think, under the circumstances, you should find somewhere else to live.'

Bianca blinked her utter bewilderment while the blood began to drain from her face. Nausea swirled in her stomach. 'But…but you said you loved me. You said you would *always* love me.'

His shrug was flippant in the extreme. 'Looks like I made a mistake. Sorry.'

Bianca thought of the kiss he'd given her yesterday morning, that awful parody of passion which had been a real goodbye kiss in a way she'd never dreamt he meant at the time.

'No…no, I'm the one who's sorry,' she said weakly, despair hot on the heels of dismay. She had never known such heartache. 'I'm sorry I ever met you...'

'Come on, Bianca, don't dramatise. It's just your pride that's hurt. You'll bounce back, right onto the next fellow. It's not as though you crave permanence, my love. Or commitment. Life is just a ball to you, remember? It's for having fun. Well, we had fun, didn't we? Don't be such a little hypocrite.'

Something rang in her whirling head—some bell which warned her that this wasn't her Adam talking.

All those moments they'd shared this past week— those warm, incredibly tender moments—flooded back into her brain, telling her that *that* was the real Adam, not this heartless stranger who was telling her oh, so casually that everything she'd ever meant to him was dead and that it shouldn't bother her one bit.

But when she looked into his face, searching for a hint of guilt or conscience, she saw nothing but a mask of stony indifference.

Bile rose in her throat and her hand fluttered up to try to stop it from going further. But in vain. 'I...I'm going to be sick,' she choked out, and, whirling, dashed for the bathroom.

She made it to the toilet bowl just in time, though there was nothing substantial to heave into it.

Afterwards she slumped against the cold tiled floor, her head resting limply against the toilet-roll holder on the wall. She felt drained, yet not nearly as despairing as she'd been a minute ago. For during her flight to the bathroom Bianca had caught a glimpse of them both reflected in the vanity mirror.

She had looked distressed, but *Adam* had looked *devastated*, his shoulders sagging, his face twisted with self-disgust.

But it was his eyes…oh, his eyes…

They'd clung to her back as she'd fled, clung with such pained regret and yearning, as though he wished he could cut out his tongue.

Which meant what? Bianca puzzled anew. He was being cruel to be kind? Or could it be that he didn't believe she really loved him and was getting out before he got in too deep?

That was more like her Adam, she conceded sadly, and her heart turned over with love and understanding for the man. She'd put him through so much over the years. Too much, perhaps. She could well appreciate his lack of faith in her.

But that didn't mean she was about to let him go— certainly not into the arms of a female vulture like that Sophie creature. He was the father of her baby, and he was going to marry her if it was the last thing he did!

'Are you all right?' Adam called casually from the bedroom.

Bianca gathered all her courage, got to her feet, rinsed out her mouth with mouthwash, pursed her lips in defiance of her pounding heart and flounced back into the bedroom, her hands finding her hips as she glared over at where Adam was sitting on the side of the bed, pretending to look totally unconcerned.

At least…she *hoped* he was pretending.

'No, I'm not all right, you unfeeling bastard. I happen to be pregnant, with *your* baby. I also happen to still love you, regardless of that appalling speech you just delivered.

'Before you ask, I haven't been on the pill since last month. That first time we made love and you didn't use protection seems to have done the impossible. Made *me* into a mother. And I have no intention of having an abortion so don't even ask.

'As I said, I love you and I want to keep our baby, and if you're halfway the decent man I think you are, you'll do the right thing and marry me.'

She scooped in a much needed breath before continuing. 'Which reminds me—I don't believe all that garbage about your not loving me. You *do* love me, Adam Marsden. I have no doubts about that at all!'

Bianca was taken aback by the black fury which swept across his face. 'And I have no doubt about that either,' he snarled, re-sashing his dressing gown as he stood up.

Bianca suspected the savage action was to keep his hands busy, otherwise they might have reached out and strangled her, so murderous was the look on his face.

'Because of course you're quite right!' he grated out. 'I do still love you—curse my stupid masochistic self to hell! I also thought I knew you pretty well, but not in my wildest dreams would I have imagined you could be this wicked. Or this coldly calculating.'

Bianca was staggered by his counter-accusations. Wicked? Coldly calculating? Anyone would think she'd deliberately gone out and got pregnant!

'Enough that you used me to back up the lies you told your mother,' he raged on. 'Enough that you told me you loved me when we both know you didn't.'

'That's not tr—'

'Shut up!' he roared. 'I won't listen to your lies any more. I can see it all now. You deliberately didn't mention protection that night till afterwards, knowing full well I'd be so carried away by finally making love to you, the only girl I'd ever loved in my whole life, that it would be the last thing on my mind. And you did it because you suspected you were already pregnant by Derek. You were hedging your bets, Bianca. You wanted an each way chance at winning a husband for yourself and a father for your baby.'

'What?'

'Oh, don't play the innocent with me. The wool's finally lifted from my eyes. You think I didn't notice the change in you these past few days? You decided you wanted Derek back, didn't you? You'd grown bored with me. But he wouldn't have you back, would he? Or marry you!

'You told him about your pregnancy last night and he gave you the shove. So it fell back onto good old

Adam to see to the aid of the party. You even thought you'd soften me up with some more sex before dropping the bombshell. One thing I'd like to know, though. Did you try that tactic with Derek last night too? I'll bet he didn't knock you back, did he? There again, he isn't mug enough to love you.'

Her hand cracked across his face with all her considerable strength. It rocked him, but Bianca couldn't see anything much through her haze of hurt and anger.

'This is *your* baby, you fool, not Derek's!' she told him, her voice shaking uncontrollably. 'I never had unprotected sex with Derek, nor any kind of sex at *all* with Derek for that matter. I was going to that weekend up at Foster, but I changed my mind. I told you before, Adam. I am not promiscuous!

'As for last night, the truth is I fainted down at the gym. Derek was there and insisted on taking me home. He really was very sweet and understanding. He even drove to an all-night chemist and bought me a pregnancy testing kit, then came back and waited while I confirmed what I had already suspected.

'I asked him to stay for a cup of coffee and he told me how happy he was that you and I had decided to stop our silly "open marriage" and have a baby. In case you've forgotten, my mother told him we were married.'

Tears pricked her eyes at the thought. For they would never be married now. 'I wasn't trying to soften you up with sex when you came home,' she said in a strangled voice. 'I wanted to make love with the father of my baby, the only man I've ever really loved.

'If I've been different the last couple of days, it was because I was worried that you hadn't mentioned marriage. I was afraid you might not want our baby. I was afraid you might not want me as your wife. I was…just…afraid…'

She started to cry then, great racking sobs which shook her body from head to toe.

Adam's arms around her sent her collapsing against him. 'Oh, Adam…Adam,' she cried. 'How could you believe all those terrible things about me?'

Yes, how could he?

Adam had never felt this rotten or this wonderful all at the same time. No one could have doubted her sincerity just now. The truth had shone from her impassioned face for all to see—but most for him to see.

She loved him. She wanted to marry him. She was going to have his baby.

His baby…

His arms tightened around her. He tried to speak but couldn't for a while, so he let his hands and lips speak for him as he stroked her back and kissed the top of her head.

'So when are you going to make an honest man out of me?' he murmured at last.

Her head rose slowly, heart-rending doubt on her

tear-ravaged face. 'You...you don't *have* to marry me, Adam. If you think that I don't really love you then perhaps we should wait a while to tie the knot...'

'No no,' he denied swiftly as panic rose in his heart. 'I don't want to wait. I want you as my wife as soon as possible.' That rebellious pout to her lips had begun to worry the life out of him.

'No, I don't think that's such a good idea. I think we definitely should wait a while...till you're sure...'

Adam groaned, then sighed his resignation to her stubbornness. He could only blame himself, he supposed. And his lack of faith in her. Besides, he'd waited this long. He could wait a little longer.

'But meanwhile we *will* be moving into a house together, won't we?' he said, trying to sound masterful.

'But of course! We have a dog and a baby to consider.'

Adam smiled wryly as he thought of that damned dog. Still, he guessed a family wasn't a proper family without a dog. He'd have to sell the penthouse if they were going to buy that really great house near the beach they'd looked at the previous weekend. Which was a shame. He'd really enjoyed his times there with Bianca.

But that didn't mean he couldn't find other places to take her. He had a feeling he'd better not ever get complacent where Bianca and sex were concerned. She'd liked the bad boy side of him far more than she would probably ever admit. He'd rather liked it himself.

He made a mental note to find out all the plush and decadent-looking hotels around Sydney where a man could take his lady-love for a night of sin. Maybe he would suss one out for tonight.

'What are you smiling at?' she asked suspiciously.

'Nothing. I was just thinking I'd like to take you out somewhere to celebrate tonight. A hotel, perhaps. We could have a romantic candlelit dinner, break open a bottle or two of champagne, then retire to the honeymoon suite.'

'But we're not honeymooners!'

'Who cares? They'll think we are. All the men will stare at you and envy me like mad. Which reminds me…there's a certain red dress I bought which I'd like you to wear…'

EPILOGUE

A WARM November sun was shining when Bianca finally emerged from the house and walked sedately down their backyard along the strip of red carpet laid especially for the occasion.

Adam stared at her and thought he'd never seen her look more breathtakingly beautiful or ravishingly radiant. Her white bridal gown was classically elegant, made of silk, straight and slender, with an off-the-shoulder neckline and a cleavage on display which made his heart beat a little quicker.

Having a baby had matured Bianca's figure somewhat.

She wasn't wearing a veil—Adam was privately surprised he'd talked her into a long white dress—though her long black hair was braided down her back with delicate white flowers set into each twist. The pearl choker and earrings he'd bought her as a wedding gift looked superb against her tanned skin.

And well they should, he thought wryly. They had cost all of his winnings so far this year. Over thirty thousand dollars.

Bianca had no idea how much they had cost. Or how much he still gambled. She'd worry if she knew.

But Adam knew what he was doing, and it gave him great pleasure to be able to afford to lavish such an expensive gift on her on this marvellous day.

Still, perhaps it was time to give some of the gambling up, especially the races. It was becoming more and more difficult to return a profit there, and, frankly, it was far too time-consuming.

He might even give up the casino as well. After all, he no longer had any need of extra money, having recently accepted a new job at Brisbane University which involved a considerable rise in prestige and salary. A house went with the job as well, which meant they could rent out this house while they lived up there.

Bianca was very excited about the move. She loved new places and new 'adventures'.

Bianca...

God, how he loved her—now more than ever. Perhaps because he was now absolutely certain that she loved him back, with a love that would last. She'd been right to make him wait. Marrying her today was going to be the best day of his life—other than the day his son had been born, of course.

He sent a quick glance over to where fifteen-month-old Tony was sitting next to his grandmother in the first line of chairs, his small chubby arms wrapped tightly around Lucky's scruffy, fluffy neck.

Adam's face filled with loving exasperation. They were inseparable, those two. He'd nearly had a fit when Lucky had first leapt up over the railing into Tony's cot a couple of months back, and settled down for an afternoon nap with his young master. But every time he'd tried to eject the dog, his son had screamed.

Dog and boy won the day, though never had a dog been so scrupulously wormed—or more often—not to mention bathed. Bianca called him an old worry-wart, and perhaps he was. Someone in the family had to do the worrying. Bianca certainly didn't. She was an eternal optimist.

He smiled over at his son, who smiled back, a wickedly naughty little grin which heralded that he was more his mother's offspring than his father's. Lord knew what would happen once Tony reached the terrible twos. He shuddered to think.

'You're supposed to be looking at the bride,' Bianca hissed as she reached his side.

'I was checking on your son,' he whispered back. 'Seeing if he was behaving himself.'

'Why is he always *my* son when you feel he needs checking on?'

Bianca smiled up into Adam's sheepish face and thought he had never looked so handsome, or so adorable. She reached up on tiptoe and kissed him.

'Hey,' he objected softly. 'That's supposed to come afterwards.'

She laughed. 'So's having children.'

'Children?' He eyed her warily. 'Are you trying to tell me something?'

'Could be. I haven't sighted a period for four months, and last night the line of my favourite test went blue again. On top of that my boobs are killing me, and while I was getting ready this morning I fainted. You know I never faint.'

'Except when you're pregnant.'

'That's right.'

Bianca was moved by the sight of Adam's joy as he grasped her hands and squeezed them.

'We'd better get married, then, don't you think?' he said thickly.

The celebrant noisily cleared her throat, indicating that she really did wish to marry this strange couple some time this century. Why they wanted everyone to think they were merely renewing their marriage vows, she had no idea! She knew for a fact that this was their first marriage ceremony. Still, hers was not to reason why—especially when she'd been paid so well for the small deception.

They finally stopped whispering and laughing, and the bride nodded for her to begin. She sighed and did so.

'We are gathered here on this lovely November afternoon, in this beautiful garden, to witness Adam and Bianca's renewal of their marriage vows. Bianca and Adam have written special words for the occasion. Adam?'

Bianca's heart contracted fiercely as Adam turned

to take her hands, his face very serious all of a sudden.

'Bianca, my darling,' he said, his voice quavering a little. 'This is a very special day for me. A day which marks the beginning of the rest of my life with you as my wife. I promise always to love you. I will never be unfaithful to you. I promise to treasure you all the days of my life, my darling. Bianca, my love, I am yours.' And he bent to kiss her.

'And you, Bianca,' the celebrant prompted, suddenly having difficulty in stopping herself from crying. How had she ever thought this couple strange? They had to be the most romantic, most in-love pair she had ever seen in her life!

'Adam, my darling,' Bianca began, just as shakily. 'I cannot hope to match those beautiful words. I am speechless with humility and wonder that you love me as you do. I…I am not worthy of you…'

Several people watching drew out handkerchiefs and there was much sniffling. Bianca's chin lifted and her eyes shone with love.

'But I will endeavour to be worthy,' she went on strongly. 'I promise always to love you. I promise always to be faithful to you. I promise never to let you down. You can count on me, my darling, just as I know I can always count on you.

'You gave me this beautiful gift today,' she said, fingering her pearls. 'But you gave me a greater gift the day you first gave me your friendship, then your undying love. Thank you, my husband.' And she reached up to kiss him.

The celebrant decided to abandon her prepared script. It just didn't seem to fit this touching moment. 'I wish to say I have never seen a couple so much in love,' she said, her eyes awash. 'And I am proud to pronounce them man and wife. May their lives be as long and as wonderful as their love for each other.'

Everyone stood up and clapped. It was much better than everyone crying. May lifted Tony up on the chair so that he could see better.

'Mum-Mum, Dad-Dad,' he said.

'Yes,' May murmured as she dashed away her own tears. 'And it's about time too.'

Did they honestly think they had fooled her all this time? She'd found out long ago they weren't really married, when she'd been staying at their unit that fortnight and picked up a photo album containing all those photographs of Adam's sister's wedding. She'd quickly guessed the reason for their deception and been very touched by it. But she was much better now. The doctors had given her a clean bill of health last month. The cancer was beaten.

Still, it wouldn't do to let on to Adam and Bianca that she knew the truth. They'd gone to so much trouble to keep deceiving her, with all their friends and Adam's relatives in on this special day. Besides, it wasn't as though she hadn't always been confident in their love and commitment to each other.

No, she would not tell them. Let them have their little secret. It didn't matter now that they were really married.

'Mum?' Bianca said, coming up to her with shining eyes and an adoring Adam on her arm. 'Before we get distracted with the party afterwards, we wanted to thank you again for minding Tony while we go on our second honeymoon.'

'My pleasure, darling. Tony and I will have such fun together, won't we?' She glanced up to find Tony had scrambled down from the chair and was running down towards his sandpit in the far corner of the garden, Lucky's little legs going hell for leather after him.

Bianca laughed. 'He'll make sure you sleep at night, that's for sure. Oh, and we have a little present for you which we hope you might like.'

'A present for me? But you don't have to reward me to mind my grandson!'

'No, it's not that kind of present.'

'Really? Now I'm intrigued. Well, what is it? Tell me.'

'There's going to be a little brother or sister for Tony some time in the New Year. Your guess is as good as mine when.'

May didn't know what to say. Her heart swelled to overflowing proportions and she hugged Bianca, looking at her proud son-in-law over her daughter's shoulder. 'Well done,' she told him, her eyes swimming. 'Oh, well done!'

P.S. It was a girl. And they called her May. Her arrival instantly turned her devil of a brother into an overly protective guardian angel. He insisted on sleeping in her room every afternoon, just in case his "lil sissie" needed something. He also insisted on his big brave guard dog joining them. Adam scowled while Bianca smiled, but boy and dog won the day. As they always did.

Medical Romance™ presents...

THE REAL FANTASY

by

Caroline Anderson

Caroline Anderson has the mind of a butterfly. She's been a nurse, a secretary, a teacher, run her own soft-furnishing business and now she's settled on writing. She says, 'I was looking for that elusive something. I finally realised it was variety, and now I have it in abundance. Every book brings new horizons and new friends, and in between books I have learned to be a juggler. My teacher husband John and I have two beautiful and talented daughters, Sarah and Hannah, umpteen pets and several acres of Suffolk that nature tries to reclaim every time we turn our backs!' Caroline writes for Medical Romance™ and Tender Romance™.

Don't miss Caroline's latest Medical Romance™

THE BABY BONDING
by
Caroline Anderson

Out in October 2003!

PROLOGUE

'How about this? "Busy general practice in bustling seaside town close to Lymington offers year's post to trainee"—blah, blah—"ten minutes from the beautiful countryside of the New Forest" et cetera, et cetera.' Tricia brandished her toast at the view through the window of the concrete tower block opposite. 'Beats this dump. Why don't you apply?'

'Lymington?' Linsey wrinkled her nose and scraped her long blonde hair back from her face. 'Funny things happened to me in Lymington. I'm not sure I want to go back—it wasn't my lucky place, really.'

Tricia's delicately pretty face screwed up with remorse. 'Oh, Lord, yes, you nearly drowned. Sorry. Forget it.'

'I fell off a boat into about five feet of water,' Linsey said drily. She leant back in the chair, arms raised above her head, and twisted her hair into a knot at her nape. Murky, weedy water, covering thick, clinging mud that had nearly claimed her life. If he hadn't been there—

She released her hair and it fell, slithering down her back like golden rain. 'It was no big deal,' she lied.

Tricia eyed her sceptically. 'If you say so. Still, you've got to train somewhere and it sounds nice. Why don't you apply? Perhaps you'll meet your mystery doctor again,' Tricia teased gently.

Linsey's mouth lifted at one corner in a reluctant smile. 'Unlikely. He wouldn't still be there—not after eight years.'

5

Tricia sank neat, even teeth into her toast and looked across at her friend. 'Why not?' she mumbled.

Linsey shrugged. There was no reason—no reason at all. Lots of doctors built up their practices in one place and stayed there for the whole of their professional lives. There was no reason at all to suppose that her mystery rescuer would be any different. The thought had a certain appeal. . .

Linsey's nose wrinkled again, but she reached across the breakfast table and plucked the professional journal out of her flatmate's hand. 'Where's the ad?'

The toast waved again. 'There—middle of the page.'

She turned her eyes to the advert. Tricia was right. The New Forest, with or without her mystery doctor, had to be better than the outskirts of Birmingham, especially for her with her love of the sea.

There were days, working here in this landlocked community, when she thought she'd die for want of the screaming of the gulls and the tug of the salt wind in her hair. She hardly ever sailed any more, but she loved to. Perhaps she'd have a chance, if she got the job.

She slid back her chair, then, scooping up the journal in one hand, she wandered out of the kitchen into the sitting room and curled up on the saggy old sofa, her long legs tucked up, bare feet under her bottom. Tricia followed her, plopping down beside her on the ancient sofa, her diminutive figure hardly denting it.

Delicate, almost fragile beauty as she was, Tricia had all the tenacity of a pit bull terrier. 'Going to apply?' she persisted.

Linsey shrugged again. 'I might.' She glanced at the date on the magazine, then at her watch. Today's, and if she moved fast she might get the letter in the post before she had to be at the hospital. She was on duty this weekend and if she didn't apply now she'd miss the boat. She had a copy of her CV and a letter of application ready in her computer. All she had to do was add the specifics of the job, juggle the wording a little to suit the occasion, print it and bung it in the post. 'Yes, I think I will.'

It took ten minutes. They drove to the postbox in Linsey's car because it was the only one with petrol in it, posted the letter of application and went on to the hospital, arriving in the nick of time.

They parted in the car park, Tricia for Obstetrics and Gynaecology, Linsey for Accident and Emergency. As she walked in, an ambulance screamed up to the entrance and within seconds the trolley was bowling through the doors, a paramedic working furiously to resuscitate someone while another ambulanceman ran alongside with a breathing bag.

'Catch,' Linsey said to the receptionist, threw her coat and her tote bag and followed the trolley down the corridor to Resus at a run. 'I'll take over,' she told the paramedic, and her hands slid over his, picking up the rhythm immediately.

'Intubate, please. Let's get some monitor leads on here fast as well.' She turned to the paramedic. 'Right, do we have any history?'

Flung head first into the grim reality of life and death, Linsey didn't give Lymington, her mystery doctor or the letter another thought.

'This one sounds good.'

Matthew Jarvis ran his eye over the profferred application letter, scanned the CV and frowned.

'What now?' Rhys growled.

He shrugged evasively. 'I'm not sure we want a woman.'

The big man sprawled across the sofa sighed with exasperation and stabbed his hand through tousled black hair, not for the first time. It had already suffered considerably throughout the sifting process they were engaged in.

'Matthew, we need a woman,' he said patiently. 'With Rosie retiring, we have to replace her with a woman. If we get a sufficiently good trainee, we could take her on. We've agreed that. Most of the others we've pulled out have been women. Why pick on this one to turn into a misogynist?'

Matthew grinned involuntarily and glanced down, a frown gathering on his forehead again. It was the name of the applicant that put him off, but he could hardly tell Rhys that without sounding like a totally off-the-wall nut case. He made himself read the letter again, and finally set it down on the miserably deficient 'maybe' pile. They really didn't have a great deal to choose from, he admitted wearily to himself, and hers was the last letter—and the best.

'OK, we could look at her,' he conceded.

Rhys unravelled his legs and stood up. 'Thank God for that. Right, I'm going home, such as it is. I'll see you tomorrow. We'll go over them all again and draw up an interview list from that bewildering selection.' His mouth tilted in a wry smile and, with a waggle of his fingers, he left.

'Such as it is'. Matthew watched through the window of the little sitting room at the back of the practice as his friend and colleague went out to his car, started it up and drove off. Was his home life falling apart still? Rhys and his wife had had a rough patch before the third baby had come along. Matthew didn't suppose another batch of sleepless nights and postnatal depression was helping either of them. He made a mental note to pay Judy a social call one day, just to check up on her. He turned back to the table and picked up the top letter again.

Linsey Wheeler. Unusual spelling. It was that, of course, that had set off alarm bells.

The only other Linsey he had known had had a catastrophic effect on his life, quite literally. One chance encounter had changed the course of history for ever.

A twinge of guilt and remorse plucked at him yet again, but he suppressed it. He had to move on.

And that reminded him. . .

He reached for the phone, jabbed in a number and leant back in the chair, the letter still in his hand. 'Jan— I'm sorry. I've been held up at the surgery.'

The voice at the other end was resigned. 'That's OK, Matthew. I understand.'

He felt another twinge of guilt and remorse, this one from a different source and touched with irritation. If only she'd yell at him, rant a bit, act as if she cared.

But he didn't want her to, of course. What he wanted was her indifference, so that his own went unnoticed.

His conscience prickling, he arranged to ring her in a few days, then hung up the receiver and turned his attention back to the letter.

Linsey.

His eyes lost focus, gazing far into the past—so far that fact and fantasy had blurred at the edges.

She had had beautiful hair. That had been the first thing he'd noticed about her. He hadn't been able to take his eyes off it. Long, golden, falling around her shoulders like a glossy curtain, slithering over one arm as she turned her head and met his eyes.

Green eyes. Jade-green, the colour of a tropical sea, crystal-clear and pure, not the murky, greasy sea he had plucked her from just moments later—the sea that had nearly claimed her life.

A shudder ran through him. If he hadn't been there, she might have died.

And Sara would be his wife.

CHAPTER ONE

LINSEY felt marvellous. The sun was shining, the gulls were screaming overhead and the salt-laden wind was tugging at her hair. Standing on the waterfront near the Royal Lymington Yacht Club, listening to the gulls and the rhythmic slap of the rigging against the masts as the boats rocked at their moorings, she felt as if she'd come home.

She looked over to the right, to the place where she had nearly drowned, and felt nothing. Good. She had been worried that it might unsettle her, but it didn't. It had all been over so quickly—all except the image of those astonishing gun-metal-grey eyes, the colour of a stormy sea.

She could still see his eyes as he'd bent over her, smoothing her hair back from her face, the gesture unexpectedly tender.

'Who are you?' she'd asked, her voice croaky and hoarse with the swallowed water, and he'd smiled like quicksilver.

'My name's Matthew. I'm a doctor. You're all right now; just rest for a moment. They've called an ambulance.'

'Stay with me,' she'd begged, hanging on his arm, and so he had, his fingers laced with hers, his other hand smoothing her hair rhythmically. His voice had been deep and soothing—a reassuring murmur that gradually replaced the thunder of her heartbeat as it steadied.

Then the ambulance had come and whisked her away,

11

but the look in his eyes had stayed with her, warming her chilled body and dissolving her fear.

He had visited her that evening, just briefly, bringing her flowers and refusing to stay.

'My fiancée's waiting,' he'd said, and she'd felt a crazy and irrational disappointment.

The following morning her parents had taken her home from the hospital, none the worse for her ordeal and only slightly sorry to miss the end of her sailing holiday.

She had never seen him or heard from him again, but she had never forgotten him, or what he had done for her.

She turned now and headed back towards her car, parked nearby in one of the quiet streets. Her interview was in half an hour, and she had to find the practice yet.

She followed the signs through Lower Pennington to Milhaven, and then turned down a quiet, leafy road off the high street. About halfway along, amongst the dentists and the orthodontists and the premises of other GPs, she found the surgery.

'Drs Jarvis, Farmer, Williams and Wilson', it said on a shiny brass plate on the gatepost. A big, double-fronted Edwardian semi-detached house with tile-hung elevations, it was welcoming and friendly, with colourful hanging baskets and pots by the front door to welcome patients. There was parking for them in what had been the front garden, and a sign pointing round the back said, 'Parking For Surgery Staff Only. Please Keep Clear.'

According to the letter in Linsey's bag, there were three men and one woman in the practice, with two nurses, a practice manager, two receptionists and a part-time accountant as well as the district nurses and midwives, chiropodist, dietician and physiotherapists attached to the practice, and the trainer was Dr J M Jarvis.

She eyed the parking space at the front, then the sign pointing to the back. The surgery was obviously still busy, judging by the number of patients' cars. She drove down the back, parked in the space labelled 'Visitor' and headed towards the front door.

As she did so a head appeared at one of the windows on the ground floor in what looked like a little extension. 'Dr Wheeler?'

She stopped. 'Yes?'

The face smiled. 'Come on in through the back door. It's open.'

She did as instructed and was greeted by the smiling face, this time attached to a plump, maternal body.

Her hand was warmly shaken. 'I'm Suzanne White, the practice manager. Come on in. The doctors are still busy in surgery at the moment, I'm afraid, but they'll be with us soon. Can I get you a cup of coffee while we wait for them?'

'Oh, please. That would be lovely after my journey.'

She followed the short, plump woman through into the kitchen. 'Have a seat, Dr Wheeler,' Suzanne suggested, and Linsey made herself at home at the kitchen table. The coffee was real, from a filter machine, and smelled wonderful. Suzanne set two mugs on the table and pulled out the chair opposite; then, seated, her dumpy hands wrapped round her own mug, she chatted cheerfully.

'Find us all right? It's quite easy.'

'Yes, no problems. The directions were excellent.' She had guessed that the directions were from Suzanne, and, judging by the slight warmth in the woman's face, Linsey thought she was right. Well, it wouldn't hurt to be on the right side of the practice manager, she reasoned, quelling the little wriggle of guilt.

'It gets a bit easier as the season comes to an end. The tourist traffic can make it all a bit confusing. Summer is usually the worst, of course. Do you know the area?'

'Only slightly. I had a sailing holiday here once, years ago.'

'Ah, a nautical type. Do you still sail?'

Linsey shook her head and smiled. 'No. I haven't had much chance in Birmingham. I'd like to start again, though, and I love to be near the sea.'

'Oh, so do I. I can't go on it, mind—I get as sick as a parrot just thinking about it; but there's something about the atmosphere—nothing else is quite like it, and nothing can take its place for me, summer or winter.' She sat back, her smile warm and relaxed. 'So, when did you decide you wanted to be a GP?'

Linsey sensed she was being interviewed now, but it didn't matter. The answer to this question was easy.

'Eight years ago—down here, actually. I met a doctor under rather fortuitous circumstances.' She gave a little laugh. Talk about understatement. 'Anyway, I was eighteen, I didn't know what I wanted to do with my life and because there's nobody medical in my family it just hadn't occurred to me. It did then, though, and I realised it was the least I could do.'

Suzanne's brow creased. 'The least you could do? In what way?'

Linsey shrugged slightly. 'I owed him my life, quite literally, and training as a doctor was the only way I could think off to repay the debt—put something back in humanity's pot, if you like. It all sounds a bit melodramatic and crazy, doesn't it, really? But at the time it seemed quite logical!'

Suzanne laughed. 'I'm sure it was, and it's as good a reason as any for going in for medicine. I'm sure a lot of people have weaker reasons.'

'I'm sure too,' Linsey agreed, thinking of some of the people she had trained with. 'Anyway, that was what I ended up doing, and thank God I did, because I discovered that I love medicine and I can't imagine doing anything else. I just wish I could thank him. I owe him more than I can ever say. I really didn't want to drown!'

'Drown?' Suzanne's eyes widened. 'I thought he'd detected some insidious disease or something!'

'Oh, no.' Linsey laughed. 'I haven't had a day's illness in my life—well, apart from breaking my leg as a child. No, he pulled me out of the river.'

'The river?' Suzanne's eyes widened even further. 'Good gracious. Tell me more about this rescue. It all sounds terribly dramatic.'

Linsey laughed softly. 'It was, for a few short seconds. I'd had a bit to drink and I fell off a boat. He fished me out of the river at Lymington.'

'I see what you mean about fortuitous! He really did save your life.'

'Oh, yes. I wasn't joking. I suppose any good swimmer could have got me out of the water and any first-aider could have revived me, and there were plenty of people there, so if it hadn't been him it would have been someone else. That's not the point, though. He made me think about medicine as a career, and it's the best thing that's ever happened to me.'

A snort behind her made her turn, and she looked up—and up—at a tall man with dark hair and laughing grey eyes. 'Clearly you've not been in medicine long enough. Still, you're just starting. Perhaps in a few years you'll be jaded like the rest of us. I take it you're Dr

Wheeler? I'm Rhys Williams. The others will be along in a tick, I expect, barring earthquake and civil commotion.'

She smiled and shook the proffered hand, liking the big, friendly man immediately, and Dr Williams hooked out a chair, reversed it and settled his large, solidly muscled body on it. His hands engulfed the steaming mug of coffee that Suzanne put in front of him, and he turned to Linsey again.

'So, you're a career doctor, are you?' he said with a grin. 'I wonder how long that'll last.'

She returned the grin. 'It's lasted so far. I see no reason why it should stop now.'

'Paperwork?' he said wryly.

She laughed. 'Every job has its downside. Look on the bright side—you could have been an accountant!'

Rhys shuddered eloquently. 'God forbid. I'll settle for endless form-filling. Ah, here's the boss.'

Still laughing, Linsey turned towards the door as another man entered, shrugging out of his sports jacket. As he did so a little shiver of awareness shimmered through her. Adrenalin, or another equally basic hormone? Both, probably.

Her eyes devoured him, taking in the lean, rangy build and powerful shoulders at a glance. He was big—not quite as tall or as solid as Rhys, but big for all that—his mid-brown hair cut conventionally short, his immaculate white shirt tapering from broad shoulders to tuck into well-cut khaki trousers that hugged his slim hips and emphasised the long, rangy legs.

She took all this in in the brief second before he met her eyes, and then without warning her heart jammed in her throat. Those eyes! It couldn't be. . .

'Matthew?' she said breathlessly.

His face was stunned for a moment, then warmth flared in his eyes—those incredible, dark gun-metal eyes that she had never forgotten.

He dropped his jacket over a chair and walked towards her as she stood up, reaching out for her hands. His fingers were warm and hard and strong—fingers that had plucked her from the jaws of death—and she clung to them as he stared at her. 'Linsey?' he said questioningly, his voice disbelieving. His eyes tracked her face, registering the eyes, the mouth, the hair. His knuckles brushed her cheek. 'My God, it really is you.'

She felt the silly grin but could do nothing to hide it. 'Yes, it is. It really is. This is amazing. Oh, Matthew— I've just been talking about you!' With a delighted laugh she flung her arms round him and hugged him hard.

After a brief hesitation his arms came up and hugged her back, then he held her at arm's length and looked at her for a moment, shaking his head slowly from side to side.

If the others hadn't been there she might have stayed there all day gazing into his eyes, but with the remnants of her presence of mind she straightened away from him and gave another little laugh.

'Wow, you look different to what I remember.'

'So do you—cleaner, for a start. And vertical. I hadn't realised you were so tall.'

She wrinkled her nose. 'Don't. Being five foot ten isn't exactly an advantage in life.'

'You can see over the crowds.'

She laughed. 'Especially at a party. Straight over the top of most of the men there.'

He looked down into her eyes. 'Not all of them.'

'No.' She returned his gaze, conscious of his height and nearness. 'No, not all of them.' She pulled herself together. 'Do you know, I've waited so long to thank you for what you did?'

He laughed awkwardly. 'You did thank me. Over and over again. So, I take it you were all right? No after-effects? Dreams—that sort of thing?'

Dreams? Oh, yes, there had been dreams—and he had starred in most of them. She could hardly tell him that, because it wasn't at all what he meant. She carefully schooled her expression. 'No. No after-effects.'

'Is this your phantom rescuer, then?' Suzanne asked curiously.

Linsey dragged her eyes from Matthew's and turned to the practice manager. 'Yes—yes, he is.' She gave a self-conscious laugh. 'My mystery doctor.'

'Hardly a mystery.' His voice was gruff, and as she looked up at him she saw that his eyes were bright with emotion. He moved away from her, clearing his throat, taking the coffee-mug Suzanne pushed into his hands.

'So,' he said at last, 'is this just coincidence that you're here?'

The silly grin was back. 'Yes. Absolutely. Well, not entirely, I suppose, in that I thought it would be appropriate to come back to where it all started, but I had no idea it was your practice.'

He looked confused, but Suzanne filled him in.

'It was here she decided to become a doctor, apparently, after you fished her out of the river.'

'Really? It's my fault?'

She nodded. 'Yes. So I hope you're going to finish what you started and offer to train me.' Her grin was irrepressible, and behind Matthew she saw Rhys snort with laughter.

'Oh, I think it would be obligatory, don't you, Matthew?'

Matthew's eyes cut to his colleague, one brow arched. 'I think it would be appropriate to find out first if we're all able to offer what the other party wants, don't you?'

Oops. Linsey realised she'd overstepped the mark, but she couldn't retract the words and she didn't want to. Instead she added to them, softening the effect with a teasing smile. 'Oh, of course. It's always possible that I may not want to train here. After all, I hardly met you. I might have imagined all those sterling qualities.'

Matthew blushed, to her amazement, and Rhys, far from looking offended by Matthew's put-down, laughed again. 'Very likely,' he said agreeably, and shot Linsey a grin. 'How long ago was it?'

'Eight years.'

'Yes, it must be,' Matthew agreed. His colour was back to normal but he was watching Linsey curiously. 'I'd just started here as a trainee myself. God, it feels like a lifetime.' He pulled himself together visibly and looked at Rhys. 'Rosie's on the drag and Tim's out on a call. Shall we have some lunch while we wait?'

Rhys nodded. 'Sure. I'm starving; I missed breakfast again. The others can join us when they're ready.'

'I've put it all out in the sun room,' Suzanne told them, and then made herself scarce while Matthew led them through into the room from which Suzanne had waved to Linsey as she'd arrived. A small extension, it overlooked the car park at the back, but it was warm and sunny, there were tall trees to offer interest and it was obviously their cherished retreat. She could imagine them snoozing there between clinics after a busy night on call, catnapping as only doctors seemed able to do.

A delicious cold buffet was set out on the low table between the wicker chairs, and at Matthew's suggestion she helped herself and then took one of the chairs, sinking down into the soft, welcoming cushions. Oh, yes, definitely a place for snoozing and retreating—but not now.

Matthew sat opposite her, Rhys on the big sofa, his long legs stuck out, the plate balanced on his lap.

He looked totally relaxed—unlike Matthew who was watching Linsey as if she were a bug under a microscope.

'So, you decided to take up medicine after you met me, is that right?'

She nodded.

'Is that a good enough reason? It seems rather fanciful to me.'

She laughed a little uneasily, uncomfortable with the criticism. She knew that he was just examining her motives, but even so. . .

'Not really. I didn't know what I wanted from life. If the truth be told I was a spoilt brat and I hadn't really given my future a second's serious thought. It was all getting a bit urgent, though, because it was the end of August and I'd prevaricated for so long that I'd lost the place I was offered at Oxford and it was a case of finding somewhere else to take me.'

'So did you start the year after?'

'No—no, that year. I rang up a few colleges and chatted to a few people and got a place in London.'

'Just like that?' Matthew said in astonishment.

She shrugged diffidently. 'I fulfilled the entry requirements.'

'Somewhat,' Rhys said through a forkful of chicken and rice. 'Four A grades at A level and an Oxbridge entrance pass. I should think they were falling over themselves to have you.'

She felt warmth steal over her skin and played with her food for a moment. 'Not really. They were a bit sceptical of my motives too. I had to work my charm a bit at the interview.'

'You must have been very convincing,' Matthew said drily.

'Apparently,' she agreed, ignoring his tone. 'They took me and I worked very hard to give them no cause to regret their decision.'

Matthew looked slightly disbelieving. 'So, like Saul on the road to Damascus, the scales fell from your eyes and you saw the light, knuckled under and stopped playing at life, is that right?'

She was astonished. Why was he so hostile all of a sudden? Because she'd made that joke about him having to take her on? Oh, hell—her and her big mouth.

'Something like that,' she replied, trying to keep her tone light.

'So why general practice?'

'Variety? I'd get bored specialising in one field. I love people and their problems and difficulties. I suppose I'm an inveterate Nosy Parker, and I can't bear people coming and going in clinics without any continuity. I thought general practice would give me a chance to get to know families and work with them over a long period of time.'

'To satisfy your curiosity?'

Lord, she'd asked for it. She should never have said 'Nosy Parker'. When would she learn to think before she spoke? 'No, not to satisfy my curiosity,' she corrected him. 'More to give me an opportunity to do the job properly.'

'And is that important to you?'

'Yes, of course.'

'There's no "of course" about it. Lots of people end

up in general practice because they're no good at anything else.'

Her mouth tightened. 'Well, I'm sorry to disappoint you but I'm not one of them.' Her voice was serious now and she gave up on any attempt to charm him with light-hearted banter. Clearly it wasn't what he wanted to hear and he was determined to think the worst of her. He probably even thought she'd applied for the job knowing he was there, intending to trade on the tenuous link between them, and he had obviously decided— probably years ago—that she was a dumb blonde and a total airhead. She would have to prove him wrong.

She looked him in the eye and went on, 'If you believe general practice is for those who couldn't make it in hospital medicine then I don't think you should be a trainer.'

She heard a muffled snort of laughter from Rhys, and Matthew's eyebrows shot up. 'I wouldn't put it quite like that,' he said crisply. 'So, Dr Wheeler, would you like to elaborate on your theme of doing the job properly?'

She could hardly miss the splinter of sarcasm in his tone. She forced a smile. 'Of course. I think continuity of care is extremely important. Without it mistakes are made, people die needlessly and suffer unnecessarily because with the best will in the world we can't write down everything we observe, and the next doctor to see the patient hasn't got the necessary benchmarks.'

'Ah, but—we have to make sure they're provided,' Matthew insisted.

'But we can't, not always, not infallibly, because so much of it is instinct and intuition.'

'Instinct? Intuition?' he said sceptically.

'I agree,' Rhys said quietly. 'That's exactly why I'm

a GP, and why I—and you, Matthew, and Rosie and Tim—go the extra mile to make sure things are followed up and dealt with. I think Linsey's understanding of the job is actually very accurate.'

'We still need to make full notes,' Matthew insisted.

'Oh, for God's sake, man, that goes without saying.'

'I don't think so. I think it needs to be clearly understood.'

'I clearly understand it,' Linsey said quietly into the fraught silence.

Both men turned to look at her.

'I wouldn't dream of making incomplete notes on a consultation just because I expect to be doing the follow-up. I wouldn't rely on my own memory and I couldn't be sure that I would be the one seeing the patient. That wasn't what I was saying. I was just trying to explain why I feel I, personally, want to be in a position to follow patients up and supervise their care to the conclusion of their treatment.'

She held Matthew's eyes in a challenging stare, defying him to differ with her again or question her motivation, and as she did so she saw the dawning of surprise—and, heavens, respect?—in their gun-metal depths.

The phone rang then, breaking the silence that stretched between them, shattering the tension and enabling Linsey to drag her eyes away from Matthew at last.

'So, tell us all about your training so far,' Rhys said easily, helping himself to more of the cold, creamy chicken mixture and tucking into it with relish.

'From the beginning?'

'Seems a good place to start,' Matthew said drily.

She gave a forced little laugh but did as she was asked,

starting at the beginning with her applications to medical colleges at various universities, her acceptance by a London college, her training, her natural leanings, the areas she had enjoyed and the areas she found difficult, when she'd made her decision to be a GP rather than a hospital doctor, and the training she had undergone since making that decision.

'Have you got an obstetrics qualification?' Matthew asked, knowing full well she had, if he'd read her application form.

'Yes. I've done my MRCOG.'

They nodded. The qualification was useful in general practice, enabling them to offer home births, contraceptive advice and other facilities related to that area. A woman with obstetric qualifications was especially valuable. It was one of Linsey's most significant assets, and she knew it. Another asset was her time in Accident and Emergency, which had a lot in common with general practice in that you never knew what was coming through the door. As a way of keeping a doctor on his or her toes it was unsurpassed.

Matthew brought it up.

'You're in Accident and Emergency at the moment?'

She nodded. 'Yes, that's right. I'm just finishing.'

'How have you found it?'

'Fascinating.' She told them about her casualty work, and how she found it stimulating even though it was very stressful.

'General practice can be stressful,' Matthew warned. 'All that continuity has its disadvantages. There's the pain of following a family through tragedy and the remorseless march of time, propping up carers, dealing with terminal illness, miscarriage, infertility, childhood cancers—emotionally it can be very, very draining.'

'I know. I don't mind—I'm not looking for an easy option. I think it's more important to do something useful; you didn't save my life so I could sit around and waste it.'

Matthew's smile was wry and a little strained. 'I don't think our actions are as carefully considered as that. I saved your life—if I did—because in that split second it was the obvious thing to do. If I hadn't, someone else would have. It was no big deal.'

'No big deal'. Exactly the words she had used to Tricia; but it was far from the truth. For her, at least, it had been a very big deal indeed, and she didn't think it had had that little impact on Matthew, either. Linsey got the feeling that there was more than modesty behind his remark. He seemed uncomfortable with the subject, as if it made him uneasy for some unknown reason. Obviously he didn't like to play the hero. Her heart softened towards him and she felt a resurgence of the affection with which she had remembered him all these years.

She wondered what it would take for him to look at her again as he had on that day, before she'd fallen in the water, when she had caught his eye. It had almost felt as if there was something between them, some magical pull that drew them together.

She nearly laughed aloud at her silliness. She'd have to stop thinking like this if she got the job. Heavens, he'd done nothing really to attract her single-minded interest, and she could hardly hold him responsible for the silly and irrational behaviour of her heart.

Anyway, he'd been engaged eight years ago, so presumably he'd been married now for years.

She almost asked, the question on the tip of her tongue before she remembered herself and clamped her lips on the words. It was none of her business. She was looking for a job as a trainee GP, not a mistress or girlfriend. This was professional. She must remember that. Just because he'd saved her life it gave her no claim on him—and anyway, the way the interview had gone so far she didn't think she stood a snowflake's chance in hell of getting the job. The problem was that she said what she felt, without editing her words in her mind— and that was not always welcome or appropriate. No, if he didn't want to offer her the job it would be her own fault. It was hardly his that he apparently didn't have a sense of humour.

She looked up at them, suddenly aware of the pregnant silence. 'I'm sorry?'

Matthew was looking at her oddly. 'I said, if we offered you the post as trainee, when would you be free to start?'

She blinked. Offered the post? Was he. . .? 'Um—the first of August,' she said hastily. 'Or any time after that.'

'OK. Rhys, anything else you want to ask Linsey?'

Rhys shook his head. 'No, I don't think so. I think you've about covered it,' he said drily.

Matthew flicked him an irritated glance and stood up, shaking Linsey's hand as she followed suit. 'Right. Well, we'll be in touch. We both have to get on now—feel free to stay and finish your lunch. There's some coffee in the kitchen, I expect. I'm sorry the others didn't make it, but that's general practice for you. Sorry to abandon you.'

Linsey thought that Matthew looked anything but sorry as he hurried out of the door. If anything he was making a hasty getaway—the faster the better. Rhys looked after him, puzzlement reflected on his face, and then turned back to her with a sympathetic smile.

'Sorry about that. He obviously decided to test you under pressure.'

She laughed. 'Yes—and I leaked like an old gas main. Oh, well. There'll be other jobs.'

'I shouldn't panic. I thought you stood up to him rather well.'

'But is that what he's looking for?'

Rhys's mouth quirked in a smile. 'Who knows? We're interviewing again tomorrow, so you should get a letter by the end of the week. If it helps at all, you've got my vote.'

She summoned a smile. 'Thanks. I don't think I've got Matthew's.'

Rhys's brow creased again. 'I wouldn't say that. He's often preoccupied. Probably something to do with a patient—I shouldn't take it personally. I'd show you the flat, but I have to go. I've got several calls to make.'

'The flat?'

'Yes, there's a flat that goes with the job—over the surgery, upstairs. It's very pretty—bit atticky, but I suppose it's all part of the charm. If you crane your neck it's got a sea view.' He grinned. 'Suzanne will show you.' He unfolded himself from the sofa, shook her hand and left, closing the door softly behind him.

Linsey sagged back against the cushions and let out a sigh of relief. As interviews went, that had been appallingly difficult. Still, even though she hadn't got the job—and she was sure she hadn't—at least she'd seen Matthew again and had a chance to thank him.

He might want to dismiss the incident, but she had no illusions about what she owed him.

She remembered again the tug of the weed at her hair, the slimy feel of it clinging round her arms, dragging her under. She shuddered with the memory. Her dress

had caught on a propeller—fortunately stationary—and
trapped her further as she struggled with the weeds and
the clinging mud around her ankles, and she could
remember the terror, the sheer blind panic of knowing
she was going to die in that cold, sinister water and that
nothing could save her.

Then, just as she was sliding into oblivion, she had
felt the firm grip of a pair of strong masculine hands
wrenching her free, and the next moment there had been
the blessed sun on her face and the tender caress of his
hand across her brow.

She might have made light of it to Tricia, but she had
been badly frightened, and Matthew had known that.
Clearly, though, however pleased he might have been
to see her again and make sure she was all right, he
wasn't going to let their slight acquaintance influence
him positively towards her. If anything, he was leaning
the other way.

Or maybe she had carried a false image of him all
these years? There was no reason, of course, why they
should get on. They had exchanged perhaps two dozen
words altogether both at the quayside and later when he
had brought her flowers in hospital. She didn't know
him. Perhaps he was just a miserable, cheerless individual. Whatever, she sensed that he didn't like her.
Another fantasy in the dust, she thought wryly. So much
for the gun-metal eyes of my dreams. Anyway, he was
married.

She put her plate down, her appetite quite gone. She
had hardly touched the delicious lunch, she realised,
so busy had she been defending herself and answering
questions. She didn't want it now. All she wanted was
to get away, to get back to Birmingham and her work
in A and E, and to find time to curl up with this week's

journals and look for another trainee post.

Skegness or Great Yarmouth or Blackpool, perhaps, if she wanted the sea. One thing she was sure of—she wouldn't be offered the post by Matthew Jarvis.

He might have saved her life once, but quite clearly he had decided that his responsibility to her started and ended there. She would have to look elsewhere to further her career.

She went and found Suzanne White. 'I'm going now—thank you for the coffee and the lunch.'

'Oh, my dear, I haven't shown you the flat yet!'

Linsey smiled. 'That's all right. I haven't really got time to look at it,' she lied.

'Well, I hope I see you again, dear,' Suzanne said with a genuinely friendly smile. 'We could do with your sunny face to brighten the place up.'

Linsey found her eyes misting over. 'Yes. Well, thanks. I hope so too. Goodbye.'

She let herself out of the back door, ran to her car and was just getting in when Matthew came out of the door.

'Are you off?'

She stood up again. 'Yes. I've got a long drive.'

He walked up to her, his eyes somehow haunted. 'I'm sorry I was a bit hard on you in there.'

She shrugged. So was she, but what could she do about it? Nothing. And nor could he. He looked awkward, staring at his hands and then back at her, his eyes belying the careful expression on his face.

'I just wanted to say I'm glad I've seen you again and that everything's all right.'

'You too,' she said, dredging up the tiniest smile. 'Well, goodbye again. I hope you find your trainee.'

She slid behind the wheel, slammed the door and reversed out without looking at him again. She caught

sight of him in the mirror as she paused at the roadside—
watching her, a thoughtful expression on his face.

She pulled out onto the road with a little spurt of
gravel, and her idol disappeared in a cloud of dust.

How appropriate. What a suitable ending for a fantasy.
She blinked the mist from her eyes and headed for
home. . .

CHAPTER TWO

'I THINK Linsey's the best.'

Matthew scowled at Rhys. 'You've made that quite obvious.'

Rhys shrugged. 'I have to work with her too, you know—maybe for ever.'

Matthew snorted. 'I don't think so. She's an airhead.'

'A dumb blonde? I hardly think so. Look at her qualifications, then look at your own—or is that the problem?' Rhys's voice was dry.

Matthew shook his head. Ego wasn't one of his problems, and his own exam results had been perfectly respectable. It wasn't her brain that worried him. 'I know she's academically gifted. That doesn't mean a thing in medicine. She has to be clever enough to have got this far. I'm more interested in her dedication and commitment, her motivation, her staying power.'

Rhys sighed. 'Have you read her references?' he said pointedly. 'She is outstanding. Nobody has said anything about her that wasn't positively dripping with accolades. And I liked her.'

'Fine. You liked her, so I have to work with her?'

Matthew knew that he was being irrational, but he couldn't discuss his feelings about Linsey—and for her—with a colleague, or even a very good friend. Admittedly, what he had seen of her was at odds with his memory of her, but eight years ago she had been flighty, light-headed and thoroughly silly—and he'd been knocked off his perch by her like a lovesick parrot.

31

He wasn't looking for an encore.

'OK, then, who else?' Rhys said, leaning back in the chair and folding his arms across his massive chest. The neutral expression on his face didn't reach his eyes, which glittered with challenge.

Damn. There he had him. There was nobody else— at least, no one who on paper or otherwise stood up to Linsey. She had made her stand and defended it well, and he found himself reluctantly admiring her for it.

'You were a pig to her,' Rhys said softly.

'Yes, I know. I apologised.'

Rhys grunted, studying Matthew's face searchingly. 'What happened between you eight years ago?' he asked out of the blue.

Matthew felt hot colour flood the back of his neck. 'Nothing.'

'You fancied her.'

'She was eighteen.'

'And I'll bet she was stunning. That's the problem, isn't it? The sexy little minx got under your skin and you can't cope with it.'

'Rubbish.' Matthew shifted uncomfortably, even more conscious of the heat reddening his neck.

Rhys's smile was knowing. 'Take her on. Keep her for the year, and have an affair with her. I think it would do you good.'

'Jan might have something to say about that,' he reminded Rhys mildly.

The rude snort that followed that remark needed no elaboration. 'Go on, Matthew. Live a little. Give your hormones some exercise for once.'

'Don't you have a home to go to?' Matthew prodded.

Rhys's face lost its animation. 'A home? You mean that shell with three whining kids and a woman who doesn't want to know me? Yeah, I've got a home.'

Matthew leant forward and put his hand on his friend's big, bony knee. 'I'm here, old man, if you want to chat.'

'Thanks.' Rhys's voice was subdued, his face shuttered. 'I think I will go, actually. Emma was sick this morning and Judy won't be coping well. I'd better go and rescue them all from each other. I'll see you tomorrow.'

Matthew watched him go, and worried. Things seemed to go from bad to worse. He must see Judy—and he must make a decision on this trainee. If Rhys and Judy were heading for a crisis, perhaps it had better be someone who was free to start soon. Rosie didn't actually leave until October, but if he could get someone before then—perhaps at the beginning of August? It never hurt to have extra cover during the silly season. People seemed to wait until they were on holiday to become ill, for some reason, and their workload always doubled in the summer months.

Yes, someone who could start promptly could well be worth considering. There were only a couple, of course, the dreaded Linsey one of them.

Lord, she was lovely. Rhys was right, needless to say. She had got under his skin eight years ago. He'd only seen her twice—the first time when she'd fallen in, the second when he'd dropped into the hospital on his way to pick Sara up for the evening, just to make sure that the subject of his heroism was doing well.

That second visit had been a mistake. She'd looked at him with those enormous jade-green eyes and thanked him in a soft, slightly throaty voice that had become woven into his dreams over the next few weeks to the detriment of his sanity—and his relationship with Sara.

Still, he was older now, there was Jan to consider and

on closer inspection Linsey was not the stuff of his fantasies. Instead she was quirky, opinionated and downright cheeky. The meek, sweet, wide-eyed, fawning girl of his fantasies had been rudely supplanted by a robust, quick-witted woman who was nobody's fool.

On second thoughts, that made her even more exciting.

He tipped back his head and groaned. Why, oh, why had she come back into his life?

There was an easy answer, of course: don't give her the job. Offer it to someone else.

And miss the chance of a lifetime?

He swore softly. The chance for what? He was committed to Jan—had been tiptoeing round the issue of marriage for months. He had no doubt that, if he'd been pushed, he would have been sleeping with her, but she'd seemed happy to let it drift, and he'd been so busy at work over the summer that there honestly hadn't been any opportunities.

Perhaps it was time to push ahead on that front, and forget about aggravating blondes with attitude. He'd find someone else for the job.

He shuffled the letters and interview notes endlessly, but came up with the same answer every time. What he didn't know was why. . .

'You've got it! You've got the job! Oh, Linsey!'

Tricia hugged her stunned friend, snatched the letter out of her hand and read it aloud.

' "Dear Dr Wheeler, thank you for attending your recent interview. We should like to offer you the post of registrar in general practice with us—salary as per scale attached, training hours by arrangement to suit schedules", blah blah, et cetera.' She dropped the letter on the coffee-table and plopped down beside Linsey on the sofa. 'The first of August? That's next week! Talk about leaving it till the last minute! You'll have to pack up and rush off almost immediately—'

'If I go.'

Tricia's pretty little jaw dropped. 'What? What do you mean, *if* you go? Of *course* you're going! Linsey!'

She shrugged. 'Am I?'

Tricia sank back into her corner of the sofa, her eyes searching Linsey's face. 'Aren't you?'

'I don't know. He was hostile.'

'Hostile? Isn't that a bit strong?'

Linsey shook her head. 'No, I don't think so. I got the distinct feeling he thought I was a bubble-brain.'

Tricia laughed. 'What? You? A bubble-brain? Give it a rest!'

'I mean it.'

Tricia's smile faded. 'Lins, that's crazy. You're the most focused, intelligent, self-disciplined person I know—'

'Oh, Tricia!' Linsey laughed and hugged her friend. 'You are so loyal! I'm lazy, bird-brained and totally self-indulgent.'

Tricia shook her head emphatically. 'Only in the flat. You used to be like that, but you've spent years getting away from it. What you don't realise is you *have* got away—you're different now—and you most certainly aren't a bubble-brain.'

Linsey shrugged slightly. 'Tell it to Matthew Jarvis. He thinks I'm too daffy to do the job.'

'So why has he offered it to you?'

'Well, funny you should mention that. I really don't know.'

'But you will take it?'

Linsey hesitated. 'I have to earn a living,' she said finally, 'and it is a lovely part of the world.'

Tricia studied her fingers for a moment. 'I'll miss you,' she murmured. 'You'll be a long way away.'

Linsey looked round the flat. 'Will you stay here?'

Tricia shrugged. 'Yes, probably. I'll see if I can get another flatmate—perhaps someone tidy?'

Linsey punched her arm gently and laughed. 'I'm not that bad any more.'

'No—but I've spent two years training you!'

'So you have.'

They shared a smile, and then Linsey bounced off the sofa and reached for the phone.

'What are you doing?'

'Accepting the job—quickly, before I talk myself out of it. Then you can help me pack.'

The traffic was awful. The last Saturday in July was the very worst time of year to make her way down through the New Forest, and by lunchtime Linsey was bitterly regretting her timing.

The motorway was chock-a-block, and when she finally left it the tailback to Lyndhurst was about five miles long and growing steadily.

She consulted her map, did a U-turn in the road and cut through the tiny villages, making a big circuit but saving herself probably at least one hot, frustrating hour of sitting in a traffic queue.

It was better then until after Brockenhurst, but the last bit into Lymington started to get very busy and she did another wiggle through the villages, cutting down through Sway and Pennington and picking up the coast road for Milhaven without having to wrestle with

Lymington on market day—and that had to be good news.

Suzanne had warned her about market day when she'd made the final arrangements to come down, and as she saw the traffic heading back into Lymington from the west, she was heartily relieved that she wasn't on call and trying to fight with the traffic on her way to an emergency.

She pulled into the car park behind the surgery and found a space with her name on it, neatly painted onto a little white board on a short post hammered into the ground. Obediently, she parked in her slot and glanced across at the only other car there.

Matthew's? Suzanne had said someone would be there to let her in, give her the keys and show her how the alarm worked. She hadn't said who, though.

Only one way to find out, thought Linsey, but her legs seemed strangely reluctant all of a sudden. What if he was still hostile? Was it all going to have been the most dreadful mistake?

She shook her head in irritation, flung open the door and climbed out of the car. She was hot and sticky, her hair was tangled to death from driving with the windows open and she hoped that there were gallons of hot water because she was going to have the longest shower in the world—just as soon as she'd found the flat and got all her stuff inside.

Matthew watched from the attic as Linsey climbed out of the car, stretching her long, slender legs and shaking her hair out of her eyes. She looked hot and cross, he thought, and incredibly beautiful.

Damn. If those jeans fitted her any tighter they'd cut off her circulation. She opened the boot of her car

and bent over, treating him to an inviting curve of
taut bottom.

He groaned and dropped his forehead against the
glass. What had he done? She was going to drive him
crazy. The libido he'd managed so effectively to stifle
with Jan's help roared healthily to life, kicking and
screaming for recognition.

He shifted uncomfortably. His jeans were nearly as
tight as hers now, damn it. She straightened, her full,
soft breasts pushing against the limp T-shirt and making
the ache worse.

'Oh, get a grip, Jarvis,' he growled. Turning away
from the window, he ran down the stairs to the kitchen
and opened the back door. 'You're here,' he said inanely,
and could have kicked himself.

She looked up over her shoulder. 'So it appears,' she
said drily. 'Did I misunderstand your letter?'

He felt a grin tug at the corner of his mouth and
stepped down onto the gravel. 'Of course not. How was
your journey?'

She gave him a withering look. 'How do you think?
It's the busiest Saturday of the summer on the roads,
and guess where everybody wants to be.'

The grin widened. 'I should have warned you.
I'm sorry.'

'I'm sorry too. I hate traffic jams. Is there a shower?'

Matthew had a sudden, crystal-clear vision of Linsey
naked under a stream of water, and his jeans tightened
further. 'Yes,' he said curtly. 'There's a shower, and the
hot water's on.'

She raised an eyebrow at his tone, but said nothing.
Instead she turned her back to him, picked up the heavi-
est of the cases and dropped it almost on his toes.

'Here—you can prove you're a gentleman. I'll take the rest.'

She picked up two smaller cases and stood waiting while he gathered his wits, picked up the case and headed for the door.

'Follow me,' he said unnecessarily, and all but ran up the stairs to the attic. He took the case straight into the bedroom, put it on the wide, solid bed and turned—straight into Linsey's soft, incredibly inviting chest. His hands came up to steady her, grabbing her shoulders and hauling her even tighter against him, and as he did so her mouth parted on a little gasp of surprise and he fell headlong into a boiling maelstrom of lust and forbidden fantasy.

Good grief, his eyes! Talk about hot and bothered. It was a wonder she hadn't melted clean away! Linsey dropped the cases and Matthew dropped her, stepping sharply backwards with a muttered oath and crashing into the wardrobe.

'Damn.' He wiggled his foot experimentally. 'What have you got in that case?'

'Books. I'm sorry. Are you all right?'

He swore softly again and rubbed the back of his head. 'I'll live.'

She felt a pang of guilt. 'Look, I can manage the rest. Why don't you give me the keys, show me the alarm and then you can go back to your wife and family?'

He stared at her. 'I don't have a wife and family.'

'Oh.' She blinked. 'I thought you were engaged.'

'I was—about a hundred years ago. Come and see the rest of the flat,' he muttered, and shot out through the door.

Linsey was rooted to the spot. Land's sakes! Well,

she'd wondered about his wife. Now she knew.

A tiny, very feminine smile played around her lips as she followed him out of the bedroom and back onto the large, airy landing that formed her entrance.

It was decorated simply but tastefully, and as she looked in turn at the sitting room, with its squashy chairs and pretty chintz, the squeaky-clean kitchen with modern units and appliances and even a washer-dryer for clothes, and the bathroom, also squeaky-clean with a white suite, gleaming chrome taps and fresh, pretty floral curtains, she knew that she was going to be very much at home here. She was pleased to see the shower over the bath. Just as soon as he went, she would take advantage of it.

She went back into the sitting room, crossed to the window, and there, if she craned her neck, was the sea view that Rhys had promised. She turned to Matthew with a smile.

'It's lovely. How much will it cost me a month?'

He looked startled. 'Nothing. It's part of the deal.'

'Oh, but that's silly!'

He shrugged. 'We have our reasons. It helps us to have someone on the premises for security purposes, to act as a deterrent. We use it sometimes for locums, as well. Anyway, it stands empty, and we can't let it because it has access to the practice.'

She looked around the sitting room again. 'It's beautifully furnished just for the odd trainee or locum.'

His mouth quirked. 'I used to live here. I've got a cottage now three miles away on the outskirts of Sway, so I don't need it any more. Anyway, I have to confess the suite isn't that comfortable!' His mouth twitched again, and Linsey let herself return the almost-smile.

Heavens, he was practically unbending! Wonders would never cease.

'So, when do I start?' she asked him.

'The first of August is on Tuesday. I should spend tomorrow and Monday getting to know the place—the roads, the practice. Poke around and look for things, and familiarise yourself with everything. Then on Tuesday I suggest you spend the day with me, shadowing me so you know what my day consists of. In fact the whole of this first week probably wouldn't be too long to do that, but I anticipate we can have you working almost independently in surgery hours after a couple of days.'

She looked at him in surprise. 'Why so long? In hospital you go in on the first day and take over from your predecessor. There's no induction time.'

He smiled wryly. 'Because I need to know you're able to do the job, and the best way for me to find that out is to let you work beside me at first.'

She arched a brow at him. 'Don't you trust me, Dr Jarvis?' she said pertly.

His reply was blunt. 'No, Dr Wheeler, I don't. Not until I've seen you working.'

That took the wind out of her sails. So, even more, did his next words.

'Why don't you go ahead and have that shower you were promising yourself? And I'll bring in the rest of your things out of the car and make you a cup of tea.'

Without waiting for a reply he turned and ran lightly down the stairs, and left her on the landing, mouth hanging open slightly. Shower? With him running in and out?

She shrugged. She was too hot to care. If he thought she should have a shower now, who was she to argue? She opened the case with her wash things in it, scooped up all the bathroomy bits and pieces and went out of the bedroom, just as he came back in.

This collision was just as spectacular. Her toiletries leapt out of her arms, tampons spraying across the landing as the box fell, and with a chuckle she sagged back against the wall and grinned at him.

'If I didn't know better I'd think you kept running into me on purpose,' she teased.

He looked up from the floor where he was busily cramming tampons back into the box, and she was fascinated to see the warm tide of colour creep over his skin.

My God, he's delectable, she thought. She bent down and took them out of his hands. 'Did you come back for anything in particular?' she asked softly.

'Car keys,' he mumbled. He straightened and stepped back, and the toothpaste tube ruptured and squirted across the landing, splattering the white wall with minty green.

He swore, comprehensively and not really very quietly, and glared at the dollops of toothpaste as they began to run slowly down the wall.

It was too much for Linsey. Folding up on the floor in a heap, she laughed until she cried, her sides aching and begging for mercy, her eyes streaming.

Around her Matthew stomped about, gathering up the remains of her wash things and dumping them in the basin in the bathroom, then going into the kitchen for a cloth to wipe the wall, all the while muttering under his breath.

When she could breathe again she looked up at him. 'Did you say something?' she wheezed, and giggled again as he glared at her. It was too much. The laughter bubbled up and over again, and she folded herself over her knees and sobbed with hilarity.

'I'm glad you're so damned amused,' he growled,

almost stepping on her fingers as he wiped the wall for the third time.

She snatched them away to safety. 'At least the wall won't get dental decay,' she said brightly, and his scowl set her off again.

At last she straightened and sat back on her heels. 'Oh, come on. Can't you see the funny side?' she pleaded.

He tried hard, but finally, to her enormous relief, his face cracked and he smiled, albeit rather ruefully. 'Keys?' he said softly.

She knelt up and delved in her jeans pocket. 'Here. There isn't much. I'll have that shower now, if you think you can manage not to knock me over this time.'

His eyes seemed to darken, or perhaps it was just a trick of the light. Anyway, with a mumbled comment about keeping out of her way he turned and was gone, leaving her kneeling in the middle of the landing surrounded by the lingering aroma of toothpaste and wondering if she'd imagined that look in his eyes.

'This is your consulting room. It's next to mine on purpose so that if you want to confer with me you can do so easily. I imagine we'll work closely together for some time.'

So he can't delegate. We'll see about that, she thought. 'Is it really necessary?' she asked.

He looked at her candidly. 'I don't know. We'll find out, won't we? Come and see the little theatre where we do our minor surgery.'

She followed him. 'Who does it?'

'Me or Rhys. No one else is qualified. You'll meet Tim this week, and Rosie, but she's leaving in a couple of months and she's only part-time.'

'Is that why you offered me the job? Because a

woman's leaving and you had to have the statutory woman doctor?'

She had stopped in her tracks and he turned and looked back at her, irritation etched on his face. 'We didn't *have* to have a woman. We felt it would be a good idea. Many women prefer to see another woman for gynae problems. Obstetrics, for some reason, is different. They don't mind when it's babies, but when it's periods and the menopause and discharges they get coy.'

'Naturally. Men, on the other hand, are always coy unless they're trying to jump your bones. Then they all but hand you a tape-measure.'

He couldn't stop the stunned cough of laughter that erupted from his lips. Oh, good, she thought, he does have a sense of humour, after all.

'Lady, you are wicked,' he informed her, but his eyes twinkled and she found herself unexpectedly drawn to him again.

Maybe her fantasy hero did exist, after all. Not only that, he was single. She had the distinct feeling it was going to be an interesting year. . .

CHAPTER THREE

MATTHEW was going crazy.

Every time he turned around Linsey was there, asking him questions, watching what he did, poking about in the files, running through the computer data, questioning everything—and it was still only Monday! God knows what it would be like once they started working together properly. He had never before come across anyone with a mind as enquiring and convoluted as hers, and he found it exhausting.

Lack of sleep didn't help either. Every time he closed his eyes she was there, singing in the shower, her voice slightly off-key, her body glistening as she slicked soap over that fabulous peach-bloom skin. Whose idea had it been to put frosted glass in the top of the bathroom door anyway? That one diffuse glimpse of her upraised arms had been enough to wreck his sleep pattern in perpetuity.

Hell.

He signed the last repeat prescription and then turned to the pile of letters awaiting signature. Just as he checked the first there was a tap on the door.

'Come in,' he growled.

Linsey popped her head round. 'Just thought I'd check the arrangements for tomorrow,' she told him.

'Eight-fifteen, in here,' he reiterated. 'I'll introduce you to my patients, and then conduct the consultations as normal.'

'And what do I do?'

'Nothing,' he said firmly. 'Absolutely nothing

whatsoever except watch and listen and answer questions if I ask them.'

'What if I disagree?'

He sighed inwardly. 'You won't.'

Her brows arched expressively, and he glared at her.

'It isn't me we're supposed to be checking up on,' he reminded her stiffly.

'But if I do disagree? If, for instance, I would have treated something differently? Surely we should discuss it?'

'Later. When the patient leaves.'

She nodded, and he had visions of five-minute consultations followed by ten-minute wrangles over the efficacy of his chosen course of treatment. He sighed again, this time audibly, and she caught her teeth in her lip. Self-doubt, or trying to hide a smile? He didn't care to consider it too closely.

'Doesn't anybody ever question anything you do?' she asked.

'Oh, yes. The patients do it all the time. I can reason with them, though,' he finished drily. He looked pointedly at his watch. 'Was there anything else?'

She pulled a face. 'Well, excuse me,' she said cheekily, and with a sniff she turned and went out, banging the door oh, so softly behind her.

He smiled. He didn't mean to, but the thing sort of snuck up on him. Damn, but she was going to be a feisty little handful.

That was a bad choice of words. His hands longed for the soft, heavy feel of her breasts. He could still feel their imprint on his chest after their first collision on Saturday.

He swore softly, dragged his mind back to the letters and forced himself to concentrate, just long enough to

finish them. Then he took himself home for the night
and prayed for oblivion. God knows, he thought, I'll
need a decent night's sleep to deal with that aggravating
witch tomorrow.

Linsey stood in bra, pants and tights and glared at the
contents of her wardrobe. For heaven's sake, it didn't
matter what she wore! She was dressing for work, not
for Matthew!

Irritated beyond belief by her own stupidity, she
snatched out the first thing she came across, only to stop
as she was tugging it over her head. A wool mix? In a
heatwave? Good grief. She put the dress back, removed
instead a cotton skirt and matching sleeveless vest-top.
It was going to be a scorcher today. In fact, her tights
were a mistake. She wriggled out of them, pulled on
the skirt and top and slid her feet into cool, strappy
sandals. There.

Now, if she could just persuade her hair to stay up in
a professional-looking bun instead of slithering down
her back as usual, she would be fine.

She headed for the stairs. Would Matthew be in a
grouch this morning, or would she see another side of
him? She laid odds on the grouch, and wasn't disappointed.

He greeted her with a reserved smile and a reminder
that she was there to observe, and so she watched him
as he checked his post, ripped open an envelope and
scanned the contents, scribbled a note for Suzanne and
took another swig of coffee.

'Riveting stuff,' she said drily after about ten minutes.

He glanced up, shook his head and apologised. 'Sorry.
I'm a bit pushed this morning—I had a couple of calls
to make on the way here. I normally get this out of the

way by eight. Grab a coffee; I'll be with you in a minute.'

She went out to the kitchen and encountered a stranger. She studied him for a second—slight, dark, late twenties—and smiled. 'You must be Tim Wilson.'

He nodded. 'And you're Linsey. Wonderful. I can have a day off at last.'

She chuckled. 'I shouldn't bank on it. So far I'm not even allowed to sharpen a pencil.'

Tim grinned. 'He'll unbend. He likes his trainees to know their place.'

'I like my trainees to know the job,' Matthew corrected him mildly from behind Linsey. 'That way I know I can rely on them. How did you get on with Mrs James?'

'Oh, OK. She's stable. I wondered if we might have to transfer her to Lymington, but I think she'll be all right in Milhaven, at least for now. I'll go and see her again later.'

Matthew nodded. 'Fine. Right, Linsey, when you're ready. . .'

She was every bit as difficult as he had anticipated. She sat there, cool and delectable and good enough to eat, her bare, satiny legs tormenting him every time she moved, and she said nothing.

Her face, however, was far from silent. Not a poker player, he thought; and after each patient came the barrage of questions.

'Why did you tell her to come back in a week if it's no better? You know it'll be better.'

'Because she's a worrier and she likes support.'

'Why did you give him a prescription? Why not just tell him he had a virus and didn't need anything?'

'Because he would just come back again and again until he had a prescription. He always does.'

This went on all morning, until at eleven-fifteen the surgery finally ground to a halt. They went into the kitchen for coffee and she started again.

'None of your reasons are medical. None of these treatments I've queried have been suggested on medical grounds!'

'No,' he replied mildly. 'But I'm treating the patient and not the condition. That's general practice—that's what your precious continuity of care gives you, Linsey: an opportunity to know your patient so well you can out-psych him or her.'

'But I can't do that yet! I would have told Mrs Bates to go home and that she'd be fine, and I would have sent Mr Dean off without a prescription for antibiotics, with an explanation of his condition. Does that make me a better doctor, or a worse one?'

'Neither. Just different. Anyway, his prescription wasn't for antibiotics,' Matthew told her with what felt to him suspiciously like childish glee. 'It was for a para-cetamol-based painkiller. They'll reduce his symptoms, he'll get better anyway, and he won't come back and waste our time.'

She rolled her eyes. 'Why not just tell him to take paracetamol and have done with it?'

Matthew smiled. 'Because he'd say it wouldn't work. He's just a big baby, Linsey. He likes to be molly-coddled. He's happy, and that means I'm happy. What have I done that's so wrong?'

'You're sneaky,' she said huffily, and he wanted to hug her.

Instead he drained his coffee and stood up. 'Come on; visits now.'

'More of the same?' she said wryly.

He grinned. 'Probably.'

It wasn't, though. One of the patients was elderly and had been suffering 'a spot of indigestion'. By the time they arrived he was in severe pain, breathless, cyanosed and obviously having a major heart attack. While Matthew arranged his admission to Lymington Hospital with its twenty-four-hour medical presence, rather than Milhaven which only had GP call-out cover, Linsey gave him an intravenous injection of diamorphine to kill the pain, and gradually his face relaxed. However, his colour was still bad and while they waited Matthew rigged up the portable oxygen cylinder he carried in his car and Linsey sat and talked to him, calming him with her quiet words.

Damn it, she was good with him, Matthew acknowledged. Perhaps her references were believable, after all. He watched, one eye on the window for the ambulance, and moments later it arrived and whisked the old boy off to Lymington.

Matthew scribbled in the notes, then pocketed his pen. 'I'll just tell his neighbour—she's got a key, so she can come in and feed the cat and keep an eye on the place. I expect she'll visit him. She's been a treasure since his wife died six months ago.'

There was no reply, and Matthew looked up to find that Linsey was standing holding a faded picture of a young couple on their wedding day. 'Is this them?' she asked, her voice a little scratchy.

Matthew looked at her carefully, then glanced at the photograph. 'Yes, it is.'

She put the picture down with great care and stared around her at the spacious but lonely bedroom. Evidence of Mr Roland's late wife was all around—pictures, a tapestry she had done, even a favourite cardigan folded on a chair, gathering dust.

'I've never seen their homes,' she said, and she sounded a little awed and somewhat sad. 'They came from out of nowhere, and we sent them back without any idea of whether they could cope and what their conditions were like.'

Matthew snorted. 'Tell me about it. We had one chap who had a prostate operation as a day case and was sent home with bladder irrigation for the first forty-eight hours! And who was supposed to do it? Me and the district nurse.'

'So what did you do?'

He sighed. 'I admitted him to the cottage hospital and he was properly looked after. I expect they knew we'd do that. Anyway, I wrote with some—ah, suggestions, and they've since changed their procedures.'

Linsey met his eyes and returned his smile. 'I'll bet,' she said softly. 'I'll just bet.'

He dragged his eyes away from hers and cleared his throat. 'Right, two more calls and then we can pop in at the hospital on our way back for lunch.'

They paused for a quick chat with the neighbour, did a post-op follow-up and another visit to a sick child with tonsillitis, and then popped into the cottage hospital.

A between-the-wars structure, it was on two floors, with two small wards and a tiny casualty unit for very minor problems, which doubled as an out-patient clinic for minor-surgery techniques by those GPs who didn't have their own facilities, Matthew explained. There were thirty beds altogether in the two wards, both mixed, although the patients were 'zoned' to give them a little more privacy.

The lady they were to check on was in the ground-floor ward at the far end, and she was lying chatting happily with the lady in the next bed.

'Hello, Mrs Simms,' Matthew said cheerfully.

'Oh, Doctor! Hello. Oh, my goodness, I wasn't expecting you—let me put my teeth in.'

She fumbled in the pot by the bed, and then gave them a toothy grin and shuffled up the bed a little. 'There. That's better. How are you?'

Matthew grinned and winked at the neighbour. 'I thought that was my line.'

She laughed. 'Oh, well—it is! And I'm much better, but I shouldn't tell you that or you'll send me home,' she confided with a wheezy giggle. Her eyes flicked to Linsey. 'Who's your girlfriend, Dr Jarvis?'

Matthew felt the colour threaten and could have strangled the old dear for her choice of words. 'I should be so lucky,' he said lightly. 'This is Dr Wheeler, who's been working in hospitals until now and is spending a year with us in general practice.'

She patted his arm. 'A whole year, eh? I expect you'll manage to charm her in that time, dear, don't you?'

She gave another wheezy cackle and Matthew found his smile was slipping a little. Linsey, bless her, moved up beside him and shook Mrs Simms's hand, relieving him of the necessity for a reply. Her words, though, did nothing to soothe him.

'It's nice to meet you, Mrs Simms,' she said with a smile. 'I expect I'll be seeing quite a bit of you one way and another, and I'll keep you in touch with his progress—although I must say he's been a bit lacking on the charm front recently. Perhaps we'll have to give him some lessons.'

He thought the old duck was going to be pushing up daisies, she laughed so much. He glared at Linsey, who simply smiled innocently and stepped back out of his way, eyes sparkling with mischief.

He arched a brow at her disapprovingly, ignored her tiny giggle of defiance and whipped his stethoscope out of his pocket. 'Right, Mrs Simms, let's have a listen to this old chest of yours and see if it's a bit clearer.' He turned to Linsey. 'She had a touch of right-sided failure and a bit of oedema, so we're keeping an eye on the chest, and her legs are supposed to be up to aid her venous return and get the oedema down. Isn't that right?'

'If you say so, Doctor. Do you want my nightie up?'

He shook his head. 'No, I can hear through the material if you'll stop cracking jokes with my colleague,' he growled gently.

She pulled a mock-guilty face, breathed in and out obediently and showed him her legs. He passed the stethoscope to Linsey. 'There's a little congestion still in the lower left lobe of her lungs. Otherwise she seems clear. Have a listen.'

She did so, frowning as she handed him back the instrument. He shook his head slightly in warning and tucked Mrs Simms back up in the bed. 'Right, my dear, I think you can go home if you promise to wear your support tights and take your water tablets. Do you think you can do that?'

'Oh, it's been so warm to wear tights, and I forget the pills—'

'I can always send you to Southampton,' he said mildly, folding up the stethoscope and returning it to his pocket.

'No—no, I'll do it. I really will, I promise!'

He smiled at her and patted her hand. 'All right. You can go home just as soon as someone can get you some food in and give you a lift, all right? How about your son?'

'I'll ask him. He's in this afternoon—could I go then?'

'Yes, if he can sort it out. I'll sign your forms and they can get your pills ready, OK? And I'll come and see you at home in a few days.'

He ushered Linsey out and made sure they were well out of earshot before he let her speak. 'Well?' he said.

'Her heart's a bit rough, isn't it?'

He smiled. 'Just a bit. I don't think she has any idea how irregular the beat is or how weak. I don't want her to know, either. She's a sweet old thing and she's near the end—I don't want her to have to worry every minute.'

He did the necessary paperwork in the sister's office on the way out, and then whipped the professional journal that Linsey had picked up off the desk from her hand and ushered her out of the door.

'Lunchtime,' he said succinctly. They reached the car and he unlocked it, and the blast of heat from the inside nearly choked him. Their eyes met over the roof. 'How about picking up a sandwich and eating it in the park over the road? Maybe we can find a patch of shade.'

She looked doubtful. 'Have we got time?'

'Just about.'

He shut the car door again, but as he did so a woman ran from the hospital entrance. 'Dr Jarvis? Wait!'

He turned towards her. 'Yes?'

'Call from the surgery—would you please go straight back there—there's an emergency come in and no one's there. Someone's collapsed with the heat and the receptionist said another patient was resuscitating her.'

He unlocked the car, jumped in, regardless of the temperature and gunned the engine, pulling away in a squeal of tyres. He just hoped Linsey was in, because there wasn't time to worry about her. He shot her a quick glance. 'OK? Sorry about that.'

She shrugged. 'That's medicine for you. One minute you're planning lunch in the park, the next you're flying along at fifty in a thirty-mile-an-hour limit to save someone's life. It's about time it hotted up—it's been a bit tame really so far.'

He laughed. 'Tame? That's general practice for you, Linsey. Old dears and tonsils.'

He swung into the surgery car park, cut the engine and ran, leaving the door hanging open. He didn't wait for Linsey. There wasn't time.

They needn't have hurried. The woman, in her late fifties and heavily obese, had succumbed to the heat and nothing and no one could bring her back. They had no idea who she was, except that she wasn't local. She had been dropped off at the gate by someone, Linsey gathered—possibly a taxi. She was wearing a wedding ring round her neck, but whether because she was divorced or because her fingers had become so swollen that she could no longer get it on they had no idea.

'No ID at all,' Matthew said in disgust. 'Oh, well, she'd better go to Lymington Hospital mortuary.'

'Don't you have a mortuary here?' Linsey asked.

'Yes, but it's not chilled, and in this heat—' He shrugged. 'We may have to keep her body some time before we can identify her, and she'll need a post-mortem, even though the cause of death is fairly obvious. That has to be done at Lymington. And in the meantime, we have to wait for someone to notice that she's missing.'

'Poor old thing,' Linsey said. 'Fancy dying like that, all alone. Do you suppose she's here on holiday?'

'Could be. We won't know, will we? I'll notify the police.'

He disappeared, leaving Linsey with the dead woman, and she searched the body yet again for any clues. There was only one—the label on the blouse was not mass-produced, nor was the garment, and it declared that the blouse was made in Sussex by Christine Cleary.

A clue? Possibly. She knew the name, and the firm. She wrote it down and gave the piece of paper to Suzanne. 'Could you give this to the police? They're a small local firm specialising in outsize clothes. It might be worth contacting them. My aunt uses them, and they're very good at remembering her name. Perhaps they'll know this lady, unless she picked up the blouse at a jumble sale or second-hand shop. They might be worth speaking to.'

Suzanne took the piece of paper and promised to hand the information on. By this time Matthew had finished with the police on the phone and the ambulance had arrived to move the body.

He shot a glance at his watch. 'Looks like lunch will be a quick cup of coffee and yet another packet of biscuits,' he said with a sigh.

Linsey needed more than that. Slender she might be, but there was a lot of her, nonetheless. 'Speak for yourself—I'm having something out of my fridge.'

He looked at her as if she held the elixir of life in her hands. 'Is there enough for two?' he said hopefully.

She chuckled. 'Maybe. I could knock up a cheese salad,' she offered.

His eyes lit up. 'Really? I'm ravenous. I didn't have time for breakfast,' he confessed.

She shook her head disapprovingly and ran upstairs to her flat, Matthew on her heels. They raided the fridge and he grated cheese while she washed and cut up the salad, then they bolted the food down and went back to the kitchen to grab a mug of filter coffee before the antenatal clinic started at two. They hadn't had time to exchange more than a word or two, but nevertheless, sharing the meal had been cosy in a way, and she hoped it might have softened him up, because there was something she wanted, and he needed to be receptive.

'Can I ask a favour?' she said, wondering how he would react.

'You give me lunch and already you want a favour?'

She blushed a little, and he laughed.

'I knew it. What?'

'Can I do your antenatal clinic?'

'No.'

Fine. That was how he'd react, of course. Why had she expected anything different?

He leant over and covered her hand with his, and a shiver went up her arm as he squeezed gently and released her. 'Watch what I do, how I work with the midwife—by all means ask questions and, if the mums don't mind, examine them, but I want to make sure you do things our way.' He looked at her, saw the set of her mouth and she could see the conciliatory words forming in his mind.

'It's not that I don't trust you.' She mimicked his voice.

He grinned sheepishly. 'It isn't. You said yourself continuity was important. Just give yourself a few days to settle in and you'll find you've got more than enough to keep you quiet. Rosie's going on holiday in a fortnight, and Tim is owed time off in a serious way. Don't worry, Linsey. Just enjoy the rest while it lasts.'

So she did. Well, in a manner of speaking. While he dealt with one patient, she read through the notes of the next, then observed to see if he followed up the way she would have done.

He did. She was relieved. After the morning's episode with the carefully nurtured psyches of his neurotic patients, she had wondered if she was cut out for general practice.

Halfway through, the phone rang.

'Would you get that, please, Dr Wheeler?' Matthew asked, continuing to palpate the distended abdomen of his patient.

She picked up the phone. 'Yes?'

'Could you ask Dr Jarvis to phone Dr Williams at home as soon as possible, Dr Wheeler?' April, the receptionist, asked her.

'Of course. Any idea what about?'

'He didn't say, but it sounded urgent.'

'I'll hand it on,' she promised.

As she cradled the receiver Matthew raised one eyebrow at her.

'Phone Dr Williams at home.'

He nodded, finished the consultation and picked up the phone.

'Rhys? Matthew. What can I do for you?'

He leant back in the chair, listening for a moment. 'Sure. What sort of problem?'

There was a short silence. 'Judy? What about her?'

Another pause, then Matthew straightened slowly. 'Gone? Where to?'

Linsey caught the anxiety in his voice, and turned to him. 'Problems?' she mouthed.

He nodded. 'Of course. I'll be there in ten minutes.'

He put the phone down, grabbed his jacket and rummaged for the car keys. 'You get your wish. Could you finish my antenatal clinic, please? And you might find you get twice as lucky and end up doing Rhys's surgery this evening, if not for the rest of the week. His wife's just left him.'

As a parting shot, Linsey thought, it was superb. The rest of the afternoon passed in a blur of activity, and as she tried desperately to do things as Matthew would have done without compromising her own judgement she found her mind straying to the big, genial man who had shown her such kindness on the day of her interview.

What kind of personal hell was he going through now? Why had his wife left him? He seemed such a genuinely decent man. Was it all a sham? Perhaps he beat her. Maybe he drank—plenty of doctors did, given the stress of the job.

The last antenatal patient came and went, and Linsey went out to Reception with the bundle of notes and spoke to Suzanne. 'Any news from Dr Williams or Dr Jarvis?'

'Yes—can you please do Rhys's evening surgery? He's on call tonight but Matthew says Tim'll do that. Will you be able to manage?'

'Of course. Where are the notes? Perhaps I should look through them first and see if there's anything I should be aware of.'

She was handed a stack of patient envelopes and went into her consulting room. Her name was on the door, she noticed, and it all looked very professional. She was qualified, her last stint had been in A and E and she'd had more than enough responsibility there.

So why were her hands clammy and her knees knocking and why was her heart beating nineteen to the dozen? All day she'd been frustrated by the lack of responsibility. So why the sudden stage fright?

Oh, well, perhaps the adrenalin would help her to

concentrate and do things right. At least she was computer-literate! So many of her hospital colleagues hadn't been.

She flicked on the monitor, tapped buttons and brought the notes of the first patient up on the screen. An elderly lady with apparently very good health, she had no immediate history that Linsey thought could be troubling her. So, no clues. Oh, well.

She checked the second patient, and the third, with the same result, and finally decided that the way to handle it was to scan the notes just before the patient came in. She could hear Matthew's voice, and was reassured to know he was just the other side of the wall and could be summoned in the event of any difficulty.

That was the difference, of course. In hospital there was always another person on the next rung of the ladder who could be referred to at a moment's notice. A GP had to make all the decisions and carry the can totally alone. It was a lonely life, she realised, and could be stressful not only because of the pressure but the tedium and very autonomy of it.

The rewards, on the other hand, were more readily visible than in hospital. Children cared for from an early stage of pregnancy would stay in the practice and become adults, and would in turn bring their children in. Family doctoring at its best.

And she was just about to taste it for the first time. . .

CHAPTER FOUR

MATTHEW was waiting for her in the kitchen when she finished her surgery just after six-thirty. He didn't say a word, just pushed a mug of coffee across the table towards her and watched in silence as she sipped it gratefully, wriggled her feet out of her shoes and sighed.

'Manage OK?' he asked at last.

She nodded.

'Any problems?'

She shook her head. 'No, I don't think so.'

He looked almost disappointed, she thought, and nearly smiled. Then she remembered why she had been doing the surgery in the first place, and the urge to smile vanished.

'How's Rhys?' she asked softly.

Matthew's face darkened. 'Shattered. Can we go up to your flat?'

'Sure.' She drained her coffee, picked up her shoes and led the way upstairs. The sun was dipping in the sky, glinting on the distant sea, and she stood in the window and breathed in the cooler evening air. Finally she turned to him as he sprawled in the big armchair that she guessed had always been his favourite.

'So, tell me about Rhys.'

He shook his head. 'I can't—not all of it. He'll have to tell you himself. I'll tell you what I can, but it's not much. Judy's gone—walked out this morning, leaving a note. The kids were with a child-minder.'

How dreadful, to come home and find that, she

thought. She perched on the edge of the sofa near him. 'No warning?' she asked.

Matthew shrugged. 'Things hadn't been wonderful for a while. I don't think he made any secret of that, but no, there was no warning that she was going, certainly not like this, without saying anything or leaving an address.'

Linsey's eyes widened. 'But what about the children? Will she come back? Is it just a temporary escape from a difficult situation?'

Matthew sighed and ran his hands through his hair, rumpling it yet again. 'No, she won't come back. She made that clear, and he made it equally clear that he wouldn't have her. That does, of course, have implications for his job until he can set up some child-care arrangements.'

He smiled wearily at her. 'It seems, young lady, that you arrived in the nick of time. If you really coped all right with that surgery, then if you're happy to take it I'd like to hand some of Rhys's workload over to you now. Tim and Rosie and I will take the follow-up cases if you could see the one-offs and temporary residents, and we won't expect you to cover his out-of-hours work, but if you could simply do his routine surgeries and daytime visits it would help enormously.'

'Of course I will,' she agreed instantly. 'I imagine I'll start first thing in the morning. I could do with a street map if I'm to do his visits.'

'Suzanne will give you one. The other problem is your tutorials, but we'll just have to fit them in—in the evening, if necessary—after work. It won't be for long, but I'm unhappy about flinging you in at the deep end without support in your first practice appointment.'

She smiled reassuringly. 'Matthew, don't worry; I can cope.'

'Timing is difficult—keeping the appointments running smoothly without getting behind. It's so easy to get twenty minutes behind—one phone call, a slightly longer consultation, and it screws up the whole day.'

'I'm used to timing. I've done clinic work.'

'Any patients you're worried about, just come and see me.'

'I will.'

'Anything you're worried about—'

'Matthew?'

'Yes?'

'Don't stress.'

His mouth closed with a snap. Shutting his eyes, he tipped his head back and sighed. 'Sorry. It's just that being the senior partner has its responsibilities, and I take my responsibilities seriously.'

'So do I, so you can relax. Are you going to eat tonight? I could fling something together for us both, if you like.'

'Me?' He sat up and shrugged. 'I was going to eat, but rather than you feeding us again, why don't I take you out for a quick bite at the pub up the road? We can eat in the garden and if we're really lucky the New Forest ponies won't come and steal it all.'

A date? Well, there's a thing, she thought. She answered his smile with one of her own. 'Sounds good. Can you give me ten minutes to shower and change?'

'Sure.' He leapt to his feet and strode across the landing. 'I'll wait for you downstairs. I've got a few things to do.'

She watched his head disappear down the stairs, and grinned. Clearly the thought of her and her toiletries

terrified the life out of him. Perhaps he thought she'd
spray him with tampons and toothpaste again.

With a chuckle, she went into the bathroom, stripped
into the laundry basket and turned the shower on full.
She washed her hair as well. It had been too hot and
sticky a day to leave it, and she could always brush it
out and leave it to dry.

She dressed in light cotton leggings and a matching
T-shirt, soft slip-on cotton shoes and a stroke of mascara.
She didn't bother with lipstick as they were going to be
eating, and she never wore eye-shadow anyway. Her
hair was tangled, of course, and took ages to comb out,
so she left it damp over her shoulders. It was still muggy,
she decided, so she would hardly catch a chill, even if
such a thing were possible.

She ran downstairs, only five minutes late, and tapped
on his consulting-room door.

'Come in,' he grunted, and she opened the door and
found him submerged in a sea of notes.

'Just sorting out tomorrow's surgery,' she was told.
'I'm almost done. Grab a pew.'

'I'll dry my hair. Come and get me when you're
ready,' she said, and ran upstairs again. Lord, the stairs
would get her fit, she thought with a smile. Up, down,
up, down.

She was on the landing, bent over double, waving the
hair-dryer at her hair, when she saw his feet behind her
through her legs. She straightened up, throwing her hair
over her head and turning. 'Ready?'

He cleared his throat. 'Um—yes. Got everything? Keys?'

She nodded, and he turned on his heel and went back
down the stairs as if the hounds of hell were after him.
Linsey chewed her lip and followed him at a more digni-

fied pace. Either he was having difficulty keeping his
hands off her, she decided, or he was scared of her. Since
she couldn't imagine Matthew being scared of anyone,
that left only one, rather intriguing possibility. . .

He was going to disgrace himself. She was glorious, her
hair gleaming gold in the evening sun, her face innocent
of make-up, her body sleek and slender yet softly curving. And that laugh!

It curled round his insides and turned him to mush.
Well, perhaps not mush. In fact, the opposite. He longed
for his tight, concealing jeans that were so good at
disguising his reaction.

They turned into the pub car park and saw a crowd
of people standing round, cameras clicking busily as
they stared at something in the middle of the road in
front of the pub.

Linsey was immediately curious, to Matthew's relief.
It took her attention away from him and might give him
time to control his libido.

'What *are* they photographing?' she asked in
amazement.

'I'll lay you odds it's a pony,' he said drily. They
crossed to the crowd and peered into the centre.

'Oh, Matthew, a foal! It can only be minutes old!'

Matthew snorted. 'Typical woman—having her baby
right in the middle of the road.' But he couldn't keep
the smile off his face, and when she turned, eyes shining,
his gut clenched and he had an almost overwhelming
urge to drag her into his arms and hug her.

And that was just for starters! He turned away from
the crowd, and with a last lingering look at the still-wet
foal Linsey followed him through the gate into the pub's
garden. There were several picnic tables scattered about

under birch trees, and because of all the interest in the foal's arrival they were able to find a table at the side of the garden, overlooking the open forest.

At least, Linsey was overlooking the forest. Matthew was overlooking Linsey, and his hormones were giving him hell. . .

It was a lovely meal. Matthew was a little preoccupied, Linsey thought, but put it down to worry over Rhys. Nevertheless, he was attentive. He told her about the practice, and how the work pattern had changed and shifted over the years, how a group of GPs had got together and installed a gastroenterology screening unit in the cottage hospital and how ulcers, bowel cancers and other related problems were now detected and sorted out much quicker.

He told her about the increase in the number of temporary residents they treated, and how the Forest was reaching saturation point with visitors, although the numbers in campsites were heavily restricted and well controlled, how the ancient paths and tracks were being destroyed because of the endless pony-trekking, and how the heathland in between the paths was steadily eroding due to the mass invasion that happened every year.

There were too many animals grazing too little grass, the recent droughts had caused even more problems, and she learned that the delightful ponies all belonged to someone and weren't truly wild at all.

'The Commoners, as the forest people are called, have the right to graze their animals on the common land. Each year in the autumn the stock are rounded up, the foals are counted and freezemarked with the owner's brand and young stock are sold on.'

'They must get killed on the road,' Linsey said, her

eyes still on the little foal who was struggling to stand with his mother's help.

'A lot of them do. The mothers cross the road, a car comes and the foals panic and try and rush across. A staggering number don't make it. I can't remember how many of the ponies are lost each year to road-traffic accidents, but it's a lot, and of course quite often, in high-speed night collisions, for instance, the occupants of the cars are hurt too.'

'But there are speed limits—I've seen yellow signs painted on the roads.'

Matthew shrugged. 'Only forty miles an hour—and that's too fast at night. Anyway, people break the limit all the time. No, the ponies are an attraction, of course, but they're also a hazard, both to themselves and to the visitors. People will feed them, and so they bite and kick and visitors get injured and blame the ponies, which is silly.'

Linsey looked at the fence around the garden. 'Do they get into people's gardens and damage the plants?'

Matthew grinned. 'Only if people leave the gates open. Nearly everyone has gates or a cattle-grid—sometimes both.'

'Do you?'

He laughed. 'Oh, yes, I've got a gate, and a stockproof hedge all round the garden—I need it. The ponies graze right up to the boundary all round.'

'Don't you have any neighbours?' Linsey asked in surprise.

He shook his head. 'No immediate neighbours, no. It's down a little wooded track and it's very much on its own. It was chosen for its isolation by the previous owner.'

'And why did you choose it?' Linsey asked, insatiably curious as ever.

His face twisted slightly. 'I didn't. He left it to me.'

Linsey felt her eyes widen. 'He left it to you? Why? Was he a relative?'

Matthew shook his head. 'No, not a relative. Not even a friend, really, until the end. He was a patient—a homosexual with AIDS-related complex. When he found out, he cut himself off from all his London friends, retreated to his little cottage and waited to die. He was here three years altogether, and he left me the cottage because he said I was the only person who understood how he felt, who didn't patronise or pass judgement or overdramatise. We used to play chess and shred up the current politics and tell awful jokes and generally pass the time.'

'Was he rich?'

Matthew shrugged. 'So-so, I suppose. He was a playwright. He was still working right up to the end. He had a brilliant mind—tortuous. And he was a very lonely man. The loneliest person I've ever met.'

'And you became his only friend.' Linsey swallowed. 'How sad.'

'I like to think I made a bit of difference.'

Linsey thought of the unknown man's situation, and how Matthew's company and acceptance must have eased his pain. 'I'm sure you did,' she murmured.

She took a big breath. 'So—tell me about it. Is it big? Small?'

'Quite small. One big sitting room, kitchen just large enough to eat in, two bedrooms and a bathroom.'

'Is it brick?'

'Good heavens, no. Wattle and daub over a timber frame, and thatch.'

'Oh, it sounds lovely! Can I see it?'

'Now?' he said, looking a bit taken aback.

'Yes—why not?'

He chuckled ruefully. 'Because I didn't make the bed this morning, I probably haven't washed up from last night and my cleaning lady comes on Wednesday.'

'So?'

'So it's Tuesday. That's bad news.'

She laughed. 'Tricia, my flatmate, calls me a pack-rat. She says I'm the dirtiest, untidiest, least domesticated person she's ever lived with, so please don't worry on my account!'

'Your flat looked fine,' he said in surprise.

'So, she's trained me! And anyway, I haven't been here long enough to get a real mess under way.'

He chuckled, and she let her smile blossom. It was good to see him relax. Maybe he was going to let her see the cottage, after all.

He tipped his head at her plate. 'Have you finished?'

She nodded.

'Right, I'll settle up and see you at the car. I expect you're going to talk to the Forest's latest arrival, are you?'

She laughed and agreed. Was she so easy to read?

'Be careful,' he warned her. 'The mother might kick if you get too close. She'll be very protective.'

So Linsey went and stood a few yards away and watched the little chap struggle to his feet, his mother nudging him with her nose to assist his unskilled efforts, and she went gooey inside when he started to suckle, his little tail wiggling furiously like a lamb's.

She heard footsteps behind her, and the mare turned her head curiously and watched as Matthew approached.

'It's a late foal,' he told her. 'It's missed the spring grass, so it'll find the winter hard unless they keep it in.

More and more people are doing that.'

'It's gorgeous.'

Matthew smiled. 'Softy,' he said gently.

'I am.' She turned away and smiled up at him, her eyes misty. She felt silly, but the little scrap had got to her. Obstetrics had always been her weakness, she thought with a little laugh. 'Come on, then. Show me your Hansel and Gretel cottage in the woods.'

It was a short drive away, less than a mile, and when they turned down the narrow, unmade track she could see what Matthew meant about isolation.

The cottage was totally invisible from the main road, and it was only as they approached that she caught her first glimpse of it.

White-painted, the thatch low down over the eaves, with little dormers like raised eyebrows interrupting the line of the roof, it was enchanting. Roses scrambled over the walls and up the thatch, and the beds around the walls were a blaze of colour.

She hopped out to open the gate and closed it again behind the car, mindful of the small group of ponies that they had passed, standing idly swishing their tails just yards away on the track. No doubt they would sell their souls to get their teeth into Matthew's garden!

He pulled up in front of the cottage and stood waiting for her as she crossed the lawn. 'Well?' he said expectantly.

She didn't disappoint him. 'It's gorgeous. Absolutely fairy-tale. I want to see inside.'

'God, what a demanding woman,' he said mildly, but he unlocked the door and ushered her in.

It was white-painted, the carpet a soft old gold, almost honey-coloured, and everything was either very pale, or dark, like the beams. An ancient oak chest stood against one wall, a grandfather clock against another. Grouped around the inglenook was a pair of sofas in pale cream, and between them was a lovely old Persian rug in soft, faded blues and golds.

'Everything is exactly as Joe left it,' Matthew told her. 'I didn't have any money to do anything, and it wasn't necessary.'

'Did he leave everything in the cottage to you as well?'

He nodded. 'Yes. I gave his personal effects to his parents, and I gather they burned them. I wish I'd kept them now, but I thought they'd want them.'

'They must have been hurt, perhaps by his unconventional lifestyle.'

'His sexuality, you mean. They never forgave him. His mother accused him of getting AIDS just to torture her.'

'How sad.' Linsey ran her fingers over the top of the oak chest, feeling the lovely mellow patina of age.

'Checking for dust?' Matthew teased.

She smiled wistfully. 'No. I just love old things.'

'I'm an old thing.'

She turned to him, her heart suddenly thudding in her chest. 'So you are,' she said lightly.

His eyes were burning up again, and without hesitation she went into his arms.

That first touch of his lips was magic.

They were soft, and yet firm, warm and generous, tentative for a moment, then suddenly more urgent. A low growl rumbled in his throat and she leant into him and parted her lips, giving him her mouth.

He took it mercilessly and without hesitation, and she felt her heart slam against her ribs as his tongue plundered the soft, dark depths. He slanted his mouth, his hands coming up to steady her face, and she could feel the uneven thud of his heart and the solid, fascinating pressure of his arousal against her softer thigh.

He shifted one leg between hers and she moaned and arched against him, desperate to eradicate the gap and be even closer—as close as she could be. She felt his hands leave her face and circle her waist, then slide up beneath her T-shirt.

He gave a ragged groan and broke away as he discovered that her breasts were bare, then he lifted her T-shirt and bent his head to suckle her breast.

Her legs nearly collapsed, and at her little cry he lifted his head and his eyes blazed into hers. 'Dear God, Linsey, you're beautiful,' he groaned, and his mouth came down on hers again, ravenous with need.

Time lost all meaning. She threaded her fingers through his hair and pulled him down harder against her mouth, arching into him, her body pleading with his.

And then suddenly, shatteringly, someone cried out his name and he leapt away.

Linsey caught a glimpse of the woman's face, ravaged with shock and pain, and then the woman was turning and running back to her car.

Matthew followed her, calling after her, but she drove away in a scrabble of gravel, leaving the gate hanging open. He stood in the driveway for an age, staring after her, and then slowly, heavily, he closed the gate and came back to Linsey.

Desire had left her now, draining away to leave her cold and sick and shaken.

'Who is she, Matthew?' she asked flatly. 'What is she to you?'

He lifted his shoulders. 'A friend—'

'She's more than a friend! Don't lie to me! I won't

be lied to, Matthew! She looked at me as if she owned you and I had taken you away from her. She looked at me as if I had killed her inside. I want to know, Matthew. I want to know who she is, and what you've said or done that gives her the right to look at me like that.'

'What the hell makes you think you've got the right to ask?' he snapped.

'That kiss,' she said bluntly.

After a moment his shoulders dropped. 'I'm sorry; you're right. I had no business kissing you like that.'

'Obviously not. Your mystery visitor would certainly agree.'

He sighed and rammed his hand through his dishevelled hair. 'Her name's Jan. We've been going out together off and on over the summer.'

'Are you sleeping with her?'

His head snapped up. 'What business is it of yours?' he asked furiously.

'Business? I'll tell you what business it is! You weren't about to stop kissing me there, Matthew, and I wasn't about to stop you, either. That kiss was going all the way, and we both know it. So tell me, and stop beating around the bush.'

She stared him down, and after a minute he turned away, his eyes closing. He had the grace to look ashamed. 'No, I'm not sleeping with her,' he said heavily. 'It's never become that serious—'

'She looked pretty damn serious.'

He sighed. 'Yes. I think perhaps she is. I hadn't realised. Look, I ought to go and talk to her.'

'Yes, I think you should,' Linsey said shortly. 'You've got some fence-mending to do and, judging by the look on her face, it's going to take some pretty fancy footwork to get you out of the mire you're in. You'd better take me home.'

She stalked out of the door, walked to the gate and held it open. The drive back was accomplished in silence, and, having seen her in, Matthew drove rapidly away in the direction of Lymington.

She didn't envy him one little bit, but it was his own fault. He had no business philandering with her if there was another woman on the scene. She went up to her flat, made a cup of tea, sat curled in the big chair that Matthew had sat in earlier and reflected on how their evening would have ended if Jan hadn't turned up.

In bed, without a doubt—unless they hadn't even made it that far. They had both been well past the point of reason.

And that was another thing. If he wasn't sleeping with Jan, then it seemed unlikely that he would have a supply of condoms to hand, and Linsey certainly didn't carry anything like that round with her. For the past few years at least, she had been too busy to hold down a relationship, and with the exception of this evening's regrettable lapse she had never found herself wanting to go to bed with anyone without knowing him very well first.

It seemed, then, that Jan might have done her a favour by turning up out of the blue. She didn't feel grateful, though—far from it. She sipped her tea, closed her eyes and groaned softly. She could still feel his lips, and the moist velvet sweep of his tongue—

She whimpered with frustration. Her body still throbbed with longing, and she was racked with a fierce urge to wrap herself around him and draw him into herself, both physically and spiritually.

She catapulted out of the chair, dumped the mug on the table and changed into her jogging gear. Damn and blast the man, she would run off the frustration.

She let herself out and jogged down the road to the high street, then down to the sea front and along the beach. It was quiet now; the trippers had mostly gone home, and apart from the odd person walking a dog she was alone. She ran to the end of the prom, then turned and ran back inland, cutting across the park and then down and back along the leafy street to the practice.

There was a light on, she saw to her dismay. Not Matthew, she thought; please, not Matthew. But it was Tim, calling in to collect some notes before a visit.

'Hi,' he said cheerily. 'That looks very healthy.'

She laughed, leaning against the reception counter and taking her pulse. A hundred and sixty-two. Fine. She let it settle and chatted to Tim for a moment.

Then she heard a door open behind her and her heartbeat picked up again. 'Linsey?'

She turned and looked at him. He looked grim, and, softy that she was, she felt sorry for him.

'Can I have a word with you?'

'Sure. See you, Tim.'

She went past Matthew, up the stairs to her flat. He followed slowly—reluctantly?

'Where have you been?' he asked, his eyes scanning her shorts and vest-top.

'Jogging. Why?'

He shrugged. 'Just wondered.' His eyes swept up and locked with hers. 'I saw Jan.'

She looked closely at him, at the faint red imprint of a hand on his cheek. 'I see you did. I gather she was unimpressed.'

'You might say that.' He sighed and ran a hand through his hair, pacing across her sitting room to stand at the window, staring out at the darkening sky. 'I shouldn't have done what I did. Whether she'd seen us or not, I shouldn't have done it. I hope you'll believe me if I tell you that I didn't take you back there with the intention of making love to you.'

'I invited myself.'

'I could have said no. Even when we arrived, I had no intention of doing what I did.'

'Kissing me?'

'Making love to you.'

'Is that what you were doing?'

'Oh, yes,' he said softly, turning towards her. 'You know that.'

Her heart thumped again.

'I just want you to know I won't do it again.'

She nodded, perversely disappointed. 'OK. Will you be able to patch things up with Jan?'

He shook his head. 'No. She's made it clear she doesn't want to see me again. We had a long chat. She's been feeling discontented with our relationship for some time, apparently, but she's never said anything.' He sighed again and turned back to the window. 'That's the second time, you know.'

She frowned, not understanding. 'The second time that what?'

'That my obsession with you has messed up a relationship.'

She found that very interesting. 'Obsession?' she said carefully.

'Obsession. After I fished you out of the river I couldn't get you out of my mind. I kept dreaming about you falling in and not being able to find you under the water. Sometimes I'd find you but I couldn't pull you free. Always, before you fell, you turned your head and looked at me, and I started to walk towards you.'

He laughed bitterly. 'I made the mistake of telling Sara about it. She was highly unimpressed—so unimpressed, in fact, that she walked out a little while later.'

'But you couldn't help your dreams!' Linsey protested, appalled that she could have ruined his life all those years ago. She knew about the dreams—oh, yes. All about them. 'You had no control over them.'

He gave a little grunt of laughter. 'No—but she didn't have to like it. Ah, well, it might never have worked anyway.'

'And Jan?'

He smiled without humour. 'Ah, yes, Jan. I was going to ask her to marry me.'

'And yet you could kiss me like that?' Linsey said in disbelief.

'Apparently. I never kissed her like that, you know. Not even remotely. I never wanted to.'

'But you wanted to kiss me.'

His eyes locked with hers. 'Yes. I wanted to kiss you. I still do, but I won't.'

She took a steadying breath. 'Do you want me to go?'

He was silent for a long time, then shook his head. 'No. It won't do any good. My relationship with Jan has been shown for what it is, and with Rhys off we need all the help we can get. You going won't help solve anything at all.'

'I just thought, if it was what you wanted. . .'

'You know what I want. I want to take that vest-top and peel it over your head, and strip those shorts off you inch by inch, and then put you in the shower and get in with you and wash every inch of you. Then I want to lift you out and dry you, and take you to bed and make love to you until you can't stand up for a fortnight.

'But I won't,' he added, 'because that wouldn't solve

anything either. So we'll work together, side by side, and I'll give you tutorials, and we'll be good kids and keep our hands to ourselves, and if we get really lucky we'll manage to sleep for a few minutes every night without being racked by lust. How does that sound?'

She almost said, Tedious, but thought better of it. 'We'll give it a try,' she said instead.

'It'll work, Linsey,' he vowed. 'It has to, because I've got to go on with my life, and I can't allow you to mess it up again.'

It was almost hurtful the way he said that. She could have told him that for years she hadn't been able to kiss anyone with her eyes open because their eyes had been the wrong colour. She could have told him that her two affairs had been boring and awful, and in the throes of the nearest that she had ever come to ecstasy she hadn't felt one tenth of what she had felt with him that evening.

She didn't, though. She simply said, 'I'm sorry.' And she was. She knew the impact she was having on his life. It was entirely mutual—and unbelievably difficult to live with.

Suddenly a year seemed a long, long time. . .

CHAPTER FIVE

BEING flung in at the deep end was often the best way to learn a job, Linsey thought. It was also the most tiring. Despite the fraught and difficult evening that she had had with Matthew, Linsey fell into bed that night and slept dreamlessly until six.

Then she got up and padded downstairs to the surgery, switched off the burglar alarm and settled down in her consulting room with a cup of coffee and the morning's notes. There were one or two patients whom she was a bit concerned about and would have liked to consult Rhys on, but she didn't like to disturb him. She didn't feel she knew him well enough to intrude on his personal problems, and Matthew could probably answer the questions.

She chewed the end of her pen and flicked through the rest of the notes—no problems. So there were just the two; the man who had had an operation for cancer of the prostate some months before, and a young woman whom Rhys was investigating for Crohn's disease, a serious bowel disorder.

She decided to shower and dress and then perhaps phone Matthew and ask him to come in early to go over them with her; she was halfway up the stairs when she heard her own phone ringing.

She ran up and answered it on the fourth ring, and was surprised to hear Rhys's voice.

'Hi,' she said, and wondered what she was supposed to know.

'Hi. Look, Linsey, I'm sorry I woke you but I was a bit worried about a couple of my patients.'

She smiled. 'You didn't wake me. I was downstairs looking at the notes a minute ago. Why don't you go first? And then I'll ask you about the two I'm concerned about.'

'OK,' he agreed, sounding relieved. 'The main one is a woman who's presented with symptoms of severe haemolytic anaemia. The thing is, I've been turning it over in my mind and there's something I can't get hold of. Could you dig out her notes and perhaps even get her back in and check up on her? Her name's Nana Dickenson—Suzanne will know her. There must be something I've missed, but I'm damned if I know what it is.'

Linsey scribbled the name down, then asked about the other patient.

'Oh, Mrs Carter. I think she's got Crohn's. Would you ask Matthew to look at her?'

'Sure—she was one of my queries. The other's Mr Joiner—he was referred for CA prostate and he's come back. You don't know what for, I suppose?'

Rhys didn't. 'Watch out for bone pain. That's the most common site for metastases—primarily the hip, spine and ribs. He's also had heart problems in the past which might be playing up again—the heat might be getting to him. If it's insidious, give it to him straight. He's very acute and won't miss a trick, and if you try and bamboozle him he'll immediately assume he's got a fortnight left to live.'

'OK,' she said, feeling far from OK. She really felt that news such as that should be conveyed by someone who knew the patient, but that was ridiculous. He might have an ingrowing toenail! She would have to play it by ear.

'Don't feel you have to cope alone,' Rhys said reassuringly. 'Ring me if you're worried. I won't mind at all.'

'I will.' She bit her lip. She could hardly ignore his situation, and not acknowledging it would be even worse. 'Rhys, I'm sorry about your problems,' she said gently.

There was a moment's silence when she thought she'd done the wrong thing, then he said, 'Thanks,' gruffly and cleared his throat. 'I'm very grateful to you for stepping in like this,' he added. 'I'll be back as soon as I can.'

'Don't panic,' she hastened to reassure him. 'I was going crazy watching Matthew work while I twiddled my thumbs. Please don't rush back on my account!'

He chuckled, just barely, but it was a chuckle nevertheless. 'Thanks, Linsey. You're a star. I'll take you out to dinner when I've got everything settled here—to say thank you.'

'You don't have to thank me—' she protested, but he cut her off.

'I do. You can have no idea how much it helps to know the practice isn't in the lurch—Oh, blast, Mark's woken up. They couldn't sleep last night, the older two. They don't understand.' He laughed bleakly. 'Damn it, *I* don't understand. I have to go. I'll be here most of the day. Remember, ring if you've got a problem.'

'I will. Thanks, Rhys.'

She cradled the phone gently. Poor man. He sounded exhausted. He probably had hardly slept all night, if at all.

She showered, dressed and breakfasted, then went downstairs again and jotted pencil notes against Mr

Joiner and Mrs Carter. She'd get Suzanne to deal with Mrs Dickenson, and in the meantime she'd check the notes and see what pathology had turned up—probably nothing but there was no harm in looking.

Matthew knocked and came in just as she was getting ready to start her surgery.

'Hi,' he murmured.

She met his eyes, then her own skittered away. She didn't want to remember that kiss—especially if there wasn't going to be another one.

'Hi,' she replied.

'Any problems?'

She shook her head. 'I've spoken to Rhys—he rang at seven-thirty.'

'How was he?'

She sighed. 'He sounded pretty rough, really. I tried to assure him I could cope, but I don't know if he believed me.'

'You don't have to,' Matthew reminded her. 'I'm just next door if you start to disappear without trace.'

She smiled at him, and her heart thudded at the answering quirk to his lips. Damn and blast, why did she find the man so attractive?

'By the way, can you tell the patients if they ask that Rhys is away for personal reasons? Don't go into details, but don't say he's on holiday, either, because he had a fortnight in June and they get uppity if we're seen to be enjoying ourselves.'

His grin was infectious and did incredible things to his eyes and her blood pressure. She sighed as he closed the door, then she pressed the buzzer for her first patient. Please God let it be straightforward. After that smile she was going to have trouble concentrating on her own name!

Her surgery was fairly uneventful in the end, except that, as Rhys had suggested might be the case, Mr Joiner was complaining of backache. He had no previous history, and Linsey's suspicions were immediately aroused.

'When are you seeing your consultant again?' she asked him.

'Tomorrow, as it happens,' he said. 'Why?'

'I'd like you to mention it to him. He can arrange X-rays as he's on the spot, and it might have some relevance to your treatment.'

His face clouded. 'You mean secondaries.'

She put her pen down and met his eyes. 'There is a slight possibility, yes,' she agreed gently. 'However, there's no need to be concerned at this stage. He'll arrange an X-ray and will discuss the result with you. It's much more likely to be a touch of arthritis or just good old back trouble, but I feel we should eliminate the possibility of anything more serious.'

He shook his head. 'No. I had a feeling it was this. I'll see him tomorrow and we'll go from there, but I had a feeling.'

'Of course, if it is, and I'm not saying it is, catching it early with radiotherapy can make a huge difference.'

He smiled gently at her. 'Don't try to soften it. I know it's curtains. I'm sixty-seven. I've had a good life. I'd rather go now, quickly, than linger on to ninety-seven like my old grandfather. He was blind, deaf and helpless for ten years before he died. Terrible. No, my dear, I don't want a lengthy prison sentence. I'd rather have the electric chair.'

He stood up stiffly and smiled at her once again, and then left, a stick and his pride holding him upright.

She filled in his notes, saw the last two patients and went out to Reception.

'April, could you do me a favour and check up on Mrs Dickenson, please?'

'Nana? Sure. She's not looking too good, you know.'

'Yes, I gathered. Have we had a blood-test result?'

April called the patient's records up on the screen, scrolled through the notes and nodded. 'Yes. Haemolytic anaemia. Red cell count is recorded as very low. Here, have a look.'

Linsey scanned the screen and pursed her lips. 'Wow. I think we'd better arrange for her admission to Lymington Hospital for a blood transfusion, just to be on the safe side, and I need to look in the textbooks.'

She pulled out a haematology reference book from the shelf and sat with it open at haemolytic anaemia, waiting for divine inspiration to strike.

It didn't. She shouldn't have been surprised.

Tim came out of his surgery, grabbed the notes of his visits and left. He had no ideas.

'I've put you down for the emergency surgery, by the way,' April warned her. 'The first patient will be here in a minute.'

'Fine,' Linsey mumbled. She was scanning the notes, and nothing made any sense.

Matthew came and added his two-penn'orth, but they still got nowhere. Then Suzanne came out of her office.

'Who are you talking about?' she asked.

'Nana Dickenson.'

'Oh, I know. Husband Tiny owns the kebab house. Well, not her husband, really. She's divorced—lives with him. They've got three children. She's Greek.'

Matthew and Linsey turned to each other and smiled. 'Favism,' they said together.

'What?' April said with a frown.

'Favism. It's peculiar to areas of the Mediterranean.

They have a fairly common genetic condition known as G6PD deficiency, and basically they're missing an enzyme that protects the red cells from attack by certain chemicals. In the case of affected Greeks, it's the chemical contained in broad beans—fava beans is the other name for them, hence the name favism.'

'So all she needs to do is have a blood transfusion, and make sure she doesn't ever eat broad beans again. And her children shouldn't either,' Matthew said with satisfaction.

'I doubt if they would,' April said, wrinkling her nose. 'Broad beans are disgusting! No self-respecting kid would eat them.'

'I'd better check. Could I have her phone number?'

She rang Mrs Dickenson and asked her if she'd eaten broad beans recently, and was told that yes, she had. Bingo! Arrangements were made for her to go to hospital for a transfusion, and then Linsey hung up.

'Are you coping?' Matthew asked her softly.

'Oh, yes. I've cured a woman of a life-threatening disease and condemned a man to death. Things are just peachy.'

His smile was gentle. 'That's general practice for you, Linsey. How about a tutorial tonight, after surgery?'

'You're on duty,' April reminded him.

He groaned. 'Right, well, how about coming out with me now on my rounds and we can do it as I drive?'

'I've got the emergency surgery.'

He looked at April. 'How many?'

'Three.'

'I'll share them. Are they here yet?'

'Two are.'

He winked at Linsey and stood up. 'Come on, Dr Wheeler. Hi-ho, hi-ho.'

The emergency case she saw was quickly and easily dealt with: a child with obvious otitis media, a middle ear infection that was making him vomit, giving him a raised temperature and generally making him feel thoroughly unwell. The eardrum was still intact but quite inflamed, and she prescribed an antibiotic syrup for the little lad, handed the scrip to his mother and sent them on their way.

Now for the last one, she thought, only to find that Matthew had taken the third patient already and she was free.

He came out a few moments later, bag in hand, and they left promptly.

'Tell me about your surgery,' he said as he turned the car out of the drive and headed for the first call.

'Oh, it was pretty much of a non-event except for Mr Joiner and his back pain.'

'Yes, I'm afraid that's probably not good news,' he agreed. 'We might be wrong.'

'And pigs fly,' she said heavily. 'He said he'd rather have the electric chair than a lengthy prison sentence.'

'Let's just hope he doesn't end up on death row for years. Lots of cancer sufferers do exactly that.'

'Maybe he'll be lucky one way or the other.'

'Maybe.'

Matthew handed her a stack of notes. 'Here. The first call is to Mrs Simms—you remember we saw her at the hospital yesterday. I want to make sure she's all right. Then there's a routine visit to an elderly man who can't make it to the surgery. He's finding the heat a bit much at the moment, according to his son. We'll see if there's any need to admit him. Then Mrs Arkwright, who's booked for a hip replacement tomorrow and just wants to chat about it.'

'And you'll visit her, just for that?' Linsey asked, incredulous.

'Of course. She's housebound, scared to death and I can reassure her and take away some of that fear. That's why I'm here. Why are you here?'

She smiled. 'I just didn't realise there was still time to reassure. In hospital it's all so fast—in, out, ten minutes for this procedure, five for that, forty minutes for another. You lose touch with what it's all about.'

Matthew's laugh was wry. 'Believe me, it's easy to lose touch in general practice, too. Anyway, I want to make sure she's fit enough before she goes in. There's no point in unsettling her if the anaesthetist is going to find she's unfit at the starting line.'

Mrs Simms was well enough, happy to be back in her own home, and although she was still very breathless when she arrived at the door Matthew assured Linsey that for Mrs Simms that was quite normal.

'She's not very well, is she?' Linsey said thoughtfully as they left.

'No, but a lot of our elderly patients aren't.'

'How can she cope at home alone?'

He shrugged. 'She can't. She has help with shopping and meals on wheels and she has a home help from social services once a week, but otherwise she muddles along. We keep an eye on her and others like her.'

So he was an old softy too, Linsey thought, and smiled inwardly. That was what continuity did for you, of course.

Mr Briggs, the elderly man with arrhythmias who was suffering with the heat, was another case. He lived with his son, and so Matthew left him there with oxygen and instructions to the son to buy him a fan and close curtains and open windows to let the air circulate but keep the sun out, and to call if there was any deterioration in his condition or if he complained of any chest pain.

'Why didn't you admit him?' she asked.

'Because he gets very confused if he goes anywhere different, and when he comes home he's often incontinent. He goes into Milhaven every now and then for respite care so that his family can have some time off, and when he comes out the stress is much worse. They told me last time they don't think they'll bother again.'

'Could they get a carer to come in so they can go away?'

'I don't think so,' he said with a shake of his head. 'Financial pressures. The old boy hasn't got any money, and his son's job isn't any great shakes. It's the daughter-in-law I feel sorry for. She's trapped there with a man she's not even related to who is terminally difficult to get on with, and she's getting carer's syndrome. It's a worry. I can tell you, after what I've seen I'd never live with my children.'

She shot him a laughing look. 'What children? Is there something else you're not telling me?'

He grinned. 'Figure of speech. If I get like that they're better off unborn.'

'What do you mean, if? You're surely difficult enough now, aren't you?' she teased.

'How did I end up with you?' he asked, pretending to be affronted. 'Legs with attitude.'

She spluttered with laughter. 'I am not.'

'You are. Right, here's Mrs Arkwright's house. We'll go and explain about her hip replacement, and then we'll head back to the surgery.'

It was a small bungalow beginning to show signs of neglect, and Linsey guessed that the owner was gradually becoming less and less able to deal with it. Matthew rang the bell and Mrs Arkwright opened the door after an age.

'Oh, Doctor! How good of you to come. Do come in,' she said in a remarkably firm voice, and hobbled back towards her chair, leaning heavily on her walking frame.

She dropped into the chair with a grimace of pain, and then carefully put her leg up on a stool and lay back, wincing. 'Oh, dear. Just give me a moment,' she said.

'They're not doing it before time, are they?' Linsey murmured.

'Absolutely not. Better now, Mrs Arkwright? I understand you're having your op tomorrow.'

'That's right,' she said. 'And I have to say it's not a moment too soon.'

'No. How have you been since I saw you last?'

'Very well. I know everybody else is complaining about the heat, but frankly it suits me. All those years in India must have conditioned me, I suppose, but I find I can cope with the heat and my leg hurts so much less.'

'Let me just have a listen to your chest and take your blood pressure while I'm here, can I? Then I'll be able to send you off with a clean bill of health.'

Linsey watched as he checked their patient over and declared her fit as a flea and ready for anything.

'So, what will they do, again? I'm sorry to be such a nuisance but I do worry about it. How will I cope afterwards?'

'You'll be fine. First of all they'll admit you and check you over, just as I have, and then they'll draw on your hip to make sure they operate on the right one, and take you down to Theatre. The operation takes about an hour, and then you'll wake up back in your bed feeling probably a lot better than you have for ages.'

She chuckled. 'I hope so. Oh, I do hope so. So, what exactly do they do?'

Matthew whipped out a pad of paper and sketched a thigh bone and the hip joint, and explained where the bone would be cut, the new ball fitted on the end and the new socket cemented into place, and he showed her where she would have stitches and how long the incision was likely to be.

'You'll be walking easily within a week, and home as soon as you can get about with sticks. You'll have to be careful not to bend too far and not to turn that leg certain ways—they'll show you that. It's just that the joint support is a bit fragile for a month or so and has to have time to heal. Once it has, you should be feeling better than you have for years. Now, who's going to come and look after you at first?'

'I've got a home help coming—one of those carer agencies are sending a lady to live in for a week. I thought it made sense.'

Matthew agreed, and after a few more moments they let themselves out. They were just pulling away when the mobile phone warbled.

Linsey answered it. It was April at the surgery, sounding a bit flustered.

'There's a young woman here who wants to see a woman doctor—she seems quite shaken up but she's adamant it has to be a woman, and Rosie Farmer's on her half-day. I wonder if you could come back, Dr Wheeler?'

'I'll check. Hang on.' She turned to Matthew and repeated the message, and a quick frown creased his brow.

'Does she say what it's about?'

Linsey checked. 'No. No idea, but she's looking distressed.'

Matthew sighed, checked the mirror and spun the wheel. 'Tell her we're coming back. So much for that nice pub lunch I had in mind!'

'I'm Linsey Wheeler. Won't you come in and sit down?'

The young woman came into the consulting room, her eyes wide and watchful. She perched on the edge of the chair and looked as if she was about to run away. Her knuckles were white where she was gripping her handbag and Linsey could see that she was very badly traumatised. She looked clean—too clean. Scrubbed.

Linsey had a very bad feeling.

'Will you tell me your name?' she probed gently.

Grey eyes turned to her. 'Clare,' she said in a harsh whisper.

Linsey nodded. It was a start. There had been no hesitation, so she was confident it was the woman's real name. 'Can you tell me what's happened to frighten you, Clare?'

Her mouth opened, but no sound came out. Linsey could see her casting around for the words, but nothing seemed to be able to make it past her lips.

Finally her eyes closed and she let out a shuddering sigh. 'It was awful,' she whispered. 'He followed me. I was going home—about midnight. I had to get my car from the car park. I heard these footsteps getting closer, and then he just—'

She broke off, biting her knuckle. Linsey gave her time, then prodded again gently. 'What, Clare? What did he do?'

'He dragged me into the bushes, and he—Oh, God, it was sick. He was so foul—I'll never be clean again—'

She broke down, her shoulders convulsing, but no sound came out. Linsey crouched beside her and put her arms gently round her. 'Shh, Clare, you're safe. It's all right.'

The woman lifted her head. 'But I'm not! How do I know I haven't caught something really awful?'

Linsey moved back to her chair but kept her hand on Clare's. 'Clare, did he rape you?'

Her eyes squeezed shut and she shuddered, then nodded slightly. 'It was disgusting. I can't get the smell of him off me. . .'

Linsey squeezed her hand. 'Have you been to the police?'

Her eyes widened and she snatched her hand back. 'No! No, I can't. I'll have to see him and testify, and I can't—'

'All right. Clare, it's all right. Will you let me look at you—just to make sure he hasn't damaged you in any way?'

Clare bit her lip, then nodded. 'OK. But just you. No police.'

'All right. But first, would you mind if I talk to a colleague? It's his practice, and I'd like him to know what's going on.'

'He'll call the police.'

'No, he won't. I promise you, he won't.'

'In here, then, so I can be sure he doesn't.'

'All right.' Linsey picked up the phone and asked for Matthew. 'Could you come in for a moment?' she asked him.

Seconds later there was a tap on the door and Matthew came in.

'Dr Jarvis, this is Clare,' she said. 'Clare, do you mind if I tell him what you've told me?'

Clare shook her head, and Linsey ran quickly through

the story, then checked with the shaken girl that she agreed.

Again she nodded.

Matthew leant back against the wall of the surgery, keeping his distance physically so that he didn't frighten her. 'Clare, I know you don't want to go to the police, but I've done some work with them in the past as a police doctor. Now, because I've done this I know the procedure for rape victims, and I know what samples and so on are needed.

'If I were to tell Dr Wheeler what to do, would you allow her to take all those samples? We could send them to the lab with an explanation of what had happened and the information that you didn't want to press charges at the moment, and they could examine the evidence and put it all on file. That way, if you ever changed your mind it wouldn't be too late.'

'Without identifying me?' she said at last.

'Absolutely. We'd tell them only what you permitted us to.'

She chewed her lip, then nodded. 'He might do it again. They might catch him, and he could be punished.' She swallowed. 'Yes, all right.'

'What about the clothes you were wearing last night?' Linsey asked. 'Have you still got them?'

She nodded. 'In the bin. I threw them out. I could keep them, just as they are.'

'Or let us have them. That might be better.'

She nodded again. 'OK. And—can I have an AIDS test?'

'That won't be necessary,' Matthew told her. 'If we can recover a semen sample, then it can be screened for HIV and hepatitis. You won't need a test.'

'Are you sure?'

He nodded. 'Certain.'

'All right.'

Matthew sat at the desk, careful to keep well away from Clare, and wrote Linsey out a comprehensive list of instructions.

Then he left, and she conducted the necessarily very intrusive examination as gently and quickly as she could. There was a lot of bruising all over Clare's body, and Linsey made a note of each bruise, especially those that looked like fingers digging into her arms and thighs. She had a few minor internal lacerations, and as she was already engaged in a sexual relationship with her boyfriend, it indicated to Linsey just how violent an attack it must have been.

She found herself growing more and more angry, and had to force herself to be dispassionate.

Finally the swabs and samples were all collected, including nail scrapings and specimens of Clare's own hair to compare with any that might be found on her clothes.

'We might need a sample from your boyfriend if you've had intercourse recently, to differentiate,' Linsey told her, but Clare's eyes widened.

'No! I can't tell him! He mustn't know! He'll say I'm dirty—'

Linsey let her cry for a while, then gave her a little hug. 'Fancy a cup of tea?' she offered gently.

Clare nodded. 'I'm taking a lot of your time.'

'That's all right. I'll leave you to get your things back on while I make the tea. In fact, if I give you some paper and a pen, why don't you sit and write down everything you can remember—about him, the place, the nature of the assault—anything at all—and then sign it, so that if you decide to press charges you've got it all written down while it was fresh?

'And,' she added, 'you might also find it helps you to work it all out of your system if you put it down on paper. Try it. It always works for me if I'm really upset about anything.'

She left Clare dressing and went into the kitchen. Matthew was there. He pushed a cup of tea towards her.

'OK?' he asked.

'She may be, one day. What a bastard. I was going to take her a cuppa.'

'I'll make some fresh. Get all the samples?'

She nodded. 'She had internal lacerations. What kind of a brute was he?'

'Where do you want me to start?' Matthew said flatly. She could tell by the very lack of expression that he was as angry as she, and it was comforting.

'Do you think she'll go to the police?' Linsey asked him.

'I have my doubts. It's traumatic enough without having to go over it again and again to the pedantic satisfaction of the judicial system.'

'But he won't be caught unless she does.'

Matthew shrugged. 'It might be a one-off. It's quite possible it'll never happen again. There hasn't been anything in the news.'

'And perhaps his other victims have also kept quiet,' she said softly.

'Um—can I come in?'

They looked up and saw Clare hovering nervously in the doorway. 'Of course,' Matthew said easily, and stood up, offering her his chair.

He went round the table, made her some tea and pushed it towards her. 'How are you feeling now?'

'Better. I think—perhaps I should go to the police. You could be right. Maybe this is happening to lots of people.' She scooped her long blonde hair back away from her face and Matthew breathed in sharply.

Her neck was bruised—a circular bruise as if the man had tried to strangle her.

'Yes, Clare, I think you should go to the police. The next victim might not be so lucky.'

'What a day.'

Matthew snorted. 'So much for our tutorial session. I'm on duty now—damn.'

Linsey gave a little half-smile. 'I could feed you again—something easy? A stir-fry?'

'Can you be bothered? I could get a take-away.'

She shook her head. 'No. Actually, I'd rather you were here. It's funny, I haven't felt at all worried about being alone in the house at night until now, but suddenly—I don't know. Am I being ridiculous?'

His eyes darkened. 'Linsey, you've got nothing to fear.'

This smile was even smaller. 'Haven't I? A rapist is on the loose, and you say I've got nothing to fear? Tell it to Clare, Matthew. I bet she won't be sleeping peacefully tonight.'

'I'm sorry the session at the police station took so long.'

She shrugged. 'It was hardly your fault. They had to have all the facts. I just hope I managed to get enough DNA material for them to get a positive ID if it happens again.'

'I'm sure you did your best. It isn't easy, especially so long afterwards.'

'Mmm. Come on, let's go and raid my fridge before

the phone rings and you have to go out.'

Matthew switched the phone through to hers and they went up to the flat, and Matthew sat on one of the kitchen chairs, tipped it back and propped his feet on the wall while he watched her.

'She was a pretty girl,' he said idly. 'Looked a bit like you.'

Linsey threw him a sideways grin. 'All blondes look the same.'

'No, they don't. When I was at my obsessive best about you, every time I saw one I looked twice. They never looked quite like you. None of them ever had that certain something that made you stand out from the crowd.'

'I thought,' she said, viciously hacking up onions, 'that you were going to avoid personal issues like that.'

'Like what?'

'Like compliments.'

'That wasn't a compliment,' he said quietly. 'That was the truth.'

She heard the chair legs hit the floor, and then his hands touched her shoulders, turning her.

'God, you're crying!' he exclaimed softly.

She laughed, a little breathlessly. 'It's the onions.'

He took the knife out of her hand, washed her fingers under the tap and wiped her eyes with a dampened corner of the teatowel.

'That's better. I don't want to think I reduce you to tears.'

And then he kissed her.

It was just like before, only better, because she knew what was coming and anticipation added to the excitement.

The stir-fry was forgotten. There was no room in her

mind for anything except sensation, and it swamped her.
The taste of his mouth, the texture of his skin, the soft,
thick mass of his hair between her fingers as she cradled
his head and drew it closer—they combined to drive all
reason from her mind.

She knew only that this was right, that she belonged
to this man and always had, and he belonged to her.
From the first moment when their eyes had met all those
years ago, they had been a part of each other, and she
could no more deny that than she could deny her own
heartbeat.

They moved to the sitting room, sprawling across the
sofa, his weight half on her as his mouth plundered hers.
His hand grazed her side, and she shifted to give him
better access. She felt the warmth of his fingers caress
her breast. They were hard and yet so gentle, cupping
the fullness, his thumb tormenting the aching peak with
soft, teasing strokes. His hips nudged against hers, his
need so obvious and yet so restrained.

'Linsey?' he said softly.

And then the phone rang, shrill and demanding. He
lay motionless against her for a moment, then with a
ragged sigh he rolled away from her and stood up, striding to the phone.

'Dr Jarvis—yes, hello, Mrs Briggs. Oh, dear. Right,
I'll come straight away. Sit him up near an open window,
and stay with him. I'll be with you in five minutes.'

He turned to Linsey. 'Phone the ambulance—here's
the number and the address. Get them over there PDQ.
It's old Mr Briggs—I think the heat has finally got to
him. Admission to Lymington—could you phone them
as well and warn them? Bless you.'

He handed her her jotter pad, muttered something
about seeing her later and ran.

So much for their second kiss. She rang the ambulance, and the hospital, and then went into the kitchen and shredded up some more vegetables. When he came back—if he came back—she'd quickly fry them with some prawns and noodles. She made a cup of tea and settled down to wait in front of the TV, and tried not to think about the rapist.

Matthew came back after an hour and told her that Mr Briggs had gone into acute left ventricular failure and was touch-and-go. 'That's the trouble with LVF— it can strike so fast, especially in a patient who's already so dodgy. Anyway, he's in. Thanks for ringing round.'

'Have you got time to eat?' she asked.

'How long will it take?'

'Four or five minutes.'

He grinned. 'I've got time.'

He had—just. As he scooped up the last forkful the phone rang, and he was off yet again.

Not quite so fast this time, though. He paused long enough to thank her for the meal, to tell her to set the alarm after him and, if she was worried, just to push the panic button in the flat.

'That'll set off the alarm here and at the police station; or, if you should feel the need to set it off silently, key in the number in reverse and it rings at the police station and my house, without making any noise here. They respond very fast to either method.'

'And do you?'

He grinned. 'Like lightning. Don't worry, Linsey, you'll be all right.' His face sobered and he drew her gently into his arms. 'One day we'll get to finish that kiss undisturbed,' he promised, and, with a gentle brush of his mouth on hers, he left.

CHAPTER SIX

ALL hell seemed to break loose in the practice over the next couple of days. Linsey, remembering her boredom and frustration during the first part of the first day, vowed never again to complain about having too little to do.

Rhys came back on Friday morning, but he was unable to stay the whole day because of a solicitor's appointment.

He looked haggard, Linsey thought sympathetically, and found time to cook him lunch in her flat.

'You're a star,' he said wearily as he cleaned the plate. 'I hadn't realised I was that hungry.'

'When did you last eat?' she asked him.

He looked at her as if she had lost her marbles. 'Eat?' he muttered. 'I have no idea.'

'Oh, Rhys—what about the children?'

He shrugged. 'I've been feeding them—beans and fish fingers and stuff like that. I don't know. I suppose I ought to go and shop but I've got an antenatal clinic this afternoon before I go to the solicitor—'

'I'll do it.'

'But you're taking on enough as it is, Linsey.'

She folded her arms and fixed him with a look. 'Are you saying you don't trust me?' she asked archly.

He laughed. 'Of course I trust you. I'd be delighted if you'd do my clinic. I'll make it up to you one day, I promise.'

She bit the inside of her cheek and hesitated.

'Yes?'

She lifted her shoulders. 'I just thought you ought to know that one or two of your patients seem to have got wind of what's going on.'

He laughed humourlessly. 'I'm sure. What have they said?'

She looked down at her hands. 'One old lady said she was glad Judy had gone and good riddance. You were far too good for her. Another. . . Well, more of the same, really.'

He eyed her sideways. 'Elaborate.'

She did, reluctantly because she didn't like repeating gossip. 'He said it was disgusting the way she'd been carrying on right under your nose, and you deserved better.'

He sighed heavily. 'Oh, well, at least they're on my side. How many said it was no wonder she'd gone off the way I neglected her?'

'No one,' she said honestly and without hesitation. 'No one at all. The only people who have said anything have been one hundred per cent behind you.'

'Of course, if it had been me screwing around I'd be called a randy old dog and I'd get away with it. Not that I mind being the injured party, you understand, but it seems somewhat unfair.'

Linsey was surprised by what seemed like a defence of his wife, and yet his choice of words showed how hurt he had been by her behaviour. 'For what it's worth,' she told him quietly, 'I wouldn't say that at all. I think infidelity in any shape or form by either party is equally unforgivable.'

His smile was wry. 'Oh, innocent, sweet girl. People are the pits. The sooner you learn that, the better. By the way, any news on that rapist?'

She shook her head. 'No, nothing. I hope the girl's

all right. The HIV and hepatitis results were negative, fortunately, so that's one less thing to worry about. I gave her a prescription for the morning-after pill to avoid any unwanted side effects,' she added drily.

'Bastard,' he whispered. 'I'd like five minutes alone with him, or any other spineless pervert who picks on the weak and innocent like that.'

She looked at him, probably six feet four, weighing half as much again as she did, and pitied any spineless pervert unfortunate enough to run into this gentle giant on a dark night. 'Go on,' she said, shooing him out kindly. 'Go and do your shopping—and remember to buy lots of fruit and vegetables.'

'Bully,' he muttered with a grin, and, dropping a kiss on her cheek, he went down the stairs to the surgery.

She watched him go from the window, backing out of his space in the car park as Matthew came in. She waved to Matthew, and he ran up to the flat.

'Hi, gorgeous. How are you?'

She smiled. 'Hi, gorgeous yourself. I'm OK. Want a cup of coffee?'

'Love one—Hey, who have you been entertaining?'

'Rhys.'

Did she imagine it, or did a flicker of jealousy cross his face? She decided to play on it. 'He was hungry and I felt sorry for him. He's rather nice, really. I wonder why she left him? All that sexy muscle and sinew—'

She was yanked hard up against his chest and kissed soundly. 'You,' he said warningly against her lips, 'are asking for trouble.'

'Oh, promises, promises,' she laughed, and with a snort of disgust he dropped her.

She straightened her shirt and smirked at him. 'I've got another antenatal clinic today.'

'Rhys's? I thought he was in.'

'I sent him to the supermarket—he was about to starve the kids to death, I think. He didn't seem to have eaten for days.'

'I'm hungry,' he told her hopefully.

'Beans on toast?'

He nodded. 'Could I? I'll have to go to the supermarket myself and stock up your larder again.' He eased himself down onto a chair and tipped it back. 'I've just come from the hospital, by the way. Mr Briggs died a little while ago.'

Linsey sighed. 'Oh, dear. Still, I suppose the time was right. He didn't seem to have much to live for.'

'He didn't. I think the family will be relieved, and then of course they'll feel guilty because they're glad it's all over. I'll go and visit them later tonight, see if I can help them at all. It's a difficult time, even when it's the right time. Oh, and I saw Mrs Arkwright. She had her op yesterday and she says she already feels much better.'

'Oh, good. It makes you realise how bad it must have been if a major operation brings relief!'

'Oh, absolutely. Some of these hips—when the socket is revealed—look so bad you wonder how the patient's been able to walk at all.' The chair hit the floor as she put the plate in front of him, and he dived into the simple meal as if he was ravenous.

She made some coffee, and sat cradling her cup and watching him eat. There was something satisfying about feeding hungry men, she decided. She'd done more of it this week than she had in a lifetime. In fact, it was rapidly becoming a habit! Matthew was right—they'd almost eaten her out of house and home. She ought to go to the supermarket and stock up.

The antenatal clinic was straightforward fortunately, and so was the evening surgery. She pulled into the supermarket car park and found a space, did her shopping and drove out again. As she did so, she thought she saw someone staring at her, but when she looked round there was no one there.

Odd. She must have imagined it. It was that rapist setting her nerves on edge. Even so, instead of taking her things up to the flat as she unloaded them, she took everything into the rear entrance, closed and locked the door and then ferried the bags upstairs after the alarm was on again and she felt secure.

Matthew was on duty that night, and she felt safe knowing that he was coming and going from the surgery, picking up patient records. She left a note for him where he couldn't miss it.

'Come up and see me some time. L.'

At twelve-fifteen, when she was lying in bed unable to sleep and watching the car headlights track across the ceiling, a set of lights swung through a different arc and she heard Matthew pull up outside, open the back door and turn off the alarm.

He found her note and came straight up, and she greeted him on the landing, dressed only in a mid-thigh-length nightshirt with pussycats all over it. He raised an eyebrow.

'Love the nightie,' he drawled, and smiled gently at her. 'What's the matter, Linsey? Couldn't sleep?'

She shook her head. 'I don't know—I'm probably being neurotic, but I thought somebody was watching me at the supermarket. It just unsettled me.'

'Do you want me to stay here tonight? I'll sleep on the sofa.'

'You could sleep in my bed,' she said softly.

His eyes darkened. 'My God, girl, you pick your moments. I've got three calls to make. They're coming in clusters tonight.'

'Can I come with you?'

'Of course. Don't you mind?'

She shook her head. 'I'd rather do that than stay here alone. I know I'm being ridiculous, but I can't help it. Do you mind the company?'

He hugged her gently. 'Of course not. Go and get dressed and come down. I'll see you in the kitchen.'

She threw on the skirt and T-shirt that she had been wearing earlier, with a cardigan in case the night was cooler, and then ran downstairs. Matthew was ready, and they went out together, setting the alarm.

The calls were fairly straightforward. There was a baby with tummy ache who burped and filled his nappy as they arrived, and immediately settled, another child of four who had been coughing constantly and needed steaming and a course of antibiotics, and a young woman threatening a miscarriage whom Matthew admitted to Southampton for observation.

It was all over and done with by two, and they drove back along the sea front. The phone was mercifully quiet, and Matthew pulled up on the prom and wound down the window. 'Listen to the sea on the shingle,' he murmured. 'I always think it sounds wonderful—so soothing.'

His arm came round her shoulder and he eased her up against him, then one finger tilted her chin gently up to meet his kiss.

'I want you, Linsey,' he said softly against her lips, and then his mouth claimed hers and she was lost. The tender magic of his kiss mingled with the music of the night, and she threaded her fingers through his hair and held him with one hand, the other seeking out the buttons on his shirt.

Her fingers found a gap and slid through, their backs brushing against the satin of his skin. There was a little hair, but not so much that she couldn't feel the warm, supple texture of his skin or the firm underlying muscles that clenched as she smoothed her hand against his chest and inched her fingers lower.

'Let's go back to the flat,' he muttered, pulling reluctantly away, and she unwillingly released him and moved back to her side of the car and fastened her seat belt. Her heart was pounding, her pulse racing.

Finally, it seemed, they were to finish what they'd started on Tuesday night—or so she thought.

However, as they turned off the high street Matthew swore softly. Blue lights flashed in the road, illuminating the front of the surgery. An alarm was sounding, and as they pulled up and got out a policeman with a walkie-talkie approached them. 'Sorry, sir, you can't go in there.'

'Of course I can—I'm the senior partner,' Matthew said shortly. 'What's going on?'

'The alarm went off a few minutes ago, sir. Signs of forced entry at the rear, and the intruder has been through the place. Perhaps you'd be good enough to turn the alarm off and inspect the damage.'

They went round the back, Linsey's heart in her mouth, and went in through the smashed back door, the policeman on their heels. Seconds later the alarm was stifled, and Matthew went through the surgery, looking for damage or anything missing.

'Drugs,' he said shortly. 'The spare stock of drugs is kept in a locked cabinet. It's been forced and the drugs are missing.'

'Which drugs, sir?' the policeman asked.

'I don't know—valium, temazepam, insulin, antibiotics, painkillers—you name it. I'll get you a complete
list off the computer.'

'Right, sir, we'll get onto it right away. And of course
we'll need to take your fingerprints so that we can identify the intruder's. Now, if you'd be kind enough to
check the other floors?'

They went through the middle floor of the house,
where Rhys and Rosie had their surgeries and where the
nurses' treatment rooms were situated, and found no
further damage. Nothing had been moved or touched in
her flat, and so it was decided to board up the door and
leave the alarm on again for the rest of the night.

'You'll come home with me,' Matthew told Linsey,
to her relief. Romance was far from both their minds.
All Linsey could think about was how close she had
come to being there when the burglar had broken in, and
how glad she was that Matthew had been on call. She
imagined that his thoughts were on the same lines, and
when they arrived at his cottage she went upstairs and
into his spare bed without a murmur.

'Rise and shine.'

She opened bleary eyes to find Matthew standing over
her, a steaming mug in his hand. The sun was shining,
the birds were singing and the break-in seemed light
years away.

She scooted up the bed, heavily conscious of
Matthew's soft, worn T-shirt that she had borrowed last
night. 'Thanks,' she said huskily, her voice unused. She
sipped the tea, blowing the steam off the top and watching Matthew as he stood at the window.

'The police have been to the surgery again. Their

forensic boys have been through it and got some prints. They need you to check your flat again, but they don't think there's any problem.'

She nodded. 'What's the time?'

'Eleven-thirty.'

'What?' She sat up straight and nearly slopped the tea. 'It can't be!'

His smile was gentle. 'You were shattered. I thought I'd let you sleep. I went in and did the emergency surgery and handed over to Rosie—it's her weekend on. I thought I'd take you back when you're ready.'

'What about the door?' she asked, wondering how she was ever going to manage to sleep there again.

'It's being replaced with a much more secure metal door and frame.'

'But when?'

'Now, as we speak. I've left the workmen there.'

'Oh.' So she would be secure—at least from that angle of attack. There were, of course, all the windows. . . Still, she mustn't be a wimp. Of course she'd be all right. This was a simple burglary, nothing to do with the rapist.

Matthew left her alone and she showered in his bath-room with an amazing power shower that nearly blasted her skin off and left her feeling invigorated and wonderful. Of course she would be all right, she told herself. It was just the accumulation of the rape and the burglary. Neither of them had been directed at her. She must stop being so neurotic.

She dressed quickly in the clothes she had had on last night, and Matthew took her back to her flat. There was a policeman there waiting to speak to her, and she took him up to her flat.

'I wonder if you could tell us if anything's missing from your flat?' he said without preamble. 'We've got several sets of prints from the burglar, and they weren't up here. Yours we've identified—they were all over the place. Also Dr Williams and Dr Jarvis. There were no other fresh prints at all, so we're almost certain that he didn't come up here.'

Linsey felt a wave of relief sweep over her. 'I'm sure nothing's missing. I haven't got anything of any value, and I keep my medical bag in my consulting room. It's still there.'

The policeman nodded. 'Right. Sorry to have troubled you. If you do notice anything amiss during the day, give us a call, but I'm pretty certain you're safe.' He gave her a reassuring smile and left, and she wandered round, picking up a cup and taking it into the kitchen, washing up the glass lying on the draining board— Glass? When had she used a glass?

She shrugged. She was getting neurotic. She went into the bedroom and made the bed, folding and tidying clothes and loading the washing machine. She looked around for her nightie with the cats on, but she couldn't find it. She shrugged again. Probably down behind the head of the bed where she'd flung it. She'd find it later.

Matthew came up and she smiled at him. 'Hi. Door fixed?'

He nodded. 'They've gone. Here's a new key for you. It's got a deadlock and bolts, so you're all secure.'

She took it. 'Thanks,' she murmured. 'Coffee?'

He smiled. 'No. I'm taking you out to lunch. How about the Ship on the quay at Lymington? They do a wonderful steak—and the wickedest puddings.'

She rolled her eyes. 'How did you know?'

He grinned. 'You wouldn't be normal if you didn't have a weakness for wicked things.'

Their eyes met and clashed.

'Like you?' she murmured.

'Hell, Linsey,' he groaned, and then she was in his arms, and they were back to square one. 'Maybe this time,' he murmured, but then the phone rang and he released her with a laugh. 'God clearly doesn't want me to have my evil way with you,' he said wryly, and scooped up the receiver. 'Jarvis.'

He shot her a glance. 'Yes, she's right here. I'll get her for you.' He held the phone out. 'Tricia.'

She took the phone, perching on the arm of the chair. 'Hi! How are you?'

'Never mind me,' Tricia said impatiently. 'Was that him?'

Linsey tilted her head so that she could see him. 'Yes,' she said, 'that was him.'

'Wow, what a voice! Like melted chocolate. No wonder you threw yourself in the river!'

Linsey laughed. 'Yeah, sure.'

'So, how's it going?'

She sighed. 'Oh, fine. We had a burglary at the surgery last night so I spent the rest of the night at Matthew's— and no, we didn't.'

Matthew's eyebrows shot up, and a grin creased his face. Linsey poked her tongue out at him and turned her back.

'Is he still there?' Tricia asked.

'Yes, he's standing on the other side of the room. Why?'

'So you can't tell me whether it's working out OK.'

'Well, I can.'

'I'll ask. Has it been difficult?'

'No, not really.'

'Is he as gorgeous as you thought? What about his wife?'

'Uh-uh.'

'No wife? He's divorced?'

'No.'

'Widowed?'

'No.'

'Single—he sounds like *that* and he's still single? Does he have genital warts or what?'

Linsey laughed helplessly. 'Not as far as I know, but I haven't looked yet.'

'Yet?'

Trust Tricia to pick that up. 'I haven't looked,' she corrected herself.

'Yet.'

'OK. Maybe I will.'

'Be careful,' Tricia cautioned her. 'Not that I don't think it's time you found someone, but you're such a softy you'll get torn to bits by him if you're not careful. Is he just a perennial bachelor?'

Linsey looked at him again. 'No, I don't think so. I think he's just fussy.'

He met her eyes, his own puzzled. 'Are you talking about me?' he demanded.

She nodded and smiled. 'He's looking cross now.'

'You sound terrified,' Tricia said drily.

She laughed again. 'Hardly.'

'So, you've got a really professional trainer/trainee relationship going there, have you?'

Linsey doubled up. 'Oh, absolutely,' she said when she could speak. 'In fact, when he's wearing his trainer's hat he's a demon. Talk about pedantic. He disagrees with everything—'

'*You* disagree, excuse me,' Matthew interrupted. 'You're the most aggravating wench.'

Tricia chuckled. 'I think you've got under his skin, my friend.'

'Hmm,' Linsey said with a twinkle. 'What an interesting thought.'

'I'm coming to see you—I want to know what this man's like and the suspense is killing me.'

'How's your job?'

'Boring. I'm going to switch to general practice. You seem to be having lots of fun.'

Linsey smiled. 'It's a case of hand-picking your trainer. They have to kiss well. I'm off now—Oh!'

Matthew snatched the phone. 'Don't listen to her, Tricia. She is the most unethical, unprofessional colleague I have ever had, not to mention disrespectful. Believe me, that's not the way to get on, and her report will reflect my opinion.'

Linsey laughed again, quite unabashed. His words might be threatening, but he had his arm around her and his hips were pressed up against her side, giving a quite unmistakable message. 'I'm sorry,' he said down the phone. 'She has to go; we're in the middle of a tutorial. I'll get her to ring you back.'

He hung up and turned to her. 'Get your things. You're coming back to my cottage for the weekend.'

Her eyes widened. 'But it's safe now.'

One brow arched. 'Not where you're going.'

A wicked little smile danced in her eyes. 'Oh, really? I'll pack.'

'You do that—and by the way, what haven't you looked for?'

She grinned mischievously at him. 'Genital warts.'

His jaw dropped, and then he laughed like a drain. 'Damn you, Linsey, you deserve everything I'm going to say in that assessment,' he said when he could speak.

She looked innocent. 'It was Tricia's suggestion. She thought that was why you might be single, seeing as you have such a gorgeous voice.'

'I have?'

Linsey shrugged. 'Tricia thought so. Personally I think it's quite ordinary.'

She went into the bedroom and started to pack, then became aware of the slow creak of boards.

The whisper was husky and chilling. 'I'll give you ordinary,' he rasped. 'I am magnificent, and by the time I've finished with you you will be mesmerised for ever!'

A cold shudder ran through her, and her hands came up to cover her face. 'God, Matthew, don't,' she pleaded.

'Linsey?'

His hands cupped her shoulders and turned her into his arms, his voice normal now and filled with remorse. 'Hell, sweetheart, what have I done?'

'Your voice—I don't know,' she mumbled into his shirt. 'Somebody walked over my grave.'

He tutted. 'I'm sorry. Come on, let's get you out of here,' he murmured. 'Grab your things.'

'I can't find my nightie.'

'You won't need it—I'll keep you warm. Let's go.'

They went, first to the Ship on Lymington quay for a delicious lunch eaten outside in the sunshine without a demon or a rapist in sight, and then back to his cottage. They lay in the garden on sun-loungers, in the shade of a little group of birches, and to Linsey's amazement she found she was drowsy.

'Go to sleep,' he told her. 'I'm here.'

Now why should that make a difference? she wondered, and dropped off to sleep.

She woke much later, and, turning towards Matthew, she saw he was sitting up on the side of the lounger and watching her. 'OK?' he murmured.

She nodded. 'Fine. How long have I been asleep?'

He looked at his watch. 'About an hour and a half.' His smile was indulgent—a rather masculine smile.

'I don't suppose you dropped off at all,' she said snappily.

He laughed. 'No. I've been gardening. Want a cold drink?'

She saw the beads of sweat on his brow, and the damp patch on the front of his T-shirt.

'It's too hot to work.'

He snorted. 'Tell me about it. I've been weeding. Why is it that during a drought the only things to grow are the weeds?'

She laughed and stood up, stretching, and his eyes fastened on the rise of her breasts and he groaned. Slowly she lowered her arms and met his gaze.

'How about a shower?' she suggested.

'I'll go now,' he said.

'No, us.'

His eyes widened, then his lips parted on a rush of air. 'What an excellent idea,' he said softly. 'Coming?'

She smiled. 'I hope so.'

'Definitely,' he replied, and took her hand in his. He was grimy and sweaty, but she didn't give a damn. She followed him, not that he gave her any choice, and in the bathroom they peeled off their clothes and went into the shower together.

The water was wonderful, pounding on their skin, adding to the excitement—at least, until it ran cold. He broke their kiss and stepped away, cutting off the water supply.

'Here.' He wrapped her in a thick, fluffy towel and picked her up, carrying her through to the bedroom.

'You'll put your back out. There's a lot of me,' she warned.

He snorted and dropped her into the middle of the bed. 'I can cope with you, you gorgeous creature,' he murmured, and began blotting her dry with the towel.

She lay there watching him, her eyes searching every inch of him, fascinated by the texture of his skin, the trailing rivulets of water that zigzagged over his chest and down his abdomen.

She traced one with her finger, right the way down to the soft nest of hair that surrounded his very masculine reaction. His eyes closed and he groaned as her finger trailed on, right to the end, and over, rubbing oh, so gently at the tiny bead of moisture on the very tip.

'No genital warts,' she murmured in satisfaction.

His choked laugh brought her eyes to his face.

'Lord, lady, you know how to ruin a moment,' he grumbled.

Her hand slid back and circled him, stroking gently, and his eyes closed. He shuddered and caught her hand, lifting it to his lips and kissing the palm, running his tongue over it and nipping the pad of her thumb.

'Matthew?'

'Mmm?'

'Take the phone off the hook.'

He reached across to the bedside table, lifted the receiver and dropped it, leaving it to dangle. Then he found a foil packet, ripped it open and handed her the condom.

'Would you?' he asked with a smile in his eyes.

'I might,' she teased, and put it on him with slow deliberation.

He groaned, deep and husky, and then she reached for him, pulling him across her.

The phone dangled, electronic beeps coming from it, and a woman's voice repeating over and over, 'Please hang up and try again.'

They ignored her. Matthew shifted his hips so that he lay above her, poised at her threshold, and kissed her, long and slow and deep. Then he eased into her, giving her time to adjust, and she lifted her hips and took him all.

A shuddering sigh went through her. 'Oh, Matthew,' she whispered, and he shifted slightly, his hand coming between them and touching her oh, so carefully, so softly, so skilfully.

It was like dropping a pebble on a still, silent pond. Her body awoke, ripples spreading out from the centre as he started to move, his body urging her on, his mouth capturing her cries as the ripples reached the banks and she shattered in his arms.

Then he stiffened, crying out her name, and gradually she felt the ripples fade, and the water became still again and silent, waiting for the next pebble to fall. . .

'I've never done this before,' she confessed.

His eyes narrowed. 'Never done what?'

'Made love to someone I don't know.'

He laughed softly. 'Linsey, you know me.'

'I feel as if I do—but then I felt I knew you years ago, and we hardly spoke to each other.'

Matthew's face went still. 'It's irrational. It's just because I saved your life.'

His expression fascinated her. Had he felt the same? His comment had been quiet, but forceful. She made her tone deliberately light. 'The Chinese say you should beware saving someone's life, because you are then responsible for it. Tricia said you're either very brave, extremely foolish or hadn't heard the proverb.'

He snorted. 'Clever girl, your friend Tricia.' His face softened again and he kissed the tip of her nose. 'Getting back to what you said, I'm glad you don't go round jumping into bed with men you don't know.'

'I did with you.'

'You know me well enough. We've spent the week together, for heaven's sake.'

'So how do you explain what almost happened on Tuesday night, before Jan came along?'

His hand strayed possessively to her breast. 'Lust,' he said simply. 'Everyone's entitled to fall off their pedestal every now and again. I guess Tuesday was your day to fall.'

His lips replaced his hand and he nuzzled her breast, licking and nibbling and driving her crazy. She pushed him away. 'Matthew, I'm trying to have a serious conversation here!'

He laughed softly and lay down beside her, his eyes on hers. 'Sorry,' he murmured, looking anything but. 'You were saying?'

'I was saying I don't know you—not well. I don't know anything about your taste in music, or what you read, or what your hobbies are; I don't know what you want from your life, or what you see in me.'

'That's not true. You know a lot about me. You know I share the same values as you, that I like the countryside and solitude, good food, continuity—'

She laughed. 'Yes. And I know you love all your patients, and you give to them far beyond the call of duty. Look at Joe. No wonder he left you this house. I know you're a man he respected. I know your patients and colleagues think the world of you, that the FHSA must think very highly of you if you're a trainer at only thirty-five; I know you have a sense of humour although you try to hide it well.'

She smiled at him and traced the lines around his eyes.

'I also know there's a deeper side of you that you don't share very easily, that you keep still and quiet and private—a side that I can only guess at. That's what I don't know. I don't know why you are as you are.'

'Is that important?'

She ran her finger down his nose, over his lips and down to his chest, dallying with the light scatter of hair. 'I don't know. I would like to know what you see in me.'

His face softened. 'A beautiful, opinionated, self-reliant woman. You fascinate me. You're difficult and awkward, and yet you tease and laugh at me and I want you anyway. You tie me in knots.'

Her hand slid lower, her palm lying flat against the taut planes of his abdomen. The skin there was pale against the darker tan of her hand, and in the hollow of his hip-bone it was unbelievably silk-like. She stroked it, then found herself distracted by his predictable response. Her fingers strayed again, sampling textures, fascinated by the contrast of satin on steel.

His breath eased out on a sigh of pleasure, and she laid her head on his chest and watched her hand torment him. A little bead of moisture appeared at the tip, and she moved her head down, her tongue flicking out to capture it.

Matthew thought he was going to die.

She bent over him, her hair like a curtain screening her from view, and her mouth cherished him with infinite care.

He needed her. Know her or not, he needed her, couldn't get her out of his mind, couldn't sleep, couldn't concentrate on anything except her.

Her tongue circled him and then tugged, suckling, taking the breath from his lungs in a gasp of ecstasy.

'Linsey,' he groaned. 'For God's sake, stop.'

She moved over him but he stopped her, the last fragments of his presence of mind focusing on the need to protect her. He handed her a condom in a foil packet and lay back, his lip caught between his teeth, dying as she slowly, teasingly caressed it on.

Then she moved over him again, drawing him into her hot, tight, secret depths. She moaned and rocked against him, and his control shattered. Grasping her hips, he drove into her, again and again, until with a little scream she fell against him, sobbing his name, her body convulsing round him.

He felt the pulsing start deep inside him, then a groan erupted from his throat as the life-force surged from him, leaving him drained.

His arms, weak and almost useless, wrapped around her and drew her still closer, and with a wordless murmur he fell asleep.

Linsey lay against him, feeling the steady beat of his heart against her chest, his arms relaxed against her ribs as he slept. It was too hot but she couldn't bear to move. She belonged here, cradled against his chest, in his arms.

So it was ridiculous. They hardly knew each other.

And yet they belonged together, two sides of a coin, like night and day, darkness and light, fantasy and reality.

She moved at last, easing away from him, taking the condoms and flushing them down the loo, putting the phone back on the hook, picking up their discarded clothes in the bathroom. Heavens, it looked like a scene from a rampant movie, she thought with a very womanly smile.

She ached, her body tender from the unaccustomed attention of a man.

And what a man.

She smiled again. He was a wonderful lover. She had known he would be, at least with her. Their souls called to each other, deny it though he might.

She pulled on his T-shirt and nothing else, and pottered about in the kitchen, clearing up a little and making some tea.

He came up behind her, pulling her into his arms, and she went without a murmur. His hand slid up her thigh and discovered her nakedness, and he groaned.

She laughed throatily and smacked his hand.

'No. Enough.'

'Are you sore?' he asked, nibbling her neck.

'A little.'

'I'm sorry.'

'I'll recover.'

'I'm glad to hear it.' His hand slid up her back, cradling her against his chest. 'You're a beautiful woman, Linsey,' he murmured, and kissed her.

The phone rang. 'Damn,' he muttered, 'I think some-one's watching us. Every time I kiss you, that phone rings!'

He picked up the receiver and barked, 'Jarvis.' His face softened.

'Sorry, Rhys. What can I do for you?'

He looked at Linsey, and his face contorted in dismay. 'Yes, of course. No problem. Linsey's here—she can help me. No, Rhys, don't worry. That's fine. Bring them over.'

He put the phone down. 'Rhys has tracked his wife

down. He wants to leave the kids with us overnight and go and talk to her.'

'Oh.'

Matthew's smile was wry. 'Look on the bright side— it'll give your body time to recover before I pounce on you again.'

She laughed. 'I think I'd rather put up with the pain. How many and what sort?'

'Mark, five, Emma, three, and Bibby, who's nearly one.'

She rolled her eyes. 'Terrific. No wonder she left.'

Matthew laughed. 'They're sweet kids.'

'Good. Shall I go and buy some fish fingers?'

He grinned. 'Yes—but I should get dressed first.'

She stuck her tongue out at him, ran upstairs and pulled on some clothes. Three kids for the weekend. So much for romance!

CHAPTER SEVEN

RHYS'S wife was in London, he told them, staying with an old friend. He had tracked her down via another friend, and she had been only too happy to pass on the information. It seemed that Judy's own friends were somewhat disenchanted with the way she had treated Rhys, a fact that Linsey thought spoke volumes.

'Are you sure you'll be all right?' he asked. 'I've written down the number where you can get me, just in case there's a crisis. If you do have a problem, please ring. I can always see Judy another time if necessary.'

'There won't *be* a crisis,' Matthew assured him. 'Just relax and go, and talk to her and forget about the children. They're in safe hands.'

Rhys's smile was strained. 'If you say so. It was you I was worried about, actually, not them. They're being rather demanding at the moment. Their mother's precipitate departure seems to have screwed them up well and truly, especially Mark. He's the worst to deal with. Emma's very quiet, on the other hand, and I'm more worried about her, in fact.'

'And Bibby?'

He smiled tenderly and looked down at the baby perched on his arm, playing with a pen. 'Bibby? Bibby's fine—aren't you, Bibbs? She'll scream blue murder when I go, but she'll settle.'

He handed the baby to Matthew, and immediately she wriggled round and cried, reaching out for her father. He called the two older ones, who were running round the garden like maniacs, and scooped them up for a hug and a kiss.

Mark looked sulky and unhappy, but Emma just clung to her father and had to be prised off. 'I'll be back tomorrow in time for tea,' he assured them. 'Don't worry.'

'Are you bringing Mummy back?' Mark asked, kicking the step with the toe of his trainers.

'I don't think so.'

'Why not?'

Rhys met Linsey's eyes and looked desperate. 'Because I don't think she wants to come back with me.'

'Why not?'

'That's what I'm going to find out,' Rhys said gently. 'I'll tell you when I get back, all right? I must go now.'

Bibby was still crying and holding her arms out for him, and Matthew's attempts to distract her with the pen were failing hopelessly.

'Just go,' he said to Rhys, and Linsey watched the big man's face crumple for a second as he hugged the children yet again, then ran to the car and drove quickly away.

'How about a bath, kids?' Matthew said brightly.

'I don't want a bath,' Mark said with scorn. 'I want to go home.'

'Emma?'

Emma shook her head, and Bibby was still straining after the car and screaming, the pen thrown to the ground.

'How about a bubble bath? I've got a special bath,' he told them. 'It has real bubbles, like blowing through a straw. Want to try? It's like sitting in a fizzy drink.'

Mark looked less anti, but Emma still shook her head.

'It could be pink water,' he said temptingly.

'Really?' This was from Emma, finally looking interested.

Linsey decided they could cope without her. 'I'm going to get supper bought. I'll make something else for us later.'

'Get a bottle of wine,' he said, and she thought she detected a touch of desperation in his voice. She grinned at him over the children's heads, and with a cheeky little wave she escaped.

The supermarket was packed, but she found fish fingers and beans for the kids, ice cream for dessert and some fresh salmon steaks and a bottle of dry white Californian wine for her and Matthew, to eat in the quiet time after the children had gone to bed.

This time nobody was watching her, and she loaded her shopping into the car and headed back to the cottage without a care in the world. OK, so they had the children for the weekend, but Matthew was wonderful, her body was in bliss and nothing could have been better.

She parked in the garden, shut the gate and gathered up the shopping, then walked in through the kitchen door to be greeted by a strange humming noise and a fascinating tide of pale pink bubbles flowing gently down the stairs. It reminded her of nothing so much as a river of lava—

'Oh, my God!' She dropped the shopping and ran to the foot of the stairs. 'Matthew? Matthew!'

He ran out of the bedroom opposite the top of the stairs, skidded on the bubbles and slithered straight down the stairs, coming to rest at her feet in a cloud of pink foam and Anglo-Saxon.

She raised one eyebrow. 'You didn't need to prostrate yourself at my feet. A simple, "Yes, dear," would have done.'

He glowered at her, and she had to bite the inside of her lip to trap the laughter. ' "Casting pearls before swine," I think my mother would have said,' he snapped sharply, and looked around in disbelief. 'What the hell is going on?' he growled, getting very carefully to his feet and wincing.

'I think the children may have found the bubble bath,' she offered.

'Oh, hell,' he muttered, and, turning round, he picked his way cautiously up the waterfall of foam and into the bathroom.

The humming ceased, and moments later there was the sound of water running away.

'It was an accident,' she heard one of the children say. Emma, probably. 'It just fell.'

'I told her not to press it again,' the other one said with deplorable lack of loyalty. Mark.

'No, you didn't!' the little one said indignantly. 'You told me to!'

Linsey followed Matthew carefully up the stairs and went into the bathroom. It was awash, the floor inches deep in pink froth, the children standing naked up to their knees in bubbles, like parasols in a milkshake. Matthew looked at her helplessly.

'I think, children, it would be a very good idea if you just went and put your pyjamas on, don't you?' Linsey said, quietly taking charge. 'Matthew, where's the baby?'

'In the cot, playing,' he told her grimly.

'Right. Off you go, and don't get into any more mischief.'

She shepherded them out of the bathroom, passed them a towel and told them to dry their feet, then turned back to Matthew.

'I suggest we get a dustpan and scoop the foam in here into the bath, then sweep the rest down the stairs and out of the back door.'

He sighed. 'Fine. I'll get a brush and the dustpan.'

'Be careful on the stairs,' she warned him, but the smile must have been lurking in her eyes.

He glowered at her. 'Don't rub it in,' he menaced. 'I am quite sore enough without you adding insult to injury.'

She crouched down and started to feel around for the bath mat. 'You'll probably tread on the toothpaste next. If I were you, I'd swear off anything to do with bathrooms,' she said sagely. 'They don't seem to agree with you—Oh!'

She found herself lying face down in the foam, the sound of Matthew's retreating footsteps echoing on the stairs.

From the doorway behind her came a tiny giggle, quickly stifled, then the sound of the door closing.

She grinned. Wretched kids. She plopped the bath mat in the basin, retrieved a small pair of leather shoes and wondered what else was submerged by the milkshake.

'Are they asleep?'

'Finally.' Linsey flopped down on the sofa, exhausted. 'Have you done anything about supper?'

He shook his head. 'I thought I'd make sure they'd gone off well and truly so they don't get to wreck the salmon as well as the house.'

She smiled tiredly. 'It doesn't look too bad now. How about the carpet?'

'Still very soggy, but I think it'll be all right. It's drying over the bench in the garden.'

Their eyes met, and he patted his knee.

'I'm too heavy.'

'Rubbish. Come here; I want to hold you.'

So she went, and snuggled against his shoulder with a sigh of contentment. 'We can't sleep together, you know—not with the children here,' she told him.

'I know. You have my bed, I'll have the sofa.'

Linsey had a better idea. 'You have your bed. That way, if the children wake up in the night, you get them, not me. And we'd better rig up a stair-gate in case they walk around in their sleep. Disturbed, unhappy children often do.'

'And if they aren't disturbed and unhappy I can't imagine why.'

'Because the mother was a waste of space and Rhys has always been the guiding light in the family?'

'Probably. He's a wonderful father. He's always taken the job very seriously, and he adores them.'

'I wonder how he and Judy are getting on?' Linsey mused.

Matthew sighed. 'Badly. They didn't get on well at the best of times, and this certainly doesn't qualify. I must say, I don't envy her. He's intending to go for custody.'

Linsey nodded. 'Good. He can afford to make sure they're properly cared for, and any woman who dumps her children with a child-minder and goes off because she's fed up, without saying a word to a soul, doesn't deserve to keep her children.'

'Did the diplomatic corps turn you down?' he said mildly.

She refused to laugh. She felt very strongly about it, and although she knew that parents were often under intolerable pressures she still found it difficult to be understanding when the repercussions were always felt by the innocent children.

Well, fairly innocent. She thought of the milkshake bathroom and smiled. 'Fancy a bubble bath?' she said to him.

He chuckled. 'No, and nor do you. I tell you what— after they've gone tomorrow I'll show you what that bath's *really* for.'

'Ooh. Promises.'

'Yeah.' He turned her head and dropped a light kiss on her lips. 'You'd better believe it.'

His hand curved round her hip, easing her against him, and his mouth settled against hers with a sigh. Heat flared between them, and after an age he broke the kiss and rested his head against hers. 'I want to make love to you,' he said huskily.

'I noticed.'

'Damn kids. They're asleep; perhaps we could—'

'No. I wouldn't feel right. Anyway, I'm sore.'

He lifted his head and tipped her chin, searching her face. 'Very?' he asked softly.

She shook her head. 'No, not very. It's been a long time.'

His smile was wry. 'I know the feeling. Oh, well, it's only twenty-four hours.'

She wriggled to her feet. 'How about supper?'

'Good idea. Then I think we ought to get to bed, because they'll be waking up at the crack of dawn, if not before.'

It didn't quite work like that. The theory was fine. The problem was that Linsey, sleeping lightly on the too small sofa downstairs, was the one to hear the thump and the sudden cry as Emma fell out of bed. She cuddled her and tucked her back in, staying there to ensure she settled, and then an hour later she heard the patter of little feet and Mark appeared at the bedroom door.

'I can't sleep,' he told her, and so she took him down-stairs and cuddled him up on the sofa under her quilt and told him stories, and gradually he drifted off.

Then the baby cried, and Linsey eased away from the little boy and ran upstairs to comfort Bibby before she woke Emma again. She gave her some warm milk in the kitchen, changed her nappy with a skill she didn't know she had and then rocked her on her lap until she fell asleep. Luckily she managed to sneak the baby back into her cot without her waking and disturbing anyone, and then crept back downstairs, pulled on her clothes and snuggled up in the chair.

Finally at six-thirty she gave up and went into the kitchen and made a cup of tea. Predictably the kettle woke Matthew, and he came downstairs, dressed only in a pair of jeans with the zip yanked up, rubbing his face and smiling sleepily at her.

'Well, they slept all right,' he said cheerfully.

Linsey looked at him disbelievingly. 'You have to be joking,' she muttered, splashing boiling water on the tea.

Matthew came up behind her and put his arms round her as she banged the kettle down.

'Aren't we a morning person, sweetheart?'

She jabbed him in the ribs with her elbow and reached down two cups. 'No, we damn well aren't—not when we've been up all night with someone else's unhappy children.'

His eyes widened. 'What?'

She told him her nocturnal tale of woe, and he hugged her gently and apologised.

'Sit down; I'll make you a cup of tea,' he said consolingly.

'I've made it,' she told him. 'You're too late.'

'I'll pour it. Sit down.'

She sat, grumpy, tired and wondering why Judy had stayed so long. Perhaps it wasn't so difficult after all to understand how someone could just up and leave.

'Have I done something wrong?' he asked quietly, sitting down opposite her.

She sighed. 'No. I was just feeling for Judy.'

'Judy?' His surprise was evident in his voice. 'If you feel for anyone, feel for Rhys. He's been holding together a rotten marriage for two years—or he thought he was.'

'Is Bibby his?' she asked.

Matthew shrugged. 'I would say so. They all look very like each other and like him—the dark hair, the grey eyes. I would think almost inevitably they're all his. Either that or her lovers look like him.'

'Lovers?'

Matthew stirred his tea. 'Lovers. In the plural. I gather it's been going on for some time.'

'Did he know?'

'Not all of it. Not the latest one, and probably not several of the others. Everybody now is in a hurry to tell him all about it, of course.'

'Is he humiliated?'

Matthew shrugged again. 'Possibly. I doubt it. Rhys doesn't have an ego problem. He's more worried about the effect on the children.'

They fell silent, thinking about the children, and as if their thoughts had woken them Mark stumbled out of the sitting room knuckling his eyes and Bibby started to cry.

The bedroom door at the top of the stairs opened and Emma appeared at the makeshift stair-gate. 'Bibby's crying,' she said unnecessarily, 'and I'm hungry.'

*   *   *

Rhys arrived at six, tight-lipped and silent. He hugged the children, his eyes filling, and took them away with hardly a word.

'Whoops,' Matthew said softly.

'Mmm.' Linsey turned to him. 'Now, about that bath. . .'

It was wickedly exciting, made more so by the suspense of the past twenty-four hours. At last Linsey sprawled, slaked, between Matthew's outstretched legs, her head lolling against his chest, and sighed.

'Beats pink bubbles,' she said with a lazy grin.

'Mmm. Definitely X-rated, though.'

She blushed, remembering some of the things they had done, and Matthew chuckled. 'Gone coy on me?'

'In the cold light of day it seems a trifle decadent,' she explained with a sheepish smile.

'Wonderfully so.' He swished water over her exposed breasts and blew on them, watching her nipples peak with the cold. 'Have you ever done a vasectomy?' he asked, idly swishing and blowing in turn.

'No—why? Do you want one?'

'Mmm. It would solve the problem of living with my children in my old age, although if one's kids were truly ghastly to bring up I suppose it would offer a form of divine retribution.'

She turned over to face him, burying her breasts in his groin. 'They were quite a handful, weren't they?'

He rolled his eyes. 'You could say that,' he agreed mildly. 'I suppose it's not so bad if you have them one at a time and get used to it. You must do most of it on autopilot.'

'Especially at three in the morning.'

He hugged her. 'I'm sorry.'

'You'll have to make it up to me, won't you?' she

said with a teasing twinkle in her eye, and rubbed her breasts against him.

His body stirred obligingly, and within moments the children were forgotten. . .

Rhys came back to work the following Tuesday, his child-care arrangements sorted out and the children safe in the care of the new nanny.

She was living in, and was apparently a marvel. Rhys was still tight-lipped on the subject of Judy, but gradually over the course of the week, as the children settled and his work began to fill the hole in his life, he started to unravel a little.

He didn't laugh, though. The fun seemed to have gone out of him, and some days he came in with an obvious hangover.

Linsey worried about him, and she knew that Matthew did too. He spent a lot of time chatting to Rhys in his consulting room, and she hoped he was able to counsel him and help him come to terms with his anger and disappointment.

She didn't think that Rhys was suffering from a broken heart. From what Matthew had said, his love had been killed a long time ago. Still, the sense of failure was the one constant that everyone reported after a marriage breakup, and Rhys was sure to hold himself responsible for having let Judy down, and ask himself why else she would have gone off like that with all those other men.

She remembered what he had said about the rapist, and thought she herself would like five minutes alone with Judy for what she had done to him and the children.

Faithless tramp. Being unable to make a relationship work was one thing. Cheating on your partner was quite another.

The very thought of Matthew with another woman sent a stab of pain through her, and she felt again for Jan, catching them kissing that night at the cottage—heavens, was it only a couple of weeks ago? How had she felt, seeing the man she loved in the arms of another woman? Linsey dreaded to think. And yet, if Jan hadn't come along and they had made love, would Matthew have ended his liaison with Jan?

Yes. She knew that. He wasn't a cheat or a liar. He had just genuinely not realised how involved Jan was with him, but he had made no commitment to her and she had said nothing, so Linsey could absolve him of blame for everything except that of being blindingly unaware of Jan's needs.

Perhaps the other woman should have made them clearer.

Like you are? she thought wryly. Oh, their sex life was wonderful, but what about the emotional side? Did he ever say he loved her?

No. He didn't, but she didn't tell him she loved him either, and if she was being honest she probably should do. She didn't want to overwhelm him, though. She was good at overwhelming people—it was what she did best—and for once in her life she wanted to do things right.

She sighed and picked up her notes. It was no good sitting here after her surgery had finished and hoping that her visits would go away. She was doing them alone now, discussing them with Matthew before and after, consulting with him before referring or admitting whenever possible, but gradually stretching her apron strings.

He didn't like it. Matthew liked to be in control. Unfortunately so did Linsey, and when she knew she could cope she found conforming to his wishes just the teensiest bit tedious.

Still, he was the boss—at least at work. He was busy with Rhys now, she discovered, so without consulting him she went out on her calls.

The first visit was to Mrs Arkwright, who had had the hip replacement and had been so slow and racked with pain when they had visited before.

This time she opened the door much more quickly, and smiled at Linsey. The lines of strain were still there, but no longer drawn so tight, and she was moving remarkably well.

'How are you?' Linsey asked.

'Oh, Dr Wheeler, I feel fantastic! It's marvellous! I can move around my home again without feeling as if I've run a marathon—I've even been for a walk around my garden! It's marvellous,' she repeated.

She was doing very well, Linsey acknowledged. The wound was healed, the stitches out and there was no sign of infection or any other problem. So long as she was careful not to turn the leg in or bend it too far in case she dislocated the new joint, she would be better in no time.

A life transformed, Linsey thought as she left. A hip replacement was so simple and yet so astonishing in its impact. It was just a tragedy that the waiting lists were so long when every day was agony for those who suffered.

Still, Mrs Arkwright was on the mend.

If only there was such a simple solution for Mr Dean. He was the man who had wanted antibiotics and to whom Matthew had given painkillers when he had a virus. Linsey smiled. They had argued about it, she remembered, and now Mr Dean was demanding a house call and saying he was still quite unwell and needed attention.

She found his house without too much difficulty, and was let in by his wife.

'Oh, Doctor, I'm glad you're here—he's been making such a fuss! He's quite unwell, you know—quite unwell.'

Linsey followed her down the hall into the bedroom at the back of the bungalow, and greeted Mr Dean, who was lying in bed looking fit as a flea but thoroughly sorry for himself. 'Damn painkillers Dr Jarvis gave me did no good at all—stupid man. Don't know what he thought he was doing. Weak as a kitten I am now, and I haven't slept through the night for weeks.'

'Have you been in bed the whole time?' Linsey asked, opening her bag and getting out her stethoscope.

'Of course he has. I've been looking after him very well,' Mrs Dean said indignantly.

'I'm sure you have,' Linsey soothed, sure of nothing of the sort. The wretched man was as well as she was, and was weak because he'd taken to bed.

'I don't like the sound of that chest,' she told him, 'and lying down is the worst thing for it. Obviously you have to go to bed at night, but I think you should have a course of antibiotics and then get yourself up and move around as much as possible. I'm sure you'll notice a great improvement in a few days if you do.'

She scribbled the prescription, shut her bag with a snap and left, smiling benignly. She managed to get into the car and drive round the corner before she allowed herself to laugh.

Matthew was just getting out of his car as she arrived back at the surgery, and she told him about Mr Dean's invalidity.

'And you weakened? You should have just told the idle heap to get his back off the bed and go and dig the garden,' he teased.

'It's not that easy. . .' she began, and then noticed the laughter in his eyes. She hit him.

'Ouch. That'll cost you lunch.'

She raised an eyebrow. 'Really?'

'Really. I'm starving.'

'We could—um—'

Matthew grinned. 'Yes, we could.'

They went in, and found Rhys sitting at the kitchen table, hunched over a cup of coffee.

'Hi, there,' she said cheerfully.

He gave her a morose look. 'Hi. Police rang—they've picked up our burglar.'

'Oh, excellent,' Matthew said. 'That's a relief. You can rest easy in your bed now, Linsey.'

'Whose?' she mouthed.

He winked and jerked his head towards the bottom of her stairs.

Linsey shook her head and then turned to Rhys. 'We were just about to have lunch. Join us?'

He lifted his head. His eyes were slightly bloodshot and he looked grim. 'I don't think so.'

'I do,' she said firmly, and got him by the arm. 'Come on. Tea, toast and a quick zizz on the sofa.'

He went without protest.

'Is he on the bottle?' Linsey asked Matthew a month later as they were trying to fit in one of their tutorials. Rhys had appeared that morning once again looking bloodshot and haggard, and she was worried about him.

'Not on a regular basis, I don't think. Just after another row with Judy or when it all gets too much.'

'Poor man. He doesn't deserve to be so unhappy.'

'We don't know the ins and outs of it, Linsey. Maybe he didn't give her what she needed.'

'No—and maybe she didn't ask. He's not psychic.'

Matthew looked at her. 'Nor am I. What do you need from me?'

She hesitated. What if she said commitment? Would he run a mile? Probably. 'How about a tutorial?' she said lightly.

He looked at her searchingly. 'Fine. What do you want to talk about?'

She scraped around in her mind for something sufficiently distracting and unromantic. 'Tell me about your endoscopy sessions and gastrointestinal screening programme.'

Matthew walked slowly along the sea front, staring out over the sparkling water at the endless little boats zipping back and forth across the Solent. He could see the Isle of Wight just a few miles away, the Needles clearly visible, marching out into the sea off the point, like lemmings.

He felt like a lemming. The urge to run away was overwhelming him, because he was scared. He was falling for Linsey, and he couldn't seem to do a damn thing about it. Their lovemaking was incredible. Every time, they reached new heights—heights he had never even dreamt of.

She was bold, too—bold and beautiful and often dominant, as diametrically opposed to the girl of his fantasies as it was possible to be. All those years ago, when she had haunted his dreams, she had been meek and submissive and wide-eyed, adoring and virginal.

The real Linsey was aggressively sexual, and

delighted in his body and her own. He was a little
shocked sometimes by her frankness, but he wouldn't
have changed her for the world. The real woman was
infinitely more exciting than the fantasy one had been.

The trouble was that he was getting addicted. She was
in his blood, under his skin, inside his mind. He was
obsessed by her, unable to think about anything except
getting her alone and tweaking the hair-trigger of her
responses.

She was fitting in well to the practice, too, and he
knew he was going to be under pressure soon from the
others to offer her the post after the year was up.

Patients were asking for her, Rosie was told a hundred
times a week how glad people were that there would be
another woman there when she left, and even the men
sought her out—a fact that made Matthew seethe with
totally irrational jealousy.

She had been with them for nearly two months, and for
most of that time they had been together every available
moment.

She still slept at the practice, for appearances' sake
as much as anything, but nobody thought anything of it
if Matthew was there as well, and, with the car park
tucked away behind the back, nobody would know
anyway.

The cottage they saved for weekends, and as the
summer came to a close and the autumn took over they
went for walks through the woods behind his house. The
trees were ablaze with colour, and as the leaves started
to fall and the evenings drew in they spent cosy hours
by the fireside.

It was wonderfully romantic—and Matthew was
beginning to panic. Every time he got close to a woman
something went wrong. Sara had left him; Ellen a few

years later had told him that he was boring. Jan had been willing to stay the course, but she'd bored him. Always, it seemed, one or other of the parties got bored. Look at Rhys and Judy, he told himself.

He knew he could never be bored by Linsey. Whatever else she might be, and she was plenty, boring wasn't ever on the cards.

It was by no means out of the question, though, that he would bore her. Once her inquisitive, convoluted little mind had extracted everything it could from their relationship, would she feel trapped? Probably. Bored? Almost certainly. He knew he didn't have the sort of scintillating personality that would be able to hold her. He was quiet, peace-loving, dedicated to his profession. He felt as if he was being sucked along in the slipstream of a magnificent mythical being, and any minute now she would change course and he would fall flat on his face.

Perhaps he should try and cool down, ease away from her, get himself some personal space.

He didn't want it. He wanted Linsey, and with shattering certainty he knew that she had the power to destroy him if she chose to do so.

He had never felt more vulnerable in his life.

Something was wrong. Matthew was quiet and distant, and Linsey, always assailed by self-doubt and unable to see her own worth, wondered if her uncharacteristically aggressive behaviour in the bedroom had shocked and repelled him.

Perhaps he didn't like it when she took the initiative? Oh, OK, physically he seemed more than happy, but was his ego being battered?

She couldn't understand her own behaviour. She was never, ever like this. She couldn't remember ever taking the initiative before—and that wasn't, by any stretch of the imagination, because her experience was so vast that any incident was lost in the mists of time. She just didn't behave like this, and she knew she was frightening him off.

A lump rose in her throat. She needed him desperately. She couldn't imagine life without him, not under any circumstances. Perhaps she should have asked him for commitment when the moment had presented itself, but she knew he'd have made light of it and run screaming.

Damn. She never cried. She wiped the tears off her cheeks angrily and stared out of the window at the glinting sea. Darkness fell earlier these days. Matthew was out, on duty. She was alone, and she didn't want to sit here alone and cry. Knowing her luck, he'd catch her.

She changed into her jogging things and let herself out of the new, supersafe back door that they no longer needed. She'd take the route along the front, up behind the park and home. It took about twenty minutes and she should be back while it was still light if she hurried.

There was a nip in the air down by the sea, and she felt the cool breeze over her heated skin and revelled in it. The summer had been too hot for running, and she was only just now getting back into the swing of it— not that she had had much time, what with Matthew being there every available minute. She'd had plenty of exercise, though.

Warm as she already was, she felt her colour rise at the thought. Lord, she'd turned into such a brazen hussy! She couldn't believe she did some of the things she did. Last week she'd covered him in honey—covered, mind you—and licked it off, inch by glorious inch.

She'd felt sick later, but it had been worth it.

She turned up by the park and pushed herself. It was

darker here, the shadows lengthening, and she didn't like this stretch of road. She always felt as if someone was following her, watching her. Ridiculous. The rapist hadn't struck again, and it seemed likely that he had been a visitor to the area. He was probably long gone. She turned onto the home stretch, powered down the road and turned into the drive with a sigh of relief.

The security lights came on automatically as she ran round the back, and she let herself in, relocked the door and punched her number into the alarm, resetting only the outside doors and the practice.

Then she went slowly upstairs to her flat, peeling off her clothes as she went, and headed straight for the bathroom. She reached for the blind before she turned on the light, and for one terrifying moment she thought she saw someone standing on the other side of the street looking straight at her.

Then a car came down the road, headlights on, and she realised that it had been the shadow of a tree.

She was getting stupid, she told herself. She snapped down the blind, flicked on the light and climbed into the shower. By the time she came out Matthew had swung his car into the car park and was running up the stairs.

His eyes tracked down her body, clad in a little towel that hardly met over her breasts, and the gun-metal turned to molten steel. She smiled and dropped the towel, walking away from him into the bedroom. To hell with playing the mouse, she thought. When he looked at her like that—

She bent over to pick up her clothes and he came up behind her, grasping her by the hips and sliding home without a word.

Her breath caught and she writhed against him, taking him deeper. With a gutteral groan he pushed her onto the bed and thrust home over and over again, his hand coming round to find the sensitive nub that ached for his touch.

She bucked against him, the waves crashing over her, shudders racking her body as the climax ripped through her. Then he fell on her, his body spent, and she laughed weakly.

'Well, hello there,' she said with the last ragged scraps of her breath.

'Hello. Had a good day?'

She chuckled. 'Better towards the end.'

He kissed her shoulder. 'Witch.'

'Any more calls?'

'No.' He eased off her and she turned over.

'Good. How about an early night?'

He hesitated, then a lazy, sexy smile escaped. 'Sounds good.'

That night, while they lay sated in each other's arms, the rapist struck again. . .

CHAPTER EIGHT

THE evening news the next day was full of it. The girl was nineteen, a student, and had been walking home from the bus at ten-thirty after an evening class. She had been brutally raped at knife-point, it was reported, and, thanks to her clear description of the attacker, they were able to say that it was likely to have been the same man who had struck before.

Women were advised not to go out at night alone, to stay in their cars and wait for help if they broke down, and to lock their doors and windows when they were in the house, day or night. It was an extraordinary thing, the reporter said, but the police had remarked how alike both girls were—tall, slim and with striking, long blonde hair.

Linsey's blood ran cold.

So, apparently, did Matthew's. 'That's it,' he said firmly. 'No night calls—neither you nor Rosie. Rhys and Tim and I will cover them.'

'Tim will love that. He and April are just getting it together. I caught them in the treatment room the other day, *in flagrante* or damn nearly.'

Matthew scowled. 'How immoderate. They should have more self-control.'

'What—like we do?' she teased, and he flushed a dull red.

'That's different; we come up here.'

'Mmm. I'm sure they all know.'

'I don't care if they do. It's none of their business.'

'Of course not,' she soothed. 'And I'll be fine doing my visits, so long as I set the alarm religiously.'

'No,' he said emphatically.

'Matthew—'

'No.'

The phone rang and she picked it up. 'Linsey? What's going on down there?'

'Oh, hi, Tricia. What do you mean?'

'This rapist! It sounds horrendous.'

She looked at Matthew. 'Mmm,' she agreed, without giving too much away.

'What do you mean, "Mmm"? He's targeting people exactly like you, chuck. You watch your step, you hear me?'

'I will. I'm very sensible. I'll be fine.'

There was a distinct and very unladylike snort. 'In a pig's eye,' Tricia muttered. 'You just be careful. What does Matthew think?'

Linsey turned her back on him. 'He's overreacting, just like you.'

'I am not,' he growled, guessing at the topic. 'I just don't want to be responsible for any injury or assault to one of my colleagues—quite apart from any personal feelings I might have on the matter!'

'Yes, and that's the trouble, isn't it?' she snapped, sick of being mollycoddled and controlled. 'You're obsessed by my body, and you can't imagine that every other man isn't too.'

There was a deathly hush, and then Matthew picked up his jacket and walked out without a word.

'Lins?'

She looked at the phone. 'Oh, God, Tricia, what did I just say?'

'Sounds like you just dropped a clanger.'

She chewed her lip. 'I think I did. God, why did I say that? I'm just as obsessed. If tall men with mid-brown hair and gun-metal eyes were being targeted, I'd have him locked up under armed guard so fast he wouldn't know what had hit him.'

'So tell him that. Go and find him and tell him you understand but that he's being over-protective. Tell him you know it's just because he loves you.'

'But I don't know that he does,' Linsey said softly. 'I really don't. I honestly think it is just my body. Every time I open my mouth, we argue.'

'You argue with me too, but I love you. You're my best friend. Just because you're argumentative and opinionated it doesn't stop people loving you, Linsey.'

Her eyes filled. 'Thanks—I think.'

'Go and find him.'

'He's gone.'

'Uh-uh, not with the rapist about. He won't have gone far. I'll bet you he's downstairs. I'll speak to you later— and take care.'

She hung up, and Linsey cradled the receiver and went slowly to the bannisters and looked over.

He was sitting at the bottom of the stairs, hunched over, his elbows on his knees, and he looked prickly and unapproachable. Linsey forced herself to go down and sit beside him.

'I'm sorry,' she said tentatively.

'You're right,' he rasped. 'I am obsessed by you. Obviously I crowd you. I'm sorry; I'll keep out of your way.'

'No!' she cried out, then said, more softly, 'No. You never crowd me. You *never* crowd me. I just hate it when people are over-protective because I'm a woman.'

He turned to her. 'You're vulnerable, Linsey. Look

at yourself.' He picked up a lock of her hair and held it in front of her eyes. 'You're just like the women he's raped. I couldn't bear it if it happened to you—'

She went into his arms with a little cry, and he crushed her against his chest and held her. 'Let me look after you,' he reasoned. 'Just until they catch him. He's a nut case. He might have a record—perhaps this time they'll get something on him.'

'And in the meantime I can't do my job. That's not fair on you and Tim and Rhys—especially Rhys. And anyway, Rosie's going any day now so you'll have all her workload. You can't take on any more.'

'All right,' he said slowly. 'All right, I'll compromise. We'll leave it as it is, but I'll stay here during the week, and when I'm on duty you'll have the burglar alarm to protect you, and when you have to go out I'll come with you.'

'But you'll be shattered.'

'No. I'll sleep in between the calls. If you're out on your own ever I won't sleep a wink at all. And you'll go shopping with me, and running with me—everything. All right? If you're outside this door between dusk and dawn, I'm with you. Agreed?'

She tutted. 'Whatever will the neighbours say?' she teased.

'Damn the neighbours,' he muttered. 'Do you agree?'

'Do I have a choice?'

'No.'

'Then I agree,' she said softly. 'Just for now, and just to satisfy your honour.'

'Thank you,' he said drily, and stood up, pulling her to her feet.

She sparkled cheekily at him. 'Don't mention it.'

He sighed and shook his head. 'You are impossible.'

'Mmm. Are you coming back up to the flat, then?'

'What, and be accused of being obsessed with your body? It's true, you know.'

She reached up and smoothed his hair. 'Oh, Matthew, I'm just as obsessed.' Her fingers threaded into the soft, sleek mass and she pulled him down to her mouth.

He groaned against her lips, but his arms came round her and lifted her against him, and only her teasing reminder of where they were and how immoderate it would be stopped him from taking her there on the stairs.

Instead he hoisted her over his shoulder like a fireman and ran upstairs to the flat, dropping her on the bed. 'He-man,' she teased. 'Well, go on, then, finish what you started.'

He undressed her, but slowly, his eyes clouded with some haunting demon, and when he moved over her his kisses, instead of being aggressive and wildly passionate, were tender and protective. He made her feel cherished—loved.

For the first time she cried, and he held her gently with arms like steel, and cradled her against the safety of his chest.

Linsey found the restriction a mixed blessing. On the one hand, of course, she saw a lot more of Matthew and that had to be a plus. On the other hand she had no time on her own, no privacy, no personal space. For such an independent and undisciplined person, it was purgatory.

Only in her surgery hours was she alone, and then Matthew wanted to discuss the patients and go over her treatment plans and possible alternatives.

Her minor surgery, to her annoyance, he did anyway, and she was present and assisted if it was required. As there was also a nurse there she seldom was required, and her fingers itched to get on the end of the scalpel.

Then she had her chance. A young woman came in complaining of heavy, irregular periods of uncertain length, weight gain and headaches. She had been on the Pill for some years and had become pregnant by accident after forgetting to take it. After a termination she had had Norplant—a contraceptive implant consisting of tiny, soft, hollow rods, filled with a slow-release contraceptive, which were injected under the skin on the inside of the upper arm and provided cover for five years.

However, it didn't suit everybody, as was often the case with any hormone, and as a result she was having the side effects that had brought her to the surgery.

'I think the implant needs to be removed,' Linsey told her. 'I'm sorry, because of course it is very convenient, but there's no point making yourself ill.'

'No,' the girl agreed. 'I felt like this once with the Pill, but of course I just stopped taking that, and I've heard such a lot about these rods being difficult to remove.'

Linsey examined them and shook her head. 'I can feel them all quite easily, although they don't show. They should be easy to get out if they were put in right, and these do seem to have been. Who did it?'

'Dr Jarvis, but I was put on your list.'

She smiled. 'That's OK. We do our minor surgery together, so he'll probably do it anyway.'

'Oh,' the girl said, 'can't you do it?'

'I expect so. Why?'

The girl grinned. 'I just think you might be more gentle; not that he hurt me at all, but you being a woman. . .' She shrugged. 'It was just a thought.'

'I'll ask him. Can you come in tomorrow between eleven and eleven-thirty? Wear a T-shirt or something sleeveless so we can get at it easily. You'll have a local anaesthetic and then we'll make a little opening and lift the rods out one by one. There are six.'

'Yes, I know. That's fine. I'll be here.'

'And then, of course,' Linsey said, 'we need to decide what you're going to use next.'

'Could I have a coil?'

'An IUCD? Yes, I think so. I don't see why not. You need to be having a period to fit it—preferably a normal one, not a hormone-induced bleed like you've been having. Wait until you're back to normal and then ring up on the first day of your period and make an appointment.'

'And can you fit that?'

'Yes,' Linsey said definitely. Her obstetrics qualification covered her for contraceptive services, and under that umbrella she intended to take out the Norplant rods.

She discussed it with Matthew that evening while she was under what she was fast coming to think of as house arrest.

'They can be difficult to get hold of,' he warned. 'There's been a lot of hoo-ha in the Press.'

'But they're so easily palpable.'

'Of course—I put them in.'

She chucked a cushion at him. 'Matthew, I'm going crazy. I can't do this, I can't go there, I have to stay in—for God's sake!'

'All right,' he agreed mildly. 'Have a go. But I'll be there—'

'Hovering.'

He smiled innocently. 'I don't know what you mean.'

In the event she was quite glad to have him there, although she managed most of the rods without any trouble. One of them, though, was difficult and evasive, and although she was stubborn and opinionated she was also aware that this was her patient's arm and she had no business scarring it for life out of pique.

Matthew, to her annoyance, managed to locate and remove it with forceps on the second try, and she ground her teeth, smiled sweetly and thanked him.

'My pleasure,' he said, eyes dancing with appreciation of her self-control.

Later he mentioned it. 'Don't feel you failed because you couldn't get that one out. There's usually one that's a nuisance, and you managed the others well.'

'It's fiddly, isn't it?'

He nodded. 'I won't fit it any more. I think the idea was superb and the principle's a good one, but if there's a problem with side effects it's much harder to remedy than just stopping taking the Pill, and in any case it has to be removed after five years, so at some time you have to deal with the tricky business of extracting the rods. It's just another risk to add to the existing ones of oral contraception.'

'Talking of which, I'm thinking of coming off it. I'm getting fat.'

He put his arms round her and hugged her. 'You're gorgeous. You're not at all fat.'

'My clothes don't fit. Will you put me in an IUCD?'

'No.'

'Why?'

'Because they fail.'

'No, they don't.'

'They do. I mean it—I don't ever want children. I'd hate you to get pregnant by accident. It's bad enough knowing either of us could get hurt in our relationship, without introducing another innocent victim.'

'So we'll go back to condoms.'

He wrinkled his nose. 'I hate having anything between us.'

'You can't feel it.'

'But I can.'

She shrugged. 'Take your choice, then, because I'm coming off the Pill.'

He groused. 'Take another sort.'

'I don't like mucking about with nature,' she argued.

'Then I'll use condoms,' he agreed. 'I don't want you having a coil—or a baby.'

She felt a tiny pang, a sort of strange, almost biological regret in the region of her womb. Would he ever change his mind?

And would he ever admit he loved her? Possibly not.

'Isn't it time we had another tutorial?' she said. 'How about non-compliance with contraceptive advice?'

'Referral to the antenatal clinic, you mean?'

And he thought she was sarcastic!

Linsey decided she wanted to learn more about the endoscopy clinic, and so the next time they had a screening session she asked to be involved.

Rhys was running it, and he was screening three patients for peptic ulcers before treating them for *Helicobacter pylori*. The procedure, a simple one requiring the patient to relax and swallow a tube with a tiny camera on the end, usually involved sedation, but, Rhys explained, because it was being carried out in the little hospital at Milhaven and not in the bigger hospital at Lymington or the even bigger teaching hospitals at Southampton, and because it was being carried out by their own family doctor, the patients rarely needed more than a local anaesthetic spray in their throats.

'The infection has already been confirmed in these

people through a blood test, and under normal circumstances we'd simply give them eradication therapy for the *H. pylori* and then follow it up with a urea breath test to see if it was eradicated. Because these patients are over forty-five, though, we routinely screen them for malignancy.'

'Hence the gastroscopy.'

'That's right. Have you done any endoscopic work in the hospital?'

'A little,' she confirmed. 'I did tons of gastric washouts when I was in A and E, though, for overdoses.'

'Want to have a go?' he asked. They were scrubbing up for the first patient, and she was surprised he should offer her the opportunity.

'Why don't I watch the first one, and then do the second?' she suggested.

He chuckled. 'Where's your confidence? Matthew been getting at you again?'

She laughed. 'Matthew? I don't know what you mean!'

'So do the first.'

She looked at him seriously. 'You mean it, don't you?'

'Of course I mean it.'

She was touched. 'OK,' she agreed. 'I will—if the patient doesn't mind.'

The patient didn't, and, although he gagged a little on the tube at first, she was gentle and patient, Rhys held his hand and talked calmly to him, and the tube slipped easily down, giving them a clear view of the wall of his stomach. They watched the screen closely as she scanned the wall systematically until she finally found what she was looking for.

'Ouch. That looks nasty—I don't wonder you've been suffering,' Rhys said with a smile. 'Right, if we could have a little snippet of that for confirmation, Dr Wheeler?'

She snipped a tiny portion of the ulcerated area with the biopsy instrument contained in the gastroscope, and then checked further to make sure that there were no other ulcers lurking elsewhere.

There weren't, and so she gently and slowly withdrew the instrument. The patient coughed and sat up, swallowing hard and shaking his head.

'OK?' Rhys asked him.

'Yes, I suppose so. Not nearly as bad as I'd thought it would be.' His smile was wry. 'Thanks, Dr Wheeler.'

She flashed him a smile. 'My pleasure. I hope it wasn't too uncomfortable.'

'Not at all. You were very gentle. Thank you.'

Her smile widened. 'Just tell the other two on the way out, would you?'

He must have done, because once she and Rhys were ready and the instruments were sterilised and prepared the next patient came in, grinned and lay down. 'Piece of cake, he said,' the man told them.

Linsey grinned. 'Absolutely. Right, open your mouth for me and I'll spray your throat with local anaesthetic, so you don't feel any discomfort when the little tube goes down. . . Lovely, well done.'

He swallowed it without a murmur, and they were getting on famously until she spotted the site of the problem.

It was quite difficult to keep her face neutral. She had seen dissected stomach tumours before in anatomy classes, and during her time in surgery she had seen growths removed. Never had she seen one so large or so badly inflamed.

'Right, I think we've found it,' she said, looking to Rhys for confirmation.

He nodded, his face impassive. 'A small biopsy will confirm the diagnosis,' he said. 'It won't hurt.'

She snipped and withdrew the instrument, and, like the other man, the patient got up, smiled at them and left quite happily. Linsey looked at Rhys as the door swung shut behind him.

'Whoops,' she said softly.

'Somewhat,' he agreed. 'That's gone too far.'

'I thought so. What will you do?'

'Refer him immediately with the result. We'll treat him for *H. pylori* anyway, but the outcome is a foregone conclusion, I'm afraid. Oh, dear.'

'Do you know him?'

He shook his head. 'Not well. I treat his wife regularly—she's on HRT. She won't take it very well. I don't think she's very emotionally robust.' He shook his head and sighed. 'Ah, well, you win some, you lose some. Let's get cleaned up and hope the last one isn't bad news too.'

'While I think about it,' Linsey said as they scrubbed up again, 'how did Mr Joiner get on with the consultant? You remember, the guy with the CA prostate who had bone pain?'

'Ah. Yes, he had secondaries. It had metastasised to the spine and his hip. He's having radiotherapy to control the pain, but it's not a cure and he knows that. It might give him a little longer, though.

'Right, let's get this last patient seen and get back to the surgery.'

Linsey was an old hand by now. The procedure went without a hitch, they found a lovely innocent ulcer, took a biopsy and sent the man on his way.

'Funny that they're all men,' Linsey commented.

'It's just the way it works. We do screen women too whenever necessary. Right, let's get back and see what's new.'

Rhys had several calls to make, but Matthew had gone out to his own calls and Linsey's, to save her patients having to wait.

She went up to the flat and launched a bit of an assault on the mess, throwing their clothes in the washing machine and dumping the breakfast dishes in the sink. Having done that, she rang her aunt in Brighton and had a chat. The woman was alone now that her husband had died, and Linsey tried to provide some emotional support in the absence of any children.

'Interesting about that woman who came into your surgery and died,' her aunt said now. 'You know, the one with the label in her shirt.'

Woman? Linsey thought. Label? Casting her mind back, she remembered the very obese lady who had collapsed on the premises. 'Oh, that woman. Christine Cleary shirt.'

'That's the one! You know I knew her, did you? Sandra Jenkinson, her name was. We met in Christine's shop and had lunch together every now and again. Mind you, she was *dreadfully* overweight.'

This last said with studied emphasis. Linsey smiled. Her aunt was very far from slender. 'I'm glad recognising that label helped identify her. They might have been searching for weeks.'

'The strange thing was nobody bothered to report her missing. It's dreadfully sad that one could die and no one pays a blind bit of notice.'

Linsey actually thought it was probably the best way. She thought of Mr Joiner and his bone cancer, and the man she had seen today with his stomach tumour, and she wondered if it was indeed better to have loved and lost than never to have loved at all.

She thought how she would feel if Matthew died, and a stab of pain shot through her, so fierce that it took her breath away. And yet she was almost certain that he had no intention of letting their relationship drift into permanence. He didn't want children—he'd made that clear—and although she had found Rhys's little ones rather a handful that weekend, actually they had been sweet and quite fascinating in between the bad bits. She thought of never having any, and found the idea very sad.

She wanted Matthew's baby.

The realisation hit her like a freight train, and she actually had to sit down to let the shock pass. Lord, she really did want his baby. Was she actually putting on weight on the Pill, or was she simply considering coming off it because that would expose her to the risk of pregnancy?

After all, Matthew had got used to being able to make love to her anywhere, anytime, without thinking about contraception. It wouldn't take much to distract him.

Was that what was at the back of her mind?

Deception?

She decided to stay on the Pill.

CHAPTER NINE

THE grip of winter began to tighten on the Forest, and with it the grip of Linsey's frustration tightened on her.

It was dark now by four-thirty and so her curfew hours stretched endlessly. Rosie had retired, the receptionists were escorted home by Suzanne's husband, and the nurses drove home alone to their families.

Only Linsey was trapped, dependent on Matthew for every breath of air or step of exercise taken after dark.

There had been no further sign of the rapist, no more attacks, nothing. Linsey no longer felt as if she was being watched. She was never alone, and never threatened by anything except the incipient demise of her own sanity.

'I cannot stand it another minute!' she said to him one night as she paced the flat. 'It's absurd! Nothing is going to happen to me—nothing! We're stuck together all day and all night like Siamese twins—it's totally ridiculous.'

'You wouldn't say that if you'd been raped,' he said mildly, used to her rantings.

'But I haven't, and I won't be, because I never get a chance!' she raged.

'That's rather the idea,' he said pointedly.

'Don't patronise me!' she yelled. 'Matthew, I'm going mad! I want to be alone! I want to be able to make my own decisions, go where I want, do as I please. I cannot tolerate having my personal freedom dictated by this madman, and I won't put up with it!'

157

Matthew's mouth tightened. 'You can and you will. I simply won't allow—'

'Won't allow? Won't allow! What do you mean, you won't allow? Who the hell are you? What gives you the right to dictate to me?'

Go on, she thought, tell me you love me. Tell me you can't bear anything to happen to me because I mean more to you than life itself; tell me you can't stand the thought of another man touching me; tell me, damn it!

'You're right,' he said at last. He didn't look at her, just went into the bedroom and packed his things that were lying about.

'What are you doing?' she asked, cold dread filling her. Yes, she wanted her freedom, but not at the expense of Matthew's company.

'Going home,' he said flatly. 'I have no control over you, no sanctions, no rights. You're an independent woman. I'm sorry. I thought I was doing the right thing. I see now I was just being autocratic and high-handed. Of course you'll be sensible—but as your trainer and senior partner I can tell you that until further notice you will not be making house calls after dark, and I would be obliged if you would take over some other duties during the day to balance the books.'

Panic filled her. 'Matthew, don't be silly; I don't want you to go! Stay—talk to me.'

'There's nothing to say,' he told her. 'I'll see you in the morning.' He left without another word, leaving her stunned.

She went into the sitting room and looked out of the window at the car park below. He was getting into his car, throwing the things haphazardly into the back, slamming the door, reversing out in a spray of gravel and skidding out of the car park in a mass of wheel-spin and fish-tailing.

She watched his empty space until the security lights went out, and then plopped onto the nearest chair, eyes wide and sightless. Her chest felt as if a steel band was wrapped tightly round it, cutting off her breathing and squeezing her heart in a ruthless hand.

He was gone. She curled into the chair, knees under her chin, eyes staring blankly. What had she done? She had just been ranting, as usual—railing against her captivity. All right, he had been ridiculously over-protective, but she had never meant him to go. Not go, with all his things, for good.

As she sat there in the empty room a cold well of pain swamped her. 'Matthew,' she whispered. Her eyes closed, tears squeezed from beneath her lids, sliding down her cheeks and plopping wetly onto her knees. She couldn't let him go like this—she couldn't!

She wouldn't. She sat up, wiping her eyes against the sleeve of her sweatshirt. She would go after him and talk to him, reason with him, move in with him if necessary, if he wouldn't come back to her.

What if he wouldn't have her?

Doubts assailed her again, but she swallowed them and stood up. Car keys—she needed her car keys. And bag. Nothing else. She could change in the morning, if he let her stay.

She ran downstairs, set the alarm again for the practice and let herself out, locking the door securely behind her. It was raining, she realised—a cold, nasty drizzle that she hadn't expected—and she hadn't picked up a coat. Still, it was only a short distance to his house.

She started the car and pulled out, and as she turned up the road she saw a shadow move on the other side, under the trees. Probably some hardy fool walking a dog. She barely registered it.

The road was wet and nasty, and she shivered and turned the heater up to maximum. It didn't make a lot of difference at first, and by the time she turned onto the road that led to Matthew's track her teeth were chattering.

What had she been thinking of, coming out without a coat?

Matthew, of course. Lord, if she'd lost him. . .

There were lights up ahead, and she slowed, puzzled. A car was parked on the verge, slewed round at a strange angle, and in the beam of its headlights she could see something else—the underside of a car?

Dear God. There had been an accident. As she drew level she saw that the car with its lights on was Matthew's, and panic clawed at her throat. She stopped, turning her car in so that she could see the upturned one, and cut the engine, leaving the lights on and switching on her hazard flashers with the last remnant of sane thought.

Then she leapt out of the car and ran.

'Matthew? Matthew, where are you?'

'Here,' he called, his voice muffled. She could see him now, lying beside the overturned car, his head in through the window. He turned towards her. 'Linsey? Get my bag from the car and come here. We've got two casualties, both trapped.'

She got his bag as he said and ran over to him, slipping and skidding on the wet leaves. 'Here.' She knelt down and passed him the bag, almost delirious with relief at finding he was all right.

'Thanks. My phone's in the car. I've rung the ambulance. Get them again and tell them to hurry, could you?

And then come back and give me a hand.'

'OK.' She ran back to the car and got the phone, then went back to him with it. 'What are the injuries?' she asked.

'I don't know. The driver's spitting teeth and bleeding copiously from various head wounds, the passenger's alive but barely—head at a strange angle, possible cervical fracture. Both are impossible to get at.'

She relayed that information, and was told that two ambulances with paramedics on board had been dispatched and the police were on their way. As she cut the connection she saw blue lights flash through the trees, and within moments an ambulanceman was running towards her.

'We need to get a line in to both of these people,' Matthew said to him. 'This one is semi-conscious; the passenger's out of it but potentially worse off. She needs a neck support before you do anything, but God knows how you'll get it on. And we need the fire brigade to lift the car off its roof so we can get at them.'

The ambulance driver made the necessary calls just as the police arrived.

She could hear the radios in the police car and ambulance burbling and crackling in the background, and lights were set up all round to give Matthew a better view.

Linsey passed him things—the giving set for the intravenous line, the bag of saline, the swabs to clear the mouth—

'Oh, my God, he's ripped his throat to pieces. The steering wheel's shattered and gone in his mouth and wrecked his palate. Possible fractured base of skull, and his mouth's swelling fast. I think I'll have to do a tracheotomy to give him an airway—that'll be jolly in these cramped surroundings.'

'I'll do it; my shoulders are smaller than yours—I can get in further,' Linsey said calmly. She didn't feel calm. The thought of climbing into that blood bath reeking of spilt petrol didn't fill her with joy and enthusiasm, but she didn't really think about it. It was her job, and she knew if she didn't get in there and do it the driver would die.

Matthew wriggled out backwards and she went in, dimly conscious of something sharp in her side. There was a light tucked under the upturned bonnet, illuminating the man's face and throat to perfection.

Not a pretty sight. She asked for the local anaesthetic, just in case he was conscious enough to feel the scalpel, but she didn't have time to give it to him. He started to gurgle, his ribs heaving helplessly, and she yelled, 'Now. I have to do it now!' The paramedic passed her a sterile pack containing a drape which she tucked round the man as well as she could, then she swiped a spirit swab over the site and quickly opened a hole in his windpipe. She found the tube in her hand, slid it in and was rewarded by the man's gasping breath.

She dropped her head onto her outstretched arm and let out a shuddering sigh.

'Done it?' Matthew asked, right behind her.

'Yes. He's OK now. I think we should get him out—if we can get the seat belt off. His feet don't seem to be trapped. It's only the passenger footwell that's collapsed.'

She wriggled out backwards, replaced by the paramedic carrying neck and back supports. After what seemed like an age he removed his head from the cabin and turned to them. 'I've supported his spine. Now we need to cut the belt and try and get him out, but he's looking a bit rough.'

'I'm not surprised,' Matthew said. 'It's an ancient car, no head restraints, sloppy fixed seat belts—a death trap.'

'Went fast enough to kill a pony,' the policeman behind them said drily.

Matthew nodded. 'I saw it there. Is it dead?'

'It is now—the vet's just been. Pregnant mare with a foal at foot. We've got the freeze-brand number and we're contacting the owner.'

'Damn, we've lost him—let's get him out,' the paramedic yelled, and, cutting the seat belt, he let the man slide to the roof of the car. Matthew grabbed one arm, the paramedic the other and, with Linsey supporting his head, they dragged the man out.

It was hopeless. Once he was out of the car the full extent of his head and chest injuries could be seen, and Linsey realised that nothing on earth could have saved him. She shuddered. What a horrible, gory end—and all because he had been driving too fast on a night as black as pitch and had hit yet another of the ponies, the innocent victims of the Forest. She looked round, and could see the foal standing some distance from its mother, nostrils flared because of the smell of blood, trying to make sense of the chaos and confusion.

'Poor little thing. It only looks a few months old.'

Matthew looked over his shoulder and grunted. 'It was lucky not to be hit too. What about the passenger?'

'Cervical fracture—probably third and fourth vertebrae,' the paramedic told him. 'I've got the collar on as well as I can. I think we're best to wait for the fire brigade before we try and get her out.'

Matthew nodded his agreement, then turned to Linsey. 'Why don't you go and wait at the house?'

She shook her head. 'I'll wait here,' she said, and shuddered violently.

He swore under his breath. 'Stupid woman, you haven't got a coat on! Here, put mine on and go and sit in the car.'

He ripped his coat off, pushed her arms down the wonderfully warm sleeves and buttoned it across her chest.

'What about you?' she protested feebly, snuggling into the cosy depths.

'I'll live. Go on.'

She stumbled up to her car, climbed behind the wheel and sat shivering while she watched the arrival of the fire brigade and the raising of the car. It was slow and laborious, but finally they raised it just enough to cut away the roof support and give Matthew and the paramedic room to ease the badly injured woman out. They had jacked open the footwell to free her, and she had broken legs, a crushed foot, almost certainly a broken neck and probably paraplegia.

Linsey wondered if they always did the right thing by saving lives. With the advent of technology and ever more powerful drugs, they seemed to have forgotten how to let people go.

She bent her head over the steering wheel and closed her eyes. She was still freezing, her hands and feet like ice, but at least she was shivering. That meant she hadn't managed to get too cold. In the icy drizzle it didn't take long to get hypothermia.

Her car door opened. 'Linsey? They're going now. We can go home.'

She lifted her head. 'Which home?' she asked him sadly. 'Yours, mine, or both?'

With a muttered oath he pulled her into his arms.

'What's the matter?' he said, and he sounded bitter. 'Miss me already?'

'Yes, as a matter of fact,' she mumbled into his shoulder.

He squeezed her and let her go. 'Come on,' he said. 'Let's go.'

His cottage was freezing. The heating was on tick-over as he wasn't there much during the week, and he fiddled with the boiler, put the kettle on and led her into the sitting room.

'Sit here,' he said, and lit the gas stove that looked like a wood-burner. 'That's the advantage of gas,' he said with a forced smile. 'It warms up quicker than wood. Stay there; I'll get you a blanket and a hot drink.'

'I'm fine,' she protested.

'I'm not. I'm cold, I'm shocked and I'm covered in someone else's blood. Frankly all I want is a hot bath, and the second it's hot that's where we're going. Now shut up and stop being independent, and just let me look after you.'

She smiled. She didn't intend to argue with him. Not again. She snuggled down in the chair, her face angled towards the fire, and slept.

He woke her up a little while later. 'Bath's ready,' he told her.

She blinked and stretched, and stumbled after him up the stairs.

'Shower first,' he told her, and, stripping their clothes off, he pushed her under the pulsing spray of the shower. He washed her hair, just quickly, then his, and then cut off the water and dragged her across the now warm room to the bath.

'Get in.'

'Yessir,' she said smartly, and climbed in, sitting

down gingerly in the piping hot water. 'Oh, bliss.'

'Indeed.' He sat down with equal caution, turned on the bubbles and lay back with a sigh.

Their legs were tangled, hers between his, her toes tucked under his bottom. 'This is wonderfully decadent,' she mumbled sleepily, and wriggled her toes.

'All thanks to Joe. I would never have dreamed of being so self-indulgent, but I have to say there are times when it has its uses.'

She lifted her lids and looked at him. His gun-metal eyes were smoky-grey, smouldering with something primitive and possessive. She pulled her toes out from under his buttocks and walked them upwards, exploring his delicate masculine anatomy with curiosity.

He watched her, eyes hooded, and shifted one leg so that his toes could do a little exploring of their own.

Her eyes widened. How could he be so skilful with his toes? She laid the curve of her instep over the tempered steel of his response and slid her foot gently up and down.

He groaned and shifted, pulling her into his arms. 'Come here, witch. I need you,' he murmured, and without another word he drew her over him and guided her into position, then slid home with a sigh. 'Kiss me,' he ordered, and she bent forwards, her wet hair surrounding them, and took his mouth in a greedy, demanding kiss that escalated their loving from a mild and curious play to a blinding passion within seconds.

The bubbles stopped, but they didn't notice. Finally her skin grew cold and he eased her down beside him into the water, pressing the switch again.

The bubbles rose up, tickling them with warm air, easing out the stresses of the evening. He turned it on again twice more, then reluctantly helped her out of the bath and took her to bed.

'Is the surgery all secure?' he asked, and she nodded. He made no further reference to the fact that she was there with him and not at the surgery, but she couldn't just let it go so easily.

'Matthew, I'm sorry,' she said quietly, her hand resting on his chest. 'I didn't mean it to sound like it did. Of course I don't want to be raped, but I'm just feeling so restricted.'

'I understand. I'm sorry too. I'll try and give you more freedom, but it really is important at the moment to look after you. Just wait until he's caught.'

She thought of her confinement, then of the terrible aching sense of loss when Matthew had gone.

'OK,' she agreed. 'I'll wait.'

And then, she thought, I'll see if he still wants to be around. . .

Christmas was rushing up at twice the speed of light. For Rhys, who was struggling to cope with a demanding job and three even more demanding children, it meant a few blissful days off with his parents in Salisbury. He hadn't wanted to ask for the time, but Matthew had insisted.

Linsey wanted to stay with Matthew, and anyway, her parents were off on Boxing Day on a cruise, enjoying their early retirement. Tim was so wrapped up with April that they were more of a hazard than an asset, and so Matthew decided that he would cover Christmas Day and Boxing Day, sharing the daytime calls with Linsey. Where possible they would ask people to attend the surgery, and they would just hope everyone was so busy having a good time that they had some peace.

'We'll have two days off at the cottage afterwards,' he promised.

They were out of luck. The calls started in the wee small hours of Christmas morning, and went on without rest until ten.

Then, as Matthew pointed out cynically, everybody's guests were arriving and so they were too busy to disturb the doctor any more.

He refused to go to bed again but instead sat in a chair, a cup of coffee in his hand, and dozed off. Linsey removed the cup carefully and let him sleep. She had a present for him—a lovely, soft cashmere sweater that had cost half her salary but was so wonderful that she hadn't been able to resist it. It could wait until he was awake.

The phone rang and he mumbled something and cracked an eye open.

'I'll deal with it,' she told him firmly, and took the details. It was the neighbour of an elderly lady who had been feeling a little off colour. Could the doctor please come; the neighbour was going out for the day and was a bit worried about leaving her.

Linsey went out, enjoying the fresh air. It was a lovely day—bright and sunny although it was cold. Perhaps they'd take the mobile phone and go for a walk after Matthew woke up.

She found the elderly patient's house and parked outside, then rang the bell. She heard a feeble voice calling, then tried the door and found it open.

'Hello,' she called as she went in. 'It's Dr Wheeler.'

'Up here, dear,' the voice warbled. 'I'm in the front room.'

The house smelt of stale urine, Linsey noticed, and a pair of sticks stood at the bottom of the stairs. A quick glance in the kitchen showed that it was reasonably tidy but the gas ring looked ancient and dangerous, and she wondered how long the patient had been incontinent.

She ran upstairs and into the bedroom, and was nearly overwhelmed by the smell. 'Hello, there. Happy Christmas. I gather you're not feeling good.'

'Oh, I'm better now,' the old lady told her. 'Oh, I had such a bad day yesterday—I felt really off colour. Then in the night I had this sharp pain, right low down—you know, dear, *there*,' she explained in a raspy whisper. 'Oh, it did hurt. Then this morning I was lying on something and I found this.'

She produced a rough yellow object the thickness of a finger and about two inches long and handed it to Linsey. 'I can't imagine what it is,' she said bluntly, 'but I'm better off without it, I can tell you.'

Linsey stared at the object in amazement. 'Miss Lucas, it's a bladder stone,' she told her. 'You must have had it in there for ages.'

The woman blinked. 'Well, how did it get out?'

Linsey wasn't sure, short of a miracle. 'You must have passed it. Perhaps I'd better have a look at you and make sure you aren't torn.'

'What, down there?' She looked scandalised.

'Miss Lucas, it's all right; I'm a doctor,' Linsey said gently.

The elderly woman blushed. 'Well, if you have to. Oh, I never thought I'd have to go through anything like this.'

She submitted to the examination with profuse embarrassment, and Linsey was glad to get it over quickly. The smell in the bed was too awful to bear.

She looked around the bleak and empty room, and then back to the frail old lady in the bed. Was this going to be her Christmas? 'Are you doing anything today, Miss Lucas?' she asked her.

'No, dear. Nothing. Why?'

'Well, because if it wouldn't interfere with your plans I wondered if we wouldn't be better to let you spend a day or two in the cottage hospital, just to get over the experience. You'd have someone to cook your meals, and you'd be able to rest and get properly better.'

Her wrinkled, rheumy eyes brightened immediately. 'I wouldn't want to be a bother,' she said briskly, but Linsey could see that the idea had appeal.

'It's no bother, not for anybody. You'll get a nice Christmas lunch there today, as well.'

She definitely brightened at that. Linsey arranged for her admission, and while they waited for the ambulance she helped Miss Lucas find a few things and put them in a case. Then she went home and changed her clothes, throwing the smelly ones in the bin.

Matthew came out of the sitting room, sniffing. 'Have you wet yourself?'

'And Happy Christmas to you too. No, I've been with a patient. She passed this in the night.'

She handed Matthew the bladder stone which she had in her pocket.

'Good God. Is she split in half?'

Linsey chuckled. 'No, but she wasn't keen to let me look at her. She was amazingly unscathed. I gave her some antibiotics and I think she'll be fine.'

'Who was it?'

'Miss Lucas.'

'Really? She's as nutty as a fruit-cake. What did you do with her?'

She smiled. 'I admitted her to Milhaven. That way

she gets a bath, a Christmas lunch and the attentions of social services.'

Matthew kissed her. 'Clever girl. Talking of Christmas lunch, what time are we eating?'

She laughed. 'Your guess is as good as mine. I'll put the turkey in for six. When we eat is dependent on the vagaries of this crazy profession, I suppose.'

He slouched against the bedroom wall and watched her dress. 'We're having a turkey for the two of us?'

She grinned. 'Only a tiny one. I thought we ought to try and do it properly.'

He laughed and hugged her. 'I've got a present for you under the tree.'

'What tree?'

He grinned. 'I thought we ought to try and do it properly,' he mimicked.

She followed him into the sitting room and there in the corner was a little artificial tree, with a string of fairy lights and a few tiny ornaments. There was a present under it.

'Hang on,' she said, and went and fetched his from the bedroom, putting it with the other one. 'Do you suppose we could have a small sherry?'

He smiled. 'Probably a small one. Have you got any?'

'Of course. Why did you think I mentioned it? Just to wind us up?'

'It wouldn't be the first time. I can think of something else you often mention when I can't do anything about it.'

She smirked and rubbed up against him. 'I don't know what you mean.'

'Hussy. Get the sherry and come and open your present.'

She did, her fingers all thumbs as she tried to peel off the sticky tape.

'Just rip it before the phone rings again,' he growled impatiently.

'Well, you open yours—Oh, Matthew!'

The box lay open on her lap, the beautifully set semi-precious stones winking in the lights of the tree. With trembling fingers she lifted the necklace from the box and stared at it open-mouthed.

'Allow me,' Matthew murmured, and, taking the necklace from her, he placed it carefully round her neck. Then he led her to the mirror.

Each stone was simply but perfectly cut into a delicate oval, set within a fine gold band and linked together so that the ovals lay end to end in a softly glittering curve against her skin. There were moonstones, topazes and amethysts, pale emeralds and delicate zircons, the colours muted and exquisite.

'Oh, Matthew, you shouldn't. . .' she began, her eyes filling, and he shushed her and smiled.

'You look beautiful in it. I knew you would—you couldn't fail.'

She looked into the mirror again, her eyes misty. 'It's the most beautiful thing I've ever had in my life,' she said, choked, and turned into his arms and hugged him. Then she sniffed inelegantly and pulled away. 'Come on, you have to open yours. I'm afraid it's going to seem awfully tame.'

He pulled the wrapper off without any hesitation and lifted the jumper out with an exclamation of delight. 'Oh, Linsey, it's wonderful! So soft—where did you find it?'

She grinned. 'Salisbury last weekend, with Tricia. I

met her there—she was staying with her parents. Put it on.'

He tugged off the one he was wearing and pulled it carefully over his head.

She eyed him thoughtfully. 'It suits you.'

'It feels wonderful,' he said, straightening the bottom. 'Like cashmere.'

'It is.'

'Linsey!' His low reproach was belied by his eyes, warm with appreciation. 'Thank you.'

He pulled her into his arms and kissed her lingeringly.

Predictably, the phone rang.

'Again?' he groaned, and answered it.

It was like that for the rest of the day. By five forty-five they had had ten calls out and eight people to the surgery, and were wondering whether they would get their meal when the phone rang again.

'Don't they have anything better to do?' Matthew grumbled, and scooped it up. 'Jarvis,' he said briskly. 'Yes? What seems to be the problem? Right, OK. Where are you? Fine. I'll be with you in ten minutes.'

He put the phone down. 'Visitors in a holiday cottage. Elderly father has chest pain—I expect he's eaten too much Christmas dinner. Chance would be a fine thing. Go for dinner at six-thirty, OK?' He kissed her lingeringly, then, with a muttered sigh he dragged himself away and ran down the stairs.

Linsey watched him go with a soppy smile on her face. Her hand went up to her necklace again, feeling the warmth of the stones against her skin. Surely he must love her? she thought contentedly. Of course he did, just as she loved him. And tonight she'd tell him.

The phone rang again.

'Hello, Dr Wheeler speaking. Can I help you?'

It was a man's voice, hoarse and rasping. 'I'm sorry to disturb you,' he said. 'It's Mr Parker—I'm a patient of Dr Wilson's. I've got some kind of throat bug, a temperature, shivering. I wonder if I might pop round to the surgery? I'm only a few doors away.'

She eyed the kitchen. She had sprouts to cook, the gravy to make, the table to lay. . .

'Are you sure?' she asked him. 'It would be a help. We've been very busy.'

'Of course. Thank you.'

The phone went dead, and Linsey ran downstairs and switched off the alarm. She'd take him through into her consulting room, she thought. She put the lights on all through the surgery and waited, and a moment later the security lights outside switched on and the intercom buzzer went.

'Hello? Who is it, please?'

'Mr Parker,' the caller's voice rasped.

'Push the door and come in, Mr Parker,' she said, and went to greet him. 'Hello, there. Could you come into my consulting room and I'll have a look at you?'

She turned away and froze at the sudden, cold sound of sliding steel. A knife.

'I don't think so, Dr Wheeler. I think I'd like to go upstairs with you to your bedroom. I watch you getting ready for bed at night, you know. You're not always very sensible about closing the curtains, especially not when your boyfriend creeps up on you.'

Linsey swallowed, praying for inspiration. 'We can't go up there,' she lied. 'The alarm's on.'

'So unset it—and don't try any fancy stuff. This knife's sharp. I use it for filleting fish. If that alarm goes off, by the time help comes I'll be long gone—and your precious Dr Jarvis won't ever want to look at you again. . .'

CHAPTER TEN

LINSEY'S hands were shaking so badly that she could hardly press the numbers on the alarm keypad. Backwards, she told herself, then the alarm would sound only at the police station and Matthew's cottage. Not that that would help—he wasn't there—but at least the police would come—if she got it right.

Nothing. No alarm. Thank God. The keypad display light went out, showing the system open. Please, God, let it work, she prayed.

'Right,' the harsh, ugly voice said behind her. 'Let's go. I want my Christmas present, Dr Wheeler. I've waited a long time, but you've made it more interesting. I thought he'd never leave you alone, but he did. I knew it was just a matter of patience.'

Linsey went slowly up the stairs, her heart pounding. Please, Matthew, come back. Please let the alarm work. Please hurry, police—

'Faster, Dr Wheeler. I'm getting impatient.'

She felt the prick of the knife against her thigh, and ran up the last few steps, the madman right behind her.

'Now, into the bedroom, nice and easy, without turning on the light—lovely. Shut the curtains. I'd hate anyone to see this. This is for me. Just me.'

He flicked the light on, and then tossed her something white—a T-shirt? She caught it automatically and stared at it.

'Put it on,' he ordered. 'Take everything off and put it on.'

She looked at him in horror. 'My nightshirt—how did you get this?'

He laughed—an ugly sound. 'I slipped in behind your not so vigilant lover one night, but before you came back to me a burglar disturbed me. I thought it prudent to make myself scarce, but I took it with me as a memento—something with your scent on to sleep with at night, and to remind me of you. Not that I've forgotten you, not for a minute. The last girl was just a distraction. Her hair was similar, you know, but not as beautiful as yours. Once I'd seen yours I realised the first girl was just a pale shadow too. It was you I really wanted all along. You should be flattered.'

She swallowed. Flattered? she thought. Try terrified. Where were the police? How could it take them so long? She'd have to waste time, distract him or something.

She took off her shoes, one by one, then fumbled with the hem of her jumper. Oh, God, she couldn't bear his eyes on her but she had to do something so that he would think she was co-operating—

'Come on!' he snarled. 'Now. I've waited long enough.'

She closed her eyes, grasped the hem of her jumper again and prayed.

Matthew couldn't find the cottage. He was sure the man had said it was down this road, but there was no trace of anything answering its description.

He drove to his cottage, meaning to phone Linsey and ask her to contact him if the man rang back, and as he got out of the car to open the gate he heard it.

Not the shrill wail of his house alarm, but the insistent beep-beep-beep of the surgery-alarm system connected to his house.

The blood drained from his face. A hoax, he thought—a hoax to get him away from the surgery, leaving Linsey alone.

'Oh, God, no,' he whispered, and, throwing the car into reverse, he shot backwards down the track, out into the lane and then forward towards Milhaven, tyres screaming, the automatic gearbox protesting at the harsh treatment.

He put his headlights on full, fumbled the magnetic flashing green light out of the glove box and plugged it into the cigar lighter, then opened the window and stuck it on the roof, all with one hand. The car swayed and steadied, and he screamed down the road at twice the legal limit, praying that nothing got in his way.

He had to get to her. Nothing else mattered. She might only have one chance.

As he turned into the high street a police car shot past him, siren wailing, and turned up the practice road. He followed it, skidding into the car park and hitting the gravel at a run.

Hands trembling, he unlocked the back door and flung it open. 'Linsey? Where are you?' he shouted, terror clawing at him.

'Up here,' Linsey called, and he ran four steps at a time up the double flight, the policeman hard on his heels.

He almost fell over them.

A man was lying face down on the landing floor, white with pain, and Linsey was sitting on him, holding his arm at an unnatural angle behind his back. In the background Matthew was aware of another insistent beep, like the alarm at his cottage.

He reached for Linsey. 'Are you all right?' he asked her, lifting her up as the policeman took over, handcuffing the man's hands behind his back.

He screamed.

'Be careful. I might have broken his arm,' Linsey said in a curiously flat voice, and turned to Matthew. 'Could you turn the oven off? I think the turkey's cooked.'

'Are you really all right?'

She dredged up a small smile. 'I will be. I thought he was going to fillet me with that knife.'

A shudder ran through her and Matthew's face hardened. 'I could kill him,' he said softly.

Linsey smiled wryly. 'I nearly did. I was so tempted. The knife was just there, but I thought, What will it achieve? Nothing.'

'So you broke his arm instead.'

'That was an accident. I only had one chance. The oven-timer went off and he spun round, thinking it was the alarm. I jumped him and yanked his arm up—rather too hard, I'm afraid.'

'Don't be,' Matthew growled. 'It's giving me great satisfaction to know he's in pain.'

'That's terrible,' she reproached him.

'So it might be. It's how I feel. When I think what he could have done to you—'

He broke off, his jaw working, and Linsey felt her eyes fill. 'Matthew?'

'Mmm?'

'Hold me?'

He stood up and came over to where she was lying on the sofa. 'Are you sure? I didn't want to crowd you after—you know.' His shoulders lifted a fraction, his eyes creased with concern.

'I've told you before—you never crowd me. Please—just hold me. I need you.'

He perched beside her on the edge of the sofa, his arms coming carefully round her and lifting her against his chest as tenderly as they would an injured child. 'Oh, God, Linsey, I thought I'd be too late,' he said unsteadily, and, burying his face in her hair, he dragged in a shuddering breath.

Her arms slid round him, clinging to him, and finally she felt safe enough to let the healing tears fall. When she finally hiccuped to a halt Matthew lifted his head and gave her a ragged smile, and she saw that his cheeks were wet.

'Don't tell me you care,' she teased, her voice uneven, and he tipped his head back and fought for control.

'Oh, God, Linsey, if you only knew how much. . .'

She laid her hand on his shoulder. 'I wish I did,' she said softly. 'I wish you'd tell me. I've loved you so much for so long, I don't think I can bear it any more if you don't love me.'

He stared at her in amazement. 'Not love you? Of course I love you. I thought you found me such a pain.'

Her brow creased. 'A pain?' she said, puzzled. 'Why?'

'Always there, following you round, trapping you—'

'It was that lunatic that was the pain, not you. I never wanted to get away from you.'

His breath came out in a shaky whoosh. 'I thought you were bored with me.'

She laughed in surprise. 'Bored? How could I be bored?'

'Easily. I'm not exactly the world's most exciting person.'

Her face fell. 'Is that what you think? That I'm expecting you to entertain me? Matthew, I love you. I don't care about being entertained. I just need to know you're there for me—' She broke off, tears welling in her eyes. 'I need you with me. I'm nothing without you.'

'That's nonsense. You're beautiful and vivacious and intelligent and kind and funny and gifted medically—you're wonderful. What the hell do you see in me?'

She smiled mistily. 'Your eyes. I used to dream about your eyes. I was obsessed by you, did you know that? I had to close my eyes if anybody kissed me because their eyes were the wrong colour.'

'You're in love with my eye colour?' he said hollowly.

She laughed and pulled him down against her. 'Amongst other things. You're quite a nice person, really, when you try, and you've got a wonderful voice, and you're super with patients, and you've got the most interesting bathroom I've ever been in—Oh, and I forgot—you don't have genital warts.'

His face was a picture. 'Damn it,' he began, and then he laughed, hugging her up against his chest and nearly cracking her ribs. 'You have no respect at all. And none of those are good reasons.'

She could hear the hesitation in his voice, the uncertainty. She smiled and threaded her fingers through his hair, cradling his head against hers. 'Did I tell you what a wonderful lover you are? How generous and thoughtful? Or that I know you'll never let me down, and you'll always be there for me, putting me first, no matter how inconvenient? Did I mention how for the first time in my life someone has actually cherished me and made me feel fragile and precious instead of huge and ungainly?'

'You aren't huge and ungainly!' he protested, lifting his head away and peering down at her.

'I've always felt it before. And loud and clumsy.'

His grin was slow but worth waiting for. 'You can be clumsy sometimes,' he admitted. 'Just a tad. And you don't ever give up.'

'Oh, no. Not if I want something.'

His face became serious. 'And do you want me? I mean really want me, warts and all, for the rest of my life?'

'Oh, Matthew, you know I do,' she whispered.

'No, I don't. I know you want me now, but I don't know that you always will. No one else ever has. They've all got bored, like Judy got bored with Rhys—'

'Please don't compare me with Judy,' she said flatly. 'I'm nothing like her, and if you think I could ever do that to you then there's no point in us going on. I'm a one-man woman, Matthew—and you're that man. I haven't wanted anyone else since I first saw you. You looked at me, and I swear I could have walked across the water to you.'

He laughed awkwardly. 'You were drunk.'

'I'd been drinking,' she corrected him. 'Not that much. I knew you were special, even then.'

'I used to fantasise about you,' he told her, 'and you were beautiful and meek and submissive—'

She laughed helplessly. 'Me? Submissive?'

His grin was wry. 'You can see why you were such a shock to me. The real fantasy was a bit stronger than the pale imaginings of my youth.'

'I should hope so. Submissive?' She chuckled. 'I should think not. I hope you're not expecting me to be a subservient wife, are you?' she added, and then could have bitten her tongue. Had he mentioned marriage? No, she didn't think so. Oh, Lord, what if he hadn't meant that?

'Good God, no,' he said in horror. 'I'm expecting you to be a thoroughly aggravating and difficult wife. You'll challenge every decision I try and make, question my judgement on every issue and generally interfere with the smooth running of our matrimonial home at every turn. What else could you do? You wouldn't be you if you didn't.'

She snuggled closer. 'Just so long as you realise what you're getting.'

'Oh, I realise,' he murmured. 'And I can't tell you how much I'm looking forward to it.'

His lips brushed hers, just gently. Too gently. He was being careful and considerate, she realised, not knowing what the rapist had done to her.

'He didn't touch me,' she said quietly.

Matthew went still. 'What?'

'The rapist. He didn't touch me. You don't have to be careful. I'd rather you weren't. I'd like you to drive me out of my mind with need for you so I forget all about it.'

'Are you sure?' he asked gently.

'Quite sure. Make love to me, Matthew—please?'

He needed no second bidding. He scooped her up in his arms, carried her into the bedroom and slowly and methodically drove her out of her mind.

For once she didn't interfere or take charge or question what he was doing; she just lay there, eyes fixed on him as she spiralled higher and higher. He took her to the brink again and again, and then finally went over the edge with her.

Then he laid his cheek against hers and their tears mingled on the pillow. . .

'You'll forgive me for not being there, won't you?' Rhys said gently. 'It's just that weddings and I don't get on at the moment.'

Linsey kissed his cheek. 'We understand. Please don't

feel bad about it. And thank you so much for your present.'

He smiled—a little quirk to a mouth that smiled too rarely. 'My pleasure. Just enjoy yourselves.'

He had given them the weekend—paid for the honeymoon suite and all meals in a lovely hotel in the New Forest. It was unbelievably generous, and to make it possible he was covering the practice from Saturday morning to Monday morning. Tim was doing Friday night, because, as he said candidly, it was no good if the groom was going to be too tired to be any use.

The wedding was very simple. Tricia was there, staying with her parents in Salisbury and delighted to meet Matthew at last.

'Keep her in line, please. I've spent two years training her to be tidy; don't let her throw it all away.'

'How could something so tiny have such a dominating influence over you?' he said to Linsey later over dinner, courtesy of Rhys.

Linsey laughed. 'Only her body's tiny. Her determination is enormous. You think I'm bad? If she wants something, she gets it.'

Matthew reached over, picked up her hand and twiddled her wedding ring. 'I haven't noticed you exactly failing to get what you want.'

She smiled lazily. 'Darling, I've hardly started.'

His eyes widened. 'Oh, God. Why did that sound like a threat?'

She laughed—a throaty, feminine laugh that made his body clench. 'Relax. You'll love every minute of it.'

Matthew wasn't at all sure he liked the sound of that. . .

EPILOGUE

LINSEY lay sprawled across the bed, her body slaked. Her mind, however, was restless. There was something she and Matthew had to talk about.

She turned on her side and faced him, running a finger gently over his chest and down to his tummy-button. Idly she picked the fluff out of it. 'Matthew?'

'Mmm?'

'You forgot again.'

He cracked one eye open, his brow furrowed for a moment, then he dropped his head back and sighed. 'Damn. Sorry.'

'That's the second time this week. You're getting careless.'

He opened his eyes again and turned towards her. 'I am? What about you? You could have reminded me.'

'You made me forget my own name. I was past caring about birth control.'

He smiled—a feral smile of great masculine satisfaction. 'That good, eh?'

She punched his shoulder. 'You know it was. It always is. Don't change the subject.'

'What is the subject?' he asked softly.

She looked down, away from those eyes that understood her all too well. 'Are you doing it on purpose?'

'Forgetting? No.'

She ran her hand over his chest. 'I just wondered.'

'Wondered what?'

She shrugged. 'If you'd changed your mind.'

He lifted her chin so that she had to meet his eyes. 'About what?'

'Babies,' she said flatly.

He searched her eyes. 'Do you want a baby?'

She swallowed. 'Only if you do. I wouldn't want to do anything you didn't want—'

His laugh cut her off. 'That's priceless,' he said when he could speak. 'You manipulate me, engineer my life, boss me about—you make Mussolini look like a regular sweetheart, and then you tell me you don't want to do anything I don't want to do? Since when?'

She scooted up the bed and folded her arms. 'Not about such a major issue,' she said grumpily. Heavens, was she really that manipulative?

He reached up and rolled her down against him, cradling her head against his chest. 'Darling, if you want a baby, we'll have a baby.'

'But eighteen months ago you wanted a vasectomy.'

He chuckled. 'Only fleetingly. Three kids were a bit much all at once. One at a time I could probably cope with. Besides—' he ran his hand up her thigh, absently caressing the soft curve of her tummy '—the caveman in me quite fancies the idea of you swollen with my child.'

She sighed with relief. 'I'm glad about that,' she said quietly, 'because the first one's due in eight months.'

He went very still then shifted his head and peered at her. 'It is?'

She watched, breathlessly as the smile lit his eyes. 'Oh, darling. . .' His hug was bone-cracking, but she didn't care. She had one more thing to ask.

'About my maternity leave.'

He shifted and looked at her again. 'Yes?'

'Can Tricia do it?'

His eyes widened. 'Tricia? The demon Tricia?'

She giggled and punched him. 'You like her.'

'I do?' he said in astonishment. 'She's worse than you.'

'Mmm. You'll feel you got a bargain in me if she's around.'

He hugged her. 'I did get a bargain—and yes, Tricia can do your maternity leave if she wants so—just until we get another doctor to take over from you.'

'I don't want to give up work, Matthew.'

'No.'

'Matthew? Matthew, don't ignore me!'

'I wouldn't dare,' he said drily. 'I wouldn't dare. . .'

Historical Romance™ presents...

MISTRESS OF HER FATE

by

Julia Byrne

Julia Byrne lives in Australia with her husband, daughter and a cat who thinks he's a person. She started her working career as a secretary, taught ballroom dancing after several successful years as a competitor, and, while working in the History Department of a Melbourne university, decided to try her hand at writing historical romance. She enjoys a game of cards or Mah Jong, usually has several cross-stitch projects on the go, and is a keen preserver of family history.

Look out for Julia Byrne's next novel – coming soon in Historical Romance™!

Chapter One

Langley Castle, near Stratford, September 1464

Has there ever been a time when she had enjoyed the colourful spectacle of a banquet? The music, the dancing, the constantly shifting crowd of chattering guests?

If so, it was beyond the reach of her memory, Nell decided as she edged past the last of the trestle tables that had been set up along both sides of Langley Castle's great hall. She paused before one of the deep window embrasures and measured the distance to the door.

A discreet exit was not going to be easy. Though the hour was growing late, the room was still crowded, and ablaze with light from the flaming torches in their iron cressets high up on the walls and the candles flickering in their table-sconces. Light that dazzled the eyes, shimmering on pearl-encrusted silks and damasks and illuminating the rich jewel-like colours of the banners and wall-tapestries. Light that glowed, dark and sullen, through glass goblets filled to overflowing with ruby-coloured wine.

In a few places the light was muted. As well as the

tables and benches, the hall was furnished with several
carved wooden screens, placed to create discreetly
shadowed corners for the benefit of those guests who
wished to conduct their little amours in some privacy.
Most of them were too drunk to bother, but lolled in
their seats, sporting openly with whomever took their
fancy. Those who could still remain upright were dancing in the centre of the hall, circling to the strains of
lute and clavichord, a hazard for anyone with escape
on her mind.

Nell dodged a couple who staggered out of the line
of dancers and wished she could be magically trans-
ported somewhere else. Preferably her bedchamber.
Her feet ached from hours of dancing, her face ached
from the constant smile she had affixed to it, and if the
unceasing cacophony of loud talk and clattering dishes,
interspersed with coarse male laughter and female
shrieks, didn't strike her deaf it would be a miracle of
saintly intervention.

"Not dancing, dear Cousin? Have all your partners
deserted you?"

A titter of spiteful laughter brought her head around
as the dancers swept past in a swirling array of movement and colour. The overblown blonde who had spoken smiled back over her shoulder, patently false sweetness on her sharp-featured countenance.

Nell smiled back just as sweetly, and refrained from
replying in kind. A cousinly exchange reminiscent of
spitting cats was more than she could cope with at present. And besides, she reminded herself, the festivities
were in honour of her imminent departure. This was
the last time she would have to put up with the way
her cousin turned every banquet into a contest to see

who could garner the most compliments or collect the most partners.

"After tonight you can have the field all to your-self," she muttered beneath her breath. Mayhap, then, she thought, Margaret would not feel obliged to wear a gown that was disgustingly tight and cut so low that Nell decided her cousin's plump breasts were about to burst free of their precarious confinement at any mo-ment. Judging by the expression of lecherous antici-pation on the face of Margaret's partner, whose ener-getic performance seemed expressly designed to hasten such a scandalous exhibition, she was not alone in hold-ing to that opinion.

Nell giggled, then abruptly sobered as she glanced down at the ermine-trimmed, silver and blue brocade gown she was wearing. Like all her cousin's clothes, its fashionable neckline was so low that it would be enough to make the boldest harlot blush. She gave the bodice a surreptitious tug and wished she had a piece of silk, or even lace, with which to cover the generous expanse of flesh thus exposed. Margaret might not have been so quick with her malicious tongue, Nell reflected, if she had known how little her cousin relished the male attention provoked by the revealing costume. Fortu-nately, since she was considerably less well-endowed than Margaret, the borrowed gown wasn't quite as shameless as it might have been. In fact, even when added to sore feet, tired eyes and deafened ears, it would not have made her presence at the banquet any more of a distasteful ordeal than usual—had it not been for one other circumstance.

Without moving her head, Nell glanced cautiously towards the screen passage at the far end of the long hall. The stranger was still there, leaning against the

wall, a big, dark shadow among the shadows cast by
the overhanging minstrels' gallery. She didn't need to
see his face clearly to know he was watching her. He'd
been watching her since she'd first noticed him standing there a little over an hour ago, tall and powerful
and unsmiling.

Despite the heat of the room, an odd little chill tiptoed down Nell's spine. There was something about the
man's stillness, about the way he just stood and
watched. Something leashed and waiting. Something…predatory.

She shivered again, then jumped as a hand came
down on her shoulder.

"Sweet Cousin! All alone? Come and dance with
me."

"Oh, Tom, you startled me." Turning, Nell managed
to slip out from under her cousin's hot, sweaty palm.
Tom had had plenty to drink by the look of his flushed
cheeks and glazed eyes, but he was still capable of
movement. Even as she tried to step away he grabbed
her about the waist and swung her into the midst of the
dancers. Pulled so abruptly off-balance, Nell was fully
occupied for several seconds in regaining her footing
and rescuing the train of her gown.

"Do we both have to caper about like drunken mum-
mers?" she gasped, catching her breath enough to resist
Tom's efforts at a high leap. It wasn't easy. He had her
clamped against his side in a position that virtually
compelled her to follow him. "This is your father's
hall, not a village maypole."

Tom roared with laughter, and leered at the gentle
swells of flesh visible above her neckline. "The leaps
have a purpose, little prude," he chuckled. "God's
nails, who'd have thought you'd turn out as frigid as a

dried-up old nun.'' The thought obviously annoyed him because the laughter vanished from his eyes, to be replaced by an unpleasant mixture of sullen resentment and frustration. ''Look about you, dearest cousin,'' he advised sarcastically. ''Your prudish morals are of scant use to you here. '''Twould suit you better to change your manner, otherwise I might taste the honey you guard so closely without the benefit of marriage.''

''What, are you still at that?'' she scoffed, not bothering to do as he bade. She had already seen enough to know that her uncle's guests were indulging their senses to the fullest. She only wished she'd managed to escape before Tom had noticed her standing alone.

''My father's intention in summoning me to Hadleigh Castle is to arrange my marriage to someone other than yourself, Cousin,'' she reminded him, unsurprised to see his scowl deepen. As her father's only child she was a matrimonial prize that Tom and his parents were loath to see slip out of their grasp. '''Tis about the only useful thing he's ever done for me since he sent me here to live,'' she finished, a slight trace of bitterness in her tone.

Tom's already heated face flushed dark red and his arm tightened around her waist, dragging her closer. ''You scornful little jade,'' he hissed in a furious undertone. ''Always thinking you're too good for the rest of us. Oh, aye,'' he added at her surprised glance, ''did you think I hadn't noticed? I watched you look down your nose at us the minute you climbed out of that litter ten years ago. Pampered little princess. But not for much longer. You're a long way from wed as yet, sweet Cousin, and your scorn will be of poor comfort when you're forced to spread your legs for me.''

''You're drunk,'' stated Nell, not bothering to con-

ceal her disgust. Tom's fingers were already digging
with bruising force into the side of her breast, but she
ignored the pressure and managed to get her elbow between them. A good jab to his ribs had him turning
purple and choking.

Nell didn't wait to see if it was in rage or pain. She
wrenched herself free and stalked off—straight into the
big, dark stranger.

Up close he was huge. The thought flashed through
Nell's mind even as her startled senses were bombarded
by the feel of large, powerful hands steadying her with
a grip that edged on painful, by the rough warmth of a
woollen surcoat against her palms, the lean, hard
strength of the body beneath. Instinctively, her fingers
curled into the solid muscles of his chest in an attempt
to lever herself away.

Merciful saints, she thought faintly. He's immovable.

"Lady Eleanor fitzWarren."

It wasn't a question, but Nell nodded automatically.
Then shivered slightly as the deep, husky tones flowed
across her nerves. His voice was as overwhelmingly
masculine as the controlled power of his hands and the
sheer size of him. The cool scent of wind and rain still
clung to him, mingling with his own clean male essence
and teasing senses that had had a surfeit of the close
smoky atmosphere of the hall and men who smelled of
stale perfume and wine. Momentarily entranced, forgetting her initial intimidation, Nell leaned closer.

"No doubt you mean to be welcoming, Lady
Eleanor, but I prefer not to be one of a crowd."

The sarcastic tone was like a pail of cold water
dashed over her. Nell gasped and stepped back, snatching her hands away as she looked up. Sweet Jesu, he
was dangerous. The predator she had imagined. Eyes

the colour of frozen amber, as fierce and intent as a hawk's, stared back at her from beneath frowning black brows. His hair was black also, cut unfashionably short and brushed back from a face of hard contours and aquiline features, with a firm, sharply chiselled mouth that only just escaped being brutal by the unexpected fullness of his lower lip.

Nell couldn't have spoken if her life had depended on it. Indeed, she could barely recall what the stranger had said to her. But it was not the compelling strength of his face or the open contempt she saw in his icy gaze that had the breath catching in her throat; it was the scar. Thin and white against his tanned skin, the unmistakable mark of violence ran down his temple in a straight line from above his left brow to below his eye, where it formed a short curve along his cheekbone. It wasn't disfiguring, but it made an already hard face look positively menacing.

"Having second thoughts, Lady Eleanor? You surprise me. You bestow your favours so indiscriminately, I wouldn't have thought this—" he touched his scar lightly "—would deter you."

This time the insult registered. Nell's breath came back with a rush. "Precisely what favours are you referring to, sir?" she demanded through set teeth.

He shrugged and folded his arms across his chest, causing a ripple of muscle to disturb the fabric of his surcoat. Nell suddenly realised he wasn't dressed for a feast and felt a surge of confidence. He was probably some upper servant belonging to one of the guests. A bodyguard, perhaps—in these dangerous times, few wealthy men travelled without several of the uncouth creatures. She would soon send him about his business.

Then, as her eyes met the stranger's, her certainty

wavered. This man looked as if he gave orders, not obeyed them. It was in the arrogant way he stood leaning against the wall, in the dangerous glitter of those golden hawk's eyes and the unrelenting line of his mouth.

"I'll admit you're more subtle than the other ladies," he drawled, the faint emphasis on the word "ladies" telling Nell exactly what he thought of the women present. "You entice with smiles and laughter, Lady Eleanor." His gaze wandered with slow insolence across the revealing bodice of her gown. "You let them stare, and occasionally whet their appetites with forbidden embraces in dim corners, before you snatch the prize away. It's been an interesting exercise in tactics to watch. Tell me, how many men do you draw into your web before you make your choice?"

"Why, you—" Nell could scarcely get the words past the tightness in her throat. She felt the most absurd desire to burst into tears, and told herself it was fury. How dared this…this…uncouth *brute* accuse her of…? When most of the women were already… When she had struggled so hard to avoid…

Her thoughts fragmented into complete turmoil under the impact of her own rage and the faint infuriating smile on the stranger's face. "You don't even know me," she burst out at last, unable to think of anything else that came even close to expressing the extent of her outrage.

"I don't have to," he dismissed. "Women like you litter the Court like beggars at a feast."

Her gaze flashed briefly to the white rose insignia embroidered on his sleeve. Memory, sharp and cold, stabbed through her. "Encouraged by your Yorkist king."

His brows went up at the fiery scorn in her tone. "So, despite this being a Yorkist stronghold, you're one of those who would rather have a drooling idiot on the throne. That shouldn't surprise me, since Henry is led around by his wife like a performing bear—in much the same manner as you lead your partners, my lady."

Nell couldn't believe what she was hearing. "I don't know who you are, *sir*—" her own emphasis was as biting as his own "—but be assured my uncle will hear of your insults."

"Rafe Beaudene," he supplied briefly. "And I wouldn't bother, if I were you." He jerked his head sideways. "Sir Edward appears to be busy."

Nell made the mistake of following his gesture. Hot colour stained her cheeks as she saw her uncle grab hold of a passing guest and pour the dregs of an ale-jug down the front of her gown. The lady shrieked and put up a mock struggle, which ended with her landing in his lap and commanding him to clean her up. Laughing raucously, he bent his head and complied. Not two places away, Aunt Maud did nothing more than titter and turn back to the gentleman with whom she was conversing. They were sipping from the same wine-cup, Nell noticed.

Conscious of reluctance, knowing what she would see, Nell searched among the crowd for her cousins. Tom was nowhere to be seen, but fourteen-year-old Edmund had cornered a maidservant. The girl's dress was down around her waist and he was openly pawing her breasts. Margaret and her partner sat nearby, indulging in much the same sort of scuffle, except that her cousin's protests were accompanied by giggles and not tears. The rest of the company were pursuing drunken oblivion or amorous adventure with equal fervour, and

Nell knew it would get worse until the guests fell asleep where they sat.

Miserably, she had to admit that the stranger's contempt for the company was justified. But *she* had no reason to be ashamed, she reminded herself. She wasn't drunk, nor was she allowing some lout to maul her the way Edmund—

A quick memory of Tom's painfully grasping fingers pulled her thoughts up short. Some of her other partners, too, had given her a few unpleasant moments before she'd managed to have herself whisked off by the next man waiting to dance with her. Nell blushed again, this time in embarrassment. Beaudene, or whoever he was, had obviously seen it all and drawn his own conclusions. And he didn't look like the sort of man to listen to explanations.

Anger flickered again. She had no need to explain. Who did he think he was to sit in judgement of her, anyway? No! She didn't owe him any explanations! But if there was one thing Nell had learned in the past ten years, it was how to defend an indefensible position. And when your opponent was intensely male, over six feet tall and unlike any man you had ever encountered, you used whatever weapons came to mind. Her chin went up.

"Rafe Beaudene?" she repeated, a languid question in her voice. "I don't believe I know the name. If you are here as bodyguard to one of the guests, I suggest you rejoin your fellows out in the bailey. I am sure their company will be more to your taste."

"Since most guards have at least some notion of honour, I'm sure of that, too," Rafe snapped, cursing the instant response of his body to the blatant feminine challenge in her. It wasn't the first time she'd had that effect on him, and he didn't like it any better now than he had earlier. Anger at his lack of control had him biting off the next words with savage inflexion. "However, as much as I would like to follow your advice, Lady Eleanor, we're stuck with each other. '''Tis your body I'm here to guard.''

The resurgence of warm colour in her cheeks had his eyes narrowing briefly. It surprised him that the little minx was capable of blushing and yet, for a moment, she seemed genuinely uncomfortable, her eyes holding a mixture of anger, shock and confusion. A trick of the light, he told himself cynically. No one who behaved as she did would be shocked or confused by anything a man chose to say to her.

He thought back over the last couple of hours, and almost laughed aloud at the notion. He'd lost count of the number of times she'd vanished with her partner of the moment into a dimly-lit window embrasure or behind a screen, to emerge several minutes later smoothing a long sleeve, straightening her gown or, on one occasion, refastening the wide belt at her waist. And then she would beckon another victim, with nothing more than a look from her dark hazel eyes, a sweep of long ebony lashes, a turn of one delicate, almost bare shoulder.

And, God damn it, watching her, he'd felt the hot pulsing of his own blood in response to her tricks. The violence of his reaction had stunned him. The slender arch of her throat when she'd laughed up at her partners, the alluring sway of her hips beneath the heavy brocade of her gown, had made him want to drag her under him—never mind where they were—and subdue the subtle movements of her body with the force of his, to watch the laughter in her eyes change to passion.

He'd stamped down on the feelings immediately, of course, but the easy control he'd always taken for granted had been forced. Even telling himself that her passion would likely be as false as her bright smiles of promise hadn't helped.

As for what he'd overheard—

Nell almost reeled beneath the fierce anger that flashed into Beaudene's eyes. It was gone almost immediately, but the dangerous expression, added to several years' experience of unpleasant innuendo and less subtle suggestion, at least convinced her of one thing. He had meant nothing more than the literal truth by the way he'd phrased that last remark.

"I'm not sure I understand—" she began cautiously, only to break off with a startled squeak when he came away from the wall with the speed of a striking adder. Before Nell had time to wonder what was going on, there was a flash of movement to her right and the victim of her cousin Edmund's attentions darted past them, making for the screen passage beyond, and escape.

Whirling about, she saw that Edmund was right behind the girl, haring across the hall and whooping as if he was on a hunt. He was almost level with them when Beaudene took one step forward and extended his arm. Edmund hit it at full speed and rebounded as if he'd run headlong into a stone wall. He sprawled on his back in the middle of the dancers, nearly taking two couples down with him and cursing viciously. There was a roar of drunken laughter from a near by crowd.

Nell didn't bother with Edmund. She glanced back swiftly at the entrance to the screen passage. The girl had halted, clutching at her torn dress and staring wide-eyed at Beaudene. There were traces of tears on her

cheeks and she looked pale. She was a mere twelve
month younger than Nell's own sixteen years, and yet
Nell felt suddenly immeasurably older.

"Go quickly, Alison," she whispered urgently, waving her hands for emphasis. "Sleep with Jacquette and
Lucy, and stay out of Edmund's way until after your
wedding."

"Aye, mistress." The maid turned and vanished before the words were finished.

"A plague on you, Cousin," roared Edmund, picking himself up off the floor. He glanced quickly at
Beaudene then advanced on Nell, clearly considering
her the less threatening opponent. "Father said I could
have the wench before she married. You think sending
her to sleep with a parcel of women is going to stop
me?"

"Probably not," Beaudene interposed coolly. He had
dropped his arm as soon as Edmund had been sent flying, but hadn't resumed his lounging position against
the wall. Now he stepped into the boy's path. "But you
may find it difficult to have her, or any woman, without
the proper equipment."

"What? Who the hell are you?" Edmund demanded,
his voice soaring to a shrill note that betrayed his youth.

"Someone who can do you a great deal of damage."

The words were uttered in a tone of such cold certainty that Nell shivered. As if he'd seen the small
movement, Beaudene glanced down at her. "The girl's
to be wed?" he asked shortly.

She nodded. "Next week. To our steward."

"Bondman, or free?"

"He's free, but—"

Beaudene turned back to Edmund before she could
finish. "If you want to function like a man when you

reach the age,'' he said with soft menace, ''you'll take warning, boy. There are enough easy women here more suited to your purpose than a maid already promised.''

''We'll see what my father has to say about that,'' Edmund blustered.

''Don't be an idiot, Edmund,'' Nell advised, deciding to enter the fray. ''Who do you think hired this...this...?'' Her voice faded away as she suddenly realised she didn't know Beaudene's exact status. His name and arrogant self-possession hinted that he was no common man-at-arms, but whether he was knighted or merely a squire she had no idea.

Temper flashed in Edmund's eyes as he turned on Nell. ''Well, if I have to settle for a strumpet, I'll start with you, Cousin. You owe me for letting that puling little ninny escape, so 'tis you who must pay the forfeit.''

''By the Rood, Edmund!'' Thoroughly exasperated, but too inured to her family's ways to protest at the insult, Nell responded only to the threat. ''As if Thomas's attentions aren't enough. Do you have to emulate everything he does?''

Her cousin's hand whipped out and fastened around her wrist. '''Ware your shrewish tongue, wench, or— *Ow!*''

''Let her go,'' Beaudene said very softly. He had moved so swiftly to counter Edmund's attack that Nell hadn't seen the hold he had on her cousin's shoulder until she heard his yelp of pain. Eyes fastened in unwilling fascination on Beaudene's hand, she watched his long fingers flex ever so slightly. She was freed at once. ''And whatever favours your brother enjoyed in the past from Lady Eleanor are now at an end,'' he finished in the same chillingly soft tone. "Do I make myself clear?"

Edmund nodded sullenly and was released. Sending Nell a look of dislike, he stumbled off, cautiously feeling his neck and shoulder.

"Come on, Lady Eleanor, we've provided enough entertainment for your uncle's guests to gape at. Let's try something more sedate like the allemande."

"The allemande?" Nell's gaze travelled in disbelief from Beaudene's mud-splashed, knee-length leather boots to his plain black hose and matching surcoat, unadorned but for the white rose and a wide fur trim. "If you think I'm going to dance wi—"

She was yanked into the dance with startling velocity.

"Is this what you call guarding my body?" she demanded indignantly, then promptly fell silent when his long fingers slid down the inside of her arm to wrap her hand in an unbreakable grasp.

The first few steps passed in a daze. Somewhere in the distance Nell could still hear the clatter of dishes, the talk and laughter of the guests, even the minstrels' lutes above her, picking out a familiar melody, but they were sounds without meaning, not real; all her senses were focused on Beaudene. For some reason, dancing with him made her feel suddenly, unexpectedly, small and vulnerable.

She had been aware of his height and size from the moment she'd cannoned into him, of course, but now that awareness was almost terrifyingly acute. He seemed to tower over her like a huge black shadow, his strength a threat—leashed, aye, but *there*—and the way her hand was totally enveloped by his was utterly unnerving. It was the only contact between them, and yet her entire body was awash with heat, as though he was touching her all over. She felt chained... captive...*possessed*. It was all she could do to follow the procession of dancers without faltering.

"What? No sparkling wit? No polite conversation? You disappoint me, my lady."

"I don't waste my wit on a hired bodyguard," Nell managed to retort. She winced inwardly at the breathless sound of her voice and hoped he hadn't noticed. What was the matter with her? Why wasn't she depressing his pretensions and making her escape?

"You are labouring under a misapprehension, Lady Eleanor. I am not for hire. Especially not by your uncle." Rafe glanced down at her just as they passed a flaring sconce-light and felt his blood surge in another rush of desire that completely drowned out her startled, questioning response. The torchlight flickered over her upturned face, casting pools of shadow in those seductive hazel eyes. Eyes like a forest at sunset, green and gold, light and dark, clear and mysterious.

Her other features held the same contradictions, he thought, frowning slightly. Her brows and lashes were dark, but the light captured the warm gleam of chestnut in the hair flowing free from the back of her headdress. Her face was fine-boned, almost fragile, the lines of cheeks, nose and jaw drawn with exquisite clarity, but her mouth was full and soft, just a fraction too wide for the current fashion of pursed lips prevailing at Court. It was a mouth made for passion, for kisses that were long and deep and utterly consuming.

God, what insanity had made him dance with her? Rafe asked himself, forcing his eyes away from that lush mouth in an attempt to subdue the throbbing tension in his body. His gaze dropped to the gently sway-

ing movement of her skirts as she stepped sedately
along by his side, and he realised suddenly how small
she was, how delicately made. The steeple headdress,
from which floated a veil of silver tissue, gave an illusion of height, but without it the top of her head
would just reach his shoulder. Her hand felt tiny in his.
Warm and soft, it quivered slightly, like a small captured bird.

Rafe's fingers tightened involuntarily. He saw her
flinch and knew he was probably hurting her, but he
couldn't seem to loosen his grip. The clenched strength
of his hold was the only thing preventing him from
dragging her into his arms so he could hold all of her,
touch all of her.

"My lands lie half a day's ride beyond your father's." His voice sounded hoarse and he forced himself to concentrate on speaking. It wasn't what he
wanted to do, but talking would serve to remind him
why he couldn't drag her into the nearest solar and take
what she'd been offering every man in sight. "Since
my return from Court coincided with your own journey,
he asked that I accompany you."

"My father?" Nell repeated, frowning. "But Tom
and several men-at-arms will be escorting me. Why
would he ask such a favour of you?" The increasing
waves of heat caused by Beaudene's long scrutiny of
her face ebbed away beneath another, different sense
of unease. Some very odd things had been happening
lately. It tended to make a girl wary of anything out of
the ordinary.

Instead of answering her question, Beaudene asked
one of his own. "Are you aware of the reason your
father has sent for you, Lady Eleanor?"

Nell made a small, dismissing motion with her free

hand. "He intends to arrange my marriage," she said briefly. "What of it?"

"You don't appear to be overly interested in the prospect."

"Why should I be? Whoever my father has in mind will only be marrying me for the wealth and lands I will inherit. Truly, I would rather be a pauper and retain my freedom."

"Spoken in the sure knowledge that you would not remain a pauper for very long," he stated sarcastically. "Easy words, my lady."

"You don't believe me?" Stung, Nell glared at him. "Once I'm married my property becomes my husband's. I will own nothing except my marriage portion, a mere third of my inheritance, *if* he honours the law. I will also forfeit the freedom of my own body. Tell me, sir, why would I have any use for marriage?"

"Would you prefer the alternative? A nunnery? Or perhaps you would rather be a man's mistress than his wife?" The supposition was loaded with contempt.

"Why not?" she flung back, tossing her head. "'Twould be less restricting than either marriage or the cloister."

A qualm shook her the moment the reckless words were out, but Nell was too angry to take them back. She glanced around the hall with scornful appraisal until her gaze rested on a couple half-hidden behind the back of a tall settle. The man was fondling his partner with an intimacy that was better suited to the bed-chamber, and though the woman laughed and wriggled invitingly as his hand disappeared beneath her skirts, exposing her plump white thighs, Nell saw her turn her head away. The expression in her eyes was one of amused tolerance.

"A perfect example," she pointed out airily, devoutly praying that Beaudene hadn't noticed how quickly she had averted her own face. At past banquets she had always managed to retire long before her uncle's guests started making such an exhibition of themselves. "They're not wedded, so at least she'll be able to seek the privacy of her own bed once he's finished."

"Not if she wants to be well-rewarded," he promptly returned. "You see, everything has a price, my lady. But perhaps 'tis as well you don't wish for marriage. The price your husband would pay for the pleasures of your body would be far too high."

"Beyond your means, that is for certain," Nell retaliated, and had the satisfaction of seeing his eyes narrow.

"I don't recall making an offer," he snapped.

"Thank the saints for that," she retorted. "Because I would have no hesitation in refusing it. And if the man my father has in mind for me is an ill-mannered, overgrown lout like you, I'll send him packing as well."

One black brow went up. "You haven't sent me packing," he pointed out in a tone that made her want to scream. "In truth, now I come to think about it, you don't have the authority to send me packing."

Nell came to a dead stop in the middle of a turn. She had to unclench her teeth so she could speak. "I don't have to continue with this ridiculous dance, however," she declared. "If you will be so good as to cease breaking my fingers, sir, I wish to retire."

"That's taking yourself off. Not nearly as satisfying as sending me packing."

"Ohhh!" Wrenching her hand from Beaudene's grasp, Nell turned on her heel and, for the second time that night, abandoned her partner, Unfortunately, this time she had ended the dance at the far end of the hall and had to negotiate her way through several couples whose progress was erratic to say the least.

By the time she reached the entrance to the screen passage, she had been jostled from side to side, had had the long points of her new shoes trampled on, and had fought off the separate advances of three drunken would-be partners. Fortunately, she hadn't had to fight very hard, and she was just congratulating herself on her easy escape when the reason for it loomed up beside her.

Angry, nervous, and feeling extremely put-upon, Nell turned on him. "Didn't you hear me? We will be making an early start in the morning. I wish to go to bed."

"An excellent idea. Which way is your room?"

"*What*?"

"Oh, don't concern yourself. I have no interest in doing more than accompanying you to your door—and then making sure none of your suitors accepts the invitation you've been putting out to follow you through it."

Nell clamped her lips shut and told herself that slapping his face and screaming like a fishwife would not help. She had to get rid of the man. There was something she had to do before she retired for the night, and she didn't want any company while she did it. Especially his.

A servant walked past carrying a platter of left-over food and inspiration dawned. "Go and have something to eat, or whatever it is bodyguards do when they're off duty," she commanded, waving a small, imperious hand. "I sleep with Margaret and my two younger cousins—*girl* cousins,'' she added for emphasis, ''*and* their nurse, so you have no need to concern yourself with my virtue.''

Beaudene's reply was to wrap his long fingers about her arm. ''A wasted effort, no doubt, but 'tis why I'm here, nevertheless. Which way?''

Furious but helpless, Nell gestured to the stairway at the end of the screen passage. ''Do you intend to accompany me to the privy as well?'' she asked with heavy sarcasm as they reached the upper gallery. ''I really don't need a bodyguard for that, you know. I've been managing on my own for quite some time now.''

''Obviously without being put over someone's knee at an age when it might have done some good,'' he said grimly.

Nell jerked her arm out of his hold and marched on ahead. Innate, if silent, honesty compelled her to admit that she had probably deserved that remark, but the knowledge did not soothe her temper one whit. ''This is my chamber,'' she managed to enunciate when they reached a door halfway along the gallery. Several chests were stacked against the wall, ready to be loaded into the baggage wagons in the morning. Beaudene stepped around them and, somewhat to her surprise, opened the door. He didn't say anything, just glanced into the room then stood aside for her to pass.

And all at once a curious feeling of reluctance swept over her. Of sudden regret at their unpleasant beginning. Beaudene might be an arrogant boor who had badly misjudged her, and he had obviously taken her in dislike, but it was equally obvious that he took his role as bodyguard seriously. And she had been so alone here. Surrounded by family and wealth and luxury, but still alone. Maybe she did need...

She looked up.

"Don't try it," he said, his eyes arctic.

Hot colour surged into Nell's cheeks. Without uttering a single word, she turned, marched into the dimly-lit room and slammed the door behind her with as much force as she could muster. "Ignorant *savage*!" she stormed. "*Brute*! *Oaf*! Stupid—"

A sleepy grumble came from one of the beds.

Nell ignored it. Her disordered mind was too busy wondering how she was going to get through the next few days. With her cousin Tom and that… that…*lout*…as escorts, she was sure it would be the worst few days of her entire life.

Chapter Two

It had been raining. Nell glanced up at the midnight sky as clouds like black wraiths scudded across the face of the moon, and hoped the next downpour would hold off for a while longer. She hadn't bothered with a mantle, but at least the night air wasn't too cold for comfort. She began to pick her way carefully around the puddles left by the recent shower, keeping to the shadows as much as possible and skirting the perimeter of the bailey rather than going straight across the open space.

Creeping out of the hall had been blessedly easy. She had half expected to see Beaudene standing guard outside her door when she'd warily opened it a crack a few minutes ago, but apparently the hour she'd waited had been enough to convince him that she was safely bundled out of the way for the night. Perhaps he'd taken her advice and gone to chase up some food. He might even drink himself into a stupor like everyone else.

The thought of his inevitable discomfort on the morrow cheered her for a moment, before she dismissed it. He didn't look like a man who relinquished control of his senses—to anything.

A dog whined nearby and she froze, recalled to her purpose. Once she reached the stables she would be out of sight, but first she had to get there without drawing the attention of the guards at the gatehouse. Fortunately, they were some distance away, and, judging by the slurred snatches of bawdy song that wafted towards her, were in much the same state as their master.

Nell gathered up her full skirts and tiptoed onwards. Not that she cared if Margaret's second-best gown trailed in the wet and mud, she thought crossly. It would serve her cousin right for slashing to pieces the gown Nell had intended to wear that evening; a nasty piece of spite that deserved retribution. But, on the other hand, she didn't need the weight of a water-logged hem dragging behind her when she returned to her chamber. One had to be practical, after all.

The stables materialised in front of her and she peered cautiously around the corner. All was still and quiet. Everyone not attending the banquet would be sound asleep by now—the guests' servants in the lodg-ing-hall across the bailey, the grooms and stableboys in the loft above the wagon-room. No one would hear her, and besides, she wouldn't be out here long. Her hand brushed over the big double doors. They were too heavy for her to open quietly; Nell ignored them and edged along the wall until she reached a smaller door at the end of the building. Easing it open, she slipped inside.

Instantly the smell of horses and hay assailed her, the mingled odours familiar and comforting. Nell felt her heartbeat slow. She hadn't realised how nervous she'd been, but when she groped on the shelf next to the door for the candle and flint she had left there ear-lier in the day, she noticed that her hands were trembling slightly. Taking a steadying breath, she lit the candle and held it aloft, glancing around as though to reassure herself that the stable was, indeed, the safe haven she had often used during the past years.

The long corridor stretched ahead of her, disappearing into darkness beyond the light of the small candleflame. Stalls were ranged on either side. Tonight most were occupied, but only the occasional shuffle or sleepy whicker disturbed the stillness as Nell glided quietly down the passage. She passed the big main doors and stopped at a stall a short distance further on. The little palfrey within lifted her head and blew gently in greeting.

Nell searched in the pocket of her gown for the apple she had brought as a farewell gift. ''Here, Chevette, is this what you're waiting for?''

At the sound of her voice, large hooves stamped angrily at the far end of the stable and there was a loud thud. Nell glanced that way to assure herself that her uncle's stallion was securely locked up. The horse was a brute, bad-tempered and dangerous, unusually nervous of open spaces, and possessed of a marked dislike for the human race, particularly women. It occupied the only stall fitted with a door, because if it saw daylight between itself and an object of dislike, it tended to charge. More than one stableboy had been savagely attacked by the animal.

''If Tom is planning to ride that seed of Satan tomorrow, we're going to have a merry time of it,'' Nell muttered, peering uneasily into the shadows. She couldn't be sure, but the door at the end of the corridor seemed to shift. As if someone had just closed it and she had caught the last few inches of movement from the corner of her eye.

"Idiot," she told herself bracingly. "You're imagining things." The door led only to the storeroom, the outer door of which was always kept locked. No one would be in there at this late hour.

Still mentally chastising herself for her nervousness, she ducked under the rope across the front of Chevette's stall while the mare was placidly munching her apple, and crouched down before the wooden manger. It was the work of seconds to reach under it and run her fingers along the space between the manger and the wall until they slipped into the rough hollow she had slowly and painfully gouged in the wood three years ago.

The crucifix hidden within fell into her hand with an almost soundless whisper of its gold and ruby chain.

With only the briefest glance at the precious object, Nell lifted the hem of her gown, fumbling for the pouch she had tied around her waist. It was awkward with her other hand holding the candle, but she didn't dare set the light down while she was in Chevette's stall. Only when the crucifix was safely out of sight again did she rise and duck back under the rope. Her heart was racing again, but this time with elation. She had done it. Now it wouldn't matter if anyone saw the faint light in the stable—an unlikely event in any case, since the windows were small and high. She could relax and turn her attention to her other reason for being here.

She reached out to stroke Chevette's cream-coloured velvety muzzle and was rewarded with an affectionate shove. "So, this is farewell, little friend. I wish you could carry me home, but 'twill be a long journey over rough country and you're far too delicate a lady to—"

This time the movement of a door was unmistakable. Nell's breath caught as a ripple of cold air brushed her face and made the candlelight flicker wildly. A small click sounded in the darkness, but not from the direction of the storeroom. She whirled at once to face back the way she had come, cursing the blackness that made it impossible to see more than a few feet beyond her meagre light.

There was absolute silence—but she was being watched. There was a presence. She could feel it. Her skin prickled all over with the primitive awareness of danger.

"Tom...? Edmund...? If that is one of you playing some stupid trick, I swear I'll throw this bucket of water over you."

Keeping her gaze fixed on the shadows, she reached under the rope again, her free hand groping for Chevette's drinking pail. The waiting stillness was nerve-wracking. She didn't know who to expect to emerge from the darkness. Edmund seeking revenge for her earlier interference? Tom intending to force his attentions on her?

Or worse! Nell's stomach clenched as she remembered Tom's words before she'd left him in the middle of their dance. She had assumed his subsequent absence meant he was indulging himself with some other woman, but had he seen her enter the stable? Had he decided to force her into a position where she would have no choice but to marry him? Merciful saints, would be actually rape her? Was he capable of it? The questions raced through Nell's mind, freezing her in her half-crouched position. Tom was capable of the act, aye. But did he have the wit for such rapid planning? Sweet Lord, where was the pail?

"A wasted gesture, my lady. I can split you where

you stand before your hand even reaches that useless weapon.''

Nell straightened slowly as a man appeared at the edge of the circle of light cast by her candle. She didn't know him. Another stranger, she thought inconsequentially. But though the man's features were unknown to her, and hazy in the dim light, the dagger in his hand was terrifyingly distinct. Her frightened gaze dropped to the weapon and she took an instinctive step back. ''Who are you?'' she whispered. ''What do you want?''

The man only smiled in answer and moved forward a pace. He made a small, sharp gesture with the knife, and light shimmered over the long blade as though caressing it. Nell edged away again. Somewhere in the back of her mind she was aware of movement as the horses in the nearby stalls shifted nervously, sensing something amiss, but she continued to retreat, watching the blade as if mesmerised. The man matched her, step for step, still not speaking.

His silence was more frightening to her than all the rest. There was a cold inevitability about it that was chilling; as though he had no doubt as to the outcome of their slow progression. She had to think! She had to get away somehow. The storeroom! If she could just reach the storeroom…hide in the darkness…unlock the outer door…

A series of angry snorts and the crashing of hooves sounded behind her and Nell glanced back involuntarily. She was almost there. She was going to escape. A shivery sense of anticipation raced through her. The man could surely see what she intended, but he was making no attempt to stop her. Perhaps he was only intent on stealing a horse. A few more steps and she would be able to reach back and—

The stallion's stall was open!

Nell froze, unable to believe that she was seeing dark space where there should have been a solid oak door. A faint glimpse of movement inside the stall convinced her. When had it happened? she wondered dimly, her gaze whipping back to face her attacker. How? Why hadn't the horse bolted out of its stall? Was it waiting for her? Holy Mother of God, she had to stop this. She had to move. But her feet felt as if they were nailed to the floor...her legs were shaking...she felt sick...

"Keep going, my lady." The man's voice was soft in the silence. He was smiling.

Did he know she was trapped? Where could she go? Forward to certain death at the hands of a thief? Backwards to be trampled beneath the hooves of an enraged stallion? For the horse would surely charge as soon as she drew level with the stall.

"Please, if you'll just go... I won't say anything... I won't tell anyone..."

"Tell them what, my lady?"

"I don't know." She made a helpless little gesture towards the stallion. "But..."

"You think I came for the horse? You're easier to deal with than that brute. Aye, I know you don't want to pass him but you will, my lady." He smiled again. "You will."

"I don't understand," she whispered. "Who...? *Why...?*"

He laughed softly, almost as though humouring her, and opened his mouth to speak. Nothing came out. An expression of stunned amazement filled his eyes. They stared into hers a moment longer, glazed and glaring, then he pitched forward to land face-down at her feet. The jewelled hilt of a dagger protruded from his back, straight over the heart.

"Don't move," said Beaudene quietly from the shadows halfway down the passage. "And don't make a sound."

Nell was quite incapable of movement. Or of speech. As one in a daze she watched Beaudene come forward and step over the body, as if it were a bundle of rags that someone had carelessly left lying there. He passed her without even a glance and slowly approached the stallion's stall.

"Easy," she heard him say, his voice very low. "Easy, boy." The murmured words continued until the stallion's snorts and stamping hooves gradually became muffled as the stall door swung closed. Beaudene moved back into the corridor, tucking something into his surcoat.

"Unusual to find a horse who feels more secure in a confined space," he muttered, as he fastened the latch and strode back to her.

The words seemed to be spoken more to himself than to her, Nell thought, but for some reason she felt compelled to answer. "Some of the grooms…think he may have been attacked out in the open…as a colt," she said faintly. "Fired upon from a distance, where he couldn't see…" Her voice trailed off. Why, in the name of all the saints, was she having this stupid conversation about a horse when she was standing here with a corpse at her feet? Had fear laid waste her wits?

Her rescuer appeared to be totally unmoved by the situation. He stepped past her, took the candle from her limp grasp and went down on one knee beside the body. Nell had to avert her gaze when his hand went to the dagger. She swallowed hard, not daring to ask any questions until she had her stomach under control. When she forced herself to look down again, Beaudene had turned the man over and was staring at his face. His own expression was grim.

"How—?" she began shakily.

"Quiet!"

The curt order succeeded in jolting her out of her shock-induced state. "What do you me—?"

"Shut up!" Beaudene rose, flashed her one savage look that raked her from head to toe, and grabbed her arm. "Unless you want to rouse everyone in the place, we'll talk away from that stallion before he kicks his stall to pieces."

"Oh, pardon me for wanting to know what's going on," she snapped beneath her breath. "How very inconsiderate of me." The anger felt wonderful, Nell discovered. She was actually beginning to feel some warmth creeping back into her body. "Are you just going to leave that…it…him…there?" she demanded as Beaudene propelled her down the passage. Chevette's head poked over the rope as they passed, her face looking enquiringly after them.

"I'll deal with it later." Beaudene came to a halt near the door and swung Nell around to face him. He wasn't gentle about it, nor did he relinquish his hold. "But before I do, you, madam, have some questions to answer. Our friend over there obviously knew you use this place for your assignations, so we'd better get your lover out of the way first. Who did you come here to meet, and where the hell is he?"

Belatedly, Nell realised that her new bodyguard wasn't quite as unmoved as she had thought. He was keeping his voice low from necessity, but it was clear

that he was blazingly angry. Instead of offering a few
kind words of comfort, he was questioning her as if *she*
was the felon. "How do you know it wasn't him?" she
flared, gesturing wildly in the direction of the corpse.

His fingers tightened so painfully that Nell gasped.
He released her arm as if she had burned him.

"Don't play your games with me, my lady. You may
be wanton, but you're not stupid enough to arrange a
tryst with your own murderer."

"Mur—" The tide of rage washed out of Nell in a
rush, leaving her weak and shaking. "What do you
mean? He was trying to steal my uncle's stallion. I must
have disturbed him. The stall was open…and the storeroom. I saw the door move, but thought I'd imagined
it."

"And then he went to the trouble of letting himself
out of the storeroom so he could come back through
this door and continue his theft while you were still
here? Don't be such an idiot!"

There was one thing to be said for his insults, Nell
reflected. They stopped her from falling apart.

"Why would he want to kill me?" she demanded
angrily. "I didn't even know the man. He was probably
going to force me into the storeroom and lock me in,
but I knew if that stupid horse saw me it would—"

"He knew that too, you little fool! Weren't you listening to him? Sweet Jesu!"

Rafe turned away from the stunned look in her eyes
and shoved his free hand through his hair. He knew he
shouldn't have said anything, but he'd had to shut her
up before she described a picture that was already sickeningly clear in his mind—a picture of soft, fragile
woman beneath the hooves of half a ton of enraged
stallion. Damn it, he had to stop thinking of her as soft

and female and desirable, and figure out what the hell was going on here.

"I don't remember," she stammered. He looked back at her sharply, hearing real confusion in her voice. "At first I thought he was—"

"Ah, yes, your lover. How soon can we expect him?"

Her eyes darkened with such fury that for a moment Rafe thought she was going to hit him. He half hoped she would try it so he could have the pleasure of subduing her. Something told him it would go a long way towards relieving his feelings.

"Well?"

"I did not come out here to meet a lover!" Her voice was shaking with rage, but every word was enunciated with great precision. "I came out here to say goodbye to my *horse!*"

She flung out her hand on the last word, drawing his gaze down the line of stalls to the palfrey looking back at them. The little mare's expression was so thoroughly disapproving and indignant that, despite the rage burning fiercely inside him, Rafe nearly laughed. The damned horse looked as if she knew exactly what was being said and that if he knew what was good for him, he'd better believe it.

"All right," he allowed, smiling reluctantly. He wanted to hang on to his anger, damn it. At the moment it was the least dangerous of the emotions rampaging through him. "I suppose I'll have to believe you, since she's telling the same story."

"Don't fall into a seizure from the effort," Nell muttered, but she was uncomfortably aware that the retort didn't have quite the force she'd intended. Beaudene's brief flash of humour had taken her completely by surprise. She hadn't thought him capable of humour, never mind that his wry smile, fleeting though it had been, had done something very strange to her insides. The quietness of the stable seemed to close in around her suddenly, making her conscious of the lateness of the hour and how alone they were.

"Well, I suppose…" She glanced down the passage, thankful that the body lay in the shadowy darkness. "I suppose we should call the guards. Not that they'll be particularly surprised." A small laugh escaped her and she began edging towards the door, knowing she was babbling but unable to stop. "'Tis all of a piece with everything else that's been happening to me lately."

The humour vanished from Beaudene's face as though it had never been. His eyes narrowed on her retreating figure and he put the candle down on the shelf with a care that was ominously deliberate. "What has been happening to you lately?" he asked, in a tone so dangerously soft that Nell halted in mid-step.

"Nothing important," she said, sending him a swift, nervous glance. "Just…accidents. Little things. Stupid things, really. I wasn't even hurt." She slid one foot sideways.

Beaudene reached out, clamped both hands around her shoulders and yanked her back so forcefully that Nell had to put her hands against his chest to stop herself colliding with him. Her startled cry was lost beneath the suppressed rage in his voice.

"Accidents have been happening to you, and you still came out here alone, in the middle of the night, just to say goodbye to your horse? Holy Mother of God! Did I say you weren't stupid? I take it back!"

"I am not stupid," she protested breathlessly, trying to push herself away. "How was I to know there would be a thief out here? We've never had one before.'' She thought briefly of the hidden pouch hanging from her waist, then shoved the image out of her mind.

''He wasn't a thief, you little idiot!'' He shook her hard. ''He was an assassin, God damn it! A hired thug—'' she was shaken again ''—and you go and make his task a whole lot easier by traipsing around as if 'tis broad daylight, in a costume expressly designed to upset a horse that already hates females!''

''How do you know he hates females?'' she asked weakly, and immediately winced at the look of impatience that crossed his face.

''One of the grooms was at great pains to tell me the details when I noticed the animal earlier. Now, shall we see if you're capable of intelligent answers as well as stupid questions? Talk!''

Talk? How could she talk when her head was beginning to spin? Heat swirled around her, heat from his eyes, from his hands, from the closeness of his powerful body. Heat that scorched, and yet lured, as flame lured a moth to its own destruction. Again, Nell tried to free herself. It was impossible; the heat and power of his body simply overwhelmed her, sapping her will, making a mockery of her efforts. ''When you take your hands off me,'' she managed, desperate enough to plead.

He released her. ''They're off.''

It didn't help. She could hardly think, let alone talk. One moment she had been feeling almost grateful— after all, he had saved her from injury or worse, even if she hadn't acknowledged it—but now... Tiny shivers were racing through her, following each other so rapidly she was sure her trembling must be visible. She had thought she knew every danger a woman faced with a man, but there was a new danger here. Something beyond her knowledge. A threat without name. A threat she had never before encountered.

"Start with the first accident," he ordered, snapping her out of her daze. "When did it happen?"

"A...a few days after my father's letter arrived," Nell stammered, forcing her brain to some sort of coherent thought. "We were hawking, and something startled my horse. She reared and I fell, but 'twas nothing. I wasn't hurt, not even bruised."

"And then?"

"Then... I think... Aye, 'twas the pennant in the hall. The standards hanging over the minstrels' gallery. One of the lances came loose and fell on me. Then, the day after that, I was locked in with the mastiffs. They hadn't been fed because my uncle intended to hunt wild boar the next day, but—"

"God's blood! And you didn't suspect anything?"

"Suspect what?" she cried. "Nothing happened. The mistake was discovered almost immediately and I was freed."

He ignored that. "So, 'tis obvious the dogs failed to make a meal of you. Were there any more so-called accidents after that?"

"Well, there was the arrow that just missed me when we were shooting at the butts, and then the broth. And today my gown, but noth—"

"Aye, nothing happened. We'll argue about it later. I hope you've said all your farewells here, my lady, because we're about to leave."

Nell gaped at him, certain she hadn't heard aright. "Leave? *Now*?" Her voice soared.

"That's what I said. Which horse were you going to ride tomorrow?"

"Rufus, but—"

"The chestnut next to your palfrey?" His gaze followed the direction of hers. "Good. He looks strong. Where's your saddle?"

"Where's my—? Have you lost your senses?" she demanded, finally recovering from her stupefaction at this abrupt turn of events. Leave? Ride off into the middle of the night? *With him*? She wasn't that mad. "You can't expect me to leave just like that," she spluttered. "Without telling anyone, without any baggage, without—"

She broke off, realising that Beaudene was taking not the slightest notice of her protests. He stepped into one of the stalls and led out a powerful-looking bay with a black mane and tail. The horse stood quietly while its bridle was fastened and the blanket smoothed into place. Beaudene reached for the heavy saddle resting atop the side wall of the stall, lifting it with easy strength and laying it lightly across the horse's back. Two leather bags followed. Not until he had tested the straps and saddle-girth did he turn back to Nell and raise an imperative brow.

"Will you listen to me?" Nell commanded, stamping her foot in frustration. "This is to act without reason! What about my baggage? I don't even have a mantle." Her voice rose to a note that was perilously close to a wail.

"Then you'll just have to make do with that gown you're almost wearing," he retorted with a distinct lack of gallantry. "Unless you can tell me which of those chests stacked outside your room holds your mantles."

Nell stared at him in dismay.

"No, of course you can't. You probably didn't even

direct your own packing. Ornamentation and coquetting is about all you're good for, isn't it, my lady?''

''There's a mantle in my chamber,'' Nell said through her teeth. ''I could fetch that, if you insist on pursuing this madness.''

''I'm not letting you out of my sight, and if we both return to your chamber what we'd fetch would be a heap of trouble. As well ask the town crier to proclaim our departure.''

''As well depart tomorrow morning, with an escort, like civilised beings,'' Nell shot back. ''There's no reason to creep away like thieves in the night, and if you think—''

''There's every reason, you little fool,'' he cut in brutally. ''We're going to be travelling for several days, and I can't watch you, and your cousin, and a round dozen of his men, every mile of the way, all day and night. We'll be safer alone.''

''In your opinion,'' she scorned. ''Why should I listen to you? Tom wants to marry me, not kill me. I'm not much use to him dead.''

''I haven't got time to argue with you,'' Beaudene dismissed. ''We're leaving as soon as I stow our friend in the storeroom. By the time he's discovered, we should have several hours' start.''

''Oh, wonderful! You expect my uncle to come after us? That should put him in a festive mood. I'll probably have a beating to look forward to. Well, you might have saved me from injury, Sir Rafe, or whatever your name is, but I don't have to obey your orders. I'm not going as far as the gatehouse with you, let alone—''

The tirade was abruptly cut off when Beaudene took a menacing step forward and captured her face in one large hand. His golden eyes blazed down into hers, fierce and implacable. "If you want to live, my lady," he said very softly, "you'll shut up and do exactly as I say. If I say we're leaving tonight, that's precisely when we leave. If I say ride hard, you'll ride harder than you've ever ridden in your cossetted, useless life. If I say walk, you'll walk. If I say crawl on your hands and knees, you'll damn well crawl on your hands and knees. Do you understand me?"

Nell was trembling by the time he'd finished, but it wasn't in fear of Beaudene. At least, she didn't think it was. His forceful insistence that they flee her family, his arrogant confidence that he was right, shook her more than she cared to admit. What if she was wrong? What if the slashed gown was the only piece of spite Margaret had indulged in, and the other incidents real attempts on her life?

It came down to a simple choice, she told herself. She either travelled with Tom and his henchmen, who would obey any order her cousin saw fit to give them, or she accepted Beaudene's protection—the protection of a man she had known only a matter of hours.

"Let me make the decision easy for you," he continued, obviously losing patience with her long silence. "You can co-operate, my lady, or I can knock you senseless, tie you hand and foot, and take you out of here slung over your horse like a slaughtered deer."

"Is that supposed to reassure me?" Nell muttered. Then cried out as he released her and drew back his fist. "All right!" She only just managed to stop herself flinching away. "I'll go with you."

"Do I have your word on that? You won't try anything stupid? You'll obey my every order?"

"Aye." She almost flung the word at him. "You don't have to keep threatening me."

The fist lowered. Nell's wary gaze followed it. Not until Beaudene's fingers uncurled did she lift her eyes to his face. With the candlelight shining directly below it, his scar stood out in harsh relief, a stark relic of violence.

"You really would have hit me," she whispered, "wouldn't you." It wasn't a question.

"Just remember that whenever you're tempted to try your hand at rebellion," he said curtly. "Now, come and help me with this corpse."

Nell swallowed as the candle was shoved into her hand. "Can't you just leave him here?"

"For the stableboys to trip over at dawn?" He sent her a withering glance. "Eventually they'll notice the horses are missing, but we'll need every minute of advantage we can get. Don't look if you're squeamish. And for God's sake, keep your mouth shut when we go past that stallion."

Turning his back on her, he strode down the corridor and picked up her erstwhile attacker. The effortless way he handled the body of a man almost as big as himself gave Nell a daunting idea of his strength. She gritted her teeth and followed, making a wide detour around the patch of blood-stained straw. She was not going to be sick, she told herself with fierce determination. She would act as if moving corpses was as commonplace to her as it apparently was to Beaudene.

They reached the storeroom door and he jerked his head, indicating that she should open it. Nell obeyed, hating him. He knew what she was feeling when her gown brushed the limp form in passing, but there was not so much as a flicker of sympathy or kindness in those hard amber eyes. He dropped the body behind a large barrel and kicked some straw over it. Then he motioned her to hold the light higher while he examined the harness stored to one side of the room.

"That's not it," Nell objected, when she saw what he had selected. The saddle in his hands looked large enough to fit three of her. She'd never stay in it. He stalked out of the storeroom without answering, forcing Nell to hurry after him. "Don't you ever listen to anyone?" she demanded in a furious whisper as he unhooked the rope from Rufus's stall and began murmuring reassuringly to the horse.

"Don't you ever stop complaining?" he countered in the same low, angry tone. "We're not going on a bloody picnic along the river. For a journey like this a side-saddle is not only uncomfortable but damned dangerous. Now, just for once in your life, you can do something useful and throw some straw over that blood."

He expected her to refuse. She could see it in the mocking challenge in his eyes, the arrogant tilt to his head. Nell tipped her own chin up and wheeled about. She'd defy him to find even one drop of blood when she was finished, she vowed passionately, kicking furiously at the straw. A nervous grumble from the stallion's stall had her going about the business more quietly.

Males! Human or equine, they were all the same. Dangerous, threatening and violent. Using intimidation to get their own way. Clearly there was no justice in a world where a woman needed one of the brutes to protect her from all the rest.

"Are you done?" Beaudene took the candle from her and cast an all-seeing eye over the straw-covered floor. "Go and wait by the horses, but stay clear of Samson."

Don't bother telling me I did a good job, Nell fumed

silently, sending a rebellious glare after Beaudene as he replaced the candle on its shelf. She took a few steps after him and found herself trading stares with the huge bay. "Samson," she murmured, hoping the animal wouldn't take it into his head to move. One well-aimed kick from those big hooves and she'd be as insensible as even Beaudene could wish.

"You can forget the charm." The hard words came from somewhere in the shadows. "You won't find Samson as susceptible as his namesake."

"Especially if he takes after his master," Nell muttered beneath her breath. She would have liked to have said the words loud, but didn't quite have the courage. Instead, she looked across at Chevette, still watching the proceedings with interest, and impulsively crossed the passage to put her arms about the mare's neck. At that moment it seemed the little horse was her only ally, her only comfort in a world that was suddenly full of danger. Her throat tightened convulsively on a wave of emotion.

"Farewell, little friend," she whispered, pressing her cheek hard against the palfrey's mane to stifle the tears that sprang into her eyes. "Be safe."

Uncomfortably aware of Beaudene's presence, Nell waited until she was sure all traces of tears had been blinked away before stepping back. She needn't have worried. At the same moment the stable was plunged into total darkness.

"Don't panic," he said, right beside her. Nell felt his hands circle her waist. He turned her towards the horses.

"What are you doing?" she quavered, unnerved all over again by his closeness in the impenetrable blackness surrounding them. She had thought dancing with him made her feel small and vulnerable, but this—

standing alone with him in the dark—was ten times worse. With the loss of sight, every other sense became almost painfully acute. Her heart thundered in her ears; with every ragged breath she drew she inhaled the scents of man and horse, and his hands…so hard and warm and strong. She trembled in his grasp, wanting to escape that overwhelming strength and yet fascinated by it, intrigued, wanting—

Horrified, Nell barely heard the small sound of shock that escaped her dry lips.

"I'm just going to lift you on to your horse." His voice, soft and deep, rasped over her taut nerves. "Can you reach the reins?"

For a moment Nell didn't think she could move. Then, slowly, she forced her arms upward, groping for the reins with one hand and the saddle with the other. The position made her feel even more defenceless. When Beaudene spread his fingers wider and tightened his hold she shivered violently and almost cried out.

"For God's sake, relax," he snarled in her ear. "I'm not going to drop you." An instant later he lifted her into the air with breathtaking ease.

Nell didn't know if it was instinct or desperation to have his hands off her that had her swinging her leg over the saddle, but, whatever it was, she found herself atop Rufus's back, shaken but secure.

"Are the stirrups all right?" His hand went to her ankle.

She immediately put her weight on her left foot, knowing that, to Beaudene, it would feel firmly in place. "They're perfect," she got out, only then realising that she hadn't taken a breath for what seemed like hours. The stirrups were far from perfect, but if he touched her again Nell knew she would probably fall right off the horse.

He moved away and she went limp with relief, grateful now for the lack of light. If he had seen the way she was blushing and trembling, her humiliation would have been complete.

A second later a faint lightening of the gloom told her he'd opened one of the big double doors.

"I'm going to lead the horses out through the postern," he said barely above a whisper. "Once we're in the woods we'll be away clear. Until then, not a sound."

Apparently taking her obedience for granted, he led the horses through the narrow opening, turned back momentarily to close the door, then faded into the shadows against the bailey wall, leading Samson. Rufus followed the other horse instinctively, their hoofbeats muffled in the long grass.

They were going to get away with it, Nell realised, as the postern gate loomed up beside her. It was locked, but that little circumstance presented no problems to Beaudene. And there were no guards posted here. Why would there be when, with the final destruction of Lancastrian hopes, there was no longer any danger of siege? The gate closed behind them as soundlessly as the stable door. A few minutes later, the dark of night gave way to the deeper blackness of the woods.

"We'll keep to the trees for a mile or so than rejoin the road," Beaudene said quietly as he mounted. "Stay close by me, Lady Eleanor. 'Tis easy to become lost without moonlight, and if I'm put to the trouble of searching for you, you'll find that saddle damned uncomfortable to sit in for the next few days."

Nell didn't bother to answer. Maybe she was becoming immune to his threats, she thought broodingly. Or maybe there were too many other things for her to worry about, like deciding whether she was relieved or apprehensive that no one had noticed their escape.

The question was still occupying her mind when the rain started again.

Chapter Three

Three hours passed in a silence broken only by the sounds of rain and swiftly travelling horses. Rafe told himself he should be grateful that he wasn't having to listen to a barrage of complaints, but some perverse whim made him want to goad his charge out of her sulks. Fortunately, disgust at his own contrariness kept him quiet. She was a duty, an obligation, nothing more.

He grimaced into the darkness. He might be annoyingly perverse where Lady Eleanor fitzWarren was concerned, but he hadn't started lying to himself. He had no obligation to her, and even less to her father. There were other reasons why he was riding along a dark road on a filthy night when he could be in a warm bed catching up on some overdue sleep. And, of course, the scene he'd walked into in the stable could hardly have been ignored, even if the little idiot had brought the danger on herself.

Rafe frowned and cast a glance at his silent companion. She had dropped back a little, but not enough to draw a comment from him. Had she really considered all those incidents she'd described to be genuine accidents? Taken alone, such a conclusion might be excusable, but together? She would have to be a complete innocent, or a simpleton, and he had already decided that Lady Eleanor fitzWarren was neither of those things.

The irony of the situation caused a grim smile to twist his mouth. The fact that she was neither innocent nor simple made everything very straightforward or very complicated, depending on which way you looked at it. And if he had any sense at all, he'd look at it the way he usually faced his problems. Head-on.

He wanted her. Badly. Despite everything else.

Or perhaps as well as everything else.

He hadn't expected it. He most definitely did not like it. But he couldn't ignore the fierce surge of desire she aroused in him whenever they touched. Touched! God, it seemed he only had to be near her.

The memory of the soft fragility of her body between his hands when he'd held her in the darkness of the stable had his fingers clenching on the reins. Only the need to get her away had stopped him sliding his hands higher, until he could close them over the sweetly rounded breasts half-exposed by her gown. A sight that had tormented him since he'd first seen her in the hall, weaving her spells. Definitely no innocent.

And she didn't want marriage.

So why not take her? And, in the process, he could even take what else was owing to him. The perfect revenge, he thought with a cold, silent laugh. Take from the daughter what the father had cheated him out of years ago. Take and give nothing in return, except the payment expected by a courtesan for the use of her body. Set her up in her chosen vocation. A swift, savage grin slashed across his face at the idea. She wanted

to be a mistress rather than a wife? Then, why not make
it so? And don't think about the rest of it.

Nell didn't want to think at all. Unfortunately, her
mind wouldn't co-operate with her inclinations. Strange
images kept dancing in her brain, making her wonder
if she was becoming delirious from the cold and wet.

Wasn't hell supposed to be a fiery place of torment,
where demons persecuted their victims with pitchforks?
After hours of hard riding, Nell knew better. Hell was
a dark, endless tunnel through a forest of moaning, rus-
tling spectres, whose weapons were stinging needles of
rain. It was chafed, aching thighs whose cramped muscles had to grip the saddle with no respite because the
stirrups were too low to support some of her weight.
And it was a confused, frightened mind that was beginning to question the wisdom of trusting Beaudene.

What sort of bodyguard forced a lady to travel in
these appalling conditions, just because *he* said she was
in danger? Why was she supposed to take *his* word for
everything? What would he say if she accused *him* of
trying to kill her, rather than Tom? Because at this rate
she would be dead of lung fever before her supposedly
murderous cousin crawled from his warm, comfortable
bed in the morning.

Nell shivered violently as a sudden gust of wind
whipped at an overhanging branch, spraying water all
over her. Not that it mattered. She was already soaked
to the skin. Her full skirts, with their ermine edging,
felt like dead weights hanging from her waist, the same
fur trim around her bodice was plastered to her chilled
flesh, her headdress dragged at its pins, making her
head throb, and the pretty silver tissue veil was a sod-
den rag that slapped against her neck with every movement of her horse.

Even if she survived this hideous nightmare, what was she supposed to change into when the rain stopped? If it ever did. She had nothing but what she stood up in. No clothes. No maid. No—

Her maid! Mother of God, why hadn't she thought of that before? She wouldn't have been alone with Tom and his men. Lucy would have travelled with her and they'd intended to sleep at religious hostels or respectable inns along the way. Instead, she was completely at the mercy of a man who was bigger than her, stronger than her, who had already threatened her with violence, who had killed a man without a single question or qualm, who—

The list stopped abruptly as Nell's heart jolted sickeningly in her chest. Other pictures flashed through her mind. Pictures that chilled the blood in her veins even as the rain chilled her flesh. She had seen no one speak to Beaudene in the hall before she'd collided with him. She had not seen her aunt or uncle acknowledge him. He had simply appeared. She knew nothing about him—except that he was arrogant, ruthless, that he killed without any sign of emotion, and considered her a loose woman.

And, God have mercy on her, she only had Beaudene's word that he had come from her father!

That last frightening realisation had Nell tugging frantically on the reins. She was not going another inch until she got some answers. And if she didn't like those answers, she would run. Away from the road where the darkness would hide her. Even a night in the forest would be preferable to stepping into the terrifying pit of danger yawning at her feet.

As if he knew the instant she stopped and why, Beaudene reined in and wheeled his horse about in the same motion. His voice was a whiplash, cracking with command. "We ride until I say stop, my lady, and that isn't here or now."

Nell leaned forward over the saddle, trying to ease her aching thighs. "Please," she whispered, her cold lips scarcely able to form the words, "I need to alter the stirrups."

She didn't care that he would know she'd been lying earlier. She didn't care if she begged. She had to get off the horse.

After an almost imperceptible pause, Beaudene nodded and dismounted. "A few minutes, no more," he said.

Nell didn't wait for him to offer any assistance. Letting herself fall against Rufus's neck, she forced her leg over the saddle and slid to the ground. Her legs almost gave way under her when she landed.

Tears of pain and weariness burned her eyes. How was she going to run away? She could barely stand. Her legs ached and quivered with strain, and the soft flesh of her inner thighs was sore and burning from contact with the hard leather of her saddle. She let her weight rest against Rufus for a moment, trying to gather enough strength to move, but the wind snatched at her veil, slapping it against the horse's flank. Rufus snorted and shied away in alarm, nearly pulling her off her feet.

"For God's sake!" Beaudene grabbed the horse's bridle with one hand and Nell with the other, while she made a futile attempt to control the veil, which had now wrapped itself soggily around her throat. "Get rid of the bloody thing, unless you want to travel the rest of the way on foot."

"Rufus isn't nervous," Nell muttered. "It just startled him for a moment. He's used to more elaborate headdresses than this.''

"Nobody could get used to such a piece of useless idiocy,'' Beaudene growled, tying the reins to a tree. He came back to Nell and started pulling pins out of her hair. In the fitful moonlight that had emerged to chase the clouds across the sky, she could see the narrowed glitter of his eyes and the hard, set line of his mouth. The combination was enough to keep her from protesting, until he ripped the veil from its moorings and tossed the limp remains of her headdress into a pile of leaves.

"What do you think you're doing?'' she demanded, lifting her hands to stop her hair from tumbling over her shoulders. "I can't ride with my hair blowing every which way.''

"Turn around.''

"Not until I know—''

"*Turn around*!''

Nell turned. She felt Beaudene's hands wring some of the wetness out of her hair, then he gathered the heavy tresses into a thick fall and used the length of silver tissue to tie it at the nape of her neck. Nell tried not to feel grateful. The relief to her aching head was wonderful, but that was no reason to trust him. An action prompted more by practicality than kindness didn't furnish any proof of Beaudene's story.

"What's amiss with your stirrups?'' he asked curtly as he stepped away.

"They need to be raised a notch.'' Nell stayed where she was, keeping some distance between them. Now, she told herself. Ask your questions now. But she wasn't quite sure where to start. With her father? With Beaudene's arrival? With his insistence that she was in danger from the relatives who had housed, fed and clothed her for ten years? Perhaps she should just vanish into the darkness without worrying about questions to which she might or might not receive truthful answers.

"You'll get chilled standing there," he said over his shoulder, before she could decide. "Walk around a bit. Keep warm."

"I wasn't warm to start with," she retorted. But she began walking up and down, stumbling at first when her stiff muscles protested at the exercise. Unfortunately her brain wasn't recovering as easily. All she seemed able to think about was how cold and wet and miserable she was.

"You'll live," was Beaudene's unsympathetic response. "'Tis September. You're not likely to freeze to death because of a few drops of rain."

Nell stopped her pacing and glared at him. "It's been raining for hours," she pointed out, ignoring the fact that the rain had now stopped. "That's more than a few drops."

Beaudene walked around to Rufus's other side. "Well, if we reach the place I have in mind before dawn, we'll be able to light a fire. I've a mantle in my pack you can wear while your gown is drying."

The deeper implications in this statement went right over Nell's head for the moment. "You mean you've had a mantle in your pack all this time, and you made me ride through that downpour until I was wet to the skin?" she cried in outrage. "How could you?"

"It was amazingly easy," he purred, coming around Rufus to stalk towards her. There was so much menace in his slow advance that Nell started to retreat. "I decided you'd prefer to have something dry to wear when you have to strip off that gown, but if you'd rather run around stark naked, my lady, I can—''

''I wouldn't,'' said Nell hurriedly. She backed into a tree and had to stop.

Beaudene didn't even hesitate. He kept walking until he was looming right over her, crowding her against the tree and forcing her to tip her head right back so she could still glare at him.

''You're trying to frighten me,'' she accused. *Trying*! He was succeeding. She could hardly breathe with the way her heart was beating in her throat, but she would die before she humiliated herself by letting Beaudene know the effect his nearness was having on her. ''But it won't work. I don't frighten easily.''

His teeth gleamed in a brief, dangerous smile. ''You don't back down, either. I'll say that for you, my lady. Not even when you were facing that knife.''

''Backing down wouldn't have saved me then, any more than it will now.''

He leaned one hand against the tree beside her head and his voice lowered to a lazy growl. ''Now? Judging by the way you're walking, I'd say you've been punished already for lying to me about those stirrups. What more do you think I'm going to do to you?''

Nell shivered. ''How can I answer that? I don't know anything about you.''

''That's true, but 'tis no cause for alarm. You'll have plenty of time to learn.'' His free hand lifted to brush back a damp tendril of hair that had escaped his earlier ministrations. ''I think we'll both learn something over the next few days.''

''What I want to know will only take the next few minutes,'' she choked out through suddenly dry lips. She had the strangest feeling they were having two sep-

arate conversations, one of which was somewhere beyond her comprehension.

"Minutes? Have all the men in your life rushed you,
little temptress? Do you tease and tantalise until they're
so wild to have you, they care nothing for your pleasure? Is that how you control them?"

"What has that to do with anything?" Nell cried,
thoroughly confused. She forced the next words out in
a breathless rush before she lost her courage. "All I
know is that you appeared in the stables at a very op-
portune time, killed a man without bothering to ask him
why he was there, and dragged me away from my family. And I want to know why."

Beaudene drew back a little. In the intermittent
moonlight Nell could see that the faintly mocking smile
on his face had been replaced by a frown. "You know
why."

"No, I don't," she denied heatedly. "You said you
came from my father, but how do I know that? And
that man… You *killed* him! You just killed him as if
it meant nothing."

"Would you rather he'd killed you, while I stood
there debating the issue with my conscience?"

"That isn't what I… How can you be so sure he was
a hired assassin? How—?"

"Because I knew him, damn it!"

Nell went very, very still. "You knew him?"

"God's blood! We don't have time for this." His
long fingers closed around her arm. "You can trust me
or not, as you please, Lady Eleanor, but you're getting
back on that horse."

"Or what? You'll knock me senseless?" Nell heard
the rising note of hysteria shatter the night-time quiet,
but couldn't control it. Every nerve was screaming a

warning at her. She was in danger from this man. If she knew nothing else, that fact was absolutely certain. "How do I know that's not what you intend doing at some other time? How do I know you didn't plan all this...that you...that you didn't hire that man yourself so you could frighten me into going with you?"

The annoyance in his eyes exploded into searing rage. "My God, if I hadn't promised the King I'd see you safe home, I'd damn well leave you to your cousin's mercies."

"The King?" she stammered. "What—?"

"Shut up, or, by God, I *will* knock you senseless. Now, move!" He jerked her away from the tree as he spoke.

Nell screamed as pain shot across the back of her head. The sound pulled Beaudene up short.

"What the—?"

"My hair," she whimpered, not caring about the tears that rushed to her eyes. At that moment nothing else mattered except freeing herself. "'Tis caught...on the bark."

"God Almighty!"

"'Tis not my fault," she said faintly, reviving the instant he pushed her back and the pressure eased.

"Just keep still, and that goes for your damned reckless tongue as well."

The warning was unnecessary. The instant Beaudene's grip left her arm, Nell forgot about talking. He stepped to the side, the better to release her hair from its entanglement. She tensed, expecting pain, but his fingers moved with surprising gentleness against her damp scalp, sending tingling ripples of warmth down her neck, across her shoulders... She almost arched her back like a cat waiting to be stroked.

She went rigid with shock, struggling to push the alarmingly delicious sensations aside. They were part of the danger, part of the reason why she had to escape. And she could run...*now*...while it was still dark and she was only a few hours from home. There might not be another chance. God knew where Beaudene might take her, and she would have to follow blindly, not knowing where she was, not knowing what he intended. He had mentioned the King. Nell remembered her only encounter with the tall, handsome victor of the fight between York and Lancaster. The memory was three years old, but still she shuddered. That was when she had vowed never to become any man's possession.

"Turn your head a little." The command came, disturbingly soft and husky, out of the darkness.

Nell obeyed. She was almost free. She could feel it. Another second and—

She ran. Strands of hair caught...tore free...making her eyes water and momentarily blinding her, but she ran, unheeding of the smarting pain. And, almost immediately, she knew it was futile. Her clothes, heavy with dampness, weighed her down. The ground, made treacherous with wet leaves and hidden roots, caused her to stumble before she had taken more than a dozen steps. Fear, wild and desperate, forced her on, but it was already too late.

Beaudene closed the distance between them as if it was nothing, his arms catching her about the waist as he took them both to the ground in a low tackle. He turned as they fell, cushioning Nell from the worst of the impact. Then, before she could recover, before she could even catch her breath, he rolled, pinning her beneath the suffocating weight of his body.

Nell fought back with every ounce of energy left in

her. She twisted frantically, tried to get her legs free, tried to lash out with her hands, but he was too big, too strong. He spread his legs, clamping hers between them. His hands snapped around her wrists like manacles, forcing her hands down to the ground on either side of her head. His weight settled more deeply into her lower body in a ruthless demonstration of sheer masculine dominance.

A scream of pure helplessness tore through Nell, only to emerge as a choked cry that was barely audible. Her breasts heaved as she struggled to drag more air into her lungs. The hidden crucifix, displaced by her writhing, dug painfully into her back.

"You can't win, so stop fighting me," Beaudene ordered, glaring down at her.

He wasn't even breathing hard, she noticed, almost sobbing as her own breath came back in ragged gasps. "Let...me...go!"

"When I think you've regained what little sense you had."

"How can I?" she cried. "When you're... you're—" She broke off, paralysed with shock, as a cascade of piercing awareness poured through her from her head to her toes. He was covering her everywhere, his powerful shoulders blocking out the moonlight, his long limbs rigid bands of muscle controlling her without effort. She couldn't move so much as an inch. His size and strength were terrifying, and yet—he wasn't hurting her. He was warm and heavy and—

Shuddering, shaken to the depths of her being, Nell stared up at the hard face above her. "Please," she whispered.

For a nerve-stretching minute she felt as though even

her heart had ceased beating. Then, very slowly, his
eyes never leaving hers, Beaudene released her wrists,
flattened his hands on the ground and lifted himself
away, hunkering back on his heels beside her.

"Just where," he began, much too quietly, "did you
think you were going?"

Nell slithered back a few inches before pushing herself up on one elbow. She was trying to think of something to say that wouldn't enrage him further when she
saw his eyes lower, and become suddenly, fiercely, intent.

Startled, she glanced down and felt her breathing
stop. The low-cut bodice of her gown had been
wrenched from the wide belt at her waist during her
struggle with Beaudene, and now hung loosely from
her shoulders, exposing one pale, rose-tipped breast.
Unable to move, terrified of what she would see, Nell
looked back at him.

In the moonlight his face was a primitive mask of
desire, his eyes narrowed to glittering slits as he stared
at her. Tension was an almost palpable force, vibrating
in the air between them. His? Hers? She didn't know,
could only feel. When he reached out a hand towards
her, Nell shrank, a thin, high sound of fear escaping
her lips. The sound of a trapped creature in the presence
of the hunter; motionless, waiting, hovering on the edge
of panic.

She saw his gaze lift to her face, the golden eyes
burning into hers before they widened suddenly, becoming arrested. He frowned, the intensity in him
changing as he registered her panic-stricken expression.

"Be easy," he said, very low. "I'm not going to
hurt you."

She didn't believe him. "If you lay one finger on

me, I'll kill you,'' she whispered. "I swear, somehow, some day, I'll kill you.''

He was still for a moment, watching her, then he moved. His hand flashed out with the same lethal speed she had seen in the hall, capturing her free arm and immobilising her. Nell went rigid, bracing herself to resist the shove that would put her flat on the ground again. He raised his other hand, his gaze lowering once more to her breast, and very gently, very carefully, pulled her bodice back into place over her shoulder. His knuckles lingered, brushing her skin in a feather-light caress before withdrawing.

''Like I said,'' he drawled softly, ''you don't back down, my lady.'' He got to his feet with a quick lithe movement and reached down to pull her upright. ''Shall we go?''

Nell nodded mutely. At that moment she was so stunned, she would have agreed to anything. She allowed herself to be led over to the horses and was again lifted into the saddle. Beaudene checked both stirrups before mounting Samson.

''This time,'' he said, reaching for Rufus's bridle to bring her horse alongside his, ''if you want to be able to walk when we stop, push your skirts between your backside and the saddle.''

The night crawled with increasing reluctance towards dawn. Beaudene kept the horses to a steady pace that ate up the miles without exhausting the animals. Occasionally, when a small hamlet or manor loomed up ahead, he would detour into the forest. Once he dismounted to lead the horses separately over a footbridge spanning a narrow river, keeping to the grassy verge so any wakeful inhabitants of the nearby village would hear nothing.

Nell scarcely noticed their route. Indeed, so stiff and weary was she that they could have ridden through London itself without arousing a flicker of interest in her. And she had long since ceased trying to fathom the reasons for Beaudene's actions, apart from dispelling any illusions that her threat to kill him had had an effect. It was a wonder he hadn't laughed in her face.

She stared numbly at the straight figure riding easily in front of her and decided the most obvious answer was the correct one. Right now he didn't have time for dalliance. And, right now, she was simply too tired to worry about later. Her head drooped, she was chilled to the bone, and every muscle ached. Wistful visions of a cosy inn and a warm bed began to flit tantalisingly through her mind. All in all, it had been an exhausting night.

"Ahh."

The short, satisfied exclamation brought Nell's head up. They were deep in the forest. Somewhere along the way, Beaudene must have led them away from the road again, for here the trees were so dense the moonlight scarcely penetrated the branches overhead. Rufus slithered down a steep bank of earth, following Samson, and Nell had to grab hold of the saddle to keep her seat. When they reached the bottom, Beaudene had already dismounted, and was leading Samson along the base of the embankment. He stopped when they'd gone about a hundred yards and began carefully moving branches aside.

Nell peered about her. Halfway up the embankment the exposed roots of an ancient beech, which had been blasted by lightning during some long-forgotten storm and now lay on its side, jutted out over a pile of rocks, hiding the entrance to what looked like a deep depression in the earth. Nell wasn't quite sure if she was looking at a hollow or a cave, but she was sure of one thing. It wasn't an inn. Suddenly, Beaudene's earlier remark about lighting a fire returned with ominous clarity.

"Why are we stopping here?" she queried, her voice husky with weariness.

"Because I haven't had any sleep in three days and there won't be much of it in the next three. A few hours now, before the hue and cry starts, may be all we'll get."

"You expect me to sleep *here*? What's wrong with an inn? Not even a peasant would—"

She stopped abruptly when he strode over to her. "For the last time, Lady Eleanor, this is not a pleasant jaunt around the countryside. Unless you want to leave a trail that a blind beggar could follow, you'll forget about inns, soft beds and warm food for the duration of this entire journey. Now, get yourself off that horse and gather something for a fire while I go back and wipe out the tracks we made when we left the road."

He was gone before Nell could gather enough breath to protest at the abrupt order, melting into the silent darkness of the wood.

She sighed and managed to slither off Rufus in an even less graceful fashion than before. "Well, 'tis just you and me," she muttered to the horse, clinging to his neck while she waited for her legs to take her weight. The circulation returned slowly and painfully. A few yards away, Samson snorted softly.

"Aye, and that great brute, too," she added. "What am I supposed to do with the pair of you? Brush you down? Water you? Did he think of you when he decided we're going to live like animals in a cave? Gather firewood, he says. How am I supposed to gather firewood when I can't see?''

Moving gingerly, she crouched down to run her hands over the ground. The light covering of leaves was slightly damp, but the sheltering trees had prevented the worst of the rain from reaching any twigs and small branches underneath. Still muttering, Nell began to build a small pile near the black entrance to their sleeping place.

''He needn't think I'm going in there on my own. I'd rather sleep in the open. How does he know there isn't a whole pack of wolves waiting to—?''

''Because I've used this place before.''

The soft, faintly menacing tone came from right behind her. Nell shrieked and leapt to her feet, spinning around so fast she nearly lost her balance.

''What do you think you're doing, sneaking up on me like that?'' she yelled. ''You frightened me out of my wits.''

''What wits?'' Beaudene retorted. ''With the noise you were making, both the Yorkist and Lancastrian armies could have marched past without you noticing. What's all this stuff?'' His booted toe pushed at her collection of bracken and twigs.

Nell opened her mouth to argue further and then decided it wasn't worth it. The possibility of warmth was too alluring. '''Tis for the fire you wanted.''

''God's teeth, woman, what kind of fire is that going to make? Couldn't you have found something bigger?''

She gritted her own teeth. ''We aren't all used to creeping around in the dark and living in caves. If you can do better, go ahead. And while we're on the subject, what about the horses? They're wet, too, you know.''

There was an odd little silence. Nell could feel him watching her, although how he could see anything of her except a vague shadow, she had no idea.

''The horses will be all right once I've rubbed them down,'' he said at last. ''Go inside. You can't tell in the dark, but there's plenty of room and 'tis dry. Just put your left hand on the wall, walk straight ahead about twenty paces and wait for me.''

''To be attacked by rats or spiders? I'd rather step off the edge of the world.''

''And I just might give you a helping—'' He bit off the rest with a muttered oath. ''Listen very carefully, your ladyship. I can't take care of the horses, and find enough dry wood to give us a decent fire so we can dry our clothes, if I have to play nursemaid to a whining, useless, pampered little princess. Now, move!''

Nell obeyed, vowing silent vengeance every step of the way. The words ''pampered little princess'' stung, more so than when Tom had used the same phrase earlier that night. She had *not* been whining. And how dared Beaudene call her useless and pampered just because she hadn't gathered the right materials for a fire? If he was so fussy, he should have given her a list. As for the horses—

Her toe struck something hard and she made a startled sound, cursing as she remembered that she was supposed to be counting her steps.

''What is it?'' Beaudene asked at her shoulder.

Nell's heart jumped into her throat before she realised he must have followed her in. She clamped her lips shut on another frightened gasp and made a second vow. Before this was over she was going to put a stop to his habit of creeping up behind her if it was the last thing she did. "I don't know," she bit out.

She felt him pass her in the darkness, then heard the sound of flint striking stone. A tiny flame appeared, illuminating a small circular fireplace at her feet. Beaudene hunkered down beside it and scooped a pile of cold ashes into his palm. He opened his hand, letting the stuff sift through his fingers.

"Is something amiss?" Shivering, Nell wrapped her arms around herself, momentarily forgetting her grievances as she saw him frown slightly.

"Someone has been here," he answered, but absently.

"Well, I suppose if you know of it, others will also," she said reasonably, not understanding his abstraction.

He shook his head. "Once the entrance is covered the keenest-eyed hunter of the King's deer couldn't find it. Even in daylight. There is only one other man who knows of this shelter."

She considered that. "A friend?"

This time Beaudene nodded. "Once. But I haven't seen him for…a long time." Abruptly shaking off his odd mood, he bent to the task of preparing a fire. "'Tis not important."

Nell was too cold and tired to pursue the matter, but, curious now, she looked around, blinking a little as the light grew stronger.

It wasn't a cave, she saw, but a small square chamber at the end of the narrow corridor they had traversed. Rocks had been piled atop each other around the perimeter of the room to form surprisingly even walls, and the floor was of beaten earth. The air was still and musty but not unpleasant, what little smoke there was from the fire drifting upwards to vanish into the darkness above her. "What is this place?" she asked wonderingly.

Beaudene glanced up from the fire and shrugged. "Some sort of ancient burial mound, I think, judging by the bones in the side chambers. Roman, maybe. Who knows?"

"Bones?" Nell peered into the shadows beyond the fire and hurriedly crossed herself. "Sweet Jesu, we can't sleep with a whole lot of corpses. 'Tis... 'tis...indecent."

"'Tis also damn wet outside, but suit yourself." He stood up and went back to the entrance where the horses waited.

Obviously he couldn't care less where she spent the rest of the night, Nell thought indignantly. She decided not to complain any further about the bones, however. She had far too many other things on her mind. And besides, if they were Roman bones perhaps it wasn't quite so bad. They'd been pagans, hadn't they?

Stifling a groan as her muscles protested, she sat down by the small fire, rubbing some feeling back into her cold hands. When Beaudene returned with their saddles and his packs, some of the chill had left her flesh, and the fur across her breasts was beginning to dry in small, matted peaks. She watched in weary silence as he placed the saddles on the other side of the fire and tossed the leather bags down beside them.

"Don't just sit there waiting for me to turn into a tiring-woman," he grated, throwing her an impatient glance. "Get out of those wet clothes."

Nell got slowly to her feet, somehow dredging up enough energy to demand a little privacy. "When you have the courtesy to wait outside."

"Not a chance, your ladyship. In case it's escaped

your notice, I'm as wet as you are, and the fire's in here." He undid his belt as he spoke, dropped it to the ground, then stripped off his surcoat to reveal an unexpectedly fine linen undershirt beneath. The shirt wasn't as wet as the surcoat, but it was still damp enough to cling to an intimidating expanse of chest, revealing the hard muscles of his shoulders and a disturbingly primitive-looking pelt of dark hair.

Nell's mouth went dry.

"Besides, 'tis a little late for modesty, isn't it?" he added, slanting a mocking glance up at her as he pulled off a water-logged boot. "I've already seen your charms." He grinned suddenly. "Well, one of them."

A tide of heat swept over Nell's face to her hairline. "A remark typical of an uncouth bodyguard," she flashed, telling herself that the fluttering in her stomach was due to embarrassment and not that unexpectedly wicked, very male grin. "And you wonder why I'm not willing to throw off my gown while you stand there mocking me!"

The second boot hit the ground. "You'll not only throw off your gown, princess, but everything else as well," he stated, turning away to pick up one of the packs. "If you sicken on this journey because you were stubborn enough to sleep in wet clothes, you'll be nothing but a damned nuisance. Now strip, or I'll do it for you."

"When men fly!"

Beaudene's head whipped around. His face was in shadow, but when he straightened slowly and set the pack down implacable determination was evident in every line of his body. Then he took a few steps forward to pin her gaze across the firelight, and Nell wondered how eyes the colour of amber could look so frigidly cold.

"I intend to get some sleep," he began very softly. "If you have a tithe the sense God gave you, you'll do the same. 'Twill be easier on you if you're warm and dry, and 'twill be easier on me if I don't have to worry about you running off. There's only one way to ensure that, little princess, and I'm big enough and mean enough to enforce it." His tone became even softer, as dark and still as the night. "Take off your clothes."

Chapter Four

The musty air in the chamber seemed to thicken, to catch in her throat, making it difficult to breathe. Across the fire Beaudene waited—the hunter, big and powerful, his eyes intent on hers. He meant every word, Nell realised. He had given her a direct order and he intended to be obeyed.

She stepped back a pace, shaking her head. "I'll take off my gown to dry it," she said huskily. "But nothing else. I'm not here for your amusement—and you know that."

One eyebrow quirked. "I'm supposed to know that because you panicked when you weren't in control earlier? The trouble with you, Lady Eleanor, is that the men in your life have been blinded by lust, slaves to their desire and therefore slaves to you, obedient to your hand on the reins."

"And you're not, I take it?" The reckless challenge was out before Nell could put a guard on her unruly tongue. But she couldn't stay silent under the lash of his scorn. It hurt. It hurt her more than she cared to admit, and instinct bade her strike back, blindly, before she weighed the risks.

"I won't be your slave," he agreed softly. His eyes glinted in a sudden flare of sparks from the fire, and Nell shivered at what had been left unsaid.

"You won't be my anything," she retorted. Unable to hold his gaze, she turned away under the pretence of unlacing her belt, striving for a show of unconcern. "Fortunately, that is one of the advantages of being one's own mistress instead of some man's wife," she tossed back over her shoulder. "A lady may choose her lovers, and I don't take mine from the ranks of body-guards."

Holy Mother of God, had she really said that? She who had never had a lover in her life was speaking as if they were legion.

"And if a would-be lover does not abide by your choice, my lady? If he decides to take you, regardless? What then?"

Nell's fingers stilled on her laces. Laugh it off, she ordered herself desperately. Laugh it off, before he sees the fear in your face, hears it in your voice. He's only a man. A man like all the others you've known.

But—sweet Lord—why was it so hard to dismiss what he said? Why was it so difficult to treat him with the carefully calculated evasiveness she had used with men since that dreadful night three years ago. Beaudene was right. They had been easy to dismiss, easy to control; each one left with the impression that, for the moment at least, she belonged to another and they would have to wait their turn.

It had been an act that had become almost second nature to her, and so well did she play the game of manipulation that only her cousin Tom, who had lived in the same house for years, had guessed the truth.

Guessed, and kept her secret, because he wanted her for himself, wanted to be the first.

And wanted her inheritance, Nell thought cynically. And as long as her game remained just that, as long as her suitors had been kept at a distance, unsure of the identity of her lover but convinced there was one, she had been safe.

Until now. Until that moment in the hall when, instead of dismissing Beaudene's insults with a careless shrug and a laugh, and then forgetting him, she had responded instinctively—as herself.

Nell looked down at her hands and saw them clenched, white-knuckled, clutching her bodice. Very deliberately she relaxed them before she turned to meet the intent, watchful eyes of the one man who had changed the rules of the game on her.

"Do you speak of yourself, sir?" she asked with feigned nonchalance. "I think not. No matter who employed you, 'twould impugn your honour to force me."

He was silent for a moment, then a slow smile of amused appreciation curved his mouth and the waiting tension seemed to leave his body. "You, my Lady Eleanor, are a worthy opponent," he informed her. "You're right. If I come from a concerned father, 'twould be an act of the most foul to betray his trust, and if I don't—" He paused and the smile turned rueful. "Well, you've just put your own trust in my honour, little princess. Only a conscienceless villain, or a fool, would use force against you in those circumstances."

"And you're no fool?" She watched him warily as he retrieved the abandoned pack and loosened its cords. He extracted a long woollen mantle of a blue so dark that it was almost black, and walked around the fire to look down at her. There were barely two paces between them.

"No," he agreed. "Nor am I conscienceless. But remember, my lady, there is more than one alternative to force, and villainy must be redressed."

"You speak in riddles," she said with a light laugh. "Are you threatening to seduce me? Surely not. You prefer not to be one of a crowd, as I recall."

"The crowd no longer surrounds you, Lady Eleanor. You stand alone. With me."

A cold ripple of dread uncurled in the pit of Nell's stomach. That Beaudene was so aware of her utter vulnerability to him made it worse, somehow. But what had she expected? she asked herself wildly. That he wouldn't notice how completely she was at his mercy? That the only weapon she could pit against his male strength was her woman's wiles?

"That makes little difference," she said, almost whispering. The effort of maintaining her cool demeanour was stripping her nerves raw, but if wit was her only defence she had to use it. Think! Reason! The men she had known hadn't cared how many lovers a woman had taken, but she thought this man would. The game was the same, she assured herself. Only the rules had changed. The realisation lent more strength to her voice.

"The crowd still exists," she pointed out. "Whether now, or in the past. As for the future, well, in sooth, bodyguards are not to my taste. That being so, instead of trying to scare me with meaningless threats, you would do better to give me that mantle so I may obey your command to remove this wet gown."

His eyes narrowed. "Why don't you just breathe

in?'' he demanded. ''And let the damn thing remove itself. Another inch should do it.''

Nell's overwrought nerves snapped. ''Why don't you stop baiting me?'' she cried, forgetting games and strategy as temper and weariness got the better of her. ''And stop leaping to conclusions while you're at it. Margaret slashed my own gown to ribbons in a fit of spite while I was bathing, and the rest were already packed away, so I had to borrow this one. And if you had the least notion of colour and fashion, Sir Rafe, instead of being an ignorant clod, you'd have known this gown was made for a blonde and not for me.''

The instant those last furious words left her mouth, Nell was wishing them unsaid. Beaudene's eyes focused on her body like a hawk sighting prey, bathing her in golden fire. She felt as if he was stripping her, as if the heat of his gaze could peel the clothes from her body one by one, leaving her naked and defenceless.

''Men don't care what colour the gown is, princess. They only see the body inside it—'' the searing fire stroked across her breasts ''—or mostly out of it, in this case. And before we go any further, 'tis Lord Beaudene.''

''Is it? Well, I'll call you 'my lord', if you stop calling me horrible names.'' Her voice wobbled desperately and the words sounded childish in the extreme, but Nell was beyond caring. She had never felt so strange. Hot and shivering at one and the same time, her breasts flushed and heavy, her nipples tingling and unbearably sensitive against the cool fabric of her gown. Not only was Beaudene playing games with her mind, he was manipulating her body as well. Without touching her!

Even when his gaze lifted to her face, the strange sensations didn't abate. She wondered how much longer her trembling legs would support her!

"You don't like 'princess'? How about 'temptress', then? 'Seductress'? 'Siren'? 'Delilah'? They suit you better than prim and proper Lady Eleanor, but—"

"Nell," she got out, unable to say more.

The single syllable had a wholly unexpected effect. The sardonic curve of his mouth softened and he tilted his head slightly, as though considering. "Nell," he repeated slowly.

As if he was tasting her name on his tongue, she thought dazedly. And another ripple of sensation feathered across her over-heated flesh at the sound of her name spoken in that dark, gravelly voice.

Then he raised a brow, mocking again. "So, what colour was the gown you were going to wear, my lady Nell? Scarlet?"

"Heaven save me. A man of humour," she muttered. "No doubt you'll be astonished to hear 'twas green and gold." And one of her favourites. Tiredness washed over her suddenly, wave after wave of fatigue breaking over her, as the events of the last day and night took their toll. She was simply too weary to fight him any more. Too weary to care what he said.

"What does it matter?" she asked bitterly, almost of herself. "Think what you like of me. You speak of honour so glibly, *Lord* Beaudene, but, bodyguard or baron, you're no better than—"

"*Don't say it!*" The snarled words slashed through the air towards her, shattering Nell's apathy. The sudden impact of emotion was stunning. Sheer unadulterated rage blazed from his eyes. For one fleeting, heart-stopping second, Nell thought Beaudene might actually strike her. Violence seemed to fill the small chamber, reaching for her, beating at her with invisible, rushing wings. She almost cried out from the fierceness of it.

Then the threat was gone. As abruptly as it had flared, the savagery in his eyes went from molten gold to frozen amber in seconds, and his taut muscles unlocked. He gave a short laugh, lifted the mantle in a mock salute and tossed it to her.

"You can trust me not to use force against you in one respect," he growled softly. "But don't push me too far, princess."

He turned away, snatched up his boots, and strode towards the dark corridor without looking back. "You've got three minutes."

Nell stayed absolutely still, clutching the cloak to her as she would a shield. Trust him? How could she trust him? He had not struck her—in truth his control seemed formidable—but that hardly reassured her. He had killed a man before her very eyes while remaining totally in control. Somehow the memory of that cool, contained violence was more frightening than an outburst of rage. And, having seen Beaudene rein in both desire and anger, how could she help but wonder just what it would take to make him unleash the full force of his emotions? And what would happen if he ever did?

She shivered at the thought. Trust him? She had once trusted another man, a man whose word should have been inviolate, and she had discovered just how much force men were prepared to use against women to have their way. Trust was for fools.

And yet...

Beaudene had held her helpless beneath him on the

road and had not so much as touched her intimately. On the contrary, he had covered her nakedness with a care that had left her speechless and shaken. And, earlier, he had gone out of his way to defend a serving-girl who meant nothing to him.

A log on the fire crackled, sending sparks flying upward, and Nell jumped, suddenly aware that she was wasting precious time. There was one thing she could count on, she thought. If Beaudene had said she had three minutes, that was precisely what he meant. And she needed to rest. Even if she couldn't sleep she still needed to rest before she could cope any further with a bodyguard who made veiled threats of seduction or worse.

And if sleep eluded her, then she would feign slumber if she had to act as she had never acted before.

But an act wasn't necessary. Even as she curled up in Beaudene's mantle, her hand closing protectively around the crucifix still hidden in its pouch, even as the feel of the jewel reminded her of the other, secret purpose of her journey, exhaustion claimed her. The black curtain of sleep fell over her like a second mantle, closing her eyes, stilling her mind. She didn't hear Beaudene return. Didn't know he stood over her, watching her sleep.

Which was not surprising, Rafe thought, because the three minutes had stretched to ten, during which time he had wondered, with growing irritation, if ten *hours* would have been enough to restore his control where this girl was concerned.

Why had he felt that wild surge of fury when she'd been about to question his honour? It shouldn't matter. She was simply a pawn, a means to an end, by whatever method he used. Seduction, or—

What? he asked himself silently, looking down at her. The more honourable course of marriage? Take a wanton to wife? Which she surely was. If he'd had any doubts on that score after her fear on the road, they'd been thoroughly allayed in the last hour. By the Rood, she couldn't have been more open about her lovers short of giving him a list of names!

And yet, lying here sleeping, the mysterious, seductive depths of her eyes hidden, she looked… bruised…fragile…unutterably innocent.

The other side of sin, he mused. Innocence.

And he was all kinds of fool for even thinking of innocence in connection with Lady Eleanor fitzWarren. That look of fragility was more likely caused by exhaustion.

Rafe went down on one knee beside her and noted the faint mauve shadows beneath her closed lashes, the pale translucence of her skin against the dark sable lining of his mantle. He'd pushed her hard tonight, wanting to put as many miles as possible between themselves and pursuit, so they could snatch this respite before an even harder day of riding. But she'd kept up—without complaint.

The thought drew his brows together. She had also given as good as he'd verbally served up, until that moment when she'd turned even paler and had seemed to droop right before his eyes.

"You have courage, princess," he murmured beneath his breath. "Even if you are spoiled and wanton, and damn near useless as a wife. And is it any cause for wonder, coming from that household?"

Annoyed with himself for the statement, Rafe got to his feet and yanked off his boots. God above, was he now making excuses for the wench? He strode around to the other side of the fire, dumped his boots, and was reaching for his open pack when he stopped cold.

There, lined up in a neat row between Nell and his baggage, were a pair of dainty leather shoes, a pair of silken hose, two gold ribbon garters, the sadly stained and muddied silver and blue gown, and a shift of the sheerest gossamer gauze.

His gaze flashed to Nell. She had wrapped herself so tightly that all he could see from his half-crouched position was a glimpse of chestnut hair, but—She was lying completely naked within the enfolding warmth of his mantle.

Desire ripped through him so savagely it nearly sent him to his knees. Slowly, as though drawn against his will, he reached out a hand and lifted the shift, letting the filmy garment drift over his fingers and back to the ground. The delicate fabric was wet and totally transparent.

A stifled sound, half-groan, half-curse, escaped him. Telling himself that she had merely followed his orders and had sensibly removed all her wet clothes did nothing to alleviate the pulsing heaviness in his loins. He wanted her so badly he ached all over.

With an effort that pulled every muscle in his body tight, he turned his back on Nell and reached into his pack for some dry clothes. God, if she could do this to him just by sleeping naked in his mantle, what would happen if—?

He snapped off the thought—before it had a chance to turn into the suspicion that his control was balanced precariously on the edge of something he'd never experienced. Something new. More than lust. More than desire.

Need?

Another stifled curse sounded, this time one of anger and self-disgust. Anyone would think she'd cast a spell on him. Need! He didn't need anyone, least of all a woman. In that direction lay weakness and the destruction of a man's will. Who knew that better than he? The only need he wanted to satisfy was physical. He'd never taken more from a woman, never wanted more. And, by God, it would be no different with Lady Eleanor fitzWarren.

Rafe tossed his wet garments aside, changed quickly and stretched out by the fire. No different at all, he told himself, closing his eyes with grim determination. And in that instant, coldly and deliberately, he decided he would have her. On his terms. The way he'd always taken a woman. Pleasure given and received, but a part of him always distant, always contained. He'd have to plan it. She was angry now, and disliked him, but that didn't worry him. Like all women, her anger and dislike would melt like snow in a spring thaw when the right incentive was dangled in front of her. They all had their price and he had the time to find hers. They would be alone for several days. It would be easy. He would have her.

And then—maybe—he'd decide whether her seduction fitted in with his other plans.

Nell woke to muted light and the knowledge that she was alone.

Completely alone, she saw, sitting up with a startled exclamation. Not only was Beaudene missing, but so were the saddles and his packs. The fire had died down to a pile of brightly glowing embers and, apart from her clothes and the confused trails of footprints crossing each other to and from the corridor, there was no sign that the chamber had ever been occupied.

Heart thumping much too fast, Nell struggled to her feet, hampered by the length of Beaudene's mantle. She grabbed up as much as she could of the heavy garment and hurried outside, speeding past the dark rectangles that led to the other chambers. Bright sunlight hit her eyes when she emerged from beneath the uprooted tree, bringing her to an abrupt halt.

The horses had gone.

For a minute Nell couldn't even think. She stared blankly at the spot where the horses had been tethered, as if their disappearance was a trick of the light and they would surely reappear at any moment. She couldn't believe Beaudene had left her. He wouldn't do that.

"He just wouldn't," she whispered, and wondered what in Christendom made her so certain of that. What gallantry had he shown her? What had he done except snap orders at her in between bouts of biting sarcasm and unnervingly enigmatic remarks?

All the questions she had shoved aside earlier in the interests of sleep now began to clamour for attention. And the only answer she had was that Beaudene had removed her from her family, taking advantage of the situation she had found herself in last night, for reasons which she suspected had more to do with his own purposes than in protecting her. This morning he could just as easily have decided she was too much trouble and left her here for Tom to find.

The sudden rush of tears to her eyes appalled her. What was she doing, crying over a rough, ill-mannered—?

"What the hell are you doing out here dressed like that?"

Nell cried out and jerked around to the side as Beaudene emerged from the trees, looking more than a little annoyed. His sudden appearance sent her heart into an even faster rhythm. And it was her own fault this time, she told herself despairingly. She had been so busy trying to conjure up horses that weren't there, she'd forgotten about his habit of creeping up on her. Unfortunately, the combination of shattered nerves and overwhelming relief did nothing for her temper.

"You're the only danger I have to worry about," she retorted. "No one else knows I'm na—" She bit her tongue, almost choking on the rest.

"Naked under that cloak," he finished, coming up to her.

Nell met him look for look, but she was trembling inside. How could she have forgotten how big he was in only a few hours? How fierce the glittering amber of his eyes; how unyielding the grim set of his hard mouth and the taut line of his jaw. His scar was clearly visible in the daylight—the mark of a warrior. He looked tough. Big and tough and dangerous.

And she had an utterly insane impulse to reach up and touch the scar with her fingertips, somehow to heal the hurt.

"I... I thought you'd gone," she stammered, thoroughly flustered.

The annoyance left his eyes, to be replaced by a quizzical gleam that was devastatingly attractive. "That gives me a very poor opinion of the men you seem to admire, princess. Have they always let you down?"

He wasn't being sarcastic, Nell decided, blinking in surprise. He sounded as if he really wanted to know.

"Those strutting popinjays!" she scorned, before she could think of the wisdom of such a reply. "They probably would have run from that thief last night, let alone abandoned me in this forest. All they care about is whether or not to have their sleeves slashed, or the colour of their hose."

His black brows shot up. "Indeed? And here I thought my lack of—uh—an appreciation of fashion was an annoyance to you."

The answer had its predictable result. Nell glared at him, effectively silenced.

His mouth relaxed into a smile that echoed the wicked amusement in his eyes. "As much as I would like to continue this interesting comparison of body-guards and popinjays, my lady, I think 'tis time you dressed." When she didn't move, he added softly, "Because if you let that mantle fall any lower, I might assume you've changed your mind about taking a bodyguard for your next lover."

"*What*?" Nell gasped and looked down. She had been so enthralled by the fact that Beaudene was actually teasing her that the precarious hold she had on his cloak had loosened rather drastically. Both her shoulders were bare, and only her fingers clenched around a fold of wool between her breasts kept her decently covered—just.

Nell made a grab for the rest of the garment and her wits. Her next lover? *Him*?

"Every man at Court will repent and become a monk before I let you lay a finger on me," she spluttered, finally retrieving her voice. Whirling, she stalked back into the corridor, uncomfortably aware that her out-raged departure was consideraby hampered by the un-

ravelling length of cloak trailing behind her, baring
more of her back with every step.

"Mannerless brute! Overgrown...*bodyguard*! How
dare he mock me so?" Muttering furiously, conscious
that she was as angry with herself as she was with
Beaudene, Nell sent a fulminating glance back over her
shoulder to make sure he hadn't followed her before
discarding his mantle and yanking her shift over her
head. She debated for a moment about whether to wear
the crucifix around her neck, then decided against it.
Beaudene might notice its sudden appearance and wonder why she hadn't been wearing it before. She fastened
the cords of the pouch around her waist. Her gown
followed. It was still damp around the skirts but she
scarcely noticed the slight discomfort.

"Next lover! Fish will walk on land first." She
pulled on her white hose, grimacing at the muddy stains
that all but obscured the dainty gold stars embroidered
on the silk. Her shoes, which had not been fashioned
with exposure to inclement weather in mind, were in
no better condition. As well as being scratched and
dirty, the long points had curled up and inwards and
stiffened, making them difficult to put on. "This is all
his fault," she ground out, teeth clenched as she balanced on one foot and tugged at the recalcitrant leather.
"Next lover! What a jest! If he was the last man left
on this earth he wouldn't be my next lover."

"If I was the last man left on this earth, you wouldn't
have a choice."

A startled squeak echoed through the chamber as
Nell lost both her shoe and her balance. She teetered
for a moment, then fell forward against the fireplace.
Her outflung hand ploughed straight into the pile of hot
ashes, sending sparks flying.

Beaudene was across the small chamber in seconds, cursing savagely as he scooped her away from the fire and up into his arms. Nell barely had time to feel the pain of her burns before they were outside and she was being carried swiftly through the trees.

Even then pain was only a vague sensation. She had never been carried in a man's arms in her life. The sudden feeling of helplessness was frightening. She wanted to struggle, to fight her way free, but at the same time she wanted to cling, to nestle into his strength. The conflicting sensations swirled around her, colliding with a dizzying awareness of the heat of his body and the coiled power of the arms that held her.

Dazed, desperately praying that he couldn't feel the way she was trembling, she scarcely noticed when they emerged into a small glade dissected by a stream. The horses were grazing nearby, already saddled.

Beaudene lowered her to the ground and grasped her left hand. "Sweet suffering saints," he ground out, examining her reddened palm before pressing her down on to the grassy bank and kneeling beside her.

Still more shaken from being carried than by her injuries, Nell peered over his arm. "'Tis not so bad," she murmured. "A few blisters. I doubt the saints will take much notice."

He sent her a look that could have raised blisters without the help of any fire, and shoved her hand unceremoniously into the stream. Nell gasped as her burned flesh reacted painfully. She would have snatched her hand back, but Beaudene's fingers tightened around her wrist, holding her still.

"I know it hurts," he said, his voice surprisingly gruff. "Try to relax. It will stop stinging in a minute."

"You must have a lot of success against enemies

with that trick,'' Nell muttered after a moment, gradually unclenching her teeth as the cool water began to take the sting away from the small wounds.

"What trick?"

"Sneaking up on people."

He looked at her, amusement flickering in his eyes. "My enemies don't spend a lot of time talking to themselves, princess. They're too busy listening for me.''

"I'll remember that," she retorted as he turned away again, but she couldn't wholly suppress the answering smile that tugged at her lips. He looked so much younger when that wicked gleam replaced the coldness in his eyes and—

He *was* much younger than she had first supposed, Nell realised with a sudden, startled little intake of air. And handsome. Why hadn't she seen that? Her smile faded as she took in the broad, high cheekbones, the straight blade of his nose, the firm line of his jaw. Against the backdrop of sunlit trees his profile had a stern masculine beauty that yet was faintly softened by the intriguing lines fanning out from the corners of his eyes. Lines that hinted at humour. While his mouth…

Nell's gaze lowered and a deep, very feminine frisson of awareness shimmered through her. He was hard and dangerous, aye, but in the passionate curve of his full lower lip she saw something that might once have been gentleness.

For the first time she found herself wondering how he'd got his scar.

"Nell?'' The husky sound of her name brought her gaze slowly upwards. One dark brow was raised in amused patience. "Your hand," he said, clearly repeating the question, "does it feel better?"

"Hand? Oh…oh…aye. 'Tis no longer stinging,''

she stammered, flushing hotly. What was wrong with her? She had been in Beaudene's company for hours now. Why was she suddenly blushing and stuttering like a fool just because he smiled at her? Why did she feel as if she was seeing him for the first time? As if she was only just now *noticing* him?

Noticing him? Had her wits gone a-begging? He hadn't exactly been invisible before! And what of all the questions she had put aside last night? she berated herself, ruthlessly dragging her wayward thoughts back to the here and now. Never mind about his scar and who had given it to him. Probably some other unfortunate female he had tormented beyond bearing. Was she to join the ranks of the addle-brained just because of a smile?

Summoning all the resolution that had seen her through the last three years unscathed, Nell forced herself to meet those disturbing eyes with their lurking smile. And, quite suddenly, in the clear light of morning, she knew exactly where to start.

''What does the King have to do with all this?'' she demanded. And watched his face go still.

Chapter Five

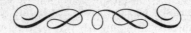

"Nothing."

For a minute Nell couldn't believe that that one brief word was the only answer she was going to get. Then, with an abrupt movement that made her start nervously, Beaudene released her wrist and rose to his feet. "Keep your hand in the water a while longer," he said curtly. "I'm going back for your shoes and to cover the entrance."

"But... Wait!" she cried, slewing around, still on her knees, as she realised he was walking away.

He had already reached the trees. He paused, glancing back, and his gaze was so hard, so cold, that a primitive awareness of a force more powerful than any she had ever encountered swept over her. So might the hawk look upon the earth from its unassailable eyrie, she thought, shivering. Proud and aloof. Invincible. And she expected to pit her will against his? "What about...what about...breakfast?" she asked weakly.

Just as he turned away, his mouth twisted into the more familiar sardonic smile. "You're soaking your hand in it."

Nell glared at the cheerfully bubbling stream washing over her hand, and didn't know whether to curse Beaudene or herself for the ease with which he had just intimidated her. Of course, if she hadn't been so shaken by his changed manner this morning, it might never have happened. Not to mention the shock of being carried off in his arms.

No! Better not to think of that. Even the memory of it caused a most unsettling sensation of weakness to flow through her limbs. And she would *not* be weak! She would have the truth. "I *will*!" she whispered, determination firming the set of her mouth. After all, she was no stranger to men who used charm—and when that didn't work, intimidation or force—to have their own way. Surely she was strong enough to stop Beaudene deciding her fate without so much as a whimper of protest or question from her? There had been secrets in that cool, distant gaze, and, by the saints, she would have them out.

And what of your own secrets? demanded an intrusive little voice inside her head.

Nell frowned and withdrew her hand from the water, examining her palm before gingerly patting it dry on her gown. The movement shifted the hidden crucifix slightly. If Beaudene had his secrets, then so did she. Even more. If he expected her uncle to follow them, he would take the most direct route to her home, for their only hope of reaching it safely lay in outrunning their pursuers. How was she to persuade him to make a detour to the cathedral at Wells without revealing a truth he might not believe? Especially when there was already a barrier of suspicion between them.

A barrier that would not be removed by blunt demands for information, she mused, as Beaudene reappeared. He moved through the trees with the purposeful stride of the hunter who knew that his prey was within easy reach. It was better not to watch that swift, almost silent approach, Nell decided. The urge to run was far too acute. And the most frightening part was that, this time, she wasn't at all sure she would run *from* him.

The unnerving thought had her quickly bending down to the stream. If water was the only sustenance available, she might as well use it as an excuse not to look at him. In truth, it would be a good idea to take a drink, if she could only stop her hand from shaking.

"Here."

The curt word brought Nell's head around, water dripping forgotten from her fingers. Beaudene's long legs, clad in dark burgundy hose and knee-length boots, filled her vision. Her shoes dangled from his hand, held by one finger hooked under the misshapen points. Not daring to glance upwards, Nell reached for them.

"Not so fast," he said, coming down on his haunches beside her. One forearm rested across the taut muscles of his thigh. "How do you expect to get your feet into the stirrups wearing these?" he asked, swinging the shoes back and forth in front of her wary gaze. "More to the point, how do you expect to get them out again?"

Nell tried to quell a feeling of defensiveness. She would not let him intimidate her again. "I wouldn't have to wear them at all if you hadn't kidnapped me last night," she pointed out. "Those shoes are fashioned for indoor use, not for riding in pouring rain."

"Ah." His mouth twitched. "My ignorance of fashion again. I cry pardon, my lady. But the problem still remains, unless…"

"Unless what?" Nell frowned intently at her maligned footwear and tried to think of a solution. It was

difficult when her wretched brain kept thinking instead
of the way Beaudene's eyes held that hint of a smile
again. Why couldn't he remain arrogant and sarcastic
and cold? Then *she* could remain angry. ''I knew you
should have let me go back—'' she began in a praiseworthy attempt to whip up some righteous outrage. It
was cut off abruptly when Beaudene drew his dagger.

Without so much as a single word of warning, he
placed the shoes on the grass, held them steady with
his free hand, and brought his dagger slashing through
the air in a swift downward arc that was so fast Nell
could have sworn the very air between them had quivered and been rent asunder. The curled-up points of her
shoes lay on the ground, sliced through as cleanly as if
he'd wielded an executioner's axe.

In the ensuing silence the gurgling stream and early-
morning birdsong filling the glade sounded unnaturally
loud. Nell picked up her shoes and examined them.
''You're very...quick...with that knife,'' she observed
faintly.

The smile that slashed across his face was predatory
in the extreme. ''In this world, princess, 'tis the quick
or the dead. And no one has succeeded in killing me
yet.''

Only by a fierce effort of will did Nell prevent her
gaze going to the scar that gave his handsome face its
hard look of danger. ''Well,'' she managed, then had
to take a deep breath before she could get the rest out,
''my toes will probably freeze, but at least I won't be
dragged behind my horse should I lose my seat.'' She
bent to put on the shoes. ''Thank you.''

''No.'' He made a quick survey of the glade. ''I'll
do it. The leather is stiff and you only have the use of

one hand. We need to be on our way again without delay.''

Something in the way he'd scanned their surroundings had Nell proffering one small silk-clad foot, then the other, without argument. As her shoes were slipped on, her own gaze followed the path Beaudene's had taken. She could not see far into the trees, but all seemed quiet.

''Would I be missed already?'' she asked. ''So early?''

'''Tis not of your family I'm thinking,'' he told her, his hand lingering on her shoe. ''After last night they're likely to be still abed, nursing sore heads. Even if they find that body, we should have another hour or two start on them.''

''Then, what?''

He shrugged, as though not greatly concerned, but the look he sent her brought all Nell's senses alert. ''There are other dangers to be encountered on the road, my lady. But I wouldn't expect you to know of them.''

''I haven't been locked away in a convent for the past ten years,'' she retorted, incensed. ''I do know something of the world.''

''Aye. The desire of men and how to use it.'' The words were angry, but a second later his voice lowered and went soft, and the hand still resting on her foot slid upwards until his long fingers closed in a warm, gentle vice around her ankle. ''But what of your own desires, princess?''

Nell amost lifted straight off the ground in shock. Tingling needles of fire raced straight up the inside of her leg to the very centre of her being. She couldn't breathe, couldn't speak. And even as her brain commanded her to move, to kick free, to break his hold, the feeling of being held captive once again swept over her.

"What are you doing?" she squeaked, forcing the words out.

Torturing myself, Rafe thought, clenching his teeth against a wave of raw need. Her immediate, unfeigned response to his touch had his blood pulsing so fiercely, so instantly, that he was almost grateful for the warnings of danger his instincts had been sending him since he'd woken. Otherwise he wasn't sure he'd be able to keep from stripping them both right now, lying Nell back on the grass and covering her with his body. Taking her, claiming her—mating like creatures of the forest, with the sun beating down on their naked flesh until its heat was lost in the hotter fires of passion. And pursuit be damned.

But even as he forced the tormenting images out of his mind, he could no more stop his fingers sliding upwards than he could stop his next breath. Under the soft silk of her hose her flesh was warm; he had to know if it would feel as soft.

"My lord?" Nell's voice, trembling and confused, pierced the fog of desire threatening to swamp his sanity. He dragged his gaze from the slender limbs exposed as her gown gave way before the slow advance of his hand, and went still when he saw her eyes.

Desire was there, soft and helpless, but overtaking it was confusion and the beginnings of fear.

Rafe's eyes narrowed. Was she playing some deep game? Did she think to hold him at arm's length by feigning maidenly nervousness? It wouldn't work when he could see the rapid pulse beating in her throat, hear the way her breath caught on each tiny gasp of air. His

nostrils flared as the faint scent of her perfume came
to him, betraying how warm her skin had become. Desire raked across his nerves like tiny claws, and he
cursed silently as he remembered that this wasn't the
time or the place to seduce her. But it would come. Oh,
aye. It would come. Of that he was very sure.

His mouth curved in a smile. "You know something,
princess? I think I just found a price you've never
thought to demand of a man. And I'm going to be more
than willing to pay it."

"Price?" Nell's mind reeled. She couldn't make
sense of his words. What was he doing to her? His
fingers still encircled her leg, lightly stroking the back
of her knee, but it was only a touch. A tiny caress.
Barely felt. How could she feel so…so…chained to the
ground, so unable to move? The sensation was frightening, but underlying it was a shivery excitement that
rippled through every nerve in her body until she
wasn't sure which emotion was dominant.

Then, with one last lingering caress, his touch was
gone, and she could breathe again.

"You forgot your garters," he said, as calmly as if
touching her had not affected him at all.

Hot colour flooded Nell's cheeks as she realised that
was probably all too true. He didn't like her, and there
was no reason to think his unsettling behaviour this
morning meant any change in that regard. She stared
blindly at the hand that reached into his surcoat to draw
out two lengths of gold ribbon. Breathing was one
thing. Rational thought still seemed beyond her. But
when his hand went to her knee again and pushed her
skirts higher, desperation jolted her brain and tongue
into action.

"No! They tie below the knee."

Golden eyes, glittering and intent, gazed straight into hers, and their expression was anything but calm. ''I don't think so.''

''Then let me. I can…''

But she couldn't. If she even tried to take over the small task Beaudene would see how badly she was trembling. All she could do was watch helplessly as he smoothed her hose up her legs and tied the garters in place. His long fingers brushed over the delicate flesh of her inner thighs and Nell had to bite her lip to stop the tiny whimper that demanded escape from her tight throat. Dear God, it was worse than before. Her heart was pounding so hard she was almost jolted by each beat, and she wanted…saints have mercy…she wanted to lie down, to feel his hands—

''There.''

The purr of satisfaction in his voice cut through her whirling senses. A satisfaction, she noticed uneasily, that was reflected in the brief smile he gave her.

Completely unnerved, Nell wondered what had gone so disastrously wrong with her plan to keep Beaudene at a distance. What had happened to his distaste for being one of a crowd? What had happened to *her* distaste at a man's touch?

Before an answer presented itself to her stunned mind, Beaudene stood, reached down for her hand and pulled her upright in one easy movement. She stiffened her knees just in time to stop herself sinking right back down again.

''Time to go, princess.''

''Aye,'' she whispered, and closed her ears to the unmistakable note of panic shaking her voice.

''Tell me about those accidents that befell you.''

The command came as Beaudene slowed the horses

to a gentler gait after several miles at the gallop. The pace had been dangerous, given the density of the trees still in full leaf, but Nell hadn't questioned it. She had been grateful for the concentration needed to follow Beaudene along a path that seemed visible only to him. She hadn't wanted to think about the meaning of the burning look he had given her before tying her garters. Even less had she wanted to think about the way she had all but melted at his touch.

Now, as they left the shelter of the trees and rejoined the road—more a wide path cut through the forest than a proper thoroughfare—she cast a quick, sidelong glance at him, wondering how much to say. He didn't seem to be in any hurry for her answer, she thought. His keen gaze scanned the woods on both sides of the road, constantly alert, and though he sat his horse with the ease of a man used to long hours in the saddle, she sensed a waiting tension in him, as though he was ready to meet an attack head-on.

What would he say if she told him that she knew what it was to live like that? Always watching, always waiting, constantly aware of danger. The sudden feeling of affinity, almost of recognition, made her uneasy, and yet curiosity stirred. Who was he, this man who could flay her with his scorn last night and tease her this morning? Who could tend her hurts one moment, then become as remote as the moon in the space of a breath? Who could kill with cold, silent efficiency, but who had touched her with a gentleness that had made her forget everything the past had taught her?

''You said something startled your horse a few days after your father's letter arrived summoning you to Hadleigh? Was anyone near you at the time?''

Nell started slightly, her cheeks warming when she realised that Beaudene's hawk-like gaze had shifted from the forest to her face. She fought back the betraying heat, hoping he hadn't been aware of the way she'd been staring at him for so long. The faint upward curve of his mouth told her that he had.

"No one was near me. I wasn't hurt. And, despite what you think, it *was* an accident. Now, tell me about the King."

His brows shot up so fast that for the first time in hours Nell felt like smiling herself—in undisguised triumph. "Did you think I would be satisfied with 'nothing' for an answer?" she asked, miraculously restored to composure at the knowledge that, for once, she had managed to take her formidable bodyguard completely by surprise. Even the narrow-eyed stare that accompanied his next question didn't shake her.

"Do you know Edward?"

She met his look coolly. "We've met."

"Indeed? It must have been a memorable meeting for the King to concern himself so closely with your safety."

"Wrong, my lord." Her chin lifted another notch. "Edward of York concerns himself rarely with the safety or honour of women. I doubt his memories of me are pleasant ones."

"Oh? What did you do? Demand favours that were beyond his power to bestow?"

The suddenly biting tone flicked Nell like a whip, but she kept her expression frozen. "Something like that."

Something like that? Rage tore through Rafe with a speed and violence that shocked him. So what if Edward had been before him? He'd known he wouldn't be the first. God's teeth, she could have lain with all condition of men, from the King to the humblest spit-boy, and it wouldn't change the only use he had for her. Why did he feel this anger, this fury, this insane urge to seek out the King and throttle the truth out of him? Like almost every other man in the kingdom he had always regarded Edward's incessant wenching with a kind of amused indulgence. Men made jest of the fact that no woman was sacred. Wives or daughters, married or virgin, all were meat to his insatiable palate, but Nell—

Had the King been her first lover? Had his friend of ten years used his legendary looks and charm to seduce the niece of a potential supporter, leaving her wanton? For, once a maidenhead was lost, it mattered not how many others came after.

He looked at her, riding proud and silent by his side, and the question gnawed at him like a cankerous growth. *Had* she gone to Edward's bed? By the fiend, *had* she known the King as well?

"Something like that," he repeated, controlling his voice with an effort. Anger would not serve him now. Anger, unleashed, destroyed rather than served. He had learned that lesson well—at the same time that he had learned never to trust a woman. "By your tone 'twas not a happy occasion. Do your sympathies lie with Lancaster, then, my lady, as did your father's? Dangerous politics in these times."

"My sympathies lie with neither," Nell stated. "Unless it be with their unfortunate wives."

The statement surprised him, but only for a moment. "Don't waste your pity," he advised. "One is a ter-magant, and the other so cold 'tis a wonder Edward doesn't freeze every time he climbs into bed with her."

Nell glared at him. "What else should he expect when he threatened to take Mistress Woodville at knife-point because she withstood his blandishments rather than compromise her virtue?"

"Aye." A short humourless laugh escaped him. "Elizabeth knew what she was about; that is for certain. From a penniless widow with two sons to Queen of England in a matter of months, and never mind that an important French alliance founders in the process."

"Just like a man to blame the woman in the case," Nell retorted hotly. "The truth is that your king thinks every woman was put on this earth for his amusement, and he couldn't bear to be bested by one. He could have left Mistress Woodville alone, he could have helped—"

She stopped dead, only to hurry into speech again when Beaudene turned an intent probing stare on her. "Henry of Lancaster might be weak— Very well, simple-minded," she amended when one black brow went up. "But at least he's not a whoremonger."

"Mayhap we have something in common then, my lady," he drawled. "You have little time for the King, and I have none at all for the Queen. On the other hand, at least cold ambition is preferable to Margaret of Anjou's viciousness. While Henry sank into the witless state he seems to prefer, she and her paramours damn near-ruined the country. As for the atrocities of her army—"

"It sounds to me as though you have little time for any woman," Nell interrupted without ceremony. "Margaret is a mother, remember? Perhaps she fights for Henry's son?"

This produced a snort of derision. "Henry's son?

Aye, and I'm the Pope. If Henry himself can wonder at the boy's begetting, what are the rest of us to think?''

''A truly fascinating question,'' Nell observed, refusing to be dragged into an argument over the paternity of the boy whose mother stubbornly persisted in calling the Prince of Wales. ''But it does not tell me what the King has to do with this journey, and why you would need to make a promise to him regarding my safety.''

He threw her an exasperated glance. ''If it sets your mind at rest, madam persistence, your father is wooing the King, hoping to be confirmed in his lands by renouncing his allegiance to Lancaster. Edward merely asked me to assure your safe journey as a sign of good faith while he considers the matter.''

''But the Court is presently at Reading, and Hadleigh Castle and your own lands in Somerset.'' She frowned, remembering that he had evaded a very similar question last night when they'd been dancing. ''Do you ask me to belive that the King and my father both expected you to travel all the way to Langley when I already had escort aplenty?''

He shrugged. ''Believe what you like. As it happens, I also have a petition awaiting Edward's attention. To travel a day or so out of my way seemed a small price to place on account towards a favourable outcome.''

''Indeed? And has your gallant escort been so rewarded?''

''Only time will tell,'' he said enigmatically. ''Now, can we move on to more pressing concerns? You said something about the standards in the hall.''

''Holy saints! And you call *me* persistent!'' When he narrowed his eyes at her, Nell capitulated. She wasn't entirely satisfied with Beaudene's explanation, but without knowing precisely *why* she felt she had missed something important, it was difficult to know what questions to ask. She heaved an exaggerated sigh. '''Twas merely one of those unchancy things. I was standing in the hall and one of the lances jutting out from the minstrels' gallery must have come loose, or perhaps 'twas never securely fastened. In any event, it fell and struck my shoulder—not with the point, fortunately.''

''Fortuitous, indeed. Was anyone up there?''

''Saints above, how should I know? The stupid thing was so heavy it knocked me to my knees, and I was buried under the banner for a full minute.''

''You couldn't have been alone in the hall. Didn't anyone see anything?''

''No one was looking up,'' Nell said drily. ''They were too busy exclaiming and wringing their hands, or trying to free me.''

He smiled slightly in rueful acknowledgement. ''So you weren't hurt at all?''

''Well—'' Nell paused and an irrepressible little gurgle of laughter escaped her at the memory ''—I sneezed a lot. That accursed banner was full of dust. Hadn't been washed in years.''

Beaudene's answering shout of laughter sent an inquisitive rabbit fleeing back into the forest and took Nell completely by surprise. Glancing sideways at him, she saw that he was still smiling, his tawny eyes alight with amusement. A little bubble of warmth burst somewhere inside her. She felt happy all at once, as though in making him laugh she had accomplished something special. The sense of recognition, tentative and fleeting, rippled through her again. Suddenly tongue-tied, she smiled shyly back at him.

"You thought 'twas your cousin Margaret indulging her spite, didn't you?" he said almost gently.

Nell hesitated, then nodded. "I still do," she murmured, hoping her insistence wouldn't shatter the fragile mood between them. "I *know* she slashed my gown, and as for the other things—'twould be just like her to slip a physic in my broth, or lock me in with the dogs, or claim she misfired at the butts. She never liked me. Nor did my aunt. Not that I was broken-hearted about it, but…" Memories flitted through her mind and she pushed them away with a little shiver. "The younger girls were all right, but Thomas and Edmund—well, you saw them."

"Aye." He looked at her thoughtfully. "Tom wants to marry you. Then your uncle must expect to gain a papal dispensation without any trouble."

"Oh, Tom is not really my cousin." Nell grimaced. "Thank the Lord. My uncle was a widower with Tom a babe when he married Aunt Maud. 'Tis Margaret, Edmund and the rest who are true kin."

"Don't be in such a hurry to thank your maker," Beaudene advised. "If there's no need for a dispensation, any plans they have to marry you to Tom may proceed apace."

"Not any longer," she pointed out.

"As you say." He smiled slightly, then stared abstractedly ahead between his horse's ears. "If something happens to you, my lady, who inherits your father's property?"

Nell frowned. "I'm not sure. There's no one on my father's side. I suppose Uncle Edward could claim it by right of my aunt."

"Your mother's sister?"

When she nodded, he went on. "And since your aunt

is presently hand in glove with the Queen their way would be clear. 'Twould then pass straight to Tom, or even the younger boy.''

"Nothing," stated Nell with loathing, "would induce me to marry Edmund! Or Thomas, for that matter.''

"You forget. We're talking about what would happen in the event of your death.''

"What a cheery subject," she muttered. "Do you think we could change it?''

"Blinding yourself to the facts won't change anything. I agree that marriage would be the easiest way of obtaining your inheritance, but if you've been holding firm in refusing I wouldn't give a groat for your life. And your father may have suspected as much,'' he added slowly.

"My father!" Nell's bubble of happiness vanished. "I haven't seen nor heard from my father in more than ten years. When it became clear that my mother would bear no more children, he set up a separate household for us in Wells so he could continue a way of life that did not take account of a wife and child. He never visited, never sent to know how we fared. I grew up listening to my mother's tears. She died when I was six, and even then he had no time for his daughter, but had servants escort me to my aunt's house. 'Tis only now that I may be useful in gaining him more wealth, or a powerful alliance, that he remembers me. Well, I am not my mother! I will not meekly obey and then spend my days weeping. *I* will be mistress of my fate!''

Her outburst was followed by a taut silence. Somewhat uneasily, Nell wondered what Beaudene was thinking, but he still seemed intent on her inheritance.

She didn't know whether to be relieved or incensed that
he had ignored her diatribe.

"Whatever your father's motives, he apparently does
not wish to see his property fall into Langley hands,
my lady. And if he made that plain in his letter to your
aunt, those accidents you so blithely dismiss as spite
could well have been aimed at delaying your departure
with a view to forcing your hand. 'Tis not so easy to
resist when you're injured or sick."

Nell sniffed. "No one forces me to anything."

Beaudene turned to look at her, eyebrows raised.

"If you are thinking of last night," she retorted,
flushing, "'twas because you confused me so that I let
you kidnap me. If it hadn't been for that thief—"

With a muttered imprecation, Beaudene reached over
and pulled both horses to an abrupt halt.

"What do you think you're doing?" Nell gasped, her
defiance crumbling with unnerving speed.

He reached back, extracted a length of rope from one
of his packs and thrust it at her. "Stripping the blind-
fold from your eyes," he grated savagely. "Look well
at that, my lady, and then tell me your assailant was a
thief. This rope came from around the neck of your
uncle's stallion, and has been cut through but for a few
threads. *Cut*, Nell, not frayed. If that damned horse had
charged, the rope would have snapped, and your fond
relatives would have thrown up their hands in horror
and blamed some hapless stable lad for using a frayed
tether. *Look at it*!"

Nell stared at the evidence literally right under her
nose. Denial was impossible. The rope clenched in
Beaudene's fist had indeed been neatly sliced through,
so that only a few strands remained. One good tug
would have been all that was needed for the stallion to

break free. Even a horse of Chevette's size and placid temperament could have done it. She could have done it herself. She looked up into Beaudene's grim face and said the first thing that came into her mind.

"Why were *you* in the stable at that hour?"

He withdrew his hand and shoved the rope back out of sight, seemingly unconcerned by the blunt question. "To collect these," he said, indicating his packs. "As I crossed the bailey I saw someone outside the stable and wondered at it. Had I known 'twas Rouget I would have moved faster."

"Oh." Nell mulled this over. "Well, you were in time. 'Tis all that matters in the end."

"I commend your equanimity, my lady."

"I don't believe in gnashing my teeth over something that's done with and past," she retorted, detecting sarcasm. "At least... Will trouble follow you for killing that man? You said he knew about the stallion. He must have been told..." She let the words trail off. Even with the evidence of the cut rope, it was still hard to admit aloud that her own family had conspired to injure or kill her because she wouldn't fall in with their plans.

Beaudene shrugged. "There'll be no hue and cry over his death. Rouget had a reputation. He was a good soldier once, but, of late, whenever he was around, people who were an inconvenience to someone would suddenly turn up conveniently dead. I doubt your uncle will confess to admitting such a man to his house. He'll probably spin the same tale of attempted thievery that you were so anxious to believe."

"But won't they know...? I mean, won't they know that *we* know...? That is to say— Oh, dear."

Beaudene laughed and leaned over to smack Rufus on the rump. He nudged Samson into a fast trot at the same time. "Don't tie your tongue in a knot. I know what you mean. But whatever your uncle suspects we know, he or your cousin will still come after us."

At her quick look of surprise, he added drily, "'Tis the only way they can cover their backs, princess. I warrant you they've already put it about that you've been kidnapped, or, more likely, run off with me."

"Run off with you! I only met you last night!" Indignation brought an angry flush to her face.

"So?" His eyes were suddenly narrowed and glittering. "Was every gallant you were cosying up to at that banquet a lifelong acquaintance?"

The question was flung at her so savagely, his amusement gone so quickly, that Nell scarcely had time to comprehend the sudden change of mood, let alone marshal any defence. Shaken, dismayed at how badly she wanted to defend herself, she could only let the storm break over her head.

"Of course they were not. Nor did it seem to matter to you. My God, I even overheard wagers running as to how long it would take a man to get you or Lady Margaret alone in a dim corner, or whether that was the night fortune would smile on one of them because you might feel like a change of lover." And, with that, Samson bounded forward under the sudden command of a booted foot.

Neither spoke again for the next several miles. Nell stared stonily ahead and told herself that she didn't want to rail at Beaudene for believing ill of her. She didn't want to explain. She didn't want to scream that he was wrong, that she had pretended to be just like her dissolute family in order to protect herself, that the most likely reason she had let him carry her off last night was because the strain of juggling men and lies and pretence, while clinging desperately to her own truth, had brought her almost to breaking-point. He'd never believe her. And besides, hadn't she deliberately fostered his low opinion of her? It was supposed to be her protection. Wasn't it?

She shook her head in despair at her confused thoughts. The problem was becoming too complicated to solve on an empty stomach. In fact, now she came to think on it, hunger was probably the cause of the hollow emptiness that had been gripping her insides since Beaudene had called her princess again, and had then flung those disgusting wagers in her face as if she had entered wholeheartedly into the business.

A cry of protest rose in her throat. Nell tried to stifle the betraying sound, but Beaudene clearly had the hearing as well as the eyes of a hawk, because he glanced around, his gaze narrowed and hard.

"Don't fall back any further, princess. We have to put a few more miles behind us before we stop to rest the horses."

"I wasn't aware that I was lagging," Nell retorted through her teeth. "But far be it from me to gainsay one who, I have no doubt, can travel for days without rest or sustenance other than a few hurried mouthfuls of water."

"Stop complaining," he ordered, but quite mildly. "I have no intention of starving you. You'd probably swoon and we'd be forever having to stop to let you recover."

"Oh, a thousand pardons, my lord. I need food occasionally. How truly heedless. How imprudent. The shame of it! How will I ever hold up my head again?"

Rafe's lips twitched. The little shrew had a trick of disarming him with humour when he least expected it.

And, for some strange reason that had nothing to do with physical desire, he was letting her get away with it. He reined Samson back until Nell came alongside, then slowed to a walk. "I'll strike a bargain with you, my lady. I won't mention your past again if you put a guard on that saucy tongue."

Nell was surprised to find herself hesitating. His words were uttered in a half-jesting tone, but surely he was proposing a truce of sorts. It would be madness to refuse and spend the next few days snapping and snarling at each other. She craved peace, not arguments, and Beaudene had the power to make this journey easy or hard on her; yet she was dithering like a witless fool because their bargain would be based on a lie.

"Of course, if you think that feat beyond your capabilities—"

"I accept," she interrupted hurriedly. Then, unable to resist the amused smile playing about his mouth, added, "What would you have done had I refused?"

His smile was suddenly very wicked and very male. "Put your tongue to better use, princess, what else?"

Nell promptly blushed a brilliant rosy hue, and the only reason she saw the faintly puzzled frown appear in Beaudene's eyes when she did so was because she was fighting to keep her gaze away from his mouth. The image evoked by his words was already far too vivid for comfort. She could almost feel the brush of his lips against hers.

"Could our bargain include you ceasing to call me 'princess'?" she managed, scarcely hearing the words over the pounding of her heart.

"But you are like a princess," he objected softly, the frown disappearing. "Beautiful, proud, wilful— recklessly so at times." The aside was tacked on somewhat drily. "Of course, you also want your own way, have never learned to follow orders without arguing, and complain about minor inconveniences, but—"

"Don't let yourself get carried away," Nell muttered, recovering from her stupefaction in a hurry. For one insane moment there she had actually thought Beaudene was praising her. Hunger was obviously making her light-headed. Pride and wilfulness were not exactly praiseworthy qualities, and she couldn't possibly look beautiful after last night's various adventures. She blushed again when she remembered the way her lips had tingled at the imagined pressure of his mouth. As if he would want to kiss someone who looked as if she'd been dragged behind her horse, rolled in the mud, and whose only comb was her fingers.

Merciful saints, what was she thinking? She didn't want him to kiss her. She *didn't*!

Fortunately for her beleaguered mind, a diversion presented itself. With a suddenness that took Nell by surprise they emerged from the forest into a sunlit green vista. At their back and curving around to the right the trees stood dark and mysterious, but ahead and on their left lay undulating hills and meadows, covered as far as the eye could see with a carpet of long grass that rippled in the breeze, swaying and springing back as though an unseen hand brushed over it again and again. The stream that had followed them through the forest, sometimes glimpsed, sometimes veering away from their path, meandered lazily across the land to spill into a small pond before disappearing around a slight incline. Beside the pond, the branches of a solitary oak, left behind when the forest had been cleared, hung low over the water, as though gazing at its own reflection.

"Oh! I know this place!" The exclamation burst from Nell's lips as memory stirred within her.

Beaudene reined in when they were halfway across the first meadow. His gaze, narrowed and intent, surveyed the scene as if he was inspecting every separate blade of grass. His dark brows were drawn together, but Nell was too excited to pay much heed to the small warning sign.

"We stopped here to eat on our way to my aunt's house ten years ago, and one of the servants allowed me to paddle in the stream. Why, that means—" she turned a delighted face to him "—that means the road to Wells is a mere mile or so to the west, beyond those trees."

"That doesn't concern us," Beaudene answered, not taking his eyes from the scene in front of them.

Nell grabbed hold of her courage with both hands and told herself to tread carefully. "Well, I didn't mention this before, because we left in something of a hurry, but... I have to stop at Wells before I go on to Hadleigh."

That got his attention. "You have to stop at Wells before you go on to Hadleigh?" He didn't sound at all receptive to the idea. In fact he sounded downright incredulous.

"Aye." She dared a fleeting glance upward. "I have to visit my mother's tomb. 'Tis in the cathedral."

There was a long minute of silence, during which time Nell refused to look at Beaudene again. When he spoke his voice was as smooth and as cold as water gliding over stone. "Have you forgotten, my lady, that several of your male relatives are probably galloping after us right this minute? This is not the time for a detour so you can say a few sentimental prayers over your mother's grave.''

Nell forgot about caution. ''But I have to—''

''The only thing you have to do is obey my orders. Something you seem to have a great deal of trouble with.''

''But I promised—''

''We are *not* going to Wells. Is that clear enough for you?''

''You don't underst—''

''*Quiet!*''

The angrily whispered command was accompanied by a bone-crushing grip on her wrist. Startled into obeying, Nell saw that Beaudene had gone very still, his gaze searching the forest behind them.

''What is it?'' she breathed, and never even questioned why she was whispering too.

''We've been followed for the past mile or two,'' he said, so calmly that for a moment the import of the words went right over her head. A second later they sank in.

''Followed!'' The word emerged as a muffled squeak. ''Then why are we chatting here instead of fleeing for our lives?''

''Because whoever has been pacing us is mounted and I don't know how fresh his horse is, whereas yours is tired and can be outrun. So far, our shadow seems merely curious, but if we take off as if the devil was at our heels he might be tempted to find out why. Our best defence is to act as if we're not worth robbing.'' His rapier-sharp gaze flicked her up and down. ''Fortunately, you look the part.''

Nell didn't know whether she'd just been insulted or not. She knew she wasn't looking her best, but Beaudene could have been improved by a bath and a shave himself.

Then an idea of such brilliance occurred to her that insults and outrage alike were forgotten. She looked hurriedly away, afraid her expression would betray her.

"'Tis just as well we have to cross these open fields for a while," he said in a voice that carried only to her ears. He released her wrist and nudged the horses forward again. "Outlaws prefer the shelter of the forest. But stay close, my lady."

Outlaws! For a second Nell quailed inwardly at what she was about to do. Then she reminded herself that she had made a promise ten years ago that came before any consideration for a bodyguard of recent acquaintance who wouldn't even listen to her. Beaudene could look after himself, and if he objected to being left behind to cope with outlaws, then perhaps it would teach him to be a little less obdurate about side-trips to Wells.

She cast a quick glance to her right, trying to estimate the distance she would have to gallop before she was out of sight. Light and shadow chased each other across the grassy hills as clouds drifted past the face of the sun and she shivered slightly. It had best be now, she thought. Before she lost her nerve.

Without giving herself more time to brood over ill omens, Nell wheeled her horse to the right and clapped her heels to his flanks. Rufus leapt forward as if he'd just left his stable, his stride lengthening into a headlong gallop within the first few paces. A fleeting prayer of thanks that Beaudene had insisted she ride astride flashed through her mind and was gone. Behind her, she heard him curse and start in pursuit, then there was nothing but her racing heart, echoing the pounding of

Rufus's hooves against the ground, and a litany of scarcely coherent thoughts.

Let him be right. Let him be right that whoever followed us will give chase. Let me be right in thinking he'll turn and fight rather than risk me being captured by outlaws. Let me escape. Keep him—

The prayer for Beaudene's safety was never finished. At the edge of the forest, directly in her path, two hooded figures rose from the grass, blood-curdling yells issuing from their throats, longbows drawn and ready.

Nell screamed and hauled on the reins so sharply that Rufus reared and nearly went over backwards. Before she could turn him to flee back the way she had come, the figures rushed forward until they were mere yards away. Both arrows were aimed, unwavering, at her heart.

Terrified, she turned to look for Beaudene. At the same moment a flash of darkness streaked past her. Snorting and skidding back on his hocks, Samson was pulled around in a sliding halt that put him between Nell and danger. But the action was only a temporary measure, she saw. Their shadow had indeed given chase. As Beaudene reached for her bridle to pull Rufus closer, another man was reining his horse in beside them.

"A chivalrous gesture, my lord," the rider drawled in a surprisingly cultured voice. His dark eyes went to Beaudene's scar and lingered. "But don't try anything else heroic. We have no wish to kill your lady. At least, not unless our leader orders it." He laughed softly.

Beaudene did not so much as glance at him. His golden eyes were fixed on Nell's face with such ferocity that she would have fled from him as well, given the choice. "Are you now content?" he snarled.

Chapter Six

"It would have happened like that anyway."

Nell huddled on a corner of the wide pallet that, apart from a crudely-fashioned table, was the only piece of furniture in the hut where she and Beaudene had been taken, and tried to sound defiant rather than defensive. It wasn't easy when her bodyguard was prowling around their quarters like a caged wolf.

He halted in front the open doorway of the hut and stared out. "No, it damn well would not have happened like that," he grated. "There was only one man lying in wait in the direction we were supposed to be going. Man!" He snorted and shook his head. "More like a boy. We could have ridden straight over him."

Nell glared at his back. "Aye, and then been shot by the others."

"A toothless old man and a girl?"

"They knew what they were doing."

"And they had a deal of assistance from you, didn't they, *princess*?" He swung around to impale her on the knife-edged rage in his eyes.

"Don't call me that!" Nell jumped up from the bed.

''You're blaming me for everything, and if you don't stop I'll—''

''You'll do *nothing*.'' As quick as a hawk striking, Beaudene took one stride towards her, wrapped a powerful hand around her arm and pushed her unceremoniously back again. He towered over her, large and menacing. ''You will sit there, my lady, and you will say and do nothing while I try to fathom what's going on here.''

Nell set her lips in a mutinous line. Apparently convinced that he had intimidated her into silence for the moment, Beaudene returned to the doorway and propped one broad shoulder against the wooden frame. He stuck his thumbs in his belt and his fingers curled into fists. By the hard set of his profile, his thoughts were not pleasant. Beyond the doorway, Nell could see a boy sitting propped against a similar rough dwelling, watching them. A small crossbow lay across his knees, its arrow nocked. She looked away, feeling slightly sick.

The open door and one small window were the only sources of light and air in the hut, but with Beaudene filling the doorway very little of either was admitted. Nell doubted that his absence would have made much difference. Fear was the reason why she couldn't seem to breathe easily, why her stomach was knotted with tension. She should have been feeling guilty for leading them into an ambush, but somehow, despite Beaudene's anger at her recklessness, she had the frightening feeling that their capture had been a little too easy. She cast a glance at him from the protection of her shadowy corner. Against the light he looked huge, his back and shoulders broad and hard with muscle, tapering to lean hips and long, powerful legs.

How had an old man, a girl, a boy younger than herself and a cripple managed to disarm him?

Of course, he hadn't known precisely who or what their captors were until it was too late. Guilt stabbed through her at last as she realised that Beaudene's first thought must have been to protect her. It wasn't a comforting realisation, but it was better than the fearful suspicions that had been tormenting her mind for the past hour; better than remembering that the only explanations she'd been given for everything had come from him alone.

But just as she felt her tense muscles relax a little, she caught sight of Beaudene's packs just inside the door. Fear hummed along her nerves again. Their horses had been tethered somewhere, and Beaudene's sword and dagger taken, but everything else was still intact. Nell swallowed and surreptitiously touched the hidden crucifix, as though she needed proof that they hadn't been searched for money or jewels. Her throat felt as if cold fingers were wrapped around it.

"We could try to escape," she suggested huskily, hardly daring to take a breath in case her voice wavered. She wasn't even sure if Beaudene knew where they were. After an hour of being led through the forest in what had seemed to be innumerable circles, her own sense of direction had been hopelessly lost.

He shot her a quick, lowering glance, then jerked his head towards the boy. "Do you expect me to kill our watchdog?" he bit out. "He's a child. Have you ever seen anyone kill a child with his bare hands, my lady?"

Another aeon of silence dragged past.

"Why…why do you suppose they haven't robbed us?" She tried again, unable to bear the sound of her erratic heartbeat any longer. "'Tis almost as if we're…guests."

"You'd better pray that's truer than you think."

"What do you mean?"

He shrugged. "Just an idea. But if I'm wrong, we're in a pother of trouble, thanks—"

"To me," she finished for him. When he turned to face her she wished she'd stayed silent.

"Enlighten me," he growled far too softly. Something leashed but violent glittered in his eyes. "Just how far did you think you would get alone?"

The tightly coiled tension in Nell snapped without warning. "All the way to Wells," she cried, leaping to her feet. "And, what's more, I still intend to go—"

The words were cut off abruptly by Beaudene's mouth coming down hard over hers.

It was anger, pure and simple. Nell could only stand there while the storm raged around her, her mouth crushed and bruised beneath the force of his, her senses stunned. She couldn't even *feel*. Her body had gone numb with shock.

When he lifted his head, only the relentless grip he had on her arms prevented her from dropping straight to the floor. Nor did he give her time to recover.

"Do you know how close you came to being killed today? *Do you*?" He shook her hard, his words battering at her senses even as his kiss had done. "God damn it, Nell, if you ever—"

"But I promised!" The desperate cry came from her heart. "You don't un—"

"Stop it!" he said thickly. "Just shut up!" The hot pressure of his mouth returned, as furious, as overwhelming as before.

Nell heard herself make a small muffled sound of

protest, and then she was weightless, helpless, her body locked to his by arms that felt like steel bands around her.

"Oh! Your pardon, my lord, my lady."

Beaudene jerked his head up and whipped around, releasing Nell so abruptly that she staggered back, hit the bed and collapsed on to it. She lifted trembling fingers to her lips and felt them part, soft and quivering, as she tried to draw air into her starved lungs. Her vision, strangely blurred, began to clear enough for her to recognise the girl standing in the doorway as one of their captors. She held a dagger in one hand and was balancing a trencher of food on her hip. Nell had never been so glad to see anyone in her life.

"I brought you something to eat," the girl said, entering and laying the trencher on the table. She straightened and cast a quick, wary glance at Beaudene, her gaze lingering for a moment on his scar. She would have been pretty, Nell thought, with her copper-coloured braids and clear blue eyes, if her face had not been so thin and tired-looking.

"If you wish you may walk outside, within the camp," the girl continued, gesturing with her free hand. "You are not…prisoners here."

"Really? What would you call us?" Beaudene's sardonic tone was so like his usual self that Nell could only wonder at how quickly he had regained his control. *She* felt as if she had just discovered what it was like to be struck by lightning.

"We mean you no harm," their captor insisted.

"I suppose that is why you carry a knife, and your children go about armed with crossbows?"

The girl's expression stilled. "Desperate times make for desperate measures, my lord. But, whether or not

Dickon relieves you of whatever wealth you carry, you will keep your lives.''

"And when is this Dickon supposed to show himself?''

"A day or two, perhaps.'' The girl shrugged. "We cannot be sure.''

She seemed about to say more, but a voice outside the hut shouted, "Bess! You're needed.'' With a quick gesture towards the trencher, she hurried from the hut.

As soon as she was gone, Nell pounced on the food, placing the trencher on the bed beside her. It was simple fare—a loaf of coarse, dark bread and some slices of cold roasted venison, accompanied by two mugs of ale—but she wouldn't have cared if the meal had consisted of a bowl of slops so long as she could use the excuse of eating to avoid meeting Beaudene's eyes. She felt him watching her, and concentrated on tearing a chunk of bread from the loaf.

"Not quite what you're used to?'' he asked, reaching down to help himself to some venison.

Nell shrugged and kept her eyes lowered.

"On the other hand, if today was a goodly example, you've probably driven any number of men to that particular act of retribution.''

Sweet Jesu! He hadn't meant the food. The morsel of bread in her mouth suddenly tasted like dried chaff. It went down with difficulty. Defiantly, Nell took another bite. "If you are talking about the way you just assaulted me, my lord, I don't wish to discuss it,'' she announced with slightly muffled dignity.

"Far be it from me to spoil your repast, princess. Just don't expect an apology.'' When she didn't rise to that bait, he picked up one of the ale cups and handed it to her. "Here, try this. 'Twill make swallowing easier."

Nell buried her heated face in the wooden beaker and tried to pretend that Beaudene wasn't standing over her, fully aware of her discomfort. She only wished *she* could remain in happy ignorance of her own humiliation. To think that earlier she had been imagining his kiss as a gentle brush of lips, a tender caress, when the reality had been a punishing onslaught that had all but paralysed her. The memory made her cringe inside. She'd been a fool! A witless, wanton fool!

"I think you're right, princess."

Nell promptly choked on a mouthful of ale. "What?" she croaked when she could speak again. Holy Saints, now he was adding mind-reading to his other diabolical traits.

"We'll have to escape. Two or more days is too long for us to kick our heels in this place. We'd better leave tonight."

Overwhelming relief nearly caused Nell to drop her cup. He couldn't read minds. No, of course he couldn't. And if he was planning an escape he could have had nothing to do with their capture, she scolded herself, feeling more foolish than ever. She took another bolstering sip of ale. "Leave. Aye. Tonight. Um…how?"

Beaudene pushed the trencher aside, sat down on the pallet and leaned back against the wall. He propped one arm on his upraised knee and stared thoughtfully through the doorway. "That ill-assorted rabble out there might have captured us, but holding us is another matter. There seem to be very few people in the camp, given the number of huts, which means most of them are with this Dickon fellow, probably off poaching the King's deer or robbing people blind, so escape shouldn't be too difficult.'' He turned a piercing stare on her, golden eyes narrowed and intent. ''Especially as, this time, you'll be on my side. Won't you, my lady?''

Nell finished her drink and set the cup back on the trencher. ''Of course,'' she said, and, taking a deep breath, forced herself to meet that compelling gaze.

The slow smile he gave her made the bed rock. Which was impossible. She wondered if she'd just imbibed too much ale.

''Good, because I'm going to need your help. That girl—Bess—said we had the freedom of the camp. They'll follow me if I set foot outside, but you won't look like a threat to them. I want you to wander about, talk to people, show Bess a friendly face. And, if you can, find out how many men are in the camp, where the horses are kept, and if anyone guards them—although I think it unlikely when they have only a babe watching us. Do you think you can do that without arousing suspicion?''

''I'm not a complete idiot,'' Nell muttered. Only where you're concerned. She rose quickly, not wholly convinced that she hadn't said that last part aloud. Beaudene was still smiling slightly, and the expression made her very nervous.

''Off you go, then. And while you're at it—'' He waited until she paused in the doorway and glanced back. ''Tell our watchdog out there to put the bow down whenever he feels like nodding off, or he'll shoot himself in the foot.''

The watchdog did not take kindly to the advice. In fact he denied any desire for sleep so loudly that Bess emerged from a nearby hut, drawn by the noise.

"Hush, Jemmie," she scolded. "You'll wake your mam." She put a hand to the boy's brow and seemed relieved at the feel of his skin. "Does your shoulder still pain you?"

Jemmie scowled and shook his head.

"The child should be abed at this hour," Nell said absently, noticing that the shadows of evening were beginning to encroach on the settlement. The air had grown cooler with the setting of the sun, and a fine mist hovered above the ground, wrapping delicate ribbon-like tendrils around the trees encircling the clearing.

At the mild comment, Bess lifted her chin, her lips parting, and Nell turned to her in quick apology. "But 'tis difficult to get them hence while daylight prevails," she added, smiling.

The girl hesitated, then an answering smile lightened her pale, weary face for a moment. "It is that, my lady. I'm Bess, by the way. Is there something…? Were you wanting—?"

"Just a little fresh air," Nell assured her. "And please call me Nell. 'My lady' is far too old and dignified, and we are much of an age, I warrant."

Bess flushed slightly and was about to reply, when a low sound came from the hut she had vacated. She turned swiftly, but Nell stayed her with a hand on her arm.

"Send the child to bed," she insisted, too low for Jemmie to overhear. "We are without weapons or horses, so surely do not need guarding, and my lord is concerned for the boy's safety."

An inspired statement, she thought, rather pleased with herself. One less pair of eyes watching them

should please Beaudene also. Which would make for a
nice change.

"I will, my lady, as soon as—"

The sound came again, followed by a harsh, racking
cough. Bess's face tightened. She whirled around and
vanished into the hut without another word, leaving
Nell staring frowningly after her.

It was very quiet.

Too quiet.

Where was everyone? she wondered, glancing about.
Where were the women and children? There was Bess,
and Jemmie apparently had a mother, but surely—?

She let her gaze wander slowly around the shadowy
clearing. The settlement consisted of a dozen huts or
more, placed in a haphazard U-formation, and as many
cooking fires. Only the two nearest her were burning,
she noticed, heating cauldrons of some sort. She could
see no sign of the horses; if they were tethered nearby
they were well-hidden. Nor were there any guards
posted, not even another child.

Of course, Jem and his mother could be the only
family in the camp, but Nell didn't think so. Despite
the fact that no lights had been kindled in the huts
against the onset of night, the place had all the appearance of a reasonably prosperous village, even if it
was in the middle of the forest. A few hens scratched
about, and there were a couple of goats in a pen behind
the cottages. She caught a glimpse of the old man who
had taken part in their ambush. He glanced up briefly
from milking one of the goats, then returned to his task
as though her presence was no cause for alarm.

And yet alarm skittered at the corners of her mind,
nudging her forward, pulling at her reluctant feet, until
she stood at the lower end of the U and could see inside

the dwellings there. At close quarters the reason for their dark air of abandonment was shockingly clear. They had been ravaged by fire, and recently.

Feeling a chill that had nothing to do with the mist that now swirled about her skirts, Nell retraced her steps to the hut Bess had entered. She halted, looking across the clearing towards Beaudene. He was watching her, standing in the shadows to one side of the doorway. She thought he nodded once, in encouragement or command. Hesitating only a second longer, she turned on her heel and stepped into the cottage.

The unmistakable odours of sickness assaulted her instantly. She paused just inside the entrance, waiting for her eyes to adjust to the dimness. When they did she saw Bess sitting on a low stool beside a pallet, her head bowed. The blanket on the pallet had been drawn up so that it covered the figure beneath from head to toe.

The chill in her veins was suddenly ice-cold. ''Holy Mother of God,'' she whispered, crossing herself. ''Is it the plague?''

Bess raised her head. It was a measure of the girl's weariness, Nell realised vaguely, that she showed no surprise at her presence. ''Naught but the plague of war, my lady,'' she answered, her voice low. ''Men fighting and killing each other whether they be kings or outlaws.''

''Outlaws did this? Oh. We thought—''

A soft humourless laugh came through the dimness. ''Did you think we were the only band of outlaws living in the forest? There are many such as we. But we were strong. We were prospering!'' Her voice strengthened suddenly and her gaze sharpened, as though focusing on Nell for the first time. '''Twas greed and envy that did this, my lady. Men who thought robbing us would be easier than waylaying wealthy travellers. They attacked at dawn five days ago—burning, raping, killing.''

"But… Surely *all* your warriors were not killed?''

"Not all, no. We drove them off. And now Dickon has taken the men who can still fight and gone after them. A show of strength, he said, so they won't come back. Who knows if our own men will come back? And how many will still be here to see it, when the wounded are dying for lack of proper care?''

Nell glanced involuntarily at the shrouded figure on the bed.

"Aye.'' Bess followed her gaze. "An arrow pierced her lung.''

"*Her*?'' Nell's breath caught. "Not Jemmie's mother?''

"No. Not yet.''

"Dear God in Heaven, is she wounded, too? Did they deliberately loose their arrows on the women and…?'' She thought of the empty, quiet clearing outside, the burned huts, and couldn't finish the question. The evidence of a massacre was all too clear.

Quick sympathy had her reaching out to touch Bess's shoulder. "You poor girl,'' she murmured. "How many are left? Have you been nursing them alone all this time?''

"Since old Meg died three days ago.'' Bess nodded. "Simpkin has been helping me, and 'tis not so many, but— Oh, my lady, even if I had the proper herbs and such, 'twould be useless. Meg was a wise-woman, she knew how to make poultices and salves, and draughts to ease their pain. She was teaching me, too, but our stocks were already poor, and are now gone as she is.''

"Well, then, we shall just have to gather more, and *I* will show you how 'tis done. Did your Meg have a garden?"

For a moment Bess stared up at her, as if turned to stone. When she finally spoke her voice was trembling with undisguised hope, and tears welled in her eyes. "No. We were going to buy them... There's a fair...crowded... We go every year...no one notices us..."

"Hush...wait." Nell pressed her hand harder to Bess's shoulder to calm the girl. "This has to be thought on. But first—" she gestured to the shrouded figure on the pallet "—this poor soul must be given Christian burial."

"Aye." Bess took a deep breath and lifted a hand to squeeze Nell's briefly. "Your pardon, lady, I forgot myself." She rose, bent to touch the still form in a gentle farewell, then gestured for Nell to precede her from the hut. "'Twill be more fitting to talk in my cottage, if you do not mind waiting until I see to the others. As to Nan here, Simpkin and Luke are preparing her grave. It does not take long," she finished with faint bitterness. "Christian burial is not for we who live secretly, hidden away from towns and churches."

There was not a lot she could say to that, Nell reflected. And it would be cruel to remind Bess of the fate of those who died unshriven when there was nothing to be done about it. "When we get to Wells I'll buy masses for their souls," she decided, not realising she had spoken aloud until she saw the tired smile again light Bess's face briefly.

"Be sure I will tell Dickon of your kindness, my lady. Now, will you wait with your lord until I may come to you?"

Nell suddenly noticed where Bess was taking her. "Holy Mother save us! We can't talk in there!" she exclaimed in a frantic whisper, grabbing Bess's arm and making a sharp left turn. She pulled her new friend into the nearest hut, barely remembering to keep her voice down when she saw two pallets against the side walls. The occupants appeared to be asleep. "And he's not my lord. Let me stay with you. He won't think anything is amiss. After all, he asked me to—" She bit her tongue on the rest.

Bess gave her a curious look.

"It matters not," said Nell hurriedly. "But 'twill be better if he doesn't know what we have planned."

"We haven't got anything planned."

"Not yet," Nell admitted. "But how much planning does it take to go to a fair and buy some herbs and cordials? How did you and Meg manage it?"

"Two or three men would go with us, my lady. They would wait in the woods while we purchased what we needed. Not only herbs, but candles, spices, wool for clothing. Why, you may buy anything you need, and when the stalls are crowded no one thinks to look closely at two women. That is…" She paused and peered doubtfully through the gloom at Nell's gown.

"Aye, you'll have to find me some clothes. No country maid would wear this, even filthy and covered in mud."

"'Tis a shame," Bess murmured, reaching out to touch the rich brocade. "Such a pretty gown to be so treated."

"Trying telling that to his lordship," retorted Nell with great feeling. "Not that I have any fondness for the wretched thing." She contemplated the rapt look on Bess's face for a moment, before asking impulsively, "Would you like to have it?"

"*Me*, my lady? Me wear such a garment? 'Twould not be... That is... Oh, I would look as fine as the Queen herself," she finished, so wistfully that Nell found herself laughing.

"Then 'tis yours," she said. "So long as you have something to replace it."

"Oh, aye, my lady. But surely you cannot mean to wear simple homespun? Although there is a velvet surcoat trimmed with miniver somewhere..."

The words tripped over each other so quickly that Nell laughed again. "The very thing. After we see to your patients, you shall show it to me. Then all that remains is to plan how we may slip away tomorrow."

"But we'll need money, and Dickon keeps it hidden." Her face, so recently hopeful, fell back into its weary lines. "'Tis only he and Simpkin who know where it is, and Simpkin will never let us go alone."

"Then I shall have to steal some coins from Lord Beaudene."

Bess's eyes went wide and startled. "Steal from your lord?"

"He's not my lord," Nell repeated absently. "He's my bodyguard."

"While you are in this camp, my lady, he had best be your lord," Bess stated, accepting this brief explanation with a praiseworthy lack of curiosity. "I'm sorry if you think it unseemly to share my cottage with him, but you'll be safer when the men return, and I'll be sleeping there also. 'Tis not as if you'll be alone with him."

Nell refrained from telling her that she had already spent one night alone with Beaudene. There were more

important things to worry about. Somehow she had to
get her supposed husband out of their hut so she could
search his packs. And if Beaudene kept his money on
his person— Nell shuddered. She didn't want to think
about how she might have to overcome that.

"Bess? Is that you?"

The faint voice from the shadows made both girls
jump guiltily. Nell recovered first. "We'll need light,"
she said briskly, turning her mind to the more immediate task demanding her attention. "And whatever
supplies you have, even if 'tis only water and clean
linen."

But water and clean linen could only do so much.
By the time full darkness had fallen, Nell had learned
just how much devastation had been visited upon the
small settlement. In every hut that hadn't been burned
lay the sick and injured: two men, both feverish and
weak from badly infected wounds, and women and
children in a like state from cuts and burns.

The children tore at Nell's heart, especially as she
was helpless to ease their pain, but what brought angry,
pitying tears to her eyes was the girl lying alone in the
hut beside Bess's cottage.

"She can't be more than thirteen," she whispered
when she had examined the girl's injuries and had
coaxed her to swallow some water. "How *could* they?
No. Don't answer that," she added with soft bitterness.
"I know only too well what men are like when they
see something they want. The last thing they consider
is youth or innocence."

"She hasn't spoken since Luke found her after the
fight," Bess murmured in the same low tone, although
the girl had turned her head away and seemed deaf and
blind to their presence. "Her wounds are not so bad,

as you see—bruises, mainly. 'Tis the shock, and the shame of it. Although, Lord knows, none of us would have her feel dishonoured. I'm here myself because my master forced me, then cast me aside when his wife discovered us. But who knows what such a one as she understands?''

When Nell looked a question at her, Bess touched her forehead. ''Simple,'' she mouthed. Then whispered, ''What if she should quicken with child, my lady? She would lose what mind she has, for certain. If it didn't kill her.''

Nell gazed down at the still girl. '''Twould take any woman to the brink of madness to bear a babe in such circumstances, let alone a child like this.''

''Meg would have known what to do,'' Bess sighed as she bent to draw the blanket up further. ''All the rest of us can do is pray.''

But would that be enough? Nell wondered rather grimly as she followed Bess from the hut. She also knew what to do. She had grown up knowing. Had often heard her aunt's friends discussing their visits to a certain apothecary to rid themselves of possible reminders of their indiscretions. And though the discussions had been conducted in whispers, though the Church condemned such a practice as a hideous abomination, a crime deserving of eternal damnation, surely, here, the circumstances were very different? Surely, here, her knowledge could do only good?

''Look.'' Bess touched her arm, distracting her from her uneasy questions and drawing her attention to the group of men around one of the fires. ''Simpkin and Luke are back. And your lord is with them. They'll be wanting their supper.''

Nell glanced up. By the light of the fire she could

see Beaudene hunkered down on his heels, talking to the other men. He looked up briefly, the light reflecting in his amber eyes as he stared at her across the flames. Half-formed plans raced through her mind like clouds before the wind. All were dangerous. All risked Beaudene's wrath. And one in particular might risk her very soul—if she had the courage to carry it out.

"See if you can keep them there for a while," she said softly. "Long enough for me to find some money, if there's any to be found."

"A wise man keeps his purse close, my lady. You may take it from me. But I'll do my best."

Bess had been right. There was no money in the packs.

Nell had just discovered that fact for herself when the door was pushed open and Beaudene strode into the hut. He pulled up short at the sight of her crouched over his belongings, candle in hand. For what seemed like an eternity, Nell could only stare up at him, frozen with dismay, before she managed to force herself to her feet.

He reached out and pushed the door closed without taking his eyes off her, leaving his hand braced against the wooden panels. "Find what you were searching for?" he enquired, in a soft tone that sent a chill down her spine.

Nell's gaze went from his face to the door and back again. Why did she have to choose this particular moment to notice how big his hands were? she wondered a little wildly. To remember the power in those long fingers when they had gripped her arms, the equally powerful restraint when he had captured her ankle.

"I... I thought to dry this," she stammered, snatching desperately at the excuse when she realised his black surcoat was clutched in her own hand. "'Tis still damp."

His eyes narrowed. "Interesting."

"Wh…what?"

"You don't lie very well."

Dear God, if he only knew. The last three years had been a lie. Something deep inside her shuddered once, uncontrollably. She was suddenly afraid. Stricken with a fear that had nothing to do with the decision she had made.

"What were you looking for, princess?"

That name! He was using it again, deliberately to—

"Money," she declared boldly. And immediately, quailed inside. Had she run mad? But she must not show her fear. She must not give him that advantage. He respected strength and—

"Money?" Beaudene's brows went up. "You're looking for payment before you deliver?"

Nell frowned. Had she just missed something while rallying her courage? "I don't expect payment for finding out about these people. Besides, I have little enough to tell you, probably less than you gathered for yourself."

There was an odd little silence. Before she could make out the expression in Beaudene's eyes, he removed his hand from the door and took a step towards her. His voice was softer than ever. "Why money, then, princess? Were you thinking of buying your way out of here?"

"No, of course not," she said, more puzzled than ever. "'Tis not for me. And we can't leave tonight, anyway."

"This grows even more interesting." He took another step forward. "Let me guess. You've decided to give your cousin a sporting chance at catching you."

"What in Christendom are you talking about?" Nell demanded, now totally confused. She remembered her light-headedness earlier. Surely the cool night air had banished any effects of the ale. Had *he* been imbibing too much? She suddenly noticed how close he was and took a step back. "You've been outside...spoken to those men. 'Tis surely obvious why we can't leave. There are people dying here for lack of proper care. They need help."

"From *you*?" His tone had her spine stiffening, as if someone had laid a whip across her back. "Good God, woman, you can't even get dressed without injuring yourself."

"I fell over this morning because of your sneaky habit of creeping up on me," she retorted through gritted teeth. "Strange though it may seem to *you*, my lord, I am not entirely useless. I have promised to help Bess nurse the sick and wounded, and that is precisely what I intend to do!"

He stared at her frowningly for a moment, then reached out and plucked his surcoat out of her hand. "Forget it, princess." He tossed the garment on to his pack with a dismissive action that spoke more surely than any words. "You can play the ministering lady of the manor some other time. Outlaws take care of their own."

"Not when they lack medicines and the knowledge of how to administer them. You don't know what it's like. The children... You haven't seen..." Oh, how could she make him listen? She whirled and dumped the candle on the table. "*You* go, then, if you fear my cousin's pursuit,'' she told him, plunking both hands on her hips. "But I'm staying here! This is not last night, my lord. You can threaten to knock me senseless all you like, but if you make one move to take me away, I'll scream loud enough to be heard in London.''

She had gone too far. Nell knew it the instant Beaudene's eyes went a fierce, glittering gold. He took one stride forward, his expression so savage that she backed against the table with enough force to set the candle rocking perilously. He shoved it aside with an impatient curse and loomed over her.

"Stop!'' she cried, struggling to keep some distance between them without touching him. It was well-nigh impossible. She would have to push him away—an impossibility in itself—or lean back on her hands, leaving her lower body vulnerable to the pressure of his. Panic fluttered in her throat. "You're trying to frighten me again, and—''

"I'm trying not to strangle you!'' he snarled, planting both hands on either side of her hips as if his grip on the edge of the table was the only thing stopping him from wrapping them around her throat. "God's blood! If a man had accused me of fearing that cup-shotten cousin of yours, he'd be choking on his own tongue!''

"I didn't mean—''

"Oh, aye, you damn well did!''

"No! I was only trying to…'' Her breath caught and she faltered, gazing up at him in unconscious appeal. "I know you're not afraid for yourself,'' she finally managed with simple honesty.

To her relief some of the fierceness went out of his eyes and he moved back a little. "So you know that much, do you?''

"Aye." Nell took a cautious breath. "'Tis your duty to me that you're thinking of, I know, but don't you see? If we tarry here for a few days, Thomas will go right past us. Why—" She stopped, and a second later a radiant smile suddenly spread across her face. Her panic and Beaudene's rage had just been entirely overtaken by a wondrous realisation. "Why, we can even go to Wells and—"

"Stop right there."

"But it couldn't be simpler!" Carried away with her plan, ruthlessly quelling a little voice in her head that was trying to remind her of the disastrous consequences of her last brilliant idea, Nell swept on. "Just think! While we're in Wells, Thomas will discover I haven't arrived at Hadleigh Castle, and *he'll* hie himself off to Wells because that's where he was to escort me first. And then, while he's searching for me there, we can take a different route home." A ripple of delighted laughter bubbled over as she thought about it. "'Tis the perfect reckoning. He'll be chasing us around in circles and he won't even know it."

Beaudene did not seem inclined to share her gleeful triumph. "And if he goes first to Wells, as you intended?"

She couldn't resist. The temptation was too much. "Why would he do that?" she asked, widening her eyes with guileless innocence. "He'll expect us to run straight for Hadleigh. Who would be foolish enough to make a detour to Wells when they're being pursued?"

Beaudene was suddenly very, very close again. "Who, indeed?" he purred with a smile as dangerous as his tone.

Nell had the grace to blush, even though she continued to watch him with unabashed hope. She was rewarded by the genuine, albeit reluctant smile that tugged at his mouth.

"I hate to admit it, princess, but that strategy is rather sound, up to a point." Before she could ask what point, he fixed her with a narrow-eyed stare that held a good deal of scepticism. "Do you have knowledge of medicines, in truth?"

"Aye." She nodded vigorously. "Our nurse at Langley taught me." Seeing the sceptical gleam still lingering, she added softly, "I was interested."

"Hmm. Damned inquisitive, more like." After another minute of intense scrutiny, he added, "So, how do you intend to obtain what you need, my lady?"

"Well, I—" Just in time Nell remembered his opinion of her lying ability. "Bess is arranging it," she amended hastily. Which was nothing less than the truth. "And she will repay you when their leader returns. He's... Did those men tell you what happened?"

"Aye, but little else." He straightened to his full height and looked down at her. "I didn't expect a wealth of information. This is an outlaw camp. People come and go, and no one asks questions. Or if they're foolish enough to do so they find their answers at the point of a dagger."

"Bess told me enough," Nell said, sobering quickly as she remembered what she had seen. "You call these people outlaws, and I suppose they do rob to survive, but would we be any different had we been abused by a master like my uncle for instance? He mistreated his people—family, servants, minstrels, it made no difference. And animals. We had a performing dog once, and a monkey. Uncle Edward bought them for my cousins' pleasure. I set them free."

"And were punished for it?"

Nell shrugged. "A beating. I would do it again."

"Aye. I verily believe you would." He reached out to tilt her chin up with the edge of his hand. "Very well, my lady, you can have one day."

"One day? But—"

His thumb lifted to press on her lower lip, silencing her. Nell went completely still.

"One day. No longer. I'll admit to some curiosity about our absent host, which accords with our staying here, but if he hasn't returned by this time tomorrow, we leave." His gaze dropped to her mouth and he moved his thumb in a slow, stroking caress across her lips before lowering his hand. "Make sure Bess knows whatever she needs to by then, because after that she'll be on her own."

Nell nodded. She couldn't speak. Mainly because she had stopped breathing again. Beaudene was still so close that she could feel the heat from his body. It seemed to wrap her around, holding her motionless until he chose to release her. Her lips throbbed where his thumb had touched and she felt strange—on edge, nervous, as though waiting…

Her gaze lifted, to find him watching her, his golden eyes shadowed by half lowered lashes, but oddly intent.

"I… There's still…" With an effort that took an incredible amount of willpower, she tore her gaze from his to glance at his packs.

"The money. I know. But first…" Still speaking, he grasped her about the waist and lifted her to sit on the table.

Before Nell could do more than gasp at this unexpected development, he placed his hands on her knees, pushed her legs slightly apart and stepped between them.

She cried out in sheer panic and tried to scramble backwards, but his hand flashed out and cupped the nape of her neck. Holding her gently captive, supporting her weight without effort, he exerted the lightest pressure to draw her close and upright again.

"No!" Her hands flew up to push frantically at his shoulders. Beneath the soft wool of his surcoat, the unyielding power of his body was terrifying. Driven by blind instinct, she swung her foot and kicked him.

He laughed, a low husky sound that made her hands cling tighter, even as she trembled with the knowledge of her own helplessness.

"A flea wouldn't have felt that," he chuckled. "Relax, princess. I'm too close for you to do any damage."

"Let me go," she ordered, in a voice somewhere between a whimper and a squeak. The aforementioned flea would have doubled over laughing, she thought hysterically. Merciful saints, she had to stop this. She had to pull herself together.

"That's better," he murmured, as she went still and struggled to think of a way out of this new predicament. The task seemed beyond her. His gentle, reassuring tone, combined with the far from reassuring vulnerability of her position, rendered her totally witless.

"You don't want to develop a kink in your neck from looking up at me," he continued softly. "Now we can talk in comfort."

"T-talk? What about?"

He smiled straight into her eyes. "Well, it seems to me that I've made most of the concessions here."

Somewhere in the whirling confusion of her mind, honesty compelled her to admit that he was right. Wariness kept her silent on the subject.

"That being so, I think a little recompense is in order."

"Rec— But I'm not... You can't..."

"That's the way it works, princess," he said softly. "Surely you know that? If you would be mistress of your fate you'll have to learn the ways of bargaining."

Bargaining? Nell stiffened, realising only then how limp she'd gone. The knowledge added to her sudden outrage, sending a healthy surge of temper through her. Bargaining! He was playing with her. Punishing her for getting them into this situation.

But just as she opened her mouth to tell him she was not so easily defeated his hand moved, stroking her beneath her hair, and she was helpless again. Weak and shivering. What was he doing to her that she couldn't fight, couldn't seem to do anything except feel? All her senses were focused on his hand—the hard strength of his fingers, the gentleness of his touch. The contrast between the two held her enthralled. And the longer he held her the more she became aware of other contrasts. How small she felt so close to his powerful body, how soft to his hardness, how utterly female to his male.

The last awareness was so strong, so *primitive*, it was frightening. Never had she been so conscious of a man, no matter how close they had been. Not even this morning, when Beaudene had been teasing her, had she been so aware of him, so aware of her own femininity.

She looked up at him, words of protest, of fear, of confusion, trembling on her tongue, and forgot every one of them. His mouth was only inches away, his lips slightly parted. Her own mouth felt suddenly soft and pliant and warm. Shaking, she forced her gaze higher, and nearly cried out at the burning intensity of his eyes. They held her, helpless, for a second longer, and then there was something...something almost puzzled...something searching.

"Strange," he murmured, so softly that she wasn't sure if he was talking to her or to himself. "You can't lie convincingly, and yet you look..."

He fell silent, then shook his head very slightly. "Perhaps 'twas because I startled you." His gaze lowered to her mouth and he bent closer. "Let's see what happens when I startle you like this, little one."

Chapter Seven

His mouth touched hers, gently, softly, and withdrew.

Braced for another assault, Nell was stunned by his tenderness. She went still, scarcely breathing, as his lips returned to stroke hers with a light, brushing movement, tantalising, tempting her with the promise of warmth, of closeness, of a gentleness she'd never expected from a man. But wanted. Oh, sweet. She wanted it, but…

Half-frightened by the unfamiliar longing that was increasing with each caress of his mouth, she tried to draw back, only to find that his hold was far too secure. Between the gentle but inexorable hand at her nape and the solid barrier of his body she was trapped. How could that be? she wondered hazily, scarcely noticing that her mouth had begun to follow his, instinctively seeking a firmer touch. She could understand helplessness when he had overwhelmed her earlier, but *this*? She trembled, and a tiny sound of mingled need and doubt caught in her throat.

''Shhh.'' he murmured. His warm breath fanned her lips with a different kind of caress, sending yet another cascade of shimmering sensations through her. ''Don't be afraid, little one. This won't be like before. I was…angry.'' His lips feathered over hers again. "Open your mouth,'' he whispered. "Let me taste you.''

"No, I—''

He stole the words as he took her mouth, in a slow possession that had her shivering uncontrollably. But not with fear this time. Had she even dreamed of a kiss like this? He left no part of her mouth untouched, claiming it with a gentle aggression that sent lightning strokes of pleasure through her with every gliding caress of his tongue against hers. Pleasure and a sweet, hot weakness that had her clinging, melting, yearning for the hardness of his body against hers. She whimpered again, the sound lost in his mouth, and felt the powerful muscles in his arms tense as though he would pull her closer.

Then, slowly, with hot, lingering touches of his tongue to her lips, he ended the kiss. His hands shifted to her wrists, unlocking her arms from about his neck, and he put her away from him, stepping back with a care that spoke of rigid control.

Nell forced her eyes open. Her lids were heavy, but her body felt light, and quivered inside with a strange heated restlessness. Dazed, she stared at Beaudene. At the powerful hands that had caged her so carefully, at the hard, sharply chiselled mouth that had kissed her with such shattering intimacy, at the eyes that—

Reality crashed back into her consciousness like a blast of cold air. And the chill went straight to her soul. His eyes were a darker gold than usual, but he watched her with an expression that held more frowning assessment than heated desire.

In painful detail she remembered the way her arms

had been clinging about his neck—she hadn't even known how they'd got there—while he had held her with nothing more than one casual hand supporting her head, the other braced on the table beside her. The chill was replaced by a wave of embarrassed heat that started at her toes and swept upwards so fast that she felt sick. She couldn't go on looking at him.

And he, it seemed, had looked his fill at her. Without a word he turned on his heel and strode to the door. As he yanked it open, he reached into his surcoat, withdrew a few coins and tossed them on to the bed. They landed with a musical tinkle that sounded to Nell like the clash of discordant cymbals.

"Your money, my lady," he said, his voice as cold as the night air coming in through the doorway. The draught was abruptly cut off when the door snapped shut behind him.

For several minutes Nell could only sit there looking at the coins glinting faintly in the dim candlelight. The heat and restlessness had faded. Now she just felt cold. She knew the money was to pay for the herbs she needed. Why, then, did she have the terrible feeling that she had just been paid for that kiss? As if she was... As if he thought...

Tears filled her eyes, turning the coins into a shimmering silver and copper blur. She swiped at her face, blinking rapidly to force them back. It was no use crying because she had been stupid enough to let herself by seduced by gentleness into a kiss. And that was all it was, she told herself stubbornly. Just a kiss. It meant nothing.

She jumped down from the table, thankful to find that her legs, so weak and trembling only minutes ago, now supported her. "See, you've already recovered from it,'' she muttered, taking some small encouragement from the fact that she could walk over to the bed and scoop up the coins. If there was more than a little bravado in the way she shoved them into the pouch holding her crucifix, Nell ignored it.

She was tired. That was the cause of her tears. Any woman would feel a trifle fragile when she'd been riding for the better part of a night and day with little food and only a few hours' sleep between. She would feel much better tomorrow. She would go to the fair with Bess and enjoy herself. It would be a morning out of time for her. A chance to relax, to be herself, away from danger and pursuit and a man who confused her more with every moment she spent with him.

Confused and frightened her, she amended, going very still as she remembered that moment earlier when she had felt something tremble deep inside herself. As if she held some secret knowledge deep within, and had shuddered away from it, retreating into the safety of ignorance.

Fanciful nonsense, she scolded herself. If she had to stand here in a pother over some man, it had better be the unknown husband chosen by her father who had ignored her for years. What was she going to do about *that*?

Nell shuddered and sat down on the bed. The thought of marriage to a stranger was suddenly more abhorrent than ever. Perhaps she should only think as far ahead as changing her clothes. A more modest gown might even stop Beaudene treating her as if she was some kind of—

No! She scowled at the door of the hut, as if he was standing immediately in front of it. She would not think of that kiss again. He had punished her—in typical male fashion, Nell reminded herself sternly—for getting her way in staying to help Bess. He'd extracted a price.

But he had given in.

Her angry scowl faded. And in its place came a wistful contemplation, a gentle, feminine wistfulness so long suppressed that she was only vaguely aware of it. What had made him so hard? Angry one moment, mocking the next. He had deliberately frightened her more than once. He seemed to despise her. And yet today…tonight…through it all, she had sensed…

What? Nell asked herself, sighing. Was she deluding herself that there was more to Beaudene than ruthlessness and an implacable will, because of the occasional glimpse of tenderness or humour? But she couldn't deny that those qualities existed. She had seen them. Felt them.

She shied away from *that* memory immediately, lying down on her side and curling up, as though protecting herself from some unseen threat. But even as she ordered herself to forget the unexpected tenderness of Beaudene's kiss, to ignore silly, girlish dreams, to banish him entirely from her thoughts until she was rested and more rational, another question hovered tantalisingly at the edges of her mind.

She thought of the scar he bore, and wondered. Had he, like her, buried the gentler side of his nature in order to survive?

How the devil had survival come down to sitting out here by the fire, trying to leash instincts that threatened to destroy years of waiting and planning? Had he been bewitched? Was he taking leave of his senses?

Rafe shifted restlessly on the hard ground and glared

at the door of the hut, as if he could see through it to the little temptress on the other side. She'd been one surprise after another today—her humour, even when she'd been complaining, her endurance, her courage, even that stupidly reckless dash across the meadow had provoked more than a twinge of reluctant respect for her determination and quick-wittedness once he'd calmed down—but that kiss! That had taken him so by surprise that he was still shaken by it more than an hour later.

His hands clenched as the memory of Nell's mouth beneath his sent a violent rush of heat straight to his loins. He gritted his teeth against the ensuing ache and willed the memory away, but for the first time in his life his vaunted self-control seemed to have deserted him. He couldn't forget how she'd tasted. Sweet and soft and unexpectedly shy. He couldn't forget the sensations aroused by his possession of that innocent, untutored mouth. Aye, untutored, damn it. She'd yielded, she hadn't responded. He was too experienced not to know the difference.

And as if that wasn't enough to raise several questions, he was beginning to recall too many other instances where she'd seemed puzzled, even totally uncomprehending, over some of the things he'd said. By the Rood, if he didn't know any better—

Rafe's eyes narrowed and he cursed softly. He did know better. Why did he forget that whenever he held her, touched her, looked into those luminous hazel eyes that held the mysteries of the forest in their depths? Her innocence was an act. It had to be. But, if that was so, why suddenly assume it now, after practically shoving the knowledge of her former lovers down his throat? And how had he known the instant she'd lied to him?

Could anyone, even a woman, act so well that she could use feigned guilt to cover an equally false innocence, which in turn covered real guilt?

God! Rafe dropped his head between his hands and stifled a snarl of sheer exasperation. His thoughts were chasing themselves around in circles within circles. Any more and he'd go out of his mind.

The image brought another scowl to his face. He raised his head and glared at the hut again. That little witch in there was more dangerous than he'd realised. In all of this he'd almost forgotten the purpose of his journey. He'd almost forgotten the burning desire for justice that had—

"Rafe?"

The soft voice came, totally unexpected, from the woods behind him. Before the single word had faded into the night, Rafe was on his feet and turning, his hand reaching for his dagger in the same swift, smooth movement. He cursed again when he remembered the dagger had been taken.

"No need for weapons, unless you've taken to killing old friends," said the voice, sounding amused. "Of course, you've still got your fists. As I recall, they were lethal enough on their own."

Rafe straightened slowly from the fighting crouch he'd assumed. The man standing in the shadows at the edge of the clearing could have been his brother. He was the same height, possessed the same lean, muscular build and his hair was as black as the night. Only his eyes were different, Rafe knew. They were a clear pale grey. His own gaze narrowed for an instant, then turned quizzical. "Dickon?" he queried, brows lifting in gentle irony.

A rueful laugh sounded. "Rather less threatening, I thought."

A brief smile flashed across Rafe's face then vanished. "Richard, what in God's name do you think you're doing living like an outlaw and leading a bloody band of cut-throats?"

The man who had once been Sir Richard Peverel stepped forward into the circle of firelight. "Better that than having my head and shoulders part company. I *am* an outlaw, remember?"

Rafe's mouth thinned. "Don't stand there babbling such folly at me. Now that Edward's firmly on the throne, do you think he'd rather see you dead because you fought for an annointed king than pardoned and giving freely of your allegiance? Mark me, he would not."

Richard made a non-committal sound and gestured with his hand. Other men emerged from the trees. With only the occasional curious glance at Rafe they dispersed, some into huts, others to gather around the second fire.

They numbered a half-dozen or so, Rafe estimated, and more than a few looked to be the cut-throats he'd called them. Simpkin came last, a faintly amused expression on his face as he limped towards them.

"So I was right to go looking for you," he said to Richard. "This is the friend you once spoke of. The man who bears the mark of a knife on his face."

"You were right," Richard confirmed drily. "But did you have to kidnap him and his lady?"

Simpkin shrugged. "You have need of him."

Rafe followed this exchange with grim attention. "You mean I have this to thank for keeping Nell and myself alive?" he demanded, indicating his scar.

"Many thanks. I suppose, had it been otherwise, we would have died in the forest when you first saw us."

"What! Me, a cripple, take on a warrior of your size? Not likely, my lord."

Richard laughed. "Is Simpkin the reason why you weren't surprised to see me just now? Apart from not hearing me, that is."

"I must be more tired 'than I thought when a great ox like you can take me unawares," Rafe retorted instantly. "But, aye, I recognised your hand in the way we were ambushed. Or rather, I hoped 'twas you. You've trained this rabble the way you once trained soldiers."

"We rabble got the task done, my lord," Simpkin reminded him rather tartly. He turned to Richard. "Sit. Bess is abed, but I'll bring meat and ale when I've checked the wounded."

"Ahh." His leader stretched and motioned Rafe back towards the fire. "A happy thought. I could eat the ox this overgrown barbarian called me."

The comment drew a smile from Rafe, but he sobered almost immediately. As they sat down, he fixed his friend with an interrogatory stare and demanded an explanation.

"I'd rather know what you're doing running around the countryside with a wife at your heels," Richard answered, yawning. "God's bones, I'm tired. But we got the job done."

"My congratulations."

The sarcastic tone had Richard's brows lifting, but he waited, not speaking.

"She's not my wife," Rafe said impatiently, but he kept his voice low and glanced warningly at the men sitting several yards distant. "I'm escorting her home."

"Well, who knows better than I that the roads are not safe for travellers? But escorting her on your own? Isn't that a little unusual?"

"The entire circumstances are damned unusual, but enough of that. What *I* want to know is how you came to this. And then I'll know how best to help you out of it," he added grimly.

Richard's soft laugh held a note of bitterness. "I'm just at the point where I might accept, my friend. Or would you rather I did not call you that?"

"Don't be a fool, Richard. You know why I chose to back Edward. The Duke of York took me into his service when I had nothing. Edward and I have been friends for years, as were you and I. Because you chose Henry of Lancaster doesn't make you my enemy now. You made your choice and honoured it to the end. There's no shame in that." He paused and stared into the fire for a moment. "God knows, in battles between kings 'tis hard to say who has the right of it and who has not."

"A pity my lord of Warwick does not hold the same view. 'Twas he who was baying for my head after Towton—I swear merely because I unhorsed him. The man was ever a pompous braggart."

Rafe glanced up again, amused. "A shrewd, pompous braggart comes closer to the mark, but I doubt he'll bother you now. He and Edward have fallen out over the Woodville alliance. Warwick has retired to sulk in his stronghold, and with good reason, I have to own. Not only was he made to look a fool at the French Court—arranging a match for Edward while the King was secretly marrying Mistress Woodville—but the Queen's relatives have overrun the Court like a plague of rats, all scurrying for their share of the pickings."

"Aye. A more ill-considered match I can't imagine." Richard grinned suddenly. "And damned inconvenient as well. If you hadn't come along, I was going to send the prettiest wench here to petition the King on my behalf. But if the gossip is true, marriage has Edward running in harness."

"Only until he gets tired of a constant diet of ice. Now, can we have a sober discussion here? What happened to you after Towton?"

"You have lost your sense of humour, Rafe. This escort business must not be much fun."

"I'm sure Nell would agree with you. Talk!"

"There's not much to tell," Richard said, capitulating with a careless shrug. "After Towton there was a price on my head. Hell's fiends, there was a price on a lot of heads, but I didn't fancy having mine adorn the archway of some city gate, so I made for that hole we know of."

"I thought so. We stayed there last night and I knew someone had been before us. 'Twas another reason why I didn't slaughter that ambitious crew of kidnappers this afternoon."

Richard chuckled. "I'll tell Simpkin to be properly grateful. Well, as you guessed, I stayed there until the hue and cry died down. It took long enough, God knows. Warwick is nothing if not tenacious. Then a little more than a year ago I fell in with these fellows. Most of them are good men, believe it or not, and the rest are controlled by the odd robbery. 'Tis not a bad life for some. Drifters from the army, runaway serfs, your true criminal—we have them all. And if a man's name is not the one he was born with, no one questions him about it."

"I daresay, but 'tis no way for you to live, Richard. Let me intercede with Edward for you."

"And live on what? A place in his hall, grateful for a few crumbs but expecting little else because I once backed a rival king? No, I thank you."

"Not at Court." Rafe hesitated, glancing at the hut before speaking again. "I may be in a position to grant you some land for your oath of fealty. You're no fool, Richard. Once you're pardoned, you can build from that."

For the first time there was a flicker of genuine interest in the grey eyes watching him. Then Richard's gaze narrowed and he said softly, "You're going to reclaim Hadleigh Beaudene. After all these years? How?"

Rafe shrugged. "Through the King, mayhap. But if not, there are other ways."

"Hmm. Do those other ways have anything to do with the girl you were hell-bent on protecting today?"

"Hell-bent? Good God! What tale did Simpkin spin you?"

"Nought but the truth," said Simpkin, coming up to them with a platter laden with chunks of venison and a brimming jug of ale. He also carried Rafe's sword and dagger, which he handed over. "You would have taken an arrow for her had we fired."

"'Tis my duty," said Rafe drily, returning his dagger to its sheath and laying the sword beside him. He turned the question on Richard before anyone could comment on that remark. "Does the fact that you're tempted to accept my offer have anything to do with the little redhead sharing my lady's hut?"

A grin that he could only describe as sheepish spread across Richard's face.

Simpkin laughed. "Accept on behalf of us all," he advised his leader with the familiarity of a trusted servant. "I, for one, grow too old for another winter spent in these woods."

"An unusual man," murmured Rafe, watching Simpkin as he returned to his place with the others. "You would have been pleased with the way he planned that ambush. I knew we were being followed, but not by more than one, nor that Simpkin had sent young Luke off to warn the others and have them waiting. And, by his speech, I'd say he's had some learning."

"Aye." Richard nodded around a mouthful of venison. "He was once a lord's fool. Was even taught his letters and how to figure. An easy life for a peasant born with a twisted foot and withered leg, one would think, but apparently the man abused him whenever the mood was upon him, so Simpkin ran away and ended up here."

He ate for a few minutes in silence, then looked directly at Rafe over his ale-cup, all traces of careless unconcern gone from his expression. "He'd probably make a good steward. And there are some others who may wish to follow me. How does that sit with you?"

Rafe smiled. "Better to end up in honest employment—even as a fool—than wind up at the end of a rope."

"Then it looks as if you've just gained yourself a fool," Richard answered quietly. He put the mug down and held out his hand. "And an oath of fealty, my friend."

The open field outside the small market town was teeming with people and animals, and alive with the scents and sounds of the fair. Wealthy merchants garbed in their finest gowns rubbed shoulders with sharp-eyed pedlars in simple homespun. Craftsmen hammered and sewed. Townswomen in brightly-hued wools and velvets compared prices with soberly-clad farmers' wives while their husbands eyed the brilliant, cloudless sky and debated how long the unusually fine autumn weather would last.

Everyone for miles around, it seemed to Nell, had chosen that morning to attend the fair.

And there was aplenty to see and wonder at. From the goldsmiths' and jewellers' precious goods, displayed in sturdy wooden booths, to trestle tables piled high with fine English wool and Flemish cloth, furs from the North and spices and sweetmeats from the faraway East. Even the spaces between the stalls and tables were occupied by people hoping to turn a profit: barbers, jongleurs, travelling players, quacks declaiming the dubious properties of whatever potion or elixir they were selling. Pie-vendors wandered through the crowd, adding their voices to the din; children and dogs abounded, darting between stalls and wagons and legs with equally reckless abandon.

And, overlooking all, the castle that held licence for the fair stood apart on its wooded rise above the town in grimly-fortified patronage.

"Do you know who lives there?" Bess asked, seeing Nell's gaze go from the grey-walled turrets above them to the uniformed men-at-arms mingling with the crowd.

"No, and even if I did, I doubt they'd recognise me like this." Nell glanced down at herself and tried to quell a growing feeling of nervousness. It hadn't been so bad at first. The unaccustomed freedom to wander at will among the stalls and booths had delighted her, as had the lavish way she had been dispersing Beaudene's money on various neccessities for their outlaw hosts.

There was, in truth, nothing to be nervous about. She looked no different from any other fair-goer. Her long hair was braided and coiled into a plain crespinette and the dusky-rose woollen gown Bess had found for her was modestly cut and worn beneath a sleeveless, fitted surcoat of moss-green velvet, neatly trimmed with miniver. She could, in fact, have passed for a respectable tradesman's daughter. Neither the soldiers in the crowd, nor the group of apprentices who had been following her and Bess around the fair, snickering and nudging each other but not venturing nearer, would suspect she was a lady abroad without male protection.

And that was the real problem, Nell admitted silently, as she waited for Bess to purchase a supply of candles. She wasn't afraid of the risk of exposure. She missed Beaudene's presence beside her.

So much for enjoying herself away from him, she thought gloomily. Somehow, in their brief time together, she had grown accustomed to his protection. After years of constant guardedness, of having to protect herself, there was something very reassuring in the knowledge that his solid strength stood between her and possible danger. He might be infuriating and intimidating, and much too complex for her peace of mind, but she could not think of one other man of her acquaintance whom she would trust with her safety, with her very life.

And that despite her suspicions that he knew more about their capture than he was willing to tell her.

Nell shivered suddenly as an insidious little question crept, unbidden, into her mind. If she trusted Beaudene with her life, did that mean she could trust him in other ways? With the secret she had guarded for years?

With her heart?

A strange stillness seemed to settle around her. The sounds and bustle of the fair faded into a dim, misty background, and all she could see was a series of images. Beaudene leaning against the wall in her uncle's hall, watching her with the golden eyes of a hawk; standing, tall and powerful, across a fire, waiting for her capitulation; blazing-eyed and furious because she had risked danger to have her way.

And, against all that, she had only one kiss. One brief moment, that for all its sweetness had left her bewildered and angry and strangely vulnerable. Why would she trust her heart to a man who had such a very unsettling effect on her? Why had the thought so much as entered her mind?

Oh, aye, he had protected her, but it was merely duty. She would do well to remember that. She might amuse him occasionally, he might be completely unlike the other men she had known all her life, but he was just her bodyguard. She was in his charge. Nothing more.

"My lady? I mean… Nell, are you all right?"

Bess's anxious countenance swam before her eyes. Nell blinked, coming back to her surroundings with a jolt. Noise and movement started up around her again, seeming to be twice as loud and bewildering as before.

"Shall we purchase something to eat, mistress?" Bess went on, obviously still concerned. She indicated a near by pie-vendor who was eyeing them with interest. "You look a little pale."

"Succulent pigeons in a coffin, ladies," the man called, sensing potential customers. He gave an ingratiating grin.

Nell repressed a shudder and aimed a weak smile somewhere between Bess and the pie-vendor. "No, I'm just a little tired, 'tis all. We'd best conclude our business and be gone."

"Aye, 'tis a long walk back," Bess agreed. She touched Nell's arm. "This way, my lady. The old woman's booth is at the end of this row, near yonder trees. And let us hope we can slip away without those dolts noting our direction." She glanced back as she spoke, frowning slightly. "I don't like the way they've been following us."

"They'll lose interest if we ignore them," Nell murmured, hoping to heaven she was right. Dismissing the apprentices from her mind, she tried to remember the list of herbs and medicines she needed to buy. That was all she had to worry about, she told herself with grim purpose. Helping Bess's people. One especially.

The reminder sent another chill whispering over her flesh. For some reason a decision that had seemed so simple and right yesterday was becoming harder to contemplate.

"The last booth, you say?" she asked, determinedly fixing her gaze on a faded green awning set a little apart from the others. She quickened her pace, suddenly aware that, a mere fifty yards away, several men-at-arms were engaged in setting up butts for an archery contest later in the day. "What is the woman's name?"

"Maudelin." Bess lowered her voice, although at this end of the row of stalls the crowd had thinned considerably. "But that's all I know. No one even knows where she lives. 'Tis said she appears at the castle, if she's needed, then vanishes back into the woods, though none have seen her go. And they say she has a pet squirrel that takes food from her lips."

''She probably tamed it,'' Nell muttered, still too busy battling with her own private demons to worry about the unearthly kind. ''But at this present moment I don't care if both she and the squirrel can fly.''

Bess looked rather awed at this reckless statement, but had perforce to remain silent. They had arrived at the front of the booth and Nell found herself subjected to a thorough scrutiny from the blackest pair of eyes she had ever seen, set like shiny little stones in a brown, wrinkled face. The woman staring at her looked as if the lightest puff of wind would blow her head over heels, but Nell didn't make the mistake of thinking the old dame was wanting in wits as well as substance. Those black eyes were shrewd and held the knowledge of ages.

''Meg is gone,'' she said without any greeting and without taking her eyes from Nell. ''And you, girl, you want something special from me.''

''We want many things, Mistress Maudelin,'' Nell answered with a calm she was far from feeling. Despite her brave words to Bess, the bent old crone was not the most comfortable person she had ever met, but she suspected that, like Beaudene, the woman respected those she couldn't intimidate. She made her tone brisk. ''To start, a lotion of comfrey or betony. Or, if 'tis not made up, then comfrey leaves, if they be freshly picked. Then, St John's wort and woundwort-cream. A little syrup of poppy. Horehound, coltsfoot, mint and bay— also in a syrup, if you have it, or steeped in spirit of wine. Mulberry leaves to make a paste for burns. Fennel and basil. And—'' she took a deep breath ''—some hyssop.''

Maudelin's black eyes narrowed, deepening the wrinkles in her lined and weathered face. ''So knowledgeable for a young lady,'' she said, giving the words a slightly mocking intonation. ''But rash. Very rash, like all the young. You should try spitting thrice in a frog's mouth, girl. Or eating bees.'' She laughed suddenly, a harsh sound that cracked in the middle. '''Tis safer for such a delicate creature as yourself.''

''I prefer something more certain,'' Nell said, holding the dame's gaze. She didn't bother to correct Maudelin's assumption that the herb she needed was intended for herself. ''And I can pay you well.''

After another long minute of intent scrutiny, the woman shrugged. ''Then choose what you will,'' she said, gesturing with a gnarled hand towards the bowls and flasks lined up at the rear of the booth. ''But later, choose wisely, girl. You think you are hard enough for the task, but there's a softness in you that few have seen. And remember, a deed once done may be regretted too late.''

Nell acted on the first statement and closed her mind to the rest, thankful that the old woman had turned her attention to Bess and was questioning her about Meg. She did not speak again until her purchases were made and stowed safely in the willow basket they had brought for the purpose. Then she had Bess's curiosity to contend with.

''What was that all about?'' the other girl pounced, the minute they were out of earshot. ''All that nonsense about frogs and bees. Does she doubt your knowledge?''

Nell shook her head and resisted the urge to look back. She knew Maudelin was watching her. She could feel that black-eyed stare boring into her back. ''Such people indulge in mysterious sayings to impress the ignorant and simple,'' she retorted, while mentally crossing herself. Then she realised that this reply was hardly flattering to Bess. "It matters not," she tacked on hastily. "If you are done here, we had best be off back to your camp. Creeping out before first light might have been easy, but saints know how we're going to explain such a long absence."

And creeping out of the camp had only been easy because Beaudene had not returned to the hut, she added silently. The possible reasons for his absence had been one of the puzzles that had kept her awake long into the night.

"We'll tell the truth," Bess said, with a blithe unconcern that had Nell staring at her in astonishment. "What can they do except yell at us? We've already done what we set out to do."

"Well, aye, but..." The words faded as Nell's mouth went dry. She had a sudden nerve-racking memory of Beaudene's reaction the last time she had roused his ire. And of the very different kiss that had come later. Somehow she didn't think he would waste a lot of time yelling; his retribution would be much more devastating. A devastation of her senses that was already beginning to tighten her nerves in half-fearful, half-tremulous anticipation. Sweet Lord, what was the man doing to her that she trembled with expectation rather than terror at the thought of his rage?

"But I think we may have a problem here first," Bess added in an undertone that succeeded in breaking into Nell's dismayed thoughts.

She looked up to see that one of the town apprentices, obviously egged on by his fellows and a considerable quantity of ale, had planted himself in their path.

"I'm in the next wrestling match," he announced in slurred accents. He waved towards the cleared space

behind him and seemed to sway in the light breeze.
''And whatever wench cheers me on can spend the
purse I'll win. For a small favour.'' He leered. ''What
say you?''

''Win!'' Bess drew herself up to her full height,
which was several inches below their inebriated swain,
and glared at him. ''Your opponent will only have to
breathe and you'll topple over. Out of our way, you
drunken oaf, or I'll call the soldiers.''

Her clear voice carried for several yards. Amid an
outburst of laughter from the passers-by the youth's
companions began jeering and shouting out crude advice.

Under cover of the noise, Nell tugged at Bess's
sleeve. ''We don't want any soldiers,'' she hissed.

''Too late,'' Bess muttered, as three men-at-arms
abandoned their archery targets and began to push their
way through the crowd rapidly gathering about the
small scene. ''Don't worry,'' she added. ''They'll cart
the lot of them off and throw them into a cell until
they're sober. You won't have to speak at all. Indeed,
'twould be better if you did not.''

''Give way there!'' The first man-at-arms to reach
them plucked an urchin out of his path, looked at Nell
and Bess, and puffed out his chest importantly. ''You
ladies havin' trouble here?'' he asked, and hiccuped.

''Oh, no,'' groaned Nell. ''He's been drinking, too.
What in heaven's name are we going to do?''

Every eye in the crowd turned to her. Too late, she
realised why Bess hadn't wanted her to speak.

''A lady!''

'''Tis a lady.''

''Dressed like that? Don't be an idiot.''

The comments rippled through the crowd like a

breeze through the grass. Almost imperceptibly the mob shuffled closer. A hand reached out and touched Nell's gown, as if testing the stuff.

Nell slapped the hand away. "Loose my gown, fellow," she ordered in her haughtiest tone. If the damage was done, she thought, she might as well try to command her way out of their predicament.

Almost instantly she realised that it wasn't going to work. The murmurs rose higher on the air like the hum of a hundred bees.

"Now, mistress, you don't want to cause any trouble," another man-at-arms began in portentous tones. He took her arm in a hard-fingered grip. "You just come along with me and—"

"I have no intention of going anywhere with you." Nell wrenched her arm free and glared at the soldier. "If you had a grain more sense than those fools, you'd take *them* away and teach them not to harass common citizens."

"That be no common citizen," shouted a voice in the crowd.

"How would you know, Martin?" yelled another. "You can't even see straight enough to tell what's female and what's not."

There was a roar of laughter.

"Them be female enough to tease us all morning," accused one of the apprentices. "And if she be a lady, what's she doing here with only another wench?"

An ominous rumble of agreement rolled through the crowd.

Encouraged by this sign of public support, the youth pressed on. "Who knows them? Who can vouch for them? More likely they're outlaws come to rob—"

He was promptly howled down by a merchant standing near by. "They paid their money, like everyone else," the man shouted, apparently taking up the cudgels of defence. "Just because you louts follow anything in a skirt—"

He got no further. Carried away by the knowledge that at least half the crowd was on his side, the apprentice rammed his fist into the merchant's fat belly. The man doubled over.

"By our Lady!" A second merchant pushed through the crowd, grabbed the strutting youth with two beefy hands and shook him like a rat. "Is this the sort of protection we pay good money for?" he yelled to his fellows as the boy's companions rushed to his rescue. "Let's teach them some manners, lads."

A second later, with what seemed to Nell like a concerted roar of approval, the field erupted into a seething mass of brawling men and crashing tables. Shrieking and yelping with dismay, women, children and dogs dived for cover behind the more solid booths.

"Saints deliver us!" Clutching her precious basket of medicines, Nell exchanged one horrified glance with Bess then looked around desperately for an escape. There was none. They were right in the middle of the madly swaying crowd, and, worse, she was staring directly into the grim face of a sober man-at-arms, who, wisely deciding against interfering in something he couldn't stop without considerable risk to life and limb, had already taken another firm hold of her arm.

"Oh, no, you don't," he growled. "You're coming up to the castle with me, mistress. Both of you can answer to the sheriff for this disturbance."

"We didn't start this," Bess protested indignantly. And before the soldier had any warning, she swung the length of wool she was carrying and caught him a blow to the side of the head.

"Run!" she shrilled as the man staggered back.

Nell, already trying to break free of his grasp, had to duck as a pigeon pie flew past her head. Her captor, equally determined to hang on was not so fortunate. Thrown off-balance by trying to avoid two more pies hurled in quick succession, which found their mark on his neck, he went down into the tangled sea of legs and feet, taking Nell with him. Her terrified scream was abruptly cut off as a large hand wrapped itself around her other arm and yanked her back to safety.

"God in heaven," grated an exasperated male voice in her ear. "Can't I leave you alone even for a few hours?"

Chapter Eight

Before Nell could do more than gasp with thankful recognition, she was jerked behind her rescuer and released. The soldier leapt to his feet with an enraged yell, met Beaudene's clenched fist head-on and crumpled. This time he stayed down.

Rafe turned to fix Nell with an extremely annoyed glare. ''When this is over, princess, I'm going to take my hand to your sweet backside so hard you'll wish you *had* been dragged up to that castle.'' He side-stepped a tun of wine as it hurtled past him and turned Nell none too gently in the direction he wanted her to go. ''Now, get over to those trees and see if you can stay out of sight!''

Using fists and feet with equal disregard for inflicting damage, he began to forge a path for them through the throng, then wheeled about to cover their retreat.

''They'll all kill each other,'' wailed Bess as Nell grabbed her hand and they sped towards the shelter of the woods.

''Good!'' Nell retorted through chattering teeth. She was still trembling and shaken from her recent fright, but she was also furious. How dared Beaudene threaten to beat her just because she had got into trouble while trying to help people?

"*Good*?" squeaked Bess. "But Dickon is in there, too, and there's a price on his head. What if he's recognised?"

"It won't happen." Nell reached the first of the trees and stopped to look back. "They're men! Far from getting into trouble they're probably enjoying themselves, and then they'll look forward to the pleasure of yelling at us. Never mind that we're the innocent parties here." She had to pause for breath, then continued as furiously as before. "Well, I, for one, am not going to let them lay this at our door. If we'd been dealing with rational beings we wouldn't have had to sneak away in the first place!"

"Oh, don't let them hear you say so, my lady. Look, they've reached those trees over there to our right, and not before time." Bess pointed in the direction of the castle, where a score of soldiers could be seen descending the rise at a run.

The fairground itself had become a shambles. Enthusiasm for the fight didn't seem to have waned in the slightest. Men-at-arms, apprentices and tradesmen alike threw themselves into the battle without regard to station, sobriety or sense. Nell winced as a farmer sailed through the air and crashed into an archery butt. He got up, shook his head, and waded back into the fray.

"Idiot males!" she fumed. "Numbskulls! They wouldn't have a brain between the lot of them."

A twig snapped behind her. "Precisely what I was going to say," grated Beaudene. "I thought I told you to get into the trees and stay out of sight, not take up a front-row stand."

Nell's head whipped around. Beaudene was striding

towards them with another man who, at first glance, looked startlingly like him. There was one rather obvious difference, however. The second man was laughing so much that he could hardly walk.

"Mistress Nell," he gasped, sobering long enough to get the words out. "My compliments. I swear I haven't had as much fun in a score of months. Nor has Rafe, probably, but he won't admit it. And judging by the look on his face he won't present me." He bowed. "Sir Richard Peverel, at your service."

Rafe threw him a furious glance and stalked past him. Wrapping his fingers around Nell's wrist, he pulled her further into the wood. "You can indulge your misplaced sense of obligation later," he growled. "We'd better get these two away, before those fools out there realise the perpetrators of the whole thing have vanished."

"Perpetrators—!" began Nell, outraged. She was interrupted from an unexpected quarter.

Bess had turned away from the battleground and was staring at Richard as if she'd never seen him before. "Sir Richard Peverel?" she repeated weakly. Then her eyes flashed blue sparks. One fist went to her hip. "*Sir Richard Peverel!*"

Richard eyed the roll of cloth in her other hand warily. "Now, Bess, lass," he placated her, "I was going to tell you."

"Don't you 'now, Bess, lass' me," Bess stormed. "You let me think… You let me believe—How *could* you, when you knew what had befallen me at the hands of your kind?"

"Damn it, that's why," Richard exploded, suddenly completely sober. "Bess—"

"Come on," Rafe murmured, yanking Nell out of

her state of shock at this unforeseen turn of events. "The horses are over here."

"But what about...? We can't just leave..." She was towed inexorably onward.

"They'll follow. Richard will soon have your little friend calmed down." He grinned at her, the expression so startling after the anger practically crackling in the air around him that Nell nearly tripped over an exposed tree-root in surprise. "All the way here he was threatening to turn her over his knee, but I rather think he may have just met his match."

"You, I suppose, still intend to carry out your stupid male threat to beat me," Nell panted. It was difficult to infuse the proper note of defiance into her voice when she was being hauled through the forest by a man whose strides were twice as long as hers. "Even though it wasn't my fault."

His grin vanished. "It damn well was your fault. Little idiot! I should beat you within an inch of your life. Mayhap then you'd learn not to throw yourself headlong into danger every time my back is turned."

"That shows how little you know," she muttered. "I've spent the last three years keeping myself out of danger—without the help of any man."

They reached the horses and Rafe stopped, swinging around to pin her with a dangerous stare. "Is that so?" he asked very softly. "And just how did you manage that, princess?"

Nell stiffened her spine and glared back at him. "It wasn't difficult. They didn't have any brains or sense either. Like you, they saw what they wanted to see and didn't look any further."

His fingers tightened around her wrist. "And you let them see what they wanted to see, didn't you? Languishing sighs, sidelong looks, admiring glances. Not to mention—''

''Admiring!'' Nell broke in without ceremony. She didn't have any desire to hear the rest of what was undoubtedly a lengthy catalogue of her faults. ''If I'd followed my natural inclinations, and laughed at those preening peacocks, they would have turned into extremely nasty small boys—except they had the strength of men.''

He was silent for a moment, his eyes intent. ''And you're too small and soft to defend yourself physically,'' he murmured. ''Is that what happened, little one? Did you learn to use men rather than be used?''

Nell discovered that her heart was beating uncomfortably fast. All at once the gently enquiring note in Beaudene's voice made her want to give in to the impulse she had felt when she'd realised who had saved her from the guard. At that moment, she remembered, she had wanted nothing more than to throw herself into his arms and feel them close around her, strong and protective. Only the fight raging around them had stopped her.

For which she should be grateful, Nell told herself now, gazing up at him. Throw herself into his arms? She didn't even know if he was still angry with her. If his punishing grip on her wrist was anything to go by, any move to fling herself at him would probably result in an accusation that she was trying to use *him*.

''I don't use men,'' she denied at last. ''I have no use for them.''

His voice went even softer. ''Indeed? Then you've never been made love to properly.''

''Love!'' Now she could hardly breathe. ''What has

love to do with the dealings between men and women?''

'''Twas merely a manner of speaking,'' Rafe said absently, intrigued by the signs of increasing female agitation. The almost imperceptible tremor in her voice was having a strange effect on him, smothering his anger beneath a growing need to hear his name spoken in that breathless, utterly feminine whisper. He took a step closer and saw her tremble.

What was she thinking? he wondered. Her chin was up and her soft mouth set in a stubborn line, but her dark-lashed eyes were wide and, in the sun-dappled forest, appeared more green than hazel. She looked as if she didn't know whether he was going to beat her or kiss her.

But he knew what he wanted. He knew what he needed. His hand clenched around her wrist.

She didn't make a sound, not one whimper, but her lashes flickered and went still.

On the edge of dragging her into his arms and kissing her senseless, Rafe froze. His eyes narrowed on the sudden pain tightening her face and his grip shifted, his hand sliding down to clasp hers. Still holding her eyes with his own, he reached out with his other hand and pushed the long sleeve of her gown halfway to her elbow. A single glance was all he needed to see the bracelet of dark bruises circling the tender flesh of her wrist. He cursed softly.

''Did I do that?''

''No.'' The faint whisper barely reached him. '''Twas the soldier. The one you hit.''

''I should have killed him,'' he said, still staring at the discoloured flesh. ''He'd have deserved it.''

Her shaky laugh washed over his senses like a caress. "For bruising me?"

"For that." His eyes returned to hers and stayed. "For frightening you." He raised her hand to his mouth and pressed his parted lips gently to the inside of her wrist. "For daring to touch you."

Her hand quivered in his, as if she would pull it away. "D-don't."

God, if her voice trembled any more he was going to—

The thought stopped abruptly when his gaze lowered to the pulse beating wildly in her throat. Was it fear or—? The question hovered at the edge of his mind for a moment, then certainty hit him like a fist to the gut. And this time there was no doubt at all overlaying it. This time there was no trace of desire in her eyes, nothing but fear and—Rafe frowned—even a hint of tears.

Stunned, he released her. "Nell?"

"I...I..." Nell closed her eyes briefly against Beaudene's searching gaze. "I think I hear the others."

It was a lie. She couldn't hear anything over the pounding of her heart. Then relief turned her knees to water as the lie became truth. A rustle of leaves and the cracking of a small branch heralded the arrival of Richard and Bess. Before they reached them, Beaudene turned quickly, shielding her.

"We'd better split up," she heard him say to Richard. "This forest will be crawling with men-at-arms before too long, and a double trail may serve to confuse them."

Richard answered. Or, at least, Nell supposed that he did. All she was conscious of was the powerful, broad-shouldered back directly in front of her and the memory of the expression in his eyes just before he'd turned away. For the first time since she'd met him, she could have sworn Beaudene had been as puzzled and unsure as she was herself.

And she could hardly blame him, Nell thought. After the almost blatant way she had thrown her supposed past in his face, she was now acting like a terrified rabbit whenever he came near her. Worse. For a mind-numbling instant there, she had actually been teetering on the brink of telling him the truth. Of telling him everything. The longing to do so had warred so fiercely with her natural caution that she'd felt rent in two, and though caution had won it had left her feeling more alone than she had ever felt before. Alone and desperately uncertain.

She moved restlessly, trying to throw off the sudden feeling of vulnerability, and the vials in her basket clinked together.

Beaudene swung around, his gaze sharpening. ''What's in there?''

''Herbs. Medicines. What we came for,'' Nell finished in a stronger tone, recalling Bess's earlier advice. She glanced towards the other girl, but Bess and Richard were already riding away. Nell seized the only other diversion available. She peered into the basket to check that nothing had been broken during her struggle with the soldier. ''They're all still intact, fortunately.''

''Give them to me,'' he ordered, his voice curt. ''I'll hand them up to you when you're on Samson.''

This was not the time to protest his lack of gallantry in letting her mount alone. Nell obeyed without a murmur. Beaudene handed her the basket, gathered up the reins and swung himself into the saddle behind her. His arms came around her, guiding Samson away from the direction Richard had taken.

Nell nearly leapt straight back to the ground in panic. To be so close to him, caged between his arms, was more than her overwrought nerves could bear. Against her back he felt warm and hard, overwhelmingly large, reassuringly strong, a threat, protection…

Saints in heaven, she wouldn't last a yard riding like this, let alone several miles. The fragile hold she had on her emotions would crumble like so much dust, and she would do something completely stupid. Like burst into tears. Cling to him. Beg him to hold her and never let her go.

"Surely…" Her voice was a husky croak and she had to start again. "Surely 'twould be better if I rode pillion—"

"The way you attract trouble? I'm keeping you where I can see you."

For one blissful second sheer disbelief had Nell forgetting everything else. "By the Rood!" she exclaimed. "What sort of trouble can I get into on the back of a horse?"

"You'd be surprised," he growled, sounding distinctly menacing.

Nell turned her head to stare at him. It was a mistake. Her cheek brushed his shoulder and his mouth was only inches away from hers. The sight drew her gaze and held it, fascinated. Contrasts, she thought again, but vaguely. How could she think when she wanted to touch him, to trace the chiselled line of his upper lip, to press her fingers to the fuller lower one?

"Keep looking at me like that, princess, and I'll demonstrate just precisely what I mean. Is that what you want?"

The soft, suddenly rough tone yanked her back to reality with jarring thoroughness. Her head whipped to the front as if he had struck her. "No," she whispered, and knew she lied.

And if she didn't say something else—*anything else*—he would know it too.

"How did you get your scar?"

The air around them seemed to go cold in an instant. Nell felt Rafe stiffen behind her and held her breath. Dear God, of all the questions she could have asked, why in the name of—?

"'Tis a long story."

Nell blinked, hardly able to believe he had actually answered her. "Good," she managed, after another nerve-racking minute of silence. "'Twill pass the time."

He muttered something that sounded suspiciously like, "That's not such a bad idea." Then he added aloud, "And not very pleasant hearing. Suffice it to say that I tried to recover something that had been stolen from me before I was old enough to fight for it."

"Someone robbed you when you were a child?" She felt as if she was poised precariously on the brink of discovery, longing to move forward, but afraid that one false step would see the treasure snatched away from her. "And then…"

"And then he tried to rob me of an eye when I confronted him, yes. Not a very heroic tale, is it?" His tone was mocking, but Nell heard the bitterness and pain behind the mockery.

"You were a child," she said gently. "But what of your father? Could he not—?"

"My father died before I had any memories of him. But since he left everything in my mother's hands, even when he was alive, I doubt I missed much."

"'Tis not an uncommon thing if a man is often away

from home,'' Nell ventured. The feeling of being balanced on the edge of a precipice was stronger than ever. "But 'tis difficult sometimes, for a woman alone. I'm sure your mother would have fought for you had she been able.''

He gave a short laugh. "Before you start wallowing in sentiment, princess, I have to tell you that my mother helped the thief in his enterprise, and then, fortunately for her, died before I knew any robbery had taken place.''

Nell was silent. She wanted to speak, to tell him that she knew what it was to be betrayed like that, to feel the pain of that betrayal, but instinct warned her that Rafe would reject any sympathy with brutal despatch.

No wonder he mistrusted women, she thought broodingly. And no wonder he had misjudged her, given the evidence at her farewell banquet. It sounded very much as if Rafe's mother had manipulated her husband to the advantage of her lover—for what other reason would a woman conspire to steal from her own son? It was also plain to the meanest intelligence that he .considered both Yorkist and Lancastrian queens to be manipulative. And when Rafe had first seen *her*, she had been juggling men right and left. The realisation was unexpectedly lowering.

"You intend to fight this man again, don't you?'' she murmured in an effort to lift the cloud of depression hovering over her. "Was that why you were at Court?''

He laughed again, softly. "I was right. You are a worthy opponent, little princess. Aye, my petition is one of the many piling up on Edward's table these days.''

"Will he grant your right to whatever it is?''

Nell felt tension stream through his body the instant

before his hands clenched on the reins. His voice went flat and hard.

"Whether he does or not, I will take back what was mine. One way or another. I have sworn an oath on it."

The cold promise of retribution in the words made Nell shiver. God send that such an implacable desire for revenge was never turned on her.

"Well... I wish you good fortune, my lord," she said, with a brave attempt at the light chatter she had once used to such good effect. "If my determination equals your own, we should both succeed in our quests."

"If you're about to mention Wells again," he promptly countered, "let me save you the trouble. The answer is still no."

An intense flash of annoyance surged through Nell. She was pathetically grateful for it. For some reason, annoyance was oddly reassuring. "But last night you said—"

"I said we'd stay here for one day. That was the extent of our bargain, my lady."

"In that case, I wonder you did not chase after me on the Wells road this morning," she flashed. "Instead of going directly to the fair."

"There was never any doubt about that," he murmured. "You had given Bess your word. But if what you're wearing was meant to be a disguise, it failed dismally in its purpose."

Totally forgetting the danger in looking at him while she was practically in his arms, Nell turned to stare upwards in utter amazement.

"I thought you hadn't noticed," she finally said in a voice that betrayed all too clearly that he had succeeded in throwing her entirely off-balance. He trusted her word!

His mouth curved in a way that sent shivers rippling down her limbs. "Oh, I noticed, princess. The problem is, so did every other man at that fair, as you discovered to your cost."

"What? But—but—I changed my clothes so I wouldn't be noticed," she spluttered. "This dress is *nothing* like the one I…you…And it even has a surcoat over it!"

"That fits you like a second skin."

Nell took several steadying breaths. "Well, I can see there is no pleasing you, my lord. First you threw my headdress to the four winds. Yesterday you slew my new shoes. And now—"

"I didn't say I dislike the dress," he interrupted. His eyes, narrowed and glittering, slid over her in a look of such intimacy that she felt suddenly, terrifyingly, naked. "Your other gown was an invitation to look." His voice lowered to a soft growl. "This one makes a man want to touch."

Every bone in her body seemed to melt in the heat that flooded her veins. Her breasts swelled and tingled. There was a strange fluttering sensation deep inside her.

She wanted him to kiss her again, Nell realised, horrified at the depth of her response. He hadn't so much as touched her, was even now watching her with that strange assessment she had seen last night—while she was quivering with anticipation.

"You forget yourself, my lord," she got out at last, tearing her gaze away from his to stare sightlessly at the forest in front of her. "You are supposed to be my bodyguard." *She* had certainly forgotten that. "Whatever your opinion of my clothes, my person or my…my actions, I will thank you to keep them to yourself.''

''And I,'' he answered beneath his breath, ''am beginning to think that I don't know much about you at all, despite your clothes, your person or your actions.''

The rest of the ride was accomplished in a silence that stretched Nell's nerves to the limit. In an effort to distract herself she brooded for a while on the second discovery of the day—that her bodyguard clearly knew the outlaw leader well. The situation should have made her mildly uneasy, to say the least, and the fact that it didn't promptly led her back to the disturbing question of trust and another flash of the strange affinity she felt with Beaudene.

She trusted him with her life, with her safety, but he threatened her in ways she could only sense. He trusted her word, but still believed her to be wanton.

They had reached an impasse, she realised with a little shiver of awareness. And, to overcome it, one of them would have to do something neither had done since childhood. Trust blindly.

She shivered again as the next logical question occurred to her. Why would she want to break such an impasse in the first place?

The task of caring for the wounded took up the rest of the day, with Nell dispensing medicines and advice and Bess following her instructions with strict attention. Nell had been grateful for the work. It had kept her mind from contemplation of a deed that had made her feel more cold and shivery inside with every passing moment, until now, with the sun hovering just above the horizon, a fine tremor had seized her hands and she felt sick to her stomach.

Bess had not seemed to notice her increasing pre-occupation, but had kept silent herself a good deal of the time. Nell wished she knew Bess well enough to mention the girl's liaison with Sir Richard, if only to offer comfort, but all she could do was brood on the inevitable result of a relationship between an outlaw girl and a knight of the realm—even if he did have a price on his own head.

Another woman at the mercy of some man, she thought angrily, even while knowing that her resentment might be misplaced. Bess was certainly capable of making her own choices, but Nell remembered the betrayal in the other girl's eyes and knew that she was in love with Sir Richard.

Holy Mother, she demanded silently, isn't there one male among them who can behave honourably when a woman is involved?

A fleeting memory of Beaudene at their first encounter, scornful and uncompromising, flashed into her mind. One, she admitted. One man. And he believes *me* to be dishonoured.

Pushing the thought aside with an effort, she paused outside the hut next to Bess's cottage and handed the basket of flasks and linens to her companion.

"There's nought to do here except dispense what comfort I may," she said, calmly enough. "You've been nursing the wounded day and night. Why don't you rest a while before we eat?"

To her relief, Bess nodded. "An hour's repose would be welcome, indeed," she said in weary agreement. "But more importantly—" she touched Nell's hand in a shy gesture of friendship "—thanks to you, my lady, I'll sleep easier tonight knowing the children will live."

Nell stepped into the dim, quiet hut with those words pounding in her head.

Children. Living. Laughing. All but one. A child who might not even exist, she told herself, stepping closer to the bed as her eyes adjusted to the muted light. She stood there for what seemed like a very long time, watching the girl who lay asleep on her side, her face turned away from the door.

Why did she hesitate? Nell wondered. Hadn't she known yesterday what needed to be done? Hadn't she already decided? The task was an easy one. Terrifyingly easy. The powder was prepared. All she had to do was mix the dose with a little syrup of wine, then waken the girl, hold the cup to her lips. She would drink before she was fully awake, unknowing, innocent of any wrong, free to live her life without the reminder of fear and shame and brutality.

Still she waited, shaking visibly now. And cold. So cold that she couldn't even feel the little bag of powdered herb clenched in her hand. She couldn't feel anything except the churning sickness in her stomach, the tightness in her throat.

There might not be a child, she told herself again. And if no child existed, there would be no harm done. No one would ever know what had passed here in any event. But if there was a child... If a babe lay snug in that fragile vessel, not yet living, but surely deserving of life; created by violence, but an innocent victim also; a soul belonging to God, but denied salvation—

"Oh, blessed Christ, I cannot do it!"

Nell sobbed aloud and clapped her hands to her mouth to stifle the sound. The bag pressed against her cheek and she lowered her hands again to stare at it. The sight of it made her almost physically ill.

"Dear Lord," she prayed in a choked whisper. "Help this innocent soul, for I cannot." And it was not of her own soul that she thought in that moment. She simply couldn't kill.

Utterly unable to think beyond that fact, she groped blindly for the pouch still tied beneath her gown, and stuffed the little bag of herbs out of sight. Then, moving very carefully, she turned and opened the door.

Beaudene was standing not two feet away. It was the first time she had seen him since they had returned to the camp in silence.

"Bess told me you were here." He hesitated, frowning at her. "Come and rest now. You've been on your feet all day tending these people."

Nell couldn't meet his eyes. She gave a jerky nod, gazing past him to the fire. Warmth. Heat. She needed it. Desperately.

"I'll sit by the fire," she murmured. Her voice was husky and she cleared her throat, stepping sideways to go around him.

"Nell?" He stopped her with a hand on her arm. "What's amiss?"

It was as well she still felt frozen, she thought vaguely. The note of genuine concern in his voice didn't affect her at all. But his hand was warm. Warm and strong and alive. She could feel the pulse beating in his fingers as they curled against the softness of her inner elbow. Or maybe it was her own pulse…or both…two hearts linked, beating as one.

"I'm just tired! That's all!" She pulled her arm free as she spoke and almost ran towards the fire, noticing too late that Richard was already seated there, sprawled against a log. She couldn't turn back. Beaudene had followed her and she didn't need to look at him to know that his intent, narrowed gaze was focused on her face.

Richard got to his feet and smiled. "Mistress Nell," he greeted her. "Bess tells me you've saved the lives of our wounded. I hope you know that, if I can ever repay you, no service would be too great to ask of me."

Nell shook her head. She didn't know if she could trust herself to speak, but unless she wanted the men hovering over her she would have to act as normally as possible.

"One man may yet die," she warned, ordering her knees to unlock so she could sit down. She edged closer to the warmth of the flames, keeping her gaze on Richard as he and Rafe seated themselves on either side of her.

Rafe picked up the wineskin next to him and handed it to her. "Here, have some of this. 'Twill put some colour in your cheeks."

"No fancy goblets, I'm afraid," Richard said, apparently feeling the need to excuse the rough amenities of the camp. He grinned. "But the wine's good, and there's roasted suckling pig for our supper."

"Roasted suckling pig," Nell repeated valiantly, while her stomach roiled. She took a cautious sip of wine and put the skin down. "Where did you get it?"

"Better not ask," Rafe put in drily.

He was still watching her. She could feel his gaze like a physical touch. What was he looking for? Was there something in her face, some lingering hint of the terrible crime she had almost committed? And how was she to get rid of the herb without his knowledge? It was far too dangerous to be left in inexperienced hands. Though it could be useful in the treatment of chest ailments, too much could kill.

Disjointed plans scurried around in her head like mice in a cage. She would have to destroy the powder. But how? Burn it? Impossible to do that without being seen. Bury it, maybe? Aye, that was it. Bury it where no one would find it, and eventually it would lose its potency. She would have to slip away from the camp and—

"Rafe tells me you have to leave in the morning."

"What?" Nell jumped, staring at Richard until the statement sank in. It seemed to take forever. "Oh. Aye. If my lord says so."

"Saints above! You must be tired. Such compliance."

"Don't tease the poor girl, Rafe. 'Tis an uneven match at the moment. Do you need me to watch your back tomorrow?"

Rafe made a negative sound. "If fortune favours us, they'll be ahead of us by now. Besides—" he paused and glanced at Nell "—we're going to Wells first."

Nell's head jerked around so fast that she nearly lost her balance. "What did you say?" She hadn't heard right, of course.

He smiled faintly. "Are you forgetting your own strategy, princess? A detour to Wells will keep us from overrunning your family's heels, or meeting them on their way back."

"Oh."

A truly intelligent answer, she thought. But what else could she say? If she asked him why he had changed his mind, he might very well change it again.

"Aye. A fond family you have there," Richard remarked. "Hiring an assassin, by God."

"He was assisted by a certain party who made a

habit of frequenting the stable at midnight," growled
Beaudene, before Nell could answer.

She scowled at him. "I went out there to say goodbye to my horse, if you recall."

"An innocent excuse," he conceded. "On that particular night."

"What is that supposed to mean?"

"It means, princess, that your relatives were very
certain of your whereabouts. So, clearly you frequented
the stable at that hour more than once."

"Someone could just as easily have seen the candle
I had left there earlier and assumed I'd slip out to see
Chevette," Nell retorted. "They knew I was fond of
her, and that I couldn't take her home."

"Why not?" asked Richard, his gaze shifting from
Nell to Rafe and back again like a spectator at a tour-
nament.

They both turned to stare at him.

"Just an idle thought," he offered meekly, but his
lips twitched.

Nell flushed, and fought down her rising temper. It
was useless to rant and rave or try to justify her actions
to Beaudene, but at least she now felt a little better.
She wondered suddenly if that had been his intention
in baiting her.

"My uncle said 'twas too long and hard a journey,"
she told Richard. "But—" She shrugged and dared a
sideways glance at Beaudene. "It hasn't been so bad."

"More likely she was too steady a mount, if they
were planning something during the trip," he said with
more than a touch of cynicism.

"I can't see Tom planning anything," Nell said
doutfully. "He's a dolt and usually has his face buried

in an ale-cup. Edmund, now, he's sharp and he's vicious enough, God knows, but—''

"He's too young," Beaudene finished for her. "I think you'll find 'twas your lady aunt who was the brains behind their ambition, princess. But don't worry, I'll get you home safely. You have my pledge on it."

"Better beware," Richard warned Nell with a grin. "Every time he said that when we were boys I always got into some sort of trouble."

"Boys. Aye. You know each other!" Nell exclaimed, abruptly reminded of her other grievance. She looked at Beaudene, her temper simmering again. "You know each other well. That is why you didn't seem overly concerned about our capture."

He merely shrugged. Just as if she hadn't been worried sick yesterday that he might have been involved, she thought indignantly.

"We were opposite numbers in the late, er, royal squabble," Richard confided. "Scouts sent out to locate the other army. Remember the day we came face to face when we discovered that bolt-hole at the same time, Rafe?" He laughed. "We hadn't seen each other for years. I don't know who received the greater shock."

"But you didn't betray each other," Nell said with great certainty. She sat back, content to let the conversation flow around her as she focused properly on Richard for the first time since their meeting. Apart from his grey eyes, his outward resemblance to Beaudene was still striking—both were tall, with the type of lean, powerful build that owed more to sheer muscular strength than bulk, and both were dark—but, as the two men began to talk of the war and their experiences in battle, she saw now that the likeness arose more from

the hard-edged ruthlessness that characterised them
than any similarity of physical feature. A ruthlessness,
she mused, that was born of a close acquaintance with
hardship and danger, and a way of life that forged a
personal code as inflexible as it was honourable.

Perhaps Bess would be safe with Richard after all,
Nell decided. If nothing else he would protect her, as
Beaudene had sworn to do in her own case.

She cast a glance at him from under her lashes, her
eyes tracing the scar at his temple as she recalled what
he had told her earlier. As though sensing her regard,
he reached out, without breaking off his conversation
with Richard, and took her hand in his, enveloping it
in a warm, strong clasp.

Heat spread through her, a sweet, melting tide of
sensation that momentarily fogged her brain. She struggled free of it, unwilling to yield again to something
she didn't yet understand. Something, she thought, almost panicked, that she *had* to understand if she was
not to lose herself to the hidden mists of danger she
had sensed today and last night. But she couldn't bring
herself to pull her hand free. His touch was too necessary, too compelling. She needed it, needed to feel
that strong, vital connection to him.

Had he known that? Had he sensed how cold and
alone she had been feeling inside?

Nell looked away, gazing blindly into the fire as a
new wave of confusion assailed her. Sweet saints in
heaven, her earlier suspicions that Rafe had had something to do with their capture were nothing compared
to the thoughts now whirling around in her head. Every
time they talked, nearly everything he said only confirmed what he thought of her, and yet at the same time
he could be so…so…

She couldn't think of just the right word. Kind was too tame. Nice was ridiculous. Gentle, maybe? Tender? But didn't tenderness imply a kind of caring?

Nell frowned as she struggled to make sense of her mental turmoil. It was almost as if Rafe sometimes forgot her supposed wantonness and treated her as if he actually liked her. Or perhaps...

A faint chill penetrated the protective warmth enveloping her. Perhaps the reverse was true. Perhaps Rafe was being gentler with her, despite his contemptuous opinion, because he wanted something.

The chill spread. Not that, she pleaded silently, not even knowing exactly what it was that she feared so greatly. Nor could she think clearly here, so close to him, touching him, his hand covering, enfolding, *caressing* hers. She realised in a sudden shocked awareness that his thumb was lightly stroking her palm.

Heat, cold, excitement, fear. The torrent of opposing sensations pouring through her was so swift, so violent, that she almost cried out from the force of the conflict. It was too much. She had to get away, had to—

"I... I think I'll walk the stiffness out of my legs." the words tumbled out so abruptly that Nell didn't realise she'd broken into the men's discussion until they both turned to stare at her. Only then did she hear the silence. It seemed to surround her.

"I'm rested now," she added, as if that explained everything. It must have explained something, however, because Rafe released her hand. Her fingers immediately curled inwards of their own volition, as though trying to hold on to his warmth. His eyes caught the small movement, then lifted to her face.

"I'll come with you," he said.

"*No*! That is—" Nell scrambled to her feet. "I won't go far. I just…"

She was rescued by Richard. "Hell's fiends, Rafe. Let Mistress Nell have some privacy. There's a stream through those trees," he advised her, waving a vague hand towards the eastern side of the camp. "Go on. We'll eat when you return."

"Aye. Thank you." Nell fled, unable to look either man in the face. Her own was fiery red.

She didn't stop until she was completely out of sight and hearing of the camp and surrounded by the quiet sentinels of the forest. Then she paused, catching her breath. In the waning light she saw some small animal flit through the bracken and vanish. A bird twittered once and fell silent. A leaf drifted down in front of her, spiraling slowly towards the earth.

"'Tis as good a place as any," Nell muttered as she watched it land. Glancing quickly about, to be sure she was alone, she knelt and brushed away other leaves. Their dark gold hue reminded her of Rafe's eyes.

Rafe. When had she started calling him that in her mind? Why did he blow cold then hot? What could he want from her? So many questions. And only one answer she was sure of. He still believed her to be wanton, to be no better than her family. That was most likely why he hadn't presented her properly to Sir Richard.

Nell sat back on her heels, staring at the small hole she had made. The realisation that Rafe *hadn't* told his friend her full name struck her with painful force. Richard had addressed her as "Mistress", not "Lady Nell". Although he had clearly been told of the danger her family posed. What was she to make of that?

Only the obvious, she concluded miserably. Rafe still

disapproved of her, so, if he was being gentler, it was because he wanted something. And all she possessed was herself.

Dear God, not that, she prayed again. But knowing, this time. Knowing, somehow, that if Rafe wanted what every other man had wanted from her, and nothing else, it would destroy something in her. Because he was different. As different from those other men as the swift, hunting hawk was from the self-important, strutting bantam. She had known that from the start—instinctively then, with utter certainty now.

And just the thought of being alone with him again had her heart shaking.

With a half-strangled sound of impatience, Nell began to attack the hole like a small, ferocious harrier. This was what came of too much thinking. Hearts did not shake. Nerves, yes. And no wonder. She had nearly been dragged ignominiously before the local sheriff; she was bone-weary from nursing people all day; she was upset by her inability to help the poor abused child back at the camp, and she had still to inform her father that she could not marry the man he had chosen for her because…because…

Well, just because!

Several more frantic seconds of digging ensued. Determined to keep her wayward thoughts on one problem at a time, Nell shook loose dirt from her hands, then stood and lifted her skirts to untie the pouch. The light was fading rapidly; she dropped her skirts and began to grope for the herb. She had to hurry. If she tarried any longer, someone would come looking for her and—

She went utterly still. The hair at the back of her neck lifted. Her entire body tingled. He was coming.

There was no sound, no warning, but she knew. She could feel him. Close.

The opened pouch fell unheeded to the ground. Nell turned, her heart in her throat, the little bag still clutched in one hand, and watched Beaudene come through the trees towards her, as big and dark and silent as the forest enclosing them.

Chapter Nine

There was nowhere to run. It was too late to hide. She could only stand there as he drew closer. Could only wait, trembling inside, as his hawk-like gaze pierced the shadows between them, sweeping over her tense face before dropping to the incriminating bag in her hand and thence to the hole at her feet.

"You were gone a long time."

The words were very soft, very gentle, but when his lashes lifted Nell felt the impact of the questions in his eyes all the way to her soul.

She struggled free of the panicked urge simply to turn and flee into the forest. She had to think, to say something. He might be starting to trust her word, but that trust was fragile. If he even suspected the truth, she would be damned forever in his eyes.

A half-truth? Would it be safe? Men knew little of physics and potions unless they were monks or clerics trained to the work. And truth had carried the day once before, she remembered. For a price.

Her heart jolted at the memory, then began to throb in a slow, heavy rhythm. "I'm sorry. I didn't realise…

But I had to—I mean, I thought I would need this herb, but as it happens I don't and 'tis not safe, so…''

His gaze never wavered from hers. ''So?''

Nell swallowed. ''I thought to bury it.''

In the heavy silence that followed the trees themselves seemed to wait for his answer. Nell wished she knew what Rafe was thinking, but his eyes gave away nothing. She could only strain to hear the slightest change in his voice that might warn her of his mood.

''What is it, this herb that is unsafe rather than healing?'' he asked.

''Oh, it can heal.'' Ignoring the question, Nell rushed into speech again. '''Tis most useful for ailments of the chest, but the dose must be measured with great care and skill and I don't have time to explain all to Bess, so…'' Once more she faltered to stop.

''Ah, I see. Its preparation must be learned over time?''

''Aye.'' She nodded quickly.

''And, since no one here is suffering from aught but burns and the wounds of battle, you decided to forgo a lesson that must needs be hasty, though you purchased the herb?''

''Aye.'' This time the affirmative was whispered.

Rafe held out his hand. ''May I see it?''

Nell's own hand shook as indecision gripped her. But it was just a powder, she reassured herself. A powder like any other. He would not know it.

She offered him the bag, praying that the waning light hid the tremor in her fingers.

He came closer and took it, his long fingers pulling the laces free so he could look inside. He lowered his head and took an experimental sniff. When his gaze lifted again to hers Nell felt the first cold knife-thrust of fear.

"What name has this herb?" he asked.

He would not know it, she repeated silently, as though reciting a magical incantation. He was a warrior. Even if he had a rough knowledge of the rudimentary treatment of battle-wounds, he would not know of internal cures. It was safe to tell him. Holy Mother of God, it had to be.

"Nell?"

"Hyssop." The name passed her lips like the sigh of the wind.

And before she had taken her next breath, she saw it. Her mistake. His knowledge. Leaping to life in his eyes amid an explosion of rage so violent it made his former anger look like mild annoyance.

"*Hyssop*!" The word hissed between his teeth. "By the fiend, it slides off your tongue as easily as the dose would slide down your throat. You don't even seek to lie."

"My—? No..."

"How often have you used it, my lady?" He overrode her faint protest as if she had said nothing, his voice harsh, flaying her, stripping flesh scorched by his fury from nerves stretched beyond human endurance. "How many times have you used the knowledge learned in your aunt's household? Once? Twice? Why throw such a useful herb aside now because you were mistaken in your reckoning? Save it for—"

"*Stop*! Stop it!" Nell flung up her hands, as though trying to ward off the relentless onslaught of words. "You're wrong. *Wrong*! 'Twas not for myself. I didn't need... I've never..."

Rafe hurled the bag to the ground with such unrestrained savagery that Nell's protest ended in a frightened cry.

"God's teeth! Do you mean to tell me that you bought it for someone else? That you were going to use your whore's tricks on one of those sick women back there?" He half reached for her, his big hands flexing before they clenched and fell back. "Does she know of your *kindness*, my lady? Or did she refuse to have her soul blackened for so foul a sin against the laws of God and man and—"

"The laws of man?" Her voice was low and shaking, but it cut across Rafe's tirade like a sword cleaving mist. His eyes were still slitted and violent, his powerful body rigid with barely contained fury, but she didn't care, no longer saw, felt only her own rage rising in a flood that swept over fear and guilt until she felt nothing else.

"Aye, you men! You men who make the laws, who stand so righteously before your women and point accusing fingers, who would condemn without hearing. Tell me what *you* would do when you look at a child…a *child*…who has been taken and used until she would rather perish where the vile creatures left her than return to her people. What good is your male honour then, my lord? Does it remove her hurt, her shame, her despair?"

"Another sin won't remove those things, either," he roared. "God damn it, Nell, I don't care what you learned in that accursed house, you must have known that at least."

In the wild storm of her emotions, the sudden pain in Rafe's voice went unnoticed. "Another sin?" she cried, anguished. "*My* sin? Is that all you can think of? Did you spare a thought for the terrible sin committed by men who do not have to live with the consequences? Do they suffer? No! Their lives continue without let or hindrance. *They* continue, sinning again and again, and women have no defence, no safety, no protection…''

Despair lanced through her again and she turned away, stumbling, blind to her surroundings, her arms held across her waist as if she had received a body-blow. ''And I couldn't do it. Oh, God save her, even knowing all that, I couldn't do it. I couldn't help her. I couldn't—'' Her voice broke.

For a moment there was nothing but the tortured echo of her own words in the silence, then strong hands cupped her shoulders from behind, holding her. ''Easy,'' he said. ''Be easy, Nell. I didn't—''

''*No!*''

His sudden gentleness was too much. Screaming, Nell wrenched herself free, fighting him even as she whirled, striking out blindly, as frantic as a wild creature caught in a trap, too desperate to be free to take heed of any hurt.

Rafe rode the glancing blow she landed on his face, then in a lightning-swift move grabbed her wrists, pinned her hands behind her back with one of his and pivoted. Before Nell realised what was happening she was immobilised between the trunk of a giant beech and the weight of Rafe's body. His free hand pressed her head into his shoulder and his mouth lowered, brushing across her hair.

''Shhh,'' he murmured, when a small, frantic sound escaped her. She was still trying to struggle and he tightened his hold, but carefully, so as not to hurt her. ''Be still. Be still, little one. Let me hold you.''

He kept his voice low, almost crooning the words, but renewed fury lashed him. God send a pox on that vicious family of hers. And on her father, who'd sent her to a place where innocence was undefended, and knowledge learned that would have destroyed what was left of goodness in anyone less strong than the girl in his arms.

She was quiet now, no longer fighting his hold, but her inner conflict still had her in its grip. The tension in her delicate frame as she struggled for control was so great he wondered that she didn't shatter like brittle glass between his hands. He fought back his own rage. There would be time enough to deal with her family, when he had her safe beyond their reach.

His head bent lower. "I'll protect you, Nell. I'll keep you safe."

He heard the words with a vague sense of surprise. How did she arouse such feelings within him? This tenderness. This need to protect. He didn't understand it, but knew beyond all doubt that he had made a vow that would never be forsworn, no matter who or what she had been in the past. It no longer mattered. He wanted her too much.

Wanted her with an urgency that was driving out his other violent emotions and increasing with each moment he held her in his arms. Not the urge to use her deliberately. He scarcely recalled that cold, measured decision to sate his physical need within her body until he was free of it and her. This was fierce, and hot, the force of it so beyond his control that as Nell abruptly softened against him, yielding to his strength with a shuddering little sigh, his body hardened in a rush that drew a harsh, agonised breath from him.

"'Tis all right," he said at once, knowing by the tremor that shook her from head to toe that she was aware of his response to her. "You're safe. I want you, but I'm not going to do anything about it.'' Not right now, anyway, he added to himself. ''You're safe with me, Nell.''

She was silent.

Very carefully he released her wrists. Her hands went at once to his chest, but she made no attempt to push him away. He flattened his hand at her back and began a gentle stroking movement. ''Do you believe you're safe with me, little princess?''

For a moment he thought she wasn't going to answer, then she stirred against him.

''Safe? Knowing you want what every other man has wanted from me?'' Her voice was low, and husky with unshed tears. ''When I can feel you—''

She stopped, appalled. But still unable to free herself, unable to trust herself to stand without his support.

His mouth curved in a smile against her suddenly burning cheek. ''Aye, a man's desire can scarcely be hidden, can it?'' he murmured wryly. ''But I'll never force you, Nell. I want you to know that. I want you to know that in my arms you're as safe as you want to be.''

Nell was too exhausted to work that out. Too exhausted by the emotional battering she'd endured in the past hour even to wonder at her own responses since Rafe had rendered her helpless. She should have been afraid, but the instant she had stopped fighting him the heat and sheer male power of his body had poured over her, drowning her in sensations that had had her all but melting against him. She could have stayed in his embrace forever, safe, protected, savouring the strength of his arms, the heavy beat of his heart against her cheek, the tightly restrained force of his desire.

A ripple of uneasiness stirred her to life. If he had

not spoken, if his desire had remained unacknowledged between them, would she have renewed her struggles or given in to the heat and power overwhelming her senses?

The fact that she didn't know the answer scared her more than the events of the past ten years put together.

"Let me go."

His soft laugh held a note that sent excitement and fear combined shivering down her spine. "If I did you would fall."

For the second time in the space of a minute Nell's face burned. He was practically taking her entire weight. She straightened so smartly that her head nearly clipped his jaw.

"There! I'm standing."

His grip shifted to her arms, steadying her before he released her. "That's good," he murmured. One hand lifted to her face and he brushed her hot cheek with the backs of his fingers. "I want you willing, princess, not weak."

"What makes you think you'll have me at all?" Nell muttered, but Rafe only smiled darkly and bent to retrieve the sack of hyssop.

Nell decided not to pursue such a dangerous discussion. That smile had struck her like an arrow piercing chainmail. She felt shattered, as though something had been torn from her, some part of herself that had been locked away all these years but had now broken free, only to be captured and held by a man who made her want things she had never thought were possible.

"When we get back to camp I'll burn this."

Shaken, she looked up to find him watching her, and the strange yearning increased, tightening the muscles in her throat until they ached. "Aye." Barely able to speak, she made a small gesture of repulsion. "Do what you will. I never want to see it again."

He nodded. "You've never used it before, have you? Despite knowing its properties."

At the note of certainty in his statement some of the tightness eased. "No. Never."

"Little fool," he growled. "Didn't you know the decision would tear you apart?"

"I refused to think of it until the last moment." She laughed unexpectedly, a sound without humour. "The witch was right. At the fair... Oh!" Her hand went instinctively to her crucifix as she spoke and a short, startled exclamation broke from her lips.

"What is it?"

The question was so abrupt that Nell almost jumped. "N-nothing. That is, my... I must have dropped..." She began peering at the ground, conscious that Rafe's gaze had sharpened again. Well, he would just have to do without an explanation, she thought tiredly. Her mind was simply not up to the task of manufacturing one.

"Is this what you're looking for?"

Straightening, Nell watched Rafe bend and scoop up the half-open pouch. Even in the near-darkness she could see that several inches of jewelled chain had spilled from its hiding place and now lay across his hand.

"Aye." She stepped forward nervously to retrieve her property. "Thank you."

He ignored her outstretched hand and opened the pouch so that the heavy gold crucifix was revealed. Nell's hand fell nerveless to her side as she watched Rafe examine the engraving on the solid bars of the cross. He weighed it in his palm.

"A valuable and unusual trinket," he murmured at last, his gaze shifting from the jewel to her face. "Where did it come from?"

Nell tried a careless shrug that felt more like a shudder. "'Tis mine, of course."

One eyebrow arched. "And you've been wearing it all this time?"

"Aye." This time her voice was firmer. It was the truth, after all.

Then her nerves jangled all over again when he shook his head.

"You've been wearing it very well-concealed, in that case, princess. Why is that, I wonder?"

"Not because 'tis stolen," Nell flashed, desperation and tiredness causing her to take refuge in temper.

To her utter amazement he laughed. "You know, I'm beginning to understand how your mind works, little one. Stolen is exactly what this is, isn't it?"

"No! It belonged to my mother and now 'tis mine. At least…" Oh, why did everything have to go wrong all at once? Hadn't she had enough to cope with today? She felt her lower lip quiver and bit down hard.

Rafe reached out, tipped her chin up and stroked his thumb across her lip, freeing it from between her teeth. "Tell me," he coaxed, cradling her cheek. "Trust me."

"I—I do," she stammered. "I do trust you, but…"

"But?"

It wasn't her secret to divulge.

"I don't know you," she almost wailed. Jerking her head back, she retreated a pace or two. "I don't know what you'll—"

"You know more of me than anyone on this earth, bar three others."

Nell drew a sharp breath. It was true. He did know

what it was like to have something of value taken from him when he'd been helpless to prevent it. He knew what it was to be betrayed. "The King, Sir Richard and the man who stole from you," she whispered.

He nodded, his eyes intent on hers.

He would wait until he wore her down, Nell realised. And at the moment she had few, if any, defences against his will. She didn't even want to fight him.

The first words came out in a rush. "My mother wore the crucifix all the time. It never left her possession. My father had given it to her, you see." She looked away, gazing into the shadowed distance as memory took her back to a childhood that had been cut brutally short. And now that she had started, it was a relief to tell the tale.

"The night she lay dying she sent the servants out of the room and made me swear by my love for her to keep the crucifix close until it could be buried with her."

"She didn't ask her priest to ensure it?"

Nell blinked, startled back into the present. "No. She sent him away also. I don't know why. He was old. Perhaps that was…"

She shrugged and continued. "She should have asked him rather than me. When the servants came back into the bedchamber my nurse took me away and I never saw my mother again. She died that night. The next morning Uncle Edward's steward arrived with an escort to take me to Langley. I wasn't allowed to attend my mother's burial, all the servants I had known were dismissed, and we left that very day. I found out later that my father had known my mother had not long to live. She had written to him, and the arrangements to take me to Langley Castle were already in train."

Rafe frowned slightly. "Has Langley never permitted you to visit Wells to fulfil your vow?"

"I wasn't even permitted to keep the crucifix," Nell told him, remembered anger and frustration breaking through her weariness to give her voice an edge. "There was no privacy at Langley. I didn't have a saint's chance in purgatory of keeping such a valuable object hidden. The moment my aunt laid eyes on it, she claimed it for herself and took it from me."

A faint smile softened his mouth. "Not without a fight, I warrant."

Nell didn't return the smile. "She has the marks to prove it."

"Hmm. I can see why she was not overjoyed to welcome you into her household, princess. Why didn't you take your claim further if it meant so much to you? Not then, but later when you grew older."

"To whom should I have taken it, my lord?" she asked softly. "Three years ago King Henry had fled to Scotland and Margaret of Anjou to France to rally more supporters. Should I have taken it to Edward of York, perhaps?"

His eyes narrowed at her tone. "Three years ago Edward had just been crowned King. Lending ear to a young girl's petition would have been just to his liking."

"Aye. It was. For a price."

Rafe's expression was suddenly very grim. "And what price was that, my lady?" As if he didn't know.

"The price I expect he demands of every woman. Of course, I was only thirteen at the time, so he drew the line at holding a knife to my throat, but when I—"

"Enough!" *Thirteen*! God, he didn't want to hear any more. The stark violence of the emotions ripping him apart was stunning. If Nell said one more word, just one, he'd be able to think of nothing except avenging her.

And how was he supposed to do that? Rafe demanded of himself in silent mockery. Challenge his king because of a years-old encounter that had nothing to do with him?

With a vicious, barely-stifled curse, he stuffed the crucifix back into its pouch and shoved it out of sight in the pocket of his surcoat. Let it suffice that she had got the crucifix back. The sooner he arranged to have it placed in her mother's tomb the better.

"What's past is past," he grated. "We won't speak of it again."

"But—"

He closed the distance between them with one swift, gliding stride and laid his fingers against her mouth. "No more," he ordered gently. And, removing his hand, he bent and kissed her.

It was the briefest caress, a fleeting brush of lips, no more, but Nell felt the impact of his tenderness in the deepest, most carefully guarded reaches of her heart.

"I'm taking you back to the camp," he murmured. "You need food and sleep or you'll never stay in the saddle tomorrow."

"I've managed so far," she felt obliged to point out, but it was a half-hearted attempt at best to regain control of her senses. She didn't want to argue with him. She was too tired, his gentleness too seductive. At this moment it didn't even seem important that she hadn't told Rafe the entire story. Or that he still had the crucifix. It was safe with him. She would ask him for it later.

He glanced down at her, the arm about her waist

keeping her close to his side as they walked back through the trees. But there was no danger in him now, she thought vaguely. Only safety and protection.

"If we leave early we should reach Wells by mid-afternoon," he said as the first of the huts came into sight. "I'll take you straight to the Bishop's palace and—"

He stopped dead, his arm tightening around her. Nell looked up to see what had caused the sudden poised stillness in his body.

"It looks like the day isn't over yet," he said very softly. "Damn it."

A few paces away, his back to them, stood Richard, confronted by what to Nell's startled gaze looked to be every man in the village. Then she saw that the crowd was divided. Three men stood a little apart from the others; the larger group included Simpkin and young Luke.

Richard half turned his head, as though he had heard Rafe's comment. "I can handle this," he said quietly.

Rafe moved closer, Nell still pinned to his side. "What's going on?"

"I announced my intention to seek a pardon and turn honest," Richard replied. "The reception was rather mixed, as you can see, and I'm afraid the rogues who prefer a life of crime are blaming you."

"Courageous of them. Perhaps they'd like to discuss the matter with me," Rafe suggested drily. Neither man had taken his eyes off the sullen trio during the exchange.

"We only want fair treatment," growled the tallest of the three. "You promised us rich pickings and one last job will provide it." From beneath a thatch of unkempt reddish hair, his eyes flickered over Nell and returned to Richard.

"What the hell does he mean by that?" Rafe asked in a voice that made Nell jump.

"I'm afraid someone overheard Mistress Nell telling Bess that you're her bodyguard." Richard sent her a quick apologetic glance. "They seem to think that a woman travelling alone with a bodyguard must be worth a considerable amount to someone.

"Aye, for her person or her whereabouts," the outlaw spoke up again. "We don't intend to hurt the wench, and there'll be a share in it for you if you like," he added, nodding at Rafe.

Nell was certain Rafe hadn't moved, but menace was suddenly emanating from him in waves. His arm fell away from her waist. He took her hand and at the same time stepped forward a pace, so that she was half shielded by his body. His right hand rested lightly on his sword-hilt. Nell couldn't see his face, but his voice would have frozen fire.

"Is this how you repay my lady for tending your women and children?"

There was a low murmur from the rest of the men. It reminded Nell of the fair just before the fight broke out. She clung to Rafe's hand like a limpet.

"None of us have women here," the trio's spokesman retorted.

"How very fortunate," Rafe said softly. "In that case there's nothing to stop you from leaving. Right now."

"Not until we get—"

"You heard him," Richard interrupted. "Take your weapons and some food and get out."

For several tense seconds the threat of violence

seemed to hover over the settlement, as if awaiting a signal. Then the men glanced from Rafe and Richard to the silent group opposite, and Nell saw acknowledgement of their weaker position cross each face in turn.

"Come on, Ned," one of the three muttered. "No wench is worth getting cut up for."

Ned apparently agreed. His mean little eyes still glared at Rafe but he backed up.

"See that they get their share of whatever money we have," Richard instructed Simpkin. Then added quietly to Rafe as the rest of the outlaws dispersed, "Take a bow with you tomorrow. There's no telling if those fools will take it into their thick heads to follow you, but they'll turn tail when they learn you don't miss what you shoot at."

Rafe nodded. He didn't seem particularly worried about the possibility of having to pick off anyone foolish enough to follow them, Nell reflected. She realised she'd been holding her breath and let it out with a long sigh of relief.

He turned to look down at her. "Come on, princess. You're almost asleep on your feet. You can eat in the hut."

"Aye. Best keep her out of sight until I have those three escorted off the premises," Richard agreed. "I'll see you in the morning, Mistress Nell." With a nod to Rafe he walked away.

"Believe me, I was in no danger of falling asleep during that little scene," Nell said with great feeling as she followed Rafe across the clearing. She remembered the expression in Ned's eyes when he had looked at her and shuddered. "Do you think I could have a bow, too?"

"No."

The blunt, uncompromising answer took her aback. "Why not?"

Rafe stopped outside Bess's hut. "Because apart from the odd scar or two I'm still in one piece, and I'd like to stay that way."

"Holy Saints! I'm not going to shoot you!"

"Good. I'm sure you'll understand that I'd like to be certain of that."

"Well! Of all the—"

The rest of her indignant protest was smothered by his hand. "I know you're not used to relying on anyone but yourself, princess," he said very quietly. "But you don't have to fight your own battles any more. I'll protect you."

He removed his hand, but Nell didn't speak. His quick understanding had surprised her into silence. But of course he understood, she reminded herself. He had been alone nearly all his life, just as she had. Had been able to rely on no one but himself, had had to fight his own battles. She wondered what he would say if she told him how very alike they were.

And then she wondered at the sudden longing that swept through her to fight his battles with him, to stand at his side, to *be* with him.

"I don't trust easily," she said slowly, carefully. "But nor do you."

"No," he agreed. "But sometimes…"

"Sometimes?" It was the merest whisper of sound.

He frowned, as though considering. "I don't know. Sometimes, little one, just lately, I've wondered if trust can be learned." He gave a short laugh and shook his head. "A question for the philosophers, no doubt, not for a soldier."

"No doubt," Nell murmured.

"Tell me—" His voice was still quiet, still gentle, but Nell sensed the moment of fragile intimacy was over. He had withdrawn from her; the part of him that might never trust a woman had been closed off again. "The camp was attacked only five days ago. This girl who was raped—you cannot know at this moment if there'll be a child from it."

"I don't." Nell drew a deep breath and tried to banish the strange wistfulness that had come upon her again. "I would never have known one way or another."

He nodded, his gaze holding hers. "But you still couldn't bring yourself to make sure of it."

When she didn't answer, he lifted his hand and tucked an escaped tendril of hair into her crespinette. His hand lingered, his long fingers tracing the line of her jaw to her chin.

"Soft little Nell," he murmured. "But don't fear that it makes you weak." His hand fell away from her face. Don't fret about the girl. We'll look after her, whatever happens. Now, go inside. I'll bring you something to eat, then you should get some sleep." He gave her a fleeting smile and walked away.

She was supposed to sleep after that exchange?

Nell entered the hut with innumerable questions battering at her brain once more. Had Rafe meant "we" in the literal sense? Had he meant that they would care for the girl together? How could that be, when he would leave her once she was returned to her father? Unless—

No. What she was thinking wasn't possible. She was the last person Rafe would want to marry. And she didn't want to be answerable to a husband anyway.

But there was no longer any real conviction in that last reminder, and Nell knew it. For just a moment out there that "we" had given her a glimpse of a future that beckoned irresistibly, that promised warmth after coldness, closeness to another after years of solitude. It was probably an illusion, Nell thought wistfully. Rafe had probably been speaking in general terms, but why not dream just once? What could it hurt? She was alone and tired and it would comfort her.

After all, an illusion couldn't harm her if she indulged it for only a little while.

Arms that were warm and strong enfolded her. Hands that were powerful but gentle stroked her hair, brushing sleep-tousled strands from her face.

Half-asleep, her eyes still closed, Nell made a small sound of pleasure and nestled closer to the warmth.

"Nell."

She murmured wordlessly and burrowed her head into the firm pillow beneath her cheek.

"Sweetheart. Wake up."

"No," she mumbled. Loath to relinquish her dream to the insistent voice trying to drag her back to reality, she spread her fingers so she could cling tighter to the bed—and frowned. "Furry," she said.

"God damn it, woman, will you wake up? I'm not made of stone!"

The hissed command jolted Nell into full wakefulness within a second. Her eyes flew open to fasten on a sight that made her heart stand still. In the very faintest lifting of the darkness she could just make out the hut's interior. All was as it had been last night, except for one thing. She was no longer alone in the bed.

Not only that. She was lying all over the bed's other occupant as if she was glued to him, her legs tangled with his, her head resting on the hard pad of muscle on his shoulder, and… Dear God, her fingers were buried in the dark pelt covering his chest.

The only thing that stopped Nell from screaming in total panic was the realisation that they were still partially clothed. She in her shift, he in his hose and undershirt. The undershirt didn't cover much, however. Its front lacing was undone more than halfway to his waist.

"R-Rafe?"

"Who else were you expecting?" he growled.

Nell flinched and tried to move away.

"No." His arms tightened and he tipped her face up to his. "Forget I said that, princess. The past is over and the future is what we make it. Once we get out of this bed, that is," he added wryly.

She hardly made sense of the words. His warm breath washing over her lips drove out every other awareness except how big and hard and *close* he was.

"Nell?"

"I—I don't think I can move," she faltered. She didn't *want* to move, but she had to. If she stayed in his arms any longer—

"You can't move?"

"No. I seem…that is, we seem to be all tangled up."

Not as tangled as we're going to be in a minute if I don't get out of here, Rafe thought, trying to remember why he couldn't take Nell here and now. The reason seemed to be buried somewhere in a mind that could only think of one thing. The need that had been growing to agonising proportions since he'd woken to find Nell, soft and warm and tantalising, lying all over him.

He shifted slightly and felt her tremble as her thigh slid between his and was trapped there. "Aye. I see what you mean," he managed, his voice sounding rough even to his own ears. "But don't worry, sweetheart. Fortunately, in a situation like this, I can do the moving for both of us."

"What does that—?" Nell began, only to break off with a startled gasp. Powerful muscles bunched and surged beneath her and before she could even blink she was on her back.

And just as imprisoned as before. More so. Rafe lay on his side next to her, propped on one forearm, so that he was looking down at her. The heat and size of him held her completely enthralled.

Her gaze dropped to her hand which, inexplicably, was still attached to his chest. How could that be? she wondered dazedly. By all the laws of nature her hand should have fallen when Rafe turned her. But instead her fingers were threading through the dark whorls of hair as if they had a life of their own. She felt the small nub of a male nipple beneath her little finger and stroked it curiously.

His breath hissed between his teeth. "You're playing with fire, princess."

"Will it warm me?" she whispered. Her gaze lifted as he made a rough sound in his throat, her eyes widening as she took in the breadth of his shoulders, the beautifully muscled contours of his chest, the sheer *maleness* of him.

"Warm you?" he repeated, his voice shaking. "God in heaven, 'twill burn both of us." Thrusting his fingers into her hair, he lowered his head and took her mouth with his.

Oh, yes.

If Nell had been able to she would have moaned the words aloud. His mouth was hot and demanding, and she knew now that she had been wanting it, wanting this, since Rafe had kissed her two nights ago. Heat. Life. She needed it, needed his strength, his touch, his taste.

Her hands slid upwards and she wreathed her arms about his neck, clinging, needing him closer. And this time, this time, he gave her what she needed. He shifted, his arms going under her back to arch her into his body as he moved to cover her completely.

Nell made a soft, whimpering little sound of pleasure as she felt his weight crush her into the bed. The kiss changed, becoming hotter, deeper, his tongue stroking over hers again and again in a slow dance of seduction and retreat until she began to respond, shyly at first, with tiny, darting touches that made him groan softly and tighten his hold, until she was utterly lost in sensation.

He lifted his weight slightly and his hand began caressing her, moving over her back from shoulder to hip, returning upwards to trace the soft indention of her waist and the delicacy of her ribs. Heat bloomed and ran before his touch. Her breasts flushed, tingled, grew heavy. Nell moved restlessly, her mouth soft and yielding beneath his, wanting…wanting…

Then his big hand closed over one aching breast, his thumb finding and stroking the velvety tip, and she almost fainted under the torrent of pleasure that flowed through her body.

"God, you're sweet," he whispered. "So sweet, so soft." His open mouth slid across her throat, nudging aside her shift, and she moved again, her hips lifting in an instinctive rhythm that echoed the throbbing deep inside her.

"Rafe," she breathed, scarcely able to speak. She felt dazed, stunned by the force of sensations she had never experienced.

"I know." He lifted his head, his eyes searching hers in the dawn light beginning to creep into the hut. "I didn't expect this," he said thickly. "I didn't expect *you*."

Nell trembled helplessly under the impact of the fierce desire in his eyes. Somewhere in a hazy distant corner of her mind a warning little voice was trying to make itself heard, but it was silenced completely when he pulled the ties of her shift free and opened it to her waist with one sweeping movement of his hand.

Nell felt his touch on her bare flesh for the first time and arched wildly, her breath splintering into mindless little cries.

But the sounds of her own response startled her, shocking her into an abrupt awareness of what was happening. This was passion, she thought wonderingly. This sweet, melting weakness; this breathless, mounting excitement; this need to give herself completely into Rafe's keeping, to trust him as she had trusted no other man, to let him lead her into the unknown world of desire. But there was something—

"Nell, sweetheart, I have to have you."

The urgent words were muttered against her throat, his hands were kneading and stroking her breasts. Streamers of fire unravelled and spread to the soft hidden flesh between her legs, but now she was torn, confused. Wanting him, but wanting *more*.

Her head turned restlessly and she forced her eyes open, struggling to understand the sudden conflict within her. And in the ray of light streaming through the unshuttered window she saw Bess lying asleep on her pallet.

Heat and desire leached out of her body in an instant. She froze, just as Rafe's hand slid down her belly and into the soft nest below.

"Rafe, no—"

"'Tis all right," he said hoarsely. "I won't rush you. I won't hurt you. Oh, God, you're so soft."

"No! We can't. Stop!" She tried to shift his hand, tugging frantically at his wrist, but his fingers caressed her warm womanflesh and she gasped in shock at the intimate invasion.

"*No!*" Desperate, torn between embarrassment, fear and the pulsing of newly-aroused desire, she began to fight him in earnest.

"Blessed Jesu!" He lifted his head, the gold fire in his eyes clear now in the morning light. The weight of his body subdued her struggles without effort. "You want this as much as I do," he grated savagely. "You can't deny it when I'm touching you like this."

"I can't… Bess!"

He went still, his eyes blazing down at her for a searing instant before they flashed to the other side of the room. A single vicious word was bitten off, his teeth coming together with a snap that was audible. In a slow withdrawal that Nell felt in every shuddering nerve-ending he removed his hand. His powerful chest expanded with the deep, controlling breath he drew in, then he pushed away from her and got to his feet in one swift movement.

Bending, he snatched his surcoat and boots off the floor and strode to the door. He jerked it open and looked back, his gaze slicing down the length of her body in the second before Nell managed to grab the blanket and pull it over her semi-nakedness.

"A good thing you remembered we weren't alone, princess," he said with biting coldness. "But God help you if I get that close again and you stop me."

The door was shut behind him with a restraint that was deadly, leaving Nell with her first taste of frustrated desire, and a desolation that went as deep as her soul.

Chapter Ten

By midday the green forests and meadows of the Avon valley had given way to the foothills of the Mendips. As they travelled further south Rafe kept to the high country, avoiding the narrow valleys formed by the outcrops of limestone that reared skyward in craggy, bracken-clad splendour.

The scenery was magnificent, but at one point the land fell away so sharply that Nell had to avoid looking down at the valley floor far below her, its cool, green dimness scarcely touched by the pale grey light of the cloudy afternoon.

The dizzy heights didn't seem to bother Rafe at all. During the past couple of hours he had left her several times to seek a higher point where he could scan the land behind and around them.

Lost in thoughts that were none too happy, Nell hadn't noticed his vigilance at first—there was no sign of human habitation on these rocky, windswept crags, no villages or even solitary dwellings—but when he reined in yet again to sweep the hills and valleys with his narrowed hawk-like gaze, she, too, looked back, a ripple of uneasiness gliding over her skin.

The land seemed empty. And yet there was life and movement here on the uplands, she thought, tilting her head back and breathing deeply of the clean air. The brushing of the breeze through the gorse and bracken, the clatter of the jackdaws, the keening cries of two kestrels high above her as they rode the wind-currents in effortless soaring flight. Somewhere, nearby but invisible, water trickled over stone, and she heard the cough of a badger.

The kestrels shimmered and blurred and Nell squeezed her eyes shut, realising she'd been staring so hard at the sky that they were watering. Then saddle leather creaked close by and her lashes flew open again.

"Stay away from the cliff-edge," Rafe advised her, nudging Samson into a walk. "These hills are like a honeycomb, full of caves and hollows where the rock has given way."

For a first remark after an enraged exit from the hut and an entire morning of silence, it was quite mildly delivered, Nell decided after a moment. Although Rafe hadn't seemed angry, she reflected, suddenly recalling the odd, considering glances she had intercepted from him during the morning. He'd appeared more lost in thought, as she had been.

The depression that had hung over her since they had said farewell to Bess and Richard seemed to loosen its hold on her mind a little. She brought Rufus up closer and tried a tentative smile.

"I remember my mother telling me stories of such caves. Caverns like underground halls and castles, where fairies ruled their kingdoms, and sailed their boats on magical lakes and rivers."

He smiled faintly. "Those stories live forever in these parts. Like the tales of Arthur."

"But he truly lived, did he not? Some say that he will come again when England is in danger, and others have seen his hounds drinking at the well at Cadbury, before following the King along the ancient road to Glastonbury."

"Hmm." He watched as she glanced back with an involuntary shiver. "Something tells me you preferred scaring yourself with tales of ghosts rather than listening to fairy stories when you were a child."

"I confess that the possibility of ghostly hounds appearing on our path is not a comforting one," she returned. "Even in full light of day."

The smile reached his eyes. "That's why you have a bodyguard, princess. But if it makes you feel any better—" he reached into his surcoat pocket and withdrew her crucifix "—I'll return this."

"Oh! Thank you." She slipped the chain over her head. "I'd forgotten…" Having had several other matters on her mind all morning.

He looked at her rather closely for a moment, and Nell fought to keep herself from blushing. Silence fell again, but this time she made no attempt to break it. What was there to say? *Why were you in my bed in the first place? Why do I wish we were there still, and alone?*

Holy Saints! She couldn't even control her own mind. Embarrassed heat suffused her entire body when she remembered the way Rafe had touched her, and her abandoned response in his arms. She gritted her teeth and fought it back once more. If Rafe was no longer angry with her she ought to be able to put the whole episode out of her mind, just as he seemed to have done.

Aye, and Arthur would reappear right that minute and dance a measure with his hounds.

A piercing yearning stabbed at her heart. She would never forget how it had felt to lie in his arms. Never forget the feel of his hands on her body. Never as long as she lived.

But would Rafe remember after he had left her? She looked at him, her yearning clear in her eyes. He had made arrangements with Richard for the others to meet him at his manor as soon as the wounded could travel, but for her it seemed that a dream and a memory would be all she would have. And it wasn't enough. It wasn't nearly enough.

The thought had no sooner crossed her mind when he turned and caught her gaze. Nell flushed and looked away at once, angry with herself. She had been staring at him like a love-struck—

"Nell?"

"I was just wondering why you've been looking behind us ever since we started riding over the top of these mountains," she said with forced brightness. "I see no sign of pursuit."

"They're hills, and you wouldn't." Without warning, he reined Samson in and reached out to catch Rufus's bridle when she would have ridden past him. "Nell—" his voice was suddenly curt "—I'm sorry about this morning. I didn't mean that to happen."

Hurt lanced through her, sharp and cutting. "Well, I dare say it would *not* have happened if you hadn't climbed into bed with me. However, there is no need to apologise. I know only too well how easily men succumb to lust, and would suggest that tonight you seek your own—"

"I wasn't the only one succumbing to lust, princess," he grated. "And I was in your bed in case some of the other men took it into their heads to hold you to ransom. Or worse."

"Oh. I see. You were there to protect me? Thank you. How foolish of me not to recognise—"

"God damn it, will you kindly shut up? You were so exhausted last night you wouldn't have known I was there at all if I hadn't woken up to find your hands all over me!"

"*What*?" She went so red with outrage and embarrassment that she thought her skin would peel right off her flesh. "I was asleep!"

"Unfortunately, knowing that didn't help."

"Well…well…" Excuses tumbled wildly around in her head. "You could have kept your shirt laced."

"It *was* laced when I fell asleep," he said through his teeth. "But it didn't stay that way for long when your little fingers got busy."

Nell wondered if anyone had ever died of shame. The possibility that she was about to do so seemed all too real.

"I didn't know…" she stammered. Holy Mother of God, she had never undressed a man when she was *awake*. How, in the name of all the saints, had she done it while asleep? Did she have the instincts of a courtesan, after all?

When she thought of Rafe's probable answer to that, it took every ounce of resolution she possessed to force herself to look at him. "My lord, you must believe—"

"Hush."

"What? But—"

"Shhh!"

Belatedly, Nell realised he was no longer looking at her. His eyes, fixed and intent, were focused on a point beyond her. She turned her head. Nothing moved in the rugged landscape except for the wind's constant ruffling of the bracken and wildflowers growing along the cliff-top.

"Do you see those horsemen on the road below us?"

She didn't see a thing, but thankfully the question successfully diverted the conversation away from the early hours of the morning. Then, as her eyes narrowed against the distance, she at last made out a group of riders, appearing then vanishing as the road snaked through the valley.

"Do you recognise any of them?"

She frowned. "'Tis too far to tell. I don't—" Her breath came in with a rush.

"Your uncle's stallion," Rafe said at the same time. His tone was grim. "With Tom on his back. Your cousin must be more of a dolt than you thought, princess. He should be at least thirty miles ahead of us by now, not bringing up the rear."

"Unless he's going straight to Wells as you said he might," Nell suggested nervously. So much for her brilliant idea of avoiding pursuit, she thought. Rafe had been right all along.

"The same thing applies. If Wells was his destination he should have been and gone long ago. 'Tis more likely that he's stopped at every town and inn along the way to make enquiries, but even so—"

"If he did that," she observed thoughtfully, "he would have stopped long enough for a drink. Several drinks."

"God's teeth! I know you said he was a sot, but—" He broke off with a sharp, dismissive gesture. "'Tis no use bemoaning the fact. Whatever he stopped for, yesterday's fair would have been right in his path, damn it!''

"Why? Do you think—?"

"I don't think. I know. Richard sent a man out at dawn to make sure Ned and his fellows had made themselves scarce. He tracked them as far as the town, and what do you think was the main topic for gossip this morning, princess?'' He fixed her with a narrow-eyed stare. "The mysterious lady who caused several of the town's good citizens to spend last night in the castle cells.''

"Oh." Nell bit her lip. Obviously there was no end to her crimes.

"Yes, oh. I'm glad you're finally beginning to comprehend the seriousness of the situation. Even Tom can figure out that if he's so close to us after the lead we had, it means we're probably in Wells or near by.''

"But we're not. At least, not yet. Couldn't we let them pass us and then—?"

Rafe shook his head, his gaze returning to track the group of riders. "Possibly, but once he's in Wells he has enough men to send them in any direction to pick up our—'' Again he broke off, this time going very still. "God damn their renegade souls to hell,'' he swore softly.

Nell's flesh went cold. "What is it?"

Without answering, Rafe drew the bow Richard had given him from its deerhide cover and reached over his shoulder for an arrow. "Get ready to ride as if all the fiends of hell are on our tail, sweetheart,'' he said, nocking the arrow and taking aim at the point where the horsemen were gradually reappearing.

He waited, not moving, keeping Samson still by the sheer pressure of his thighs alone. Then, as the last man came into view, he gently released the arrow and watched it find its mark seconds later.

"Ride!" he yelled, and slapped Rufus on the rump.

Clinging with hands and knees, Nell obeyed, urging Rufus into a gallop. Behind and below them she could hear faint shouts and knew they'd been seen, but she didn't look back. Beside her, Rafe kept pace, riding easily, with one hand guiding Samson and his bow in the other.

"Where are we going?" she gasped, the wind nearly whipping the words from her mouth.

"We have to get off this cliff while they're scrambling for cover and wondering what's happening," he shouted back. "There are only one or two paths safe enough for the horses. If they get to them before we do, we're stuck, but if we reach lower ground we can dig in and fight."

"*Fight*! But they didn't know we were up here," she shrieked. "Why did you—?"

The way suddenly became steeper as the land dipped, and she had to concentrate on keeping Rufus's head up as he slithered on his hocks.

"Easy," Rafe commanded. "We'll make it. See that formation of rocks yonder, where the valley opens out? That's where we'll wait."

"And then what?" She was still yelling, fear and anger combining to shred any attempt at control.

"Then we see if our chances have improved. That was Ned I shot. Without him, the other two might back off and we'll have only seven to cope with."

Only seven?

Nell fixed her eyes on the rocks several hundred yards distant and halfway up a sloping hillside, and rode as she had never ridden before in her life. She would worry about fights and how the outlaws had come into the picture later.

They hit level ground and Rafe urged Samson to a faster pace. Rufus followed gallantly, but by the time they came to a plunging, snorting halt both horses were breathing hard from the final uphill run and Rufus's sides were dark with sweat.

Rafe leapt from the saddle, yanking his sword free of its scabbard before he had hit the ground. "Get the horses over there between those two standing stones," he ordered as Nell dismounted on shaky legs. "Then come back here and keep your head down."

She obeyed, fuming.

"Do you mind telling me why we're doing this?" she demanded when she returned to Rafe's side. He was waiting, half-hidden by a stone that stood shoulder-high, and they were surrounded by others of varying shapes and sizes, piled one on top of the other. Several more boulders were scattered about the hillside, the crest of which stretched in a long ridge that joined the cliff on the other side of the gorge.

Rafe's dark brows were set in a frowning line as he examined the crest and the narrow entrance to the valley.

"Well?"

"No, 'tis not well at all," he answered. "I can pick off the first two, maybe three men to come through that gap in the hills, but the others will dive for cover. We'll be safe from fire from that direction, but there's nothing to stop one or two of them from circling around on the other side of that ridge. You'll have to watch the rocks behind us, princess, and yell the second you see anyone."

Nell barely heard the instructions. She ground her teeth. "That isn't what I meant."

He shifted his gaze from the valley entrance and looked at her. "For God's sake, think, Nell. You've been alone with me for two full days and three nights. What do you think your cousin will do to you if you fall into his hands?"

"There was little danger of that before you fired that arrow and announced our presence," she retorted, not answering his question.

"That might have been true if Tom hadn't met up with Ned and the others." He went back to watching the gap, half leaning against the boulder, an arrow ready nocked but pointing earthwards. His sword was propped beside him, its naked blade gleaming silver in the afternoon light. "I'd wager Tom or his men heard the talk about the fair and started asking questions, and Ned was none too happy about losing a leader who helped him to easy money and then told him to leave. Put those circumstances together and what do you get, princess?"

This time she stayed silent.

"I'll tell you," he continued inexorably. "You get a dissatisfied outlaw who knew when we were leaving the camp and where we were going. And you get him meeting up with a man who was very probably offering money for any information about you. Not only that—" his eyes flashed swiftly to hers "—Ned knew the location of Richard's camp. He could have betrayed him."

Nell's breath caught. "Do you think he has already?" she asked, suddenly appalled as his words sank in. She slumped against the nearest boulder, feeling sick. She was to blame for all this. If anything happened to Bess and Richard and the others it would be her fault.

"I only went to the fair because I wanted to help," she murmured brokenly. "I didn't mean…"

Rafe crossed the small space between them with one long stride, captured her face with his free hand and kissed her, quick and hard. "No, I don't think Ned went that far," he stated, looking into her startled eyes for a moment.

He returned to his post and took up his watchful stance again. "Ned had a price on his head, too, sweetheart. 'Twould have been safer to seek revenge against us by joining up with your cousin than by betraying Richard."

"But now he won't do either." Nell looked at Rafe, standing so still, the bow in his hands. Relaxed and yet alert, waiting like the predator he was. "Will you kill the other two?"

"Aye."

And that was all she needed to know. He would kill her cousin and his henchmen, also, if it was necessary to keep her safe.

"I'm glad I'm with you," she whispered.

He smiled at her then, a swift, slashing, dangerous smile that hit her like a bolt from a crossbow. "Don't worry, little one. I've been in worse corners than this. We'll be all right. If I can wound your cousin we'll be rid of the danger for good."

The words had barely left his mouth when Nell heard the thundering hoofbeats of several horses. The riders burst through the valley entrance and reined in sharply, milling about as they looked over the apparently empty land.

Why didn't Rafe fire? she wondered impatiently. The

men were little more than a hundred yards away, well within range of his longbow, and were obviously arguing about their next course of action. She craned further around the base of her rock and spied Tom in the middle of the group. One of the men pointed to the rocks and said something, and she ducked back again.

"Those two outlaws are still with them," she observed, trying not to sound terrified.

"So I see. Your cousin must have offered them a substantial reward."

For some reason this calm answer pulled her already straining nerves tighter. "I thought you said outlaws take care of their own."

"Aye. Well, apparently Ned and his cohorts have never heard of that particular philosophy. That's right," he crooned before she could respond. "Just a little closer. Another step and—"

Rafe straightened, brought the bow up and fired in a movement so fast it was blinding. A scream of pain rent the air. Before it had died away, he had sent three more arrows after the first.

Stunned by his speed, Nell could only crouch in the grass, listening to the confused sounds of yells and the neighing of panicked horses as their riders leapt for whatever cover they could find on the exposed hillside.

"Fiend seize it!" Rafe wheeled back behind the boulder and reached for another arrow.

"What happened?"

"I killed one of those outlaws and hit two of your cousin's men, but Tom managed to flee back to shelter."

"Leaving his men?"

"Don't sound so shocked. Did you think a man who hires assassins to do his work is anything but a coward?

Stay down! Three of them have bows. When nothing else starts flying from here, we're going to have a hail of arrows falling around us.''

Several of the missiles went whistling overhead even as he spoke.

"Damn!" Rafe scowled after them. "I could wish their aim was better."

Nell stared at him, wondering if she was losing her mind. Or perhaps she was living in some crazy nightmare and would soon wake up. "You want us to be *hit*?"

"Of course not. I want more ammunition."

Dear God, that was why he had stopped firing when Tom had retreated. He couldn't afford to loose an arrow unless he was sure of it finding its mark.

"We could sit here for hours," she realised aloud. Dismay had her voice shaking. "No one out there is going to move just so you can shoot him."

"I think Tom's patience will run out before too long," Rafe answered with a brief, reassuring smile. "As for his cowardice, it might work in our favour."

"How so?"

"Men won't risk their lives for a craven who has shown he'll abandon them to save his own skin. Not only that. He still has a man with him behind that entrance, but he hasn't given any order for covering fire so the others can retreat safely."

That left six men out in the open, Nell thought, two of whom might only be wounded, not dead.

"What are we going to do?" she asked.

"Wait. 'Tis all we can do for the moment. Except to pick off anyone foolish enough to show himself."

"And if those men out there crawl closer without making a target of themselves? What then?"

He grimaced. "I was hoping you wouldn't think of that, princess. Let's just say I'll need more arrows than I have to pin them down and persuade them to change their minds."

"*Nell*!"

Rafe's head whipped around as Tom's voice bellowed across the space between them. He risked a quick glance past the boulder to make sure the men flattened in the grass hadn't moved.

"Nell? Can you speak? Can you answer me?"

"Nice touch," Rafe growled sardonically. "Puts the idea in his men's minds that I have you under duress."

"But won't they learn our exact position if I answer?"

He shook his head. "They saw me when I fired at them, sweetheart. Answer him, but keep your eyes on those rocks above us while I watch the front. This could be meant to distract us."

She nodded and took a deep breath. "I'm not a prisoner, Tom," she shouted. "So you might as well go back home. I don't need you."

From the corner of her eye she saw Rafe grin. "Good girl," he said. "Make him angry enough to forget caution."

She certainly seemed to have done that. Tom's voice when he yelled out again had a distinct edge to it.

"Nell? You're a fool if you stay with Beaudene. He's a killer, a murderer. He killed the man my father hired for extra protection."

"You mean the man your father hired to kill me!" Nell shouted back. "I saw the cut rope, Tom."

"'Twas Beaudene's plan to use the horse, but when it didn't work, he decided to make some money out of you. Why do you think he let those outlaws capture you? They're his friends.''

She flicked a quick glance at Rafe, then went back to examining the rocks. He wasn't smiling now. His eyes were narrowed, his face tense. Did he think she would believe anything Tom said? she wondered vaguely.

''Ned told me what happened,'' Tom went on when she didn't answer. ''How you nursed them. He was going to the sheriff to free you when he found me instead.''

''You're the fool if you think I'll believe that,'' Nell cried huskily. Her voice was getting hoarse from all the yelling and she cleared her throat. ''I was there. I know what—*Rafe*!''

Her warning scream was still echoing around the rocks when Rafe turned and fired. The shadow that had suddenly loomed above her wavered then became a man. He pitched forward, hit the rocks and bounced off to roll down the hillside.

At the same moment, a series of battle cries told Nell that the others had taken advantage of the situation to try to pin Rafe down so they could rush his cover. She heard him cursing steadily as he returned their fire, but her eyes were fixed on the body that had come to rest against a boulder some distance below them. The man didn't move. Beside him lay his longbow, and a deer-hide quiver.

She glanced back at Rafe. The hail of arrows had stopped again, and there was a raw graze along his jaw.

''You were hit!''

''*'Tis* nothing. Stay where you are.''

''But—''

''The arrow was spent, Nell. It rebounded off one of

the rocks and just caught me. 'Tis not even bleeding now.''

He was right, but— Once more she fought down rising fear. "Did…they get any closer?"

"Aye." His tone was still terse. "Damn their eyes. I think I hit one or two, but I couldn't get a clear shot without getting killed myself. Still, your cousin is now alone behind that cliff, so they can't try that particular diversion again."

But they might try something else, Nell thought. She looked at the arrows in Rafe's quiver. There were five. Not enough to stave off another attack. Not even to kill each man singly if the wounded could still fight.

She bit her lip, her gaze returning to the body wedged against the rock. From where he stood, Rafe couldn't see it, but it was only about fifty feet away. If she moved very fast, she could reach it, grab the quiver… She wouldn't think about getting hit. It was her fault they were in this mess, and if Rafe was wounded or killed because of her she wouldn't be able to bear the pain and guilt.

Taking a long, steadying breath, she got to her feet. "I'm going after those arrows," she said quietly.

He didn't turn his head. "Don't be an idiot. They're scattered all over the—*Christ Jesu!*"

Nell was already racing down the hill, staying as low as she could. Cursing, Rafe leapt into the open and fired arrow after arrow, his aim so deadly that one man jerked and went still and the others flattened themselves even further.

"Run!" he roared as she grabbed the quiver and turned back. He caught her arm as she reached him and flung her behind the rocks, hurling himself after her.

Nell lay gasping for breath. "They didn't shoot back," she panted. "I thought they would."

He came up on one knee beside her, wrapped his hands around her upper arms and shook her furiously. "By God, I ought to—" He stopped, crushed her against him and held her hard. A second later she was free. With one searing glance from blazing gold eyes, Rafe got to his feet, shrugged off his empty quiver and snatched up the one Nell had retrieved.

"What are you going to do?" she gasped, more breathless from his anger than her own exertions.

His mouth set hard. "Finish this." He turned away, nocked an arrow and took careful aim.

But not at the men still trapped in the open, Nell realised suddenly. She scrambled to her feet to watch. The arrow soared high, seeming to touch the clouds, then plummeted to earth just short of the place where Tom was hiding.

"Curse it!" Rafe fired again, and again the arrow soared skyward. "Come on, you bastard," he muttered. "Fly!"

"What—?" Nell began. She was cut off by a startled yell and a horse's angry squeal. Tom's stallion burst into the open, plunging and bucking, completely out of control.

"You hit it!" she exclaimed, incredulous.

"Not at this range, when I couldn't even see it." Rafe's voice was tight with grim satisfaction. "But that shot was obviously near enough to panic the brute into running, which is what I wanted." He fired again, sending the next missile straight past the horse's face just as Tom got its head up.

The stallion reared, pawing the air, then put his head back down and went into a frenzy of bucking. Tom managed to hang on for a few seconds before he was sent flying. He landed with a sickening thud and lay still, one arm at an odd angle.

"Stay here," Rafe commanded. Picking up his sword, he sheathed it and strode out of their shelter, readying his bow as he went.

Nell waited until he was several yards ahead, then followed.

The men on the ground had scrambled out of the stallion's path when the horse had bolted after throwing Tom, apparently considering the greater risk lay in being trampled rather than shot. They now watched Rafe's approach with varying degrees of wariness.

He stopped a few feet away and looked them over, his eyes cold. Two appeared unhurt, one had an arrow through his leg, another was unconscious but breathing, and Tom was doubled over, groaning. The rest weren't going to move again short of a miracle.

"On your feet," he ordered the two uninjured men. "Leave your bows on the ground. You've got five minutes to pick up your dead and wounded and start back to Langley. And make sure you don't turn around. If I even think you're following us, there'll be no one left to see that Master Tom gets home in one piece."

"Bastard!" spat Tom. He struggled to sit up, his eyes bloodshot and glaring. "You won't get away with this. My father will go to the King and—"

"Let him," Rafe interrupted without ceremony. "You gave yourself away the minute you mentioned that stallion in connection with the rope. Something you wouldn't have known if you hadn't planned it, since the rope in question is in my possession."

"We only intended to delay Nell's journey," Tom muttered, turning sullen. "But the stubborn jade had

the devil's own luck. 'Twas her father's fault. He
shouldn't have taken her from us. And now my arm's
broke. I can't ride. How—?''

Again Rafe cut him off. ''A pity it wasn't your neck.
'Twould be no more than you deserve after ordering
your men to open fire at the risk of hitting a girl to
whom you no longer have any rights.''

''More rights than you, Beaudene, as you'll discover.'' Tom's mouth twisted with spiteful satisfaction.
''My father sent a rider direct to Hadleigh. How do you
think fitzWarren will react when he learns his precious
daughter has been alone with you all this time? She'll
be marked as your wh—''

The vicious word was never uttered. With no com-
punction whatsoever, Rafe drew back his foot and silenced Tom with a brutal kick to the jaw, knocking him
nearly senseless.

There was movement to his right and he wheeled,
bringing the bow up. ''Don't even think about it,'' he
said, eyes slitted with menace.

The men backed off. Looking as sullen as their master, they got to work rounding up horses. They were
ready to depart just after the five minutes was up, a
very groggy Tom being the last to be helped into the
saddle.

Rafe looked at him, not bothering to hide his contempt. ''Tell Langley that if you, or he, or any other
member of your family comes near Lady Nell fitz-
Warren again, I will assume 'tis with the intent of doing
her harm and I will act accordingly. Is that clear?''

Tom glared blearily back at him. Nursing his jaw, he
opened his mouth to reply, then glanced past Rafe and

shut his lips on whatever he'd been about to say. Nodding stiffly instead, he gave his men the signal to start.

Rafe watched them go, thankful the process had been so easy. He had taken a risk, assuming that the men wouldn't fight if Tom was taken out of the reckoning, but they still could have turned on him. There had been three men capable of using a bow—or a knife, come to that. He hadn't left them entirely weaponless to face the journey back to Langley.

Then he turned and saw the other reason why his adversaries had decided to be so amenable.

Nell was waiting motionless in front of the rocks. She had retrieved a dead man's bow and an arrow, and was standing ready to fire, the weapon aimed steadily at the place where Tom had been.

Something unbearably poignant tightened inside Rafe as he took in the sight of her. She looked like a young Viking queen, ready to fight at the side of her warriors. Her crespinette had fallen off when he'd grabbed her and hauled her behind the rocks again, and her long hair flowed free in the wind, a bright chestnut banner against the green of her surcoat. She stood slightly side-on to him, the bow held in a grip that was practised and sure. His throat tightened again when he saw that the weapon was at least half a foot too long for her. And yet, despite that, despite the strain and fear she had to have felt, she had been willing to fight with him, to risk her life to help him.

He walked slowly towards her, knowing that with every step he moved closer to a destiny he no longer wanted to question.

She wasn't looking at him. As he drew nearer, he saw that her eyes, huge in her delicate face and darkened to the shadowed green of a hidden woodland pool, were still fixed on the point where the arrow was aimed. He made his voice low, so that he wouldn't startle her, but tension was gathering, racing through his body like wildfire out of control.

"You can put the bow down now. They've gone."

Nell blinked, and looked at the weapon as if she'd never seen it before. Carefully she eased her hold on the drawn bowstring and let the arrow fall. "A good thing I didn't have to use it," she murmured. "'Tis heavier than I'm used to."

She felt strange, unsettled, as if not quite sure what to do or say next. Nor could she look at Rafe, although she sensed his gaze hadn't wavered from her face. She mustn't let him see her eyes. That was the only clear thought in her head. If he did, if he looked into her eyes, he would see the sick terror that had seized her when he had walked into the open, thinking Tom beaten.

But he hadn't known her cousin as she did. Tom might have been hurt, but he was vicious and stupid, a combination as volatile as it was dangerous. Rafe could have been killed.

Dear God in heaven he could have been *killed*.

"'Tis over," she whispered, as though reassuring herself. "We're safe."

"Over?" Rafe's tone was suddenly so harsh that Nell jumped, her gaze flying involuntarily to his. "Safe?" The bow was wrenched from her grasp with such speed she barely registered its absence. Rafe flung it to the ground and thrust his hands at her. They were shaking.

"Look at that!" he ground out raggedly. "I've been like this since you made that insane, suicidal dash for those arrows, and knowing you're safe isn't stopping me thinking about what could have happened to you.''

Nell started to shiver deep inside. His eyes. Those fierce hawk's eyes were filled with emotions that were primitive, savage, all restraints of civilisation gone.

''Rafe,'' she breathed. Just that, his name. She took a step towards him, her hand lifting to touch the graze on his jaw, and something else flashed in that burning gaze. The ruthless purpose she had sensed before, unleashed at last, and unstoppable.

He reached for her, sweeping her up into his arms without warning. Then, his eyes holding hers, he turned and carried her back into their shelter among the stones.

Chapter Eleven

Nell was trembling when he laid her on the grass and knelt beside her, but she could no more have stopped him than she could stop the frantic rhythm of her heart.

He didn't love her. She knew that. It was only passion, a primitive urge to couple, born of danger and the threat of death, but she would take it. She would have this moment. She would have this to remember when he was gone; the way he touched her face with his fingertips, as if he didn't trust himself with a firmer caress, the fine tremor still in his hands as he swiftly unlaced her surcoat and then her gown and shift. The almost agonised expulsion of air as he parted the fabric and watched the rosy tips of her breasts peak in the cool air.

Just for a moment shyness threatened to overwhelm her, a ripple of trepidation at the awareness that she was lying half-naked beneath his gaze. But then his long fingers closed over her soft mounds and fire streaked through her, drawing a whimpering sound of pleasure from her throat. Her head went back and she wanted to close her eyes, to abandon herself to the clever, knowing caress of those powerful hands, but now something apart from shyness held her back, something deep within her that clamoured for acknowledgement.

His face. It was in his face. Hunger. Desire. But more.

She forced her blurred vision to clear, struggling to understand, and shivered uncontrollably when she saw the fierceness in his eyes, the sharp-edged mask of passion tautening his face. Men had looked at her with desire before today, but this…this *intensity*, this utterly focused need was terrifying. He would demand— *take*—everything she was.

And in that moment she knew with mind-shattering clarity that there was nothing he would demand that she wouldn't give. Willingly, passionately. Somewhere, some time in the past few days, she had fallen in love with him, with his fierceness, his moments of gentleness, the vulnerable boy he had once been, the strong man he had become. Her body, her heart, her very soul were his. Absolutely. Irrevocably. For all time.

''Rafe,'' she said again, and this time there was full knowledge, trust, love.

He made a rough sound in his throat and came down over her, his mouth hard and urgent on hers, his tongue plundering deep, deeper, until she was kissing him back as frantically, her arms around him, small hands probing the powerful muscles of his back, learning him, savouring his strength.

She couldn't think any longer, couldn't speak or breathe, but it didn't matter. He had stolen everything, but she was alive as she had never been before. While he kissed her, caressed her, awakened her body once more to his touch, she lived only for him. He groaned against her mouth and she felt the vibrations of sound echo all through her body.

"You're mine," he said hoarsely. "Mine! I don't care who…"

He swept her skirts upwards as he spoke and his words ceased to make sense. She cried out when his fingers found her, touched the soft, melting centre of her womanhood, stroked, circled. She was mindless, drowning in exquisite sensation, almost sobbing with pleasure.

Rafe tore his mouth from hers, wanting to see her, wanting to watch her as he touched the sweet heat between her thighs, but the lure of her parted lips, swollen and moist from his kisses, defeated him, tormenting him with images of the deeper possession to come. He couldn't wait. He was burning, aching, shuddering uncontrollably with the need to have her.

Dimly he realised that he could be endangering them both by taking her here and now, but instincts, wild and savage, were driving him. He had to take her, make her his, brand her with his body until she remembered no other man but him. He lifted his weight slightly to free himself of his clothing and it was like tearing his own flesh away to be apart from her for even that brief moment.

His arms closed around her again and he pressed her legs wider, groaning harshly as he felt the silky warmth of her body begin to enclose him. He buried his face in her hair, fighting for control. She was so small. Small and tight. "Oh, God, I can't wait. I can't wait. Nell, I have to—"

Her sharp cry tore through the mists of passion as he thrust into her with the full force of his body. Rafe froze, his breathing hoarse and broken, hardly able to believe the evidence of his senses.

"Nell? My God!" He raised his head, his fingers spearing into her hair to hold her still for his shocked scrutiny. She gazed up at him, her hazel eyes luminous with tears that she instantly blinked away.

"It doesn't matter," she said urgently. And he felt the truth of that in the sudden pulsing of her body around him. "It doesn't… Oh, Rafe. Don't stop. *Please* don't stop."

A ragged sound that could have been a laugh or a groan was torn from him. "Stop? God, I couldn't stop now if there was a loaded crossbow at my head. Nell, sweetheart…" She was innocent! She was *his*! The thought nearly drove him over the edge. Only the knowledge of her innocence, and the feel of her, soft and fragile beneath him, gave him back the will to leash his strength, to take her slowly. For her he could be gentle. Only for her.

He felt her tremble, felt the involuntary tensing of her body as he withdrew slightly, and touched her face with a tenderness he hadn't known he possessed. "'Tis all right, sweeting," he whispered. "I won't hurt you again." He began kissing her, easing her back into passion with gentle stroking movements of his body. "Relax. Just relax for me."

Relax? When he was seducing her so gently, so sweetly. When all her senses were filled with him, overwhelmed by him. She had never imagined such closeness. She felt bound, linked to him forever by the unbreakable chains of this most intimate act, her will gone, her very self merged with his, no longer separate.

And the sweet, pulsing ache grew and grew until she couldn't bear it any more. He began to move more forcefully, and tension coiled tighter within her. Impossibly tighter. It was like being caged by fire and yet she had no desire to be free. The unrestrained force of his hunger was too powerful, burning away everything but the need to belong to him. Her heart raced so fast it must surely burst; she heard her own voice almost sobbing, pleading, felt her body arching helplessly beneath his and wondered distantly how he could do this to her. If she hadn't trusted him so deeply the total loss of control would have terrified her.

Then his arms tightened around her with crushing strength and she felt the edge of his teeth against the side of her throat.

''Nell. *Nell*...''

The sensation was too much. She barely heard the anguished sound of her name. The tightening coil of tension seemed to spring open and a torrent of voluptuous pleasure flooded every part of her body. She was helpless. Blind. Deaf. Exquisite sensation blotted out everything, throbbing through her in wave after wave of ecstasy, until, gradually, the waves became ripples that drew his name from her with every sighing breath she took.

Sound came back first. The wind moaning softly through the rocks, the twitter of a bird, the faint restless movements of the horses.

Nell lay motionless, listening to the sounds of reality as her heartbeat returned to normal and the delicious sense of utter relaxation that had enfolded her began to fade. And in its wake came tension, coldness, dread. Ice touched her skin, a creeping chill that spread from her head to her heels as the realisation of the completeness of Rafe's withdrawal seeped into her consciousness.

She was alone again. He had straightened her clothing while she had lain almost senseless with bliss, covering her against the autumn wind, but she no longer felt the wonderful weight of his body, was no longer protected by the hard strength of his arms, no longer engulfed by the fire of his passion. He had withdrawn from her totally, was no longer touching her at all, although she sensed he was near.

One of the horses stamped and snorted, making harness jingle, and Nell turned her head in that direction. Rafe was lying on his back beside her, one arm flung across his eyes. His other hand lay clenched in the grass at his side.

The longing to reach out and touch him, to entwine her fingers with his, to hold on, *somehow*, to that feeling of being one with him, was almost overwhelming. But the way he was lying...

Could he not bear even to look at her?

All at once she felt sick with nerves. What in Christendom was she supposed to say? What *could* she say when she had just given herself to a man whom she'd met only three days ago? Three days! And for most of that time he had considered her to be a nuisance at best. Holy Mother, what was he thinking, lying there so still and quiet? Did he regret what had happened?

Aye, of course he would, she answered her own question immediately. He didn't love her. He didn't even trust women in general. He had thought her experienced and was probably now cursing her for deceiving him. She wouldn't be able to endure it. His resentment. His disgust. Even if he blamed himself, in part or entirely, the knowledge of his regret would burn through her memories of this one time together until there was nothing left but ashes and heartache.

Nell clenched her own fists as determination flowed into her. She would not have this spoilt. She would not be made to feel shame because she had given herself to the man she loved, even if he didn't want or know of her love.

She sat up, and with shaking hands began to lace up her gown. Her crucifix gleamed up at her from the grass. Rafe must have removed it, she thought, slipping it over her head, and in the heat of their passion she hadn't even noticed. Beside her, he stirred as if he'd felt her movement, and she knew he was watching her.

"The wind blows cold," she observed, with a composure that Edward's notoriously ice-cold queen would have envied. "And 'twill be dark soon. We should be going."

He came up off the ground as if propelled by a catapult, taking her hands and pulling her to her feet in the same movement. "Don't," he said, taking her in his arms and pressing her head into his shoulder. "Just...don't."

Nell stood quietly within his embrace but she didn't soften against him. Let him apologise for this, she thought grimly, and I'll hit him.

She felt his head bend to hers. "Are you all right?" he asked, very low. His hand began stroking her back in a movement that was probably meant to be soothing, but only succeeded in pulling her already straining nerves tighter. Concern for her physical comfort was the last thing she needed.

"Of course I'm all right," she muttered, lying through her teeth. "Why wouldn't I be? You... We..."

Her courage quailed at the thought of describing the incredible pleasure he had given her.

After a moment of silence he gave a short laugh. "I don't wonder you find it impossible to describe. I went at you like—" His breath hissed out and he held her tighter.

Sudden awareness hit Nell like a bolt of lightning. He was regretting the *way* he'd taken her, not the act itself. At least...

Oh, blessed Lord, let it be so.

"Like a man who had just seen us through a very real threat to our lives," she murmured, lifting her head so quickly that she took him unawares. The piercing intensity in his eyes almost made her falter. Shy colour tinted her cheeks but she looked up at him unflinchingly. "You didn't hurt me."

When he raised a disbelieving brow, her colour deepened. "Well, only for the veriest moment."

His hands shifted to cup her shoulders, his eyes watching the movement as his fingers caressed the delicate bones beneath her clothes. "But you're so small and I was— Sweet Jesu, Nell, I must have scared you witless."

"Witless, indeed," she muttered, lowering her gaze to stare fixedly at his surcoat as she remembered her utter abandonment to ecstasy. "But not from fear."

In the deafening silence that followed, Nell wished she could be struck mute. When was she ever going to learn to guard her unruly tongue? "I... I mean... I might not have been as shocked as you would expect because...well, at Langley..."

"Aye, Langley." He released her shoulders and took a step back.

Nell risked one fleeting glance upwards and almost

shrivelled inside at the sternness in his face. Now she had made everything worse. "A girl could hardly remain ignorant there," she whispered.

"No." His agreement was cool, giving nothing away. "But knowledge is not experience. You were innocent. God's *teeth*!" he exploded suddenly, turning away and raking a hand through his hair. "Everything pointed to you being—"

"What you thought me," she finished.

He stood with his back to her for a minute, then wheeled about and wrapped his hands around her arms. "You never denied it," he accused, giving her a little shake. "From the moment in the stable when I asked the whereabouts of your lover, you didn't deny a thing. Damn it, Nell, you answered me as if there *was* a lover. That first night on the road you taunted me with your supposed lovers. And then there was the hyssop. I thought… God, at that stage I didn't know what I was thinking, but when I discovered your knowledge of the herb any uncertainty I had about your past was gone, even though you'd never used it. Why else would you need such knowledge? I thought."

"How did you know of it?" she asked abruptly, curiosity on this point momentarily diverting her.

His eyes were hard for just an instant. "My mother used it," he told her flatly. "I was very young but I can remember her taking it, the odour of it. Eventually it killed her."

Nell's breath caught in her throat. How was she ever going to overcome so much distrust and bitterness learned at such a young age? The immensity of the task overwhelmed her—before she remembered that she wouldn't have to worry about it. Rafe would be gone after he delivered her to her father.

"And what was I seeing that night in your uncle's hall?" he went on, as if the detour in their discussion had never taken place. "What did I hear?"

Nell sighed, the sound soft and a little sad. "A lie," she said quietly. "A lie I enacted from the night the King tried—" She broke off and shook her head. "'Twas the only way I could protect myself. It worked but 'twas becoming harder. I had to watch, all the time. Never to be alone with a man, but to bestow a smile here, a few words there. Even a kiss, if 'twould get rid of…" she faltered, shuddering, and let the words fade away, but Rafe wasn't finished with her.

"Edward," he said. "Why didn't you tell me the truth then, Nell? When you told me about the crucifix."

"I tried," she retorted, her chin coming up as indignation lent her strength. "You wouldn't let me finish."

He smiled slightly in wry acknowledgement. "Your dislike and contempt for Edward were so great I thought 'twas because he must have forced you to trade your virtue in exchange for your mother's crucifix. I couldn't listen to the rest. If I had I would—" he gave a short laugh and shrugged. "I don't know. Throttled him, maybe."

Nell smiled, too, but faintly. "A good thing I escaped the King's attentions, then," she said. "'Twas when Edward was visiting my uncle. He did try to force such a bargain from me, and when I refused he became angry and tried to use force of another kind, until I shamed him by pointing out how spoilt he was, that because no woman had ever refused him he thought he could even rape with impunity.

"I was so angry, so…*distressed* that a king would behave so, that I went straight up to my aunt's chamber and stole the crucifix back from her. Then I marched

through the hall in full view of everyone and made a
hiding place for it in the stable.''

"That's why you were out there that night?"

She nodded. "Aye. If I had stopped to think about
any of it, I probably wouldn't have succeeded, but no
one noticed anything amiss. They were too drunk, as
usual, and Aunt Maud never wore the crucifix; she just
took it from me for spite."

"But she might have noticed its disappearance any
time these past three years, which means you've lived
with the risk of discovery as well as everything else.
Because you had a vow to fulfil."

She made a small gesture of assent, but when she
would have turned away at the finality in his tone he
reached for her and drew her close again. "Nell," was
all he said, but in the murmured sound of her name she
heard regret and understanding, and something else she
couldn't recognise.

He held her like that for a heartbeat of silence. Nell
thought his lips brushed her hair once, before he released her and stepped back.

"We really do have to reach Wells before dark," he
said, his voice deep and husky. "I'll get the horses."

Nell watched him turn away, then bent her head and
finished lacing her surcoat. She shouldn't feel so lost
and desolate because he hadn't said anything about the
future, she scolded herself. He might have regretted
taking her maidenhead, but why should he feel anything else for her? She hadn't expected him to.

But she had! Merciful saints, deep down she had!
Despite everything she had told herself—that she'd
known he didn't love her, that she had only wanted one
moment out of time with him—she hadn't expected his
indifference to hurt so much. She hadn't known. In her

innocence she hadn't known how much more devastating it would be to see him walk away after they had been so close.

He led the horses over to her and she carefully kept her expression blank. It took a considerable effort, and for the first time she was grateful for the years spent learning control. Not that she felt shamed by what had happened. She had no intention of marrying the man her father had chosen for her, or marrying anyone else come to that, so the loss of her virginity didn't matter, but—''

"Come on, princess, up with you."

The command broke through her preoccupation. Nell blinked and found herself confronted by Samson's solid bulk. Rafe lifted her into the capacious saddle and mounted behind her before she could question the arrangement. She looked back as he nudged Samson into a walk, to see Rufus following on a makeshift leading-rein.

"Why—?"

"This will be more comfortable than riding astride for you, sweetheart," he murmured, and bent to brush his mouth across her cheek. "Are you very sore?"

Nell felt herself flush bright scarlet all the way down to her breasts. She jerked around to face the front. Holy saints, she had blushed more in the last hour than in her entire life. If only Rafe wouldn't keep taking her unawares with such embarrassingly intimate questions.

Then she remembered the heart-shaking intimacy that had led to the question, and her control tottered as an echo of sensual pleasure hummed through her.

"No," she gasped in a hopelessly breathless voice. "I told you…you didn't hurt me."

His arms tightened around her and he settled her

more closely against him. "'Twill be better for you next time, little one, I promise you. Much better."

Nell's eyes widened. She only just managed to stop herself turning to stare at him. Better? There was better than that sweet, melting, utterly thrilling— Next time!

Her heart stopped beating, she was sure of it. Next time? He was going to…? Did he mean to…? What in the name of all the saints was he…?

Her thought process shattered. She didn't dare ask for clarification, but if she didn't ask *something*…

"What…what shall we do when we get to Wells?" she stammered, practically unable to recall why she had wanted to go there in the first place. "You said something…last night…about the Bishop's palace."

"Aye. We'll find accommodation for the night in the guest dorter and I'll arrange for you to visit your mother's tomb in the morning."

"Thank you," she whispered, truly grateful. A measure of sanity returned and she closed her hand protectively around the jewel beneath her surcoat. "I wish I didn't have to part with this," she confided. "'Tis all I have left of my mother, and though, as I grew older, I thought her weak for loving my father so blindly, she loved me also, and I her."

"Is that why you set your face against marriage, Nell? Because of your parents?"

"That and what I saw at Langley."

"Well, I can hardly wonder at that, but don't fret, princess. You're far from weak, and if that taste of you I had was any example, I'll never give you cause for tears because I've gone to another woman."

She hadn't heard aright. Either that or she had left her wits back there at those rocks. "I beg your pardon?" she asked in a very polite, very small voice.

"We're getting married," he explained calmly. "In fact, before we worry about accommodation or anything else, we're going to hunt up the Bishop or one of his priests and have our betrothal vows witnessed."

The only thing Nell could think of to say to that pronouncement was that he hadn't asked her to marry him. Which was so absurd that she dismissed it immediately.

"Why?" she finally produced, and decided she really had lost her mind.

He seemed to hesitate, and she felt him go very still against her for a fleeting second before he relaxed again. "The usual reasons. I've been considering marriage for some time. Every man needs sons, and they need their mother to be honourable and strong as well as their sire. You are that, Nell. 'Tis a rare quality in a woman, and one I value."

The words made her heart melt, but some perverse demon was still driving her, goading her to probe his reasons for wanting to marry her.

"I don't know your situation," she began, choosing her words as carefully as he had seemed to do. "But I am an heiress. My father may well object, since he has already chosen a husband for me, and if I disobey him, you could find yourself taking a pauper to wife."

"You don't have to concern yourself with that," he answered curtly. "I'll handle your father, and in any event, I'm not in need of a wealthy wife."

While she was still considering that, he added, "You needn't try to think up any more objections. We're getting married."

Indignation stiffened her spine, even as she longed to agree. "Are we?"

"We are. Make up your mind to it, princess. Apart

from any other cause, I could have got you with child. 'Tis reason enough.''

And a reason she hadn't even considered until now. Her hand went to her belly in wonder at the thought of a small being within. Rafe's child. Her baby. His. Part of them both.

It was no less prosaic a reason for marriage than the others Rafe had given her, but did it matter? She knew her hesitation was only caused by the last remnants of her distrust of men, her fear of being so vulnerable, of virtually becoming a man's property. But this was Rafe. The man she loved. Hadn't she already realised that one of them would have to trust blindly?

Aye, she thought, and like her mother, like most women, she would take that risk for love. And, mayhap, one day in the future, Rafe would learn to trust her also. Even...one day...if she loved enough, he might love her in return.

"All right," she said at last. "I'll marry you."

"Many thanks," he returned drily. Then, when she giggled suddenly, he bent to nuzzle her hair and she felt his lips, warm and seductive, on her throat.

"Don't be afraid of me, sweeting. I know you felt pleasure before, but 'twas only a ripple compared to the pleasure you gave me. I couldn't even—'' He lifted his head, strain and a certain puzzlement clear in his voice. "I've never lost control like that with a woman. Never! Holy saints, we were still clothed; I barely touched you, barely took enough time to prepare you—'' He took a deep breath and held her hard for a moment. "It won't be like that again."

"You knew I...'' Nell hadn't even heard the rest. She was blushing wildly yet again and knew he could see the hot colour staining her face.

He laughed softly and stroked a finger down her cheek, leaving more fire in his wake. "I could feel it," he murmured wickedly. "And I can't wait to feel you around me again."

Nell decided, rather belatedly, that it was a great deal safer to remain silent until she was no longer sharing a saddle with her betrothed. Otherwise, if the conversation continued on its present deliciously dangerous path, Rafe would also feel the half-nervous, wholly-thrilling shivers of anticipation coursing through her.

But she nestled closer within the circle of his arms and laid her head on his shoulder, and, for the first time in ten years, allowed a warm little glow of hope and tentative happiness to light the depths of her heart.

Chapter Twelve

Late the following morning, Nell stood in the grave-yard beside the cathedral at Wells, blinking a little after the taper-lit gloom of the vault where generations of her maternal ancestors lay at eternal rest, and wondered what Rafe was doing.

Since their arrival in Wells on the previous evening, and the exchange of betrothal vows before they had so much as rested after the rigours of the day, they had spent very little time together. While Rafe had been closeted with the Bishop, regaling that shocked cleric with the tale of Nell's treatment at the hands of her family, she had been shown to a guest-chamber, where a girl fetched from the town had waited upon her. Then, after a meal and a blissful hour's soak in a tub of hot water, she had had only enough energy left to tumble into bed.

She had slept the sleep of the exhausted, not stirring until her maid had knocked on the door with the news that Father Simeon, the priest assigned to escort her, was waiting in the ante-chamber and would be at her disposal all morning.

The good father had turned out to be an elderly,

plump little individual, whose greying tonsure and faded blue eyes belied a sprightly nature. He had heard her confession—couched in very vague terms; pronounced a penance—negligible—and had accompanied her to Mass in the cathedral. He had also been of considerable help in other ways.

Nell turned on the thought as the clunk of the vault's lock sounded behind her. Father Simeon met her gaze with a smile.

"Is there somewhere else I may escort you, my lady?" he enquired politely. "A walk in the cloisters before dinner, perhaps? Or, if you prefer a moment of prayer now your task is done, the Lady Chapel is quiet at this time of day."

"Thank you, Father." Nell returned the smile warmly. "I fear I have kept you from your duties overlong, but I could not have managed without you. You have my heartfelt gratitude, especially for your kindness in finding that little casket in which my mother's crucifix could be sealed."

"'Twas a small enough service, dear lady," Father Simeon demurred.

But Nell shook her head. "'Twas more than that. I confess I was not looking forward with any pleasure to the prospect of having the tomb itself opened."

"Departed souls deserve their privacy," agreed Father Simeon comfortably. "And your lady mother will surely rest easier now her final wish has been granted at last."

"I'm glad 'tis done," Nell sighed. "I thought I would miss having something of hers, but now 'tis gone I feel more relieved than anything."

The priest nodded. "'Twas not an easy task to lay on a child. And now…?" He paused, enquiring again.

"And now I may just sit here awhile, if 'tis allowed. The morning is fine and—" she coloured slightly "—my lord will know where to find me."

"Ah." Father Simeon smiled with cheerful understanding. "And 'tis not my company you'll be wanting when he does," he said, a most unpriestly twinkle in his blue eyes. "In which case I had best hie myself off to the meeting in the chapter-house. God bless you, dear child."

"Thank you again, Father." Nell watched as the little priest hurried across the grass towards the imposing bulk of the cathedral.

He turned to wave before he vanished through a door and she waved back, feeling more at peace than she had done in years. And with the peace was a growing sense of anticipation. For the first time the future held promise, and she couldn't wait for it to begin.

Suddenly restless, she walked across the graveyard and around to the west front of the cathedral. Here, carved in tier upon tier on the façade of the building, were statues of the saints, fashioned with painstaking diligence and detail. Here also, she could watch for Rafe while affecting a fascinated interest in the statuary above her. He had said he would see her on the morrow and the day was already half done. Surely he would be here soon.

What would he think of her? she mused, looking down at herself with purely feminine concern. Her hair was in neat braids but bare of any headdress to lend elegance to her appearance. She still wore the dusky rose gown and moss-green surcoat. They had been brushed, and her shift and hose had been laundered, but the outer garments were still travel-stained, and as for her shoes…

Nell lifted the hem of her skirts and contemplated the sight of the tips of her toes peeping from her decapitated footwear. The interlude by the stream seemed to have happened a long, long time ago.

"Something else amiss with your shoes, little princess?"

Nell yelped and jumped about a foot in the air. She whirled around to find Rafe grinning at her—and forgot all about scolding him for creeping up on her again.

Somehow his height and powerful build always managed to take her breath away. He was wearing his black surcoat again. The sombre colour should have made him appear unobtrusive, at least, but the stark severity of the garment seemed rather to emphasise the leashed strength beneath it. And now, in full daylight, Nell could see the subtle gleam of the fine gold thread at his wrists, on the high collar, and outlining the white rose badge.

Her widened gaze travelled slowly upwards again. Like her, he was bare-headed, his midnight-dark hair ruffled by the breeze. The strong, masculine contours of cheeks and jaw were more starkly revealed with the disappearance of several days' growth of beard, the outline of his mouth both clean and sensual. The scar on his temple made him look hard and dangerous, but in his golden eyes she saw memories that sent little darts of fire winging through her body.

"You'll have to stop doing that," she said weakly.

His smile was slow and infinitely disturbing. "What's that? Wanting you?"

"No," she gasped, nearly strangling on the knot of nervous excitement building in her throat. She swallowed hard. "Creeping up on me. If you intend to make a practice of it, my nerves will be shattered before the year is out.''

Or a lot sooner if he didn't stop looking at her as if they were…and he was about to…

''Well, at least you weren't talking to yourself, princess. That's a start.'' His smile flashed again, then he released her from the sensual spell of his eyes, shifting his gaze to the cathedral.

''I thought I'd find you inside, studying the more humorous carvings, rather than contemplating these saintly figures,'' he went on, saving her from having to think of a response that would have been hopelessly incoherent at best.

But the remark set her to gathering her scattered wits. Not for anything would she admit that she'd stayed outside to watch for him.

''I saw them many times as a child,'' she murmured. ''My favourite was the carving of two dragons biting each other's tails. But, best of all, my mother used to bring me here to watch the clock strike the hour. I would wait and wait, it seemed like forever, and then the four knights would at last come charging out to knock each other off their horses. I never tired of it.''

''Aha! So that's what you were waiting for.''

Nell kept her expression serene with an effort. ''Isn't it amazing that a clock made more than one hundred years ago can show the phases of the moon as well as days and hours and minutes?'' she observed chattily.

''Amazing,'' Rafe agreed, the lines of amusement deepening around his eyes. ''And if you will accept my escort, my lady, we may go and marvel at such a wondrous invention.'' He offered her his arm,

Nell regarded him suspiciously. ''Are you laughing at me?''

He came a step closer, took her hand and tucked it into the curve of his arm. "Considering where we are, it seemed safer than kissing you," he said softly, beginning to stroll with her towards the cathedral entrance.

"My lord—" the protest was faint but valiant "—you should not speak so. We are in a church."

"Not quite, but you're right about one thing. 'Tis far too public a place for what I have in mind. Next time I kiss you, little one, I intend to make sure we won't be interrupted for a long time." His voice lowered and went dark. "A *very* long time."

She had been right that first night also, Nell decided, hoping her suddenly trembling legs wouldn't collapse under her. Lord Rafael Beaudene was a dangerous man. Extremely dangerous. She just hadn't known in what way until it was far too late.

"I must thank you, my lord," she began, determined to put a stop to his nerve-racking style of conversation before he discovered just how weak she was where he was concerned. She wanted his complete trust and love before that happened. "'Twas kind of you to arrange for Father Simeon to accompany me this morning."

He paused just inside one of the entrance arches and looked down at her. "I thought you would rather have a priest with you."

"Aye." Nell smiled shyly and began to relax. She should have known better.

"So, sweetheart, now that your vow is fulfilled, do you think you might trust me enough to tell me the true reason why your mother was so insistent on taking that crucifix with her to the grave?"

"I... I...what...?" Her brain seemed to freeze.

"Did she never tell you? Did you not investigate?"

"Investigate? I don't know what you mean," she faltered. "My mother only…"

He glanced around quickly, then released her hand and framed her face with both of his. "We're already lovers," he urged gently. "I'm going to be your husband. Trust me with this."

She had to, Nell thought despairingly. She had to trust him, and by her trust hope to draw him closer.

"I don't know what you mean by investigate," she repeated more surely. "I was only a small child when the crucifix was given to me, and all I remember is my mother telling me that it must never fall into the wrong hands. Then, later, I did wonder if it perhaps held something. The cross itself was…different."

"Go on." He was watching her intently, as if he would draw the rest from her by sheer will alone.

"That's all. I didn't want to see if it opened. Not that I had a lot of time to search for a latch or a clasp, but it didn't matter. If the cross indeed held a secret I thought 'twas probably something to do with the wars between York and Lancaster, and if my father had behaved dishonourably, which seemed all too likely from what I knew of him, I didn't want to know of it. I would not have agreed with my mother's desire to shield him, but I had promised her."

He nodded slowly and took his hands from her face, touching the tips of his fingers to the sides of her throat. His thumbs lightly traced the delicate line of her jaw and met just beneath her chin.

Heat burst inside her, flowing all the way to her toes. "Rafe? Do you…?"

"Aye," he said instantly. "I believe you, and you're right. It no longer matters. We have to—"

Footsteps hurrying along the path beside the wall

interrupted him. There was something urgent in the sound, Nell thought vaguely. Then, just as one of the Bishop's servants skidded into the arched entrance where they stood, Rafe stepped away from her.

"Oh, my lord, my lady, thank the saints I found you." The man paused for breath, then bowed low to Nell. "Your pardon, my lady, but you must return to the palace at once. Your father has arrived and requests your presence immediately."

"You were not surprised by my father's arrival," Nell observed as she and Rafe approached the bridge across the moat surrounding the Bishop's palace.

Nor had he hurried her. Whatever urgency had sent the servant searching for them in such haste, Rafe had seemed singularly unimpressed.

"I had warning," he explained. "Your uncle sent a rider express to Hadleigh with what tale we can only imagine. But it makes no difference, Nell. fitzWarren has no power over you now. We've said our betrothal vows before witnesses, and 'tis as binding as any marriage. A fact your father knows full well."

She nodded, looking pensive. "And what else did Tom say to you? I meant to ask before, but… Why did you kick him?" she amended hastily, remembering just how thoroughly she had been distracted at the time.

Rafe slanted an amused glance down at her. "He said something I didn't like."

The bland answer had her frowning at him indignantly. "Well, that was patently obvious, but what?"

"Nothing important." He stopped walking and raised the hand he held to his lips.

Nell steeled herself. "Nothing important? You nearly broke his jaw over noth— Merciful saints." Her knees went weak. He was brushing the backs of her fingers across his mouth, over and over, and now he was pressing them closer, tasting the line between each finger with the tip of his tongue. She was going to faint. She was going to collapse and melt right here on the bridge.

"Stop that," she said weakly. "'Tis not fair. Every time we argue about something, all you have to do is touch me or kiss me and—Oh, no!" she groaned in mortification as she realised where her nervous babbling was taking her.

But Rafe dropped her hand, turned her about and propelled her rather abruptly through the open door of the palace. "You certainly pick the most inconvenient times to rouse a man's baser instincts, princess," he growled. Then, as she looked back at him, he grinned wickedly. "But don't worry about it. I'll remember what you just said."

Her pulse was still racing like a fleeing hare when they stepped over the threshold of the solar where her father was waiting.

She wasn't sure what she had expected, Nell thought a second later, but it wasn't the obese, pallid man, clad in an ankle-length tunic of dark grey wool, who remained seated by the fire, watching them cross the room towards him.

The solar was a cosy apartment, with woven rugs on the floor, tapestries depicting scenes from the religious life on three walls and a fireplace set into the fourth. Two tall, arched windows let in the light, and there were tables and chairs aplenty, but Nell was blind to these comforts. Her gaze remained fixed on her father's face while she searched for a reason why her mother had loved this man so completely.

He had probably been handsome once, she conceded,

and standing he would be almost as tall as Rafe. But his height and the piercing regard of his hazel eyes were the only traces left of the young man who had charmed women so easily. Everything else had softened, gone to seed. The lines about the mouth were dissatisfied, the cheeks flacid, the once-firm jaw slack. Deep pouches of dissipation pulled at his eyes and his skin had an unhealthy parchment hue. A life of self-indulgence had taken its toll.

"Well, girl, you don't favour your mother much," he remarked as she and Rafe halted on the other side of the fireplace. His voice was strained, as though it was an effort to speak. "Not in colouring nor meekness, if I'm any judge. I notice you don't curtsy."

"I owe you nothing, least of all meek, unthinking respect," she returned, meeting his cold stare with one equally as indifferent. "As for my mother, I wonder you even remember her."

Her scorn was evident, but the words were spoken without heat. He's nothing, she realised, and suddenly the anger and bitterness she had harboured towards her father seemed to have vanished, gone for good. She didn't need it, didn't need to pray that divine retribution would overtake him one day. The man sitting in front of her had destroyed himself.

He made a noise that betokened mocking agreement and looked at Rafe. "You'll have your work cut out breaking that spirit, Beaudene. I'm surprised you still want her." His thin lips twisted in a parody of a smile.

"Lady Nell will tell you she is mistress of her own fate," Rafe said coolly. He stood, half leaning against the chair opposite her father's, his hand still clasping hers. "I have no intention of breaking her spirit."

"Hrrmph. New-fangled nonsense, but I haven't got

the time to argue about it. Have to get ready to meet
my Maker.'' He glanced briefly at Nell, and frowned.
''Since 'tis obvious she's taken no hurt, despite the
Canterbury tale that fool from Langley poured into my
ear, we can dispense with her presence.'' His mouth
twisted again. ''No doubt you'll want to discuss the
marriage contract with me, Beaudene.''

''Your concern for your daughter is touching,
fitzWarren, but, aye, we do have something to discuss.'' He smiled down at Nell and gave her hand a
gentle, reassuring squeeze. '''Twould be best if you
return to your chamber, my lady. Have your maid bring
you something to eat.''

The gleam in his eyes belied the formality of his
address, but Nell didn't return the intimate smile.
Something was wrong. Something had jarred. She
wasn't sure what it was. A remark? A certain tension
in the air? Nothing in the conversation struck her as
wrong or strange, given her father's disposition, and yet
she felt this definite sense of unease, almost of dread.

''Rafe, I…'' She half turned towards him, keeping
her voice low so as not to be overheard, but he fore-
stalled her, pressing a finger quickly to her lips.

''Hush, sweetheart. Let me handle this. 'Twill be all
right, I promise you. Trust me.''

Nell sighed. He trapped her with that every time.

Worried, her stomach full of butterflies, though she
knew not why, she nodded acquiescence and freed her
hand. She looked once at her father, who was watching
with a cynical expression on his face, then, without a
word to him of acknowledgement or farewell, she
turned and left the room, pulling the door closed behind
her.

And halted before she had gone a dozen paces.

"I'm surprised you still want her."

Still want her.

Still…?

Why still? She frowned, trying to pin down the elusive source of her unease. It wasn't the word itself—her father had most likely meant to pass comment on her defiance, although he must have known that Rafe couldn't break their betrothal, short of a papal dispensation, even if he had taken a sudden, instant dislike to her behaviour.

Could the "still" have meant a longer time-span? That was impossible, surely. And there had been mockery, too, in her father's tone. What if it hadn't been meant as a subtle jab at her manners, but a direct strike at Rafe?

Her hands began to tingle as though a thousand pins were piercing her flesh. Nell tucked them under her arms, hugging herself, her eyes staring blindly ahead as certainty hit her. It had not been mockery she had heard. It had been malice. Her father had made that remark as if he had *known* Rafe would still want her. As if he was sure Rafe would want her had she been pock-marked, shrewish and devoid of any manners whatsoever. As if…

She went cold all over. As if Rafe would still want her had she been the wanton he'd first assumed her to be.

Without even thinking about it, she spun on her heel and retraced her steps to the door. She had opened it a little more than an inch when her father's raised voice had her hand freezing on the latch.

They hadn't heard her over the angry tirade. Nell managed to unclamp her fingers from the latch, but that was all she was capable of doing. Unable either to step forward into the room or retreat, she listened.

"If you hoped to force my hand in this by betrothing yourself to Eleanor before you returned her to me, you're a fool, Beaudene. I don't take well to threats of scandal. A lesson I thought I'd taught you nine years ago."

"You gave me this scar nine years ago, fitzWarren." In contrast to her father's, Rafe's voice was calm, and as cold as ice. "The only lesson I learned from that was to wait until I was in a position of sufficient power before going against an adversary who was without honour."

"You arrogant bastard, I—"

"Oh, I'm no bastard. You of all men should know that. My father was still alive when you seduced his wife, if you recall. Any bastards my mother might have borne were killed by the same evil means that took her life."

"Alise made her own decisions," fitzWarren blustered. "You can't blame me for her death."

"No. I suppose even a sewer rat like you drew the line at outright murder, but it didn't stop you and my mother forging the deeds that gave you title to Hadleigh Beaudene."

"Fiend seize you, I *had* right. Who do you think helped your mother run the place after your father died?"

"That's easy," Rafe said. "The man who posed as her paid seneschal, but was really her lover. The man who couldn't marry her because he was already wed to another. The man who used lies to banish me from my birthright after she died, leaving me with nothing except the clothes on my back."

"I could hardly help being wed to another," fitz-Warren muttered sullenly. "Until Eleanor was born, I thought the woman was barren. But, curse it, she was still my lawful wife. What could I do?"

"You could have divorced her on the grounds of her inability to bear children. But you didn't want that, did you, fitzWarren? A wife in the background left you free to dishonour other women without the threat of having to marry them. On the other hand, you had already wasted your wife's marriage portion, and most of her inheritance, so you had to look around for another source of easy wealth."

"Don't run away with the idea that Alise was a young innocent, Beaudene. There she was with a husband twenty years older who expected her to produce a brat every year. That wasn't for her. She was a ripe plum, waiting to fall."

"And you made sure you caught her."

"A man has to grasp opportunity when it presents itself." Her father made a scornful sound, as though suddenly more confident. "But why drag this up again? Nothing's changed. When Henry was put back on the throne nine years ago your claim was thrown out, because you'd sided with York. And 'twill be no different now that Edward's in power."

"You think not?"

"I know not, Beaudene. For the simple reason that you have no proof of forgery, and never will. Our last meeting was conducted without witnesses and so is this one. 'Tis your word against mine. Edward's father might have picked you out of the stews of London where I…shall we say…mislaid you, but he couldn't help you when I held title free and clear, and nor will Edward. He wants a peaceful kingdom, an end to lurk-

ing threats from the red rose. He's not going to hand
Hadleigh Castle back to you, leaving me with an excuse
to help finance Lancaster's next rebellion. That's why
he sent you to Langley to look Eleanor over. That's
why he suggested you marry her to settle any dispute.
And though I agreed at the time, I'm not so sure…''

"Don't stop there, fitzWarren,'' Rafe encouraged
silkily. "Take as much rope as you want.''

Her father laughed. "As you wish. You see, I haven't made up my mind to the match yet. You're not
much more than the adventurer I was. That estate York
deeded to you is smaller than Hadleigh, and you can't
have amassed a fortune putting down rebellions for Edward. No. Now that I see how Eleanor's grown to be
a beauty, I might look for a better alliance.''

"You forget what I just said about positions of
power, fitzWarren. The balance has shifted. I'm no
longer a homeless seven-year-old child, or a fifteen-
year-old youth burning too hot over past injustice to
fight successfully for his future. You can look all you
like for another match, but 'twill avail you nought. You
see, 'tis not merely your honour at stake here—a com-
modity you don't possess in any measure—but—''

"You're bluffing, Beaudene.''

"But your immortal soul,'' Rafe continued relent-
lessly. "How do you feel about burning in hell for all
eternity, fitzWarren?''

She was going to be sick. She couldn't listen to any
more. She had to get away, before someone came into
the hall and found her standing there, ashen and shaking.

Somewhere in the distance Nell heard her father
shouting again, but she was concentrating too hard on

backing away from the door for the words to have any meaning. She couldn't think, could scarcely breathe for the vice-like fist clutching at her throat. Her heart felt as if a sharp dagger had been plunged into it, and the knife was twisting...twisting...

Oh, God, the pain was terrible. She could hardly move. The effort of putting one foot in front of the other was agonising. The stone staircase leading to her chamber appeared before her and she had to put a hand on the wall for support while she dragged herself upwards, moving slowly, like an old woman.

When she finally reached the haven of her chamber one hand was pressed to her breast, as if to stop her heart from shattering. Her breath was coming in sobbing gasps, and she could barely focus her burning eyes enough to close the door.

There was still the small ante-chamber to cross, but she couldn't go any further. Leaning against the wooden panels at her back, Nell let herself slide downwards until she was crouched on the floor, doubled over in silent, unrelenting agony.

Rafe had lied to her. *Lied*! Asking all those questions about her inheritance, showing concern for her safety, but only because he needed her alive to regain his lands. Knowing all the time that he was the husband her father was considering, passing judgement on her— looking her over. Oh, Holy Mother save her. *Rafe*.

The knife twisted cruelly and she whimpered. How long would it last? This anguish. This terrible sense of betrayal. Surely pain this crippling would have to ease. People didn't die because their hearts had been torn apart from loving someone who intended to use them. She would have to go on living. She would have to function.

But not yet. Dear God, not yet! She wasn't capable of returning to the hall, of facing Rafe and acting as if nothing had happened, as if happiness was still possible. She had to think. Her brain felt almost as shattered as her heart, but she had to think.

Her father! What had he done?

Nell covered her face with her hands, blocking out sight in an attempt to clear her mind. If she had heard aright, he had caused his lover to betray both her husband and son and after her death he had taken that son—sweet Jesu, a child of seven—and abandoned him to fend for himself; he had stolen and lied and committed felony after felony for his own gain.

Her father was the thief Rafe had faced as a boy, the man who had stolen from him, who had almost taken his eye when confronted by the victim of his crimes. Her father was the man Rafe had sworn to defeat, his first step being his petition to the King. And Edward's answer had been to ''look her over''.

She was nothing more to the man she loved than an instrument of revenge and justice. The daughter of his bitterest enemy. The one woman he would never be able to love.

Her hands fell from her face and she slowly straightened so she was sitting against the door. Through the half-opened doorway to the inner chamber she could see a corner of the curtained bed and the table beside the window, flanked by two high-backed chairs. A flask of wine and a trencher of bread and meat had been laid on the table, and Nell quickly averted her gaze. Even the thought of food made her feel sick, but she took a shuddering breath, clenched her hands and forced herself to her feet.

She would not grovel on the floor any longer, bemoaning her fate. An anguished little sound escaped her and she almost doubled over again. Her fate? That was a jest. Rafe had probably laughed himself silly when she had declaimed that she was mistress of her fate. And then, without a second's hesitation, without so much as a hint of anything permanent between them, she had melted in his arms.

She cringed inside when she remembered how easy had been his conquest. He hadn't even had to go to the trouble of seducing her. He had looked, reached out, touched. And she had given herself completely.

Had he ever really wanted her? *Her.* Nell. Or had physical desire been another weapon wielded cold-bloodedly to further his plans? Had she been more correct than she knew when she had described his loss of control yesterday as a reaction to the danger they had faced? And had he then turned it to his advantage? Giving her all those reasons for marriage when all the time—

Knuckles rapped imperatively on the wood at her back, ripping through the tangled web of questions and making her heart lurch violently. Nell wheeled, backing away from the door as if a spectre from hell loomed on the other side. She didn't want to see anyone, she didn't want to—

''Nell?'' Rafe, his voice sharp with command. ''Open the door.''

She shook her head, as if he could see her, and continued backing into the other room, trying to remember if she had locked the door. She couldn't face him. Not like this. Filled with pain and the agony of betrayal. Torn apart by hurt pride, understanding, rage, love. She had to think. She had to decide what—

The door crashed open under the impact of an impatient hand on the latch and Rafe strode into the ante-chamber. He took one look at her face, slammed the door shut and locked it, then reached the solar in three long strides.

Nell went utterly still, freezing like a hunted animal in the presence of danger.

He stopped just clear of the doorway, his face set hard, eyes blazing with implacable determination. "How much did you hear?" he demanded, and slammed the second door shut with the flat of his hand.

Chapter Thirteen

Nell backed away so rapidly that she was up against the window before she knew it.

"How…did you know…?" Her voice was raspy, choked with unshed tears. She hadn't expected the sight of him to affect her so badly. She needed to be calm to survive this, but hurt was welling up within her, battering at her defences, crying to be free. She wanted to scream, to throw herself at him, clawing and kicking, to relieve the awful pressure of pain and rage and despair building inside her.

"The solar door was open." He had halted as soon as she'd retreated and now stood watching her, big and dark and immovable, framed by the grey stone arch behind him. "You're the only person who would open it again and not come into the room, and the only reason for that would be if you'd overheard enough to upset you."

"Upset me?" She laughed, a shrill, brittle sound that had her biting her lip in an effort at control. "Aye, you could say I'm somewhat upset. Being lied to does that to me."

"I have never lied to you," he said harshly. "I may not have told you the whole truth, but—"

"Is that not a lie?" she cried, unable to maintain her calm in the face of his denial. "Right from the start you've lied by omission. From that first night when you said you were there to escort me home. 'Twas the truth, aye, but you forgot to add that your other purpose was to look me over, didn't you, my lord? Why was that, I wonder? Afraid I would refuse you?"

His tawny eyes bored into hers. "As I recall, you were planning to refuse regardless of who the bridegroom turned out to be, but I didn't say anything then, because there was no need for you to know my reasons for considering a union with you."

"No need!" Her voice soared and nearly cracked. "That was the rest of my life we were talking about. I had every right to know why I was being *looked over*!"

"Will you stop throwing that phrase at me?" he yelled suddenly. He clenched his fists, and his eyes shut briefly in a visible bid for patience. "Neither Edward nor I used it, no matter what your father said."

"I don't care what phrase was used!" she screamed back. "The intent was the same." And, without warning, words were pouring from her in an uncontrollable stream as her frail shell of composure shuddered, cracked and was rent asunder. "But you didn't like what you saw, did you? No wonder you were so angry that night. 'Twas because you were being forced to marry a woman you despised to have your birthright restored to you. Nor was that the only time you lied to me. You said my father had promised to renounce his allegiance to Lancaster if the King would confirm his title. Sweet Lord, why didn't I suspect then? All those questions you asked about Hadleigh, and what would happen in the event of my death. Did you think I would be so grateful for your efforts in keeping me alive that I wouldn't care if 'twas in your own interests?''

She laughed again, wildly, mockingly. ''What a predicament for you. Faced with the same situation as Tom. Both of you trying to put me in a position where I would be forced to marry you, without getting me killed in the process. But you had more to lose, my lord. You even said so. One of the few times you told me the truth, I expect. My aunt *is* close to the Queen, and had Uncle Edward counter-petitioned to marry me to Tom, your revenge might have received quite a check. Especially since you believe the Queen is capable of bending Edward to her will, manipulation of males being such a dangerous female trait. What were you planning to do in that event? Seduce me?''

Something flashed in his eyes and Nell almost staggered back against the wall, gasping as if she'd received a mortal blow. ''You did,'' she whispered in horrified comprehension. If he had admitted it aloud she would not have been more certain. ''You did! That was why you were…gentler. Why you let me help Bess…why you…''

She couldn't go on. Her protective rage had been torn from her by the shocking realisation that Rafe had, indeed, made such a cold-blooded plan.

''Are you done?'' he asked with ominous quiet, when she didn't say any more. ''I hope so, because I'm only going to say this once. No one was forcing me to marry you. Nor have I ever lied to you. fitzWarren did petition the King, exactly as I told it, and 'twas that which prompted my own action, though I'd hoped to have more time to find the witnesses I needed to call fitzWarren into court. Edward then suggested the marriage to both your father and I as a means of protecting you, so you wouldn't be left destitute, but if for some reason I didn't want to marry you, he would have backed me in a civil claim.''

She just looked at him, disbelieving, her eyes dry and burning in her white face, pain crouching like a wild beast inside her, snarling, merciless, waiting to spring free the moment she let down her guard.

He must have seen it, seen her disbelief at least, because his voice softened and he took a step towards her. ''Nell, use your common sense. Of course our marriage will make everything quick and tidy, but, if worst comes to worst, there is nothing to stop Edward rejecting your father's petition and restoring title to me on the simple grounds that fitzWarren fought on the side of Lancaster.''

''Nothing to stop him?'' she echoed, incredulous. ''No, only his bride of four months. Apart from any other consideration, she was the widow of a Lancastrian, and is known to favour her family and friends beyond measure. You said yourself that Edward will do anything for her. No—'' she looked away, speaking almost to herself ''—marriage to me was your only sure way. There were too many risks otherwise. Elizabeth's influence on behalf of my father or my uncle, the fact that you had no proof, no witnesses...'' She paused, vaguely struck by the word. ''Witnesses?''

Rafe gestured impatiently. ''Old serfs who had been at Hadleigh Beaudene when your father first arrived there. 'Twould have been unlikely, however. He was very careful to be rid of anyone who posed a danger to him.''

''Even the child of his dead mistress,'' she whispered, raising stricken eyes to his. "The rightful heir. Oh, Rafe…"

The beast inside her stirred, a claw reaching for her heart, and she forced it back, praying he hadn't heard her. "Well, it doesn't matter any more. None of it matters. Indeed, this whole discussion is unnecessary and—"

"At least we agree on that," he muttered. "Nell, little one—"

She flinched visibly at the endearment and he stopped dead, his eyes narrowing.

"Don't," she begged. "I understand why you planned as you did. I do, truly. But you don't have to be…be nice…any more. You can take my father into court and win your lands back that way. You don't have to marry me."

His brows snapped together. "What?"

"Take my father into court," she repeated, her voice beginning to shake. "You have your witness. Me. I heard what was said between you. Hadleigh is yours by right of birth. You don't have to marry me for it."

"I already know that," he grated. "'Tis what I've just been telling you. What you heard doesn't change anything. It doesn't make any difference to us, Nell."

"How can you say that?" she cried, anguished. Pain shuddered through her again and she barely suppressed a whimper. Didn't he understand what she was trying to do? Didn't he know how impossible this was for her? "I'm the daughter of the man who wronged you so grievously he can never be forgiven, and to regain what you've lost you intend to ally with him—your worst enemy, a man you despise. Do you think I want to look at you one day, when I am no longer a means of revenge and justice, and see hatred or resentment in your eyes?''

''God damn it, I have never thought of you as a means—'' He stopped abruptly, and the sudden flash of memory in his eyes struck Nell like an open hand to her face. She turned whiter still, the sudden roaring in her ears almost drowning out her own choked words.

''No, you can't deny it. The same way you can't deny that you planned to seduce me.''

''That,'' he said through his teeth, ''was a separate issue entirely. And I ceased thinking of you as an instrument of revenge days ago. As for justice, it can be achieved through other means. In fact—''

''Then go ahead and achieve it through those means,'' Nell shrieked. She couldn't bear it. She couldn't take any more. The pain was too much. Claws raking at her heart, tearing, rendering…''Prove you didn't lie to me. Prove you didn't intend to use me. *Prove it*!''

''All right,'' he said very calmly.

She went still, staring at him.

''We'll go to Edward. You can give him your deposition, he'll pass judgement in my favour and that will be the end of it.''

Nell's eyes widened. She couldn't believe he had said that, and yet…

''Do you mean that, in all honour?''

''If you insist on it. But before you make your decision, princess, think on this. The minute the wax has set beneath the King's seal, I'll have us wed by the nearest priest.''

''Married?'' She hardly dared breathe the word.

''That's right.'' His voice was still calm, chillingly so. ''We can waste all that time so you can prove to yourself that I'm as easily manipulated as any other man, and end up just as wedded as if we'd been married here in Wells without any trouble or unnecessary delays at all.''

''I… I can't…'' She frowned and put a shaking hand to her brow. She was getting confused. Somehow Rafe had turned the tables on her and she was no longer sure of anything. Manipulate him? She had wanted only to right the shameful wrong her father had done, without destroying herself. Was that so terrible?

''Aye, put like that, your objections do sound like the rantings of a hysterical female, don't they, Nell?'' he said, obviously mistaking her long silence. ''Which is why we're not going to do it that way.''

''What do you mean?'' she whispered, suddenly afraid. His glittering eyes held an expression that made her mouth go dry and turned her limbs to water.

This was not the passionate lover of yesterday, nor even her fierce protector, but the man she had met at Langley. Cold, hard, ruthless.

He started slowly across the room towards her, his fierce golden eyes locked on hers. ''I'm sorry you had to find out about your father the way you did,'' he said very softly, ''but I'm not letting his crimes disrupt our lives any longer. When you calm down, you'll know I'm right.''

''No! Wait!'' Eyes wide, completely unable to move, Nell clutched the top of the nearest chairback with quivering fingers and watched his slow advance.

''We don't have time to wait.'' He stopped less than a foot away from the chair she was clinging to, and his voice hardened. ''There's still the possibility of a child, if you recall, my lady. Doing things your way could take several months, and no child of mine will be born a bastard.''

It wasn't pain that hit her this time, but a healthy bolt of rage. She was trembling so violently with it that the chair shook.

''And you call women manipulative! My plan to save us both from a marriage of cold necessity, if indeed I ever had one, pales in comparison to your own to trap me into such a situation. Is that why you took me in such haste yesterday? To ensure my agreement to an immediate wedding? Well, it won't work. You can—''

Her tirade was abruptly cut off when he reached out, yanked the chair out of her grasp and tossed it aside as if it weighed no more than a feather.

Nell barely noticed the crash when it landed. Jerked off-balance by the force with which he'd pulled the chair out from under her fingers, she staggered forward against the unyielding wall of his chest with an impact that drove the breath from her lungs. Before she could recover, she was trapped in his arms, held so tightly that she could feel every hard male inch of him pressed to her softer frame.

She lifted her head to protest and her throat closed up. His eyes were savage, slitted, molten with fierce intent. They stared down into hers, blazing even hotter when her lips parted.

''Don't say another word,'' he snarled, his voice so hoarse she would hardly have recognized it. ''Not one word, princess. I know yesterday was a shock to you, and over too damned soon, but I thought you knew I wanted you, at least. Obviously I was wrong, and—'' he bent, swinging her up into his arms with a swiftness that shocked her ''—you still need convincing.''

Nell stiffened, trying to hold herself rigid as Rafe carried her over to the bed. But her pulse was racing so fast she thought she might faint, and she began to shiver, even as the intense heat of his body wrapped around her.

''You're going to force me?'' she got out, unable to believe he would actually go to such an extreme. ''You know I'll never forgive you. Never! Is that what you want? For me to hate you?''

Just for a second his face tightened with an emotion too fleeting for her to recognise. Then he laid her on the bed and came down over her, the weight of his body keeping her pinned there.

''No,'' he murmured. ''No force.'' And this time there was no anger in the voice rasping over her nerves, only gentleness. His big hands framed her face and he looked down into her eyes as his mouth lowered slowly to hers. ''There's too much passion in you to make force necessary, sweetheart.'' His lips brushed hers. ''What do you think is tearing you apart right now? You're hurt and angry, I know, but there's more between us than cold necessity. I'm going to show you...''

She would not succumb, Nell vowed fiercely as Rafe began kissing her more deeply. Nor would she fight him. He would get no pleasure from this, neither conquest nor willing surrender. She would be as cold, as unfeeling, as passionless as the stone statues on the cathedral.

The vow lasted all of ten seconds. Rafe's mouth moved on hers with a gentle cherishing that crushed every vicious claw piercing her heart. Rage didn't have a chance; hurt reached out to be healed. He had never kissed her like this. As if kissing her was all. As if he needed. As if he *craved*.

Her lips softened and parted and she was powerless to stop the gentle, insistent invasion of his tongue. He filled her mouth, tasted, possessed. Her blood warmed, slowly...slowly. She put her hands to his shoulders, intending to push him away, and the solid strength beneath her fingers made her moan silently instead. Somewhere her mind was screaming. Not like this. *Not like this*! But he was warm and strong and she loved him. *Loved* him.

When this kiss ended it was so gradual that for a moment Nell lay dazed, her breathing light and fast. Then her lashes lifted and the brilliant gold of his eyes slammed into her with a force that left her senses reeling. Triumph, desire, sheer male determination to claim his woman. She read them all, and a silent cry of despair welled up inside her.

He had won. He would take her, and she would marry him, regardless of his reasons, not knowing if he would ever return her love.

Oh, he wanted her. She believed that. But for how long?

She gazed up into his eyes, searching desperately, forgetting in her distress that he would not trust his heart easily, and saw only the reflection of herself lying helpless in his arms. He would win this particular battle every time, for she could never withstand him, never leave him. She needed to be close to him in the only way he seemed to want, and he would only have to touch her.

And, dear God in Heaven, he had known that. Oh, weak fool that she was, she had told him so herself not an hour ago, and he had, indeed, remembered.

It was too much. Defeat shrouded her in utter misery. She had tried to fight for the future she wanted and had been betrayed by her own body, and as Rafe bent his head to kiss her again the first hot tears seeped from the corners of her eyes and ran down to the pillow.

''You're mine,'' he whispered against her trembling mouth. ''Mine! Say it!''

But she couldn't speak. Couldn't respond to the fierce urgency in his command. She felt his mouth touch the wetness on her cheek, felt him lift his head, and she tensed, turning her face away, closing her eyes and pressing her cheek into the pillow. But the silent tears were coming too fast to be hidden, and she knew he could feel the tremors shaking her body.

He went still for the space of a heartbeat, then caught her chin in his hand and swiftly brought her face around to his again.

''Nell? Oh, God, sweetheart... Don't...

Taking her face between his hands, he began pressing frantic little kisses to her eyes, as though trying to stop the flow. ''Don't cry. Darling, please. I didn't mean... I only wanted to show you... I *had* to show you. We belong together. I can't let you go. Anything else you want, I'll do, but not that. Not that!''

Somewhere through the jagged edges of pain the anguished sound of his voice reached her, but she still couldn't speak. Her throat was too tight. He was kissing her too desperately—her eyes, her mouth, her cheeks. Words of need, of love, poured over her as if he had wanted to say them forever.

''I know you don't love me yet, but you will. You will! I'll make sure of it. Oh, God, don't cry any more. My darling, my heart. I love you...love you...''

His mouth, hard and shaking, salty with the taste of

her tears, covered hers, and with a wrenching sob Nell started kissing him back, her arms clinging around his neck until she couldn't breathe for the emotions filling her heart. The transition from despair to shock to tremulous hope was simply too rapid, too frightening. She wrenched her mouth free, buried her face in his shoulder and wept uncontrollably.

The storm didn't last long. Rafe held her against him as if he was afraid she would be torn from his arms at any minute, murmuring to her over and over, until finally she was calm.

"I'm sorry," he said hoarsely. "I'm sorry. I never wanted to hurt you, but you said we didn't have to marry and I panicked. I knew it was true that I couldn't force you and I panicked."

Nell tried to find her voice. "You? Panic?" was all she could manage in a husky croak.

He turned her gently on to her back and leaned over her, his fingers threading through her hair, brushing tear-drenched tendrils aside.

"Nell, look at me."

Hesitant, still afraid to believe that Rafe had said he loved her, she raised her eyes to his face. And then she had to believe. The depth of emotion shimmering in her eyes made her heart stand still.

Aye, shimmering, she thought in wonder. This man who had been forced to survive the streets of London at a horrifyingly young age, who had grown into a warrior as ruthless as he was honourable, was showing her a vulnerability she had never even guessed at.

"I can't lose you," he said urgently, holding her gaze. "You mean too much to me. You're the one woman I didn't think existed. The other half of myself. My heart."

At the deep note of tenderness in his voice fresh tears welled in Nell's eyes. She blinked them back, smiling shakily up at him, and he bent to kiss her, his possession of her mouth slow and gentle and deep.

''My little princess,'' he murmured minutes later. ''How could you have doubted after the time we've spent together? Don't you know yet how very alike we are?''

If she had any doubts remaining after his kiss, those words would have dispelled them forever. ''I've known that for days,'' she whispered, her heart mirrored in her eyes for him to see. ''Oh, Rafe, I love you so. Why do you think I agreed to marry you? Why do you think I let you…yesterday…?''

She broke off, blushing rosily when his hard mouth curved in a smile as wicked as it was tender.

''Let me? My innocent little darling, you didn't *let* me make love to you yesterday. I didn't even give you a chance to say yea or nay. You were practically in shock, and as for me—'' his smile turned rueful ''—an entire army of villainous cousins wouldn't have stopped me. I'd just seen you risk your life to help me, and all I could think of was making you mine in every way possible.''

''You would have stopped,'' she said with absolute certainty. ''If I had truly wished it.''

''You have a touching if misplaced confidence in my control when I have you in my arms, sweetheart.''

''In your honour,'' she corrected softly, putting a hand up to his face. ''Tis the first side of you I fell in love with. After that, the rest was inevitable.''

His eyes flashed with a sudden blaze of emotion, desire and tender love combined, and his arms tightened convulsively. ''Oh, God, Nell, I didn't know until yesterday how much you meant to me. I'd wanted you since the moment I saw you, but when you went racing after those arrows—''

He stopped, shook his head and added in a low voice, ''If you had been so much as bruised I would have killed every one of those men, including your cousin. I knew then that what I felt was more than desire, but I'd never let a woman come that close, never wanted to protect her with my life or trust her with my honour. I wasn't ready to call it love, until I realised what you'd overheard. Then I knew. Sweet Jesu, how I knew! I couldn't get up here fast enough to see how much damage had been done, and when I thought I'd lost you, I just went mad. All I could think of was holding on to you, showing you how it could be between us, when what I should have done was shown you this.''

He sat up as he spoke, drawing Nell up with him and taking a folded sheet of parchment from his surcoat pocket. She could tell by the deep creases in the paper that it was very old.

''You found that in the crucifix,'' she whispered, knowing immediately what had happened. ''So it did conceal something.''

''Aye. After you left it with me the other night, I found the hidden catch. This was inside the cross.'' He handed the document to her. ''Read it.''

She took it with some reluctance, looking up at him, troubled. ''Rafe, I don't need to know what secret this holds. I trust you. I didn't mean all those terrible things I said. I know you wouldn't lie for your own gain, or try to trick me into marriage. 'Twas just…hearing all the dreadful things my father had done… I couldn't imagine how anyone would *not* want revenge and…'twas just too much.''

"Or not enough." He leaned forward to brush her lips in a fleeting gesture of reassurance. "That's why I want you to read it, love," he said gently. "At first I didn't want you to be hurt by the truth about your father, but, since you heard some of it, you should know it all. We should start on equal footing, you and I. We should *both* know I'm marrying you because my future is meaningless without you beside me."

A warm glow spreading through her at that last remark, Nell spread the parchment open and began to read.

"'Tis a confession," she said, amazed, a few seconds later. "My father's confession, in his own hand, of all he did to rob you of your lands. The forgery of transfer of title from the Beaudenes to the fitzWarrens. The way he dismissed the long-time servants when your mother died so his way was clear to eliminate you. Merciful saints, he even hopes for redemption because he didn't kill you outright. And then he finally remembers to tack on his unfaithfulness to my mother."

A disturbing thought occurred to her. "Do you think my mother knew of this?" she faltered, frowning worriedly up at Rafe.

"No," he said, with such assurance that Nell believed him instantly. "fitzWarren told me he wrote this confession when he moved your mother to Wells a year after you were born, as can be proved by its date. He told me all, in fact. Did you know that you and your mother never lived at Hadleigh Castle, but at the manor she had inherited from her father? He used to visit her there after my mother died, and probably before, if the truth is known.

"Then, after years of a barren marriage, his wife was suddenly with child, and in the expectation of a son of his own he took me to London, and conveniently mislaid me in one of the meanest parts of the city. Apparently he regarded the birth of a daughter as divine punishment for his sins, and when no more children were forthcoming he decided to protect his soul by concealing that confession in the cross he gave your mother. He told her it had to do with his support of poor, mad Henry and that since the Duke of York was protector of the realm at that time, his life would be endangered if the document ever came to light."

"Holy saints!" Nell exclaimed weakly.

"Aye. I don't think the man has ever told the truth in his life, except now, with the threat of death looming over him."

"What will you do with him?" she asked. "Accuse him publicly?"

Rafe shook his head. Taking the confession from her, he tossed it on the floor, propped his back against the carved bedhead, and settled Nell close to him again. "I might have needed revenge once, sweetheart, but not any more. That document is just to keep your father from troubling us. As for his punishment, 'twill come soon enough. The man is ill. If he sees the year out 'twill be a miracle. I've given him two days to return to Hadleigh, clear his trappings out of the place, and move as far from us as possible. Oh, and before he leaves Wells, he is to send your uncle's man back to Langley for your baggage and Chevette."

"Chevette! Oh, Rafe." She raised shining eyes to

his face. "You're going to ask my uncle for Chevette? Oh, thank you."

He grinned down at her. "Might as well blackmail everyone into giving us what we want while we can. Anything you'd like from the King when I inform him he's not to come near you again unless I'm with you?"

Nell smiled, so happy she would have forgiven the entire world its sins. "I don't want revenge either," she said. "As long as I have your love, I have everything I need. Although—" She stopped suddenly, remembering something she had wanted to do—holy saints!—was it only four days ago? "There is a *little* thing..."

"Name it."

"You will have to let me go first," she said demurely.

He looked at her. "For a minute. If you're lucky." He opened his arms.

Nell rose on her knees beside him and let her gaze travel over his face, from the quizzical expression in his tawny eyes to the amused set of his hard mouth, and then lower to the width of his shoulders and chest. She remembered how her breasts had felt, crushed against the powerful muscles beneath his surcoat, remembered the strength in his arms, the intimacy of his touch.

With an inward shiver, she reined in her wayward thoughts. There would be time later to touch, to savour his strength, but first—

Her gaze returned to Rafe's face and she lifted her hand towards him. The amused expression had vanished from his eyes. Nell shivered again, hesitating when she saw the smouldering heat that had replaced it. "May I—?"

"Anything," he said at once, his voice a low growl deep in his throat. "Whatever you want."

She edged closer and her hand touched his cheek, but the position threatened her balance. His eyes on her face, Rafe took her free hand and placed it on his shoulder, so she could brace herself. The muscle beneath her fingers was as hard as steel.

Her lips parted slightly as the heat from his body surrounded her. Love, desire, tenderness—all swirled within her. All for Rafe. Her hand touched his cheek again, and with the tips of her fingers she traced the scar on his face, from his brow to the short curve below his eye. Then she leaned closer and retraced the path with her lips.

"I'm so sorry," she whispered. "So very sorry."

His arms closed around her, holding her against him with a fierce strength that was yet heart-meltingly tender. "It doesn't matter any more. My little darling. You won't regret marrying me. You won't regret trusting me with your love. I swear it. We've both been scarred by the past, even if all the marks don't show, but the future is ours."

He moved suddenly, with the unexpected swiftness that always managed to surprise her. Before Nell had taken her next breath, she was flat on her back, gazing bemusedly up at him. "Starting now," he growled, and lowered his mouth to hers.

"But…the Bishop…"

It was the only protest Nell managed to utter before Rafe was kissing her with the same intensely focused need she had felt in him before, kissing her until she was soft and melting inside, until she couldn't remember why she would ever want to protest.

His hands moved over her, even as she surrendered to the magic of his kisses, unlacing, shifting, sweeping their garments aside until she lay naked in his arms for the first time. Felt the burning heat of his body enfold her, felt the softness of her breasts crushed against the deliciously abrasive hardness of his chest. And, like his mouth, his hands cherished, worshipped, aroused.

Shyness intruded just once, when he raised himself slightly on one forearm to let his gaze move slowly down the length of her body. Nell murmured softly as warmth tinted her cheeks, and he bent swiftly to her mouth again.

"Hush," he whispered. "You're so beautiful. So beautiful, my darling. My princess. Let me love you. Let me…"

His dark voice was so strained and hoarse that it would have startled her had she been thinking clearly, but his hands started to trace the path his eyes had taken, and she could only feel. His long fingers found and circled her breasts, shaping their soft contours, teasing the rosy buds that responded to his touch in a tingling rush that sent lightning flashes to every quivering nerve-ending.

Leaving her wanting more of the thrilling caresses, his hand moved lower, flattening on the gentle curve of her belly, pressing and kneading lightly in a movement that was both sensual and possessive. Nell's hips lifted in a response she couldn't control, and a small cry of longing shuddered through her. He had given her pleasure yesterday, but this… She was drowning in sensations never before imagined.

"Shhh," he soothed, trailing tiny kisses along her jaw, then moving to the soft flesh beneath her chin. "Slow, this time, sweetheart. Slow."

With lips and tongue he tasted her throat, her neck, the delicate bones below, moving with nerve-racking slowness towards her straining breasts. His tongue curled around a velvety nipple, teasing over and over, making her writhe beneath him in frustrated need. Then, just when she thought she could not stand the sweet torment any longer, his mouth closed hotly over the throbbing peak, and at the same time his fingers parted the soft curls between her legs to stroke her body with earth-shattering gentleness.

Ecstasy burst inside her almost immediately. She arched, an almost soundless cry parting her lips, no longer herself but a pulsing, throbbing creature of fire and pleasure.

It went on forever. He gave her no rest, no respite, but with mouth and hands took her from peak to peak until, when she was almost senseless with pleasure, when she thought there could be no more, he raised himself above her and, with a look of love so intense she could hardly bear it, he filled her body with his. Took her heart. Gave her his own.

It was a joining so complete that she no longer had any awareness of two separate beings. Every breath, every whispered word of love, every heartbeat was theirs, shared. Every touch, every meeting of lips, of hands, of warm, naked flesh was a link binding them more closely. And when the final release came, when his life-force merged with hers, their souls met for one single, timeless moment of shared ecstasy.

* * *

Two weeks later, wrapped warmly against the brisk autumn wind in a sable-lined mantle of dark gold velvet, Nell stood in the courtyard of the inn near Wells where she and Rafe had been staying since their marriage, and watched the last of her chests being loaded on to the baggage wagon.

A few yards away Samson and Chevette, already saddled, awaited their riders. Next to the bay's huge bulk Chevette looked more like a child's pony, but she didn't seem to mind the close proximity of the larger horse, even though Samson was standing with his head arched over her withers.

Indeed, if anything, Nell mused, suddenly realising that Samson had been assuming that particular stance since the little palfrey had arrived three days ago, Chevette looked rather smug.

''Are you ready to depart, sweetheart?'' Rafe asked, coming up behind her. He didn't stop walking until he was close enough for her shoulder to brush his chest. ''They're expecting us at Hadleigh before the supper hour.''

Nell smiled up at the hard face of her warrior husband, and marvelled at the softer light that filled his eyes every time he looked at her. That, and his need to be within touching distance of her whenever they were together, had her utterly enthralled.

Of course, it had its disadvantages also, Rafe had informed her only last night. She was now so sensitive to his presence that, much to her glee and his pretended disgust, he could no longer creep up on her.

He looked down at her now and his eyes lingered, narrowing thoughtfully. ''Why are you smiling like that?''

The smile grew. "Do you see anything familiar?" she asked, glancing to the side.

His gaze followed hers. He was silent for a moment, then, "You don't have withers," he muttered. "And I don't *hang* over you."

Nell giggled. "Of course not."

Rafe continued to watch the horses. "Poor old Samson," he observed, with patently false gloom. "Another warrior brought to his knees by the female of the species."

"Indeed?" Nell bent a minatory look on him. "I don't think I've ever seen you—"

But Rafe wasn't listening. "On the other hand, if he's going to be distracted… Euan," he called to his young squire, who was contemplating the unenviable task of separating Chevette from her protector. "Leave the palfrey's reins tied. I'll take my lady up before me on Samson for the first few miles. You can stay with the baggage wagon."

"Aye, my lord." Relieved of duty, the boy scampered off to fetch his own mount.

"But I was looking forward to—" Nell began, only to be stopped by a gleam in her husband's eyes that she had no trouble in recognising.

"Do you recall that I once promised to show you how much trouble you can get into on the back of a horse, my lady?" he murmured in the dark velvet voice that never failed to make her knees go weak.

And to think she'd just been picturing the interesting spectacle of her erstwhile bodyguard on *his* knees. A mind-numbing suspicion suddenly occured to her. Surely he didn't mean to…? On a *horse*? He couldn't! She wouldn't!

But, when Nell looked up into those intensely glittering hawk's eyes, she knew that if he could, she would.

"Do you know something, my lord?" she asked, her frown promising dire retribution even as a deliciously wanton shiver of excitement coursed through her. "I am not precisely sure how or when it happened, but somehow I seem to have ended up no longer mistress of my fate."

"Of course not. Do I look like a fool?" Rafe grinned at her, his expression wicked and very male. "But never mind, little princess. You can be mistress of my fate instead. Console yourself with the reflection that 'tis a lifelong occupation."

Nell tilted her head and pretended to consider. "That," she finally pronounced, "will do perfectly well."

And with a smile of dazzling brilliance she launched herself into Rafe's arms and into their future.

* * * * *

Modern Romance™
...seduction and
passion guaranteed

Tender Romance™
...love affairs that
last a lifetime

Sensual Romance™
...sassy, sexy and
seductive

Blaze Romance™
...the temperature's
rising

Medical Romance™
...medical drama on
the pulse

Historical Romance™
...rich, vivid and
passionate

27 new titles every month.

With all kinds of Romance for every kind of mood...

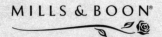

MILLS & BOON®

Don't miss *Book Twelve* of this BRAND-NEW 12 book collection 'Bachelor Auction'.

MILLS & BOON

Bachelor
AUCTION
Who says money can't buy love?

Who says money can't buy love?

best man
in Wyoming
Margot Dalton

On sale 1st August

*Available at most branches of WH Smith,
Tesco, Martins, Borders, Eason, Sainsbury's,
and all good paperback bookshops.*

BA/RTL/12V2

Tender Romance™
...love affairs that last a lifetime

Four brand new titles each month

Take a break and find out more about Tender Romance™ on our website
www.millsandboon.co.uk

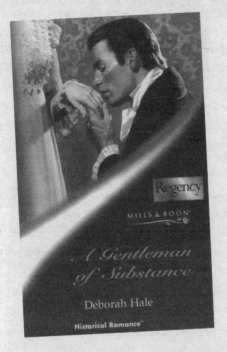